THE LIGHT GAZER

Amanda Luper

Amanda Luper

This is for those who found *her*—the girl who made sense of the madness, who was both mirror and flame. For the kisses that saved you, the touches that claimed you, and the moment you finally knew: this is who I am—wild as fire, and finally free.

The Light Gazer contains mature themes and is intended for adult readers (18+). This book is fiercely queer, emotionally charged, occasionally filthy, and crafted for those who believe sapphic love deserves to take up space—boldly, tenderly, one page at a time.

If that's you?

Welcome home.

CONTENTS

PROLOGUE: A SPARK IN THE ASHES OF YEARS

1945

The old man ran his fingers over the silver patterns on the small box. The Clockery smelled like oil and wood shavings. Time moved differently here—everywhere except on him. Outside, the world kept moving, but he sat alone by candlelight. If he opened the box, would she still be there? Or had she been gone longer than he remembered?

He picked up the wooden trinket box. It felt heavier than it should. His vest and white shirt belonged to a different time, sleeves rolled up to his elbows. His hair had gone thin and gray, but his green eyes still looked sharp, for now.

Tiny designs adorned the box, the interior clockwork visible through a side dial displaying numbers. He traced them with his finger, wanting to open it but afraid to try.

"I want to see her again," he whispered.

He noticed his glasses sliding down his nose as he looked at the small key next to the box. When had he put it there? Had it always been there? The key looked worn, like many people had used it before him. He picked it up.

The box felt like it was alive in his hands. He stared at it, confused. Hadn't he already opened this? Or was that a dream? He tried to remember, but the memory slipped away.

He saw the key and picked it up again. When he put it in the lock, the room seemed to hold its breath. Click. The lid opened. Light came from inside.

It wasn't just reflected by candlelight—this was something else. It swirled like fog trapped in glass, crooning. His chest felt tight.

The light spilled out, floating into the air like a slow breath. It lit up the wrinkles on his face and threw shadows on the bookshelves. Pictures flashed in the glowing mist—blurry and unclear.

His heart beat faster. He saw fancy old furniture, candlelight, and a woman's face. Then something else made his pulse race, a window to another time, or another dimension. He couldn't remember.

"Little Lark..." he said without thinking. Why did that name feel familiar? Who had he called that? A daughter? No, that wasn't right. But he was sure she had been here once. The more he tried to remember, the more it faded. Had she been real?

The light got brighter, filling the room. A low mechanical sound hummed underneath everything. He turned the key the other way and twisted the small dials on the box. Gears clicked like a puzzle solving itself. The walls shook. Shadows moved. The humming got deeper, vibrating through the entire shop.

The lid snapped shut, then burst open again with force, tearing a hole between worlds.

A shape formed in the swirling light—a clear outline against the glow. The old man stepped back. Broad shoulders, a long coat moving in the strange wind. A tall man with onyx hair and eyes the color of emerald and aged whiskey stepped through. The air turned frigid.

The gears clicked once more. The sound had changed. Someone had found him.

"Well, congrats, my guy. You opened it. Yet again." The voice sounded tired and amused at the same time.

The old man's legs gave out. He grabbed the counter to stay up. His mind felt like it was falling apart. Had this happened before? Was this new? Was this a memory? "I just wanted to see her again," he said, his voice rough.

The stranger tilted his head and smiled. "Yeah, and I just wanted a quiet life, but here we are. Now come on—I can't keep babysitting you through the decades."

Before the old man could answer, the light grew brighter. It swallowed them both, and the room disappeared in a flash of white.

Silence.

The derelict shop was empty again. Only his trinket box remained, its glow fading.

1

ONLY IN PORTLAND

PRESENT DAY

The lights were back.

Dani squinted into the trees across the riverbank, now swallowed in shadow. "Sneaky little shits," she muttered, shifting her iced coffee to her other hand. Her gaze swept left, then right. There—barely there. Faint shimmers of light clung to the trunks like fireflies, as if someone were slipping through the gravestones with a lantern too small to be real.

"Hold still," she hissed under her breath. The last of the golden light kissed her skin, setting her jawline aglow. She will see them. She could feel it—like the universe holding its breath inside her chest.

Every September 21st, she stood beneath the green arches of St. Johns Bridge, eyes fixed across the river, waiting for something that always appeared. She'd glimpsed those strange lights before—in other quiet, shadowed places—but here, beneath this bridge, they consistently returned with a steady, haunting rhythm.

The worst part? No one else ever saw it. Not even Mary.

The river caught the last threads of sunlight, glowing gold beneath a blanket of creeping fog that curled over the water like slow, soft breath. The sharp scent of pine and damp earth in the air.

The cool chain around her neck pressed against bare skin. Her shirt was unbuttoned, sleeves pushed past her elbows, revealing the tight tank top underneath—like she'd walked straight off a soccer field and into an open mic night featuring sad girl guitar covers.

Behind her, Mary lay sprawled across their worn, crocheted blanket, laughter spilling from her like sunlight itself—a queen in a world Dani couldn't touch.

"Oof," Mary muttered, frowning at her wrist. "My watch is doing that glowy thing again." The antique watch filled with cogs and gears swirled softly with a blue pulsing glow. Mary chalked it up to electromagnetic frequencies from the cell phone towers or a dying battery. It always glows on this day.

She snapped open her golden opera glasses and gave Dani a slow once-over. "You look like you just got thrown out of a ladies' book club for seducing someone's wife."

Dani didn't answer right away. Mary always said things like that. Pretty little comments with enough edge to leave you wondering if it meant something.

The way Mary's copper curls caught the light didn't help. The jacket, a vintage piece with fragile buttons, cinched her waist. Her perfume was lavender, soft, and stubborn. Dani knew the scent like muscle memory.

Soon it would disappear with her.

Off to college.

Away from this.

"Mock me all you want," Dani said, voice dry as old parchment. "But when this becomes a Netflix docuseries, I'll be the brooding main character. You? The comic relief."

Mary sighed—long and theatrical—then dropped her glasses to her chest like a wounded starlet.

"This has always been your bizarre little fixation, Detective Dani. I'm just here for the ambiance."

Dani arched a brow. "You mean the free food. You've never said no to Thai."

"How dare you? I came for the intrigue. The romance. The completely unhinged chance you might uncover a glowing ghost wife." Mary gasped, hand pressed dramatically to her heart.

Dignifying it with a response is not Dani's style. But the smallest twitch of her mouth gave her away.

Mary gestured lazily toward the river, voice soft but teasing. "You ever think about how we're sitting right across from a graveyard?"

"Oh yeah," she replied dryly, "super normal thing to bring up on a chill night out." Dani drifted, her thoughts elsewhere. Why did Mary always joke like that?

Unbothered, Mary grinned, cupping her hands around her mouth. "Hi, Grandma! Hope the afterlife's treating you well!"

"I swear to God, if she answers, I'm sprinting to the train and never looking back." Dani growled.

"Grandma, if you're out there, give us a sign. I don't know... throw Dani into the river or something." Mary was always teasing, but tonight, something about it landed differently.

A flutter of movement.

A brighter glow shimmered between the trees across the riverbank.

Dani paused to concentrate and focus her eyes.

Her fingers curled around the tiny silver key resting at her neck, cool and steady against her skin. She always reached for it when things felt off. Or maybe right. Hard to say these days.

"Do you see that?" she asked, voice sharp with hope.

Mid-chew, Mary held a veggie roll inches from her mouth until Dani's elbow struck with chaotic precision. The roll went flying, cabbage spraying across the blanket like green confetti.

Mary blinked, first at the river, then at the mess. "Hard to tell with all this cabbage in my eyes."

Dani shoved the binoculars to her. "Just look."

"If it's raccoons holding a town hall, I'm out of here." Mary raised the lenses to her eyes.

Of course, Mary isn't taking it seriously. She never does.

Under the St. Johns Bridge, they'd found each other at twelve—awkward, dirt smudged, unafraid. A friendship forged from nothing, lasting far longer than it probably should have.

And she didn't know what scared her more, the lights coming back or Mary walking away.

Dani had been kicking a soccer ball alone, aiming for the concrete steps, while Mary raced around with a pack of sugar-high birthday kids and a tail of little boy admirers. The ball slipped wide, smack—right into Mary's shin.

She grinned and booted it back.

Dani caught it clean. "Nice pass. You play?"

"Only if tripping over my own feet counts."

That was enough.

The birthday chaos faded behind them, their footsteps soft against the damp earth, moving together with no need for words.

Then Dani caught sight of it.

She squinted toward the riverbank, at first thinking it was headlights flickering on the water—but the glow drifted oddly. Slow, uneven, as if hesitant to settle. It hovered just above the surface, like a restless spirit searching for something lost.

"What is that?" she breathed, the question barely escaping her lips.

Mary followed her gaze, frowning. "Probably just trees... or maybe a boat."

"No." Dani gripped Mary's sleeve tighter, her voice sharp. "There. Under the trees. Near the graveyard."

They slipped down the slope, feet sliding on slick stones and grass. Dani nearly tumbled forward, but her eyes stayed fixed on the faint lights pulsing through the shadows on the far bank—soft, alive, like something breathing beneath the night's quiet.

"Right there—look!" Dani urged, pointing into the darkness.

Dani... there's nothing there."

But the lights were real—bright and steady, just like the stars scattered overhead.

Humoring Dani for years, Mary played along. Nights spent chasing lights in different places, borrowing her father's telescope, dragging skeptical friends into the cold. But after so many empty evenings, the magic had slipped through her fingers.

Now, she came just for Dani.

"Well. This has been fun. I still saw nothing, but I'm glad you did." Mary twisted the timepiece on her wrist again. Beneath the glass, the soft teal glow flickered once—then faded.

"There's this clock shop I pass every day along the rail. You should see it sometime—feels like it's stuck in another century."

"Speaking of the rail... I better hustle for the bus, or I'll miss the next one." Mary gave a lazy smile, but her fingers were already gathering the scattered pieces of her evening.

"Wait—where's that fancy little trinket box you promised me?" Dani asked as she reached for her bag.

"Ugh, I completely forgot!" Mary smacked her forehead, then grinned. "No, wait—I didn't. Just needed a dramatic moment." Dropping her bag, she rifled through the side pocket with exaggerated fuss, muttering to herself. After a brief struggle, she produced something no larger than a jewelry box.

"This," she said, holding it out between them, "is yours. Consider it repayment for that corset I swiped from your grandma last Christmas."

"Where the hell did you find this?" Dani stood eyes wide.

"Great-grandma Cleo's. You remember—after she passed, when I helped clear out her things?" Mary pressed the box into Dani's hands, her thumb grazing Dani's palm.

Dani's mind buzzed with the weight of the small gesture, but Mary's smile stayed effortless, like this was all perfectly ordinary. Like she hadn't just lit a fire inside Dani and stepped away from the flames.

"Open it," she whispered.

Tracing her thumb over the carvings, the wood was smooth and warm beneath Dani's skin. Someone shaped every edge with obsessive care—tiny cogs nestled into the corners, half-hidden between elegant Edwardian swirls, as if a watchmaker had poured centuries of quiet devotion into something no one touched.

On the right side, a small number dial rested flush against the grain. The digits read 1905—locked in place, unmoving. Just beneath a pale green gem set into the lid, a slender keyhole waited, sharp-edged and silent.

It looks like someone had stolen it from a fairytale. Or a vault.

She tried the lid. It didn't move.

Turning the box over, she checked the sides, searching for some hidden mechanism. Nothing.

"You too, huh? I couldn't open it, either. Guess it's a mystery for future-you to solve." Mary chuckled.

Crouching to gather what remained of her dinner, Mary brushed cabbage from the blanket with a theatrical sigh. "We should probably head out. I require more food—since mine is currently fertilizing the grass."

She checked her watch again. The gears beneath the glass pulsed with that familiar, soft teal glow, faint but steady—like something breathing just beneath the surface.

"Man," she muttered, angling it toward the fading light. "Cleo really had a thing for weird clocks."

"Not shocking. That was her version of tech." Dani replied. "We want all the new gadgets now; it was probably the same back then."

Mary tapped the watch face, "Some mysterious hot guy gave it to her. A tragic, doomed romance. At least, that's the version my mom swears by. But knowing this family?" She snorted. "They probably embellished half of it just to be dramatic."

"So that's where you get it. Cleo—the original drama queen." Dani smirked, nudging her.

"Careful," Mary snorted, her voice a thread of laughter in the cooling dusk. Her fingers drifted to the edge of her watchband, stroking the worn leather as if it might hum beneath her touch. "I'm not the only one with a borderline hoarder-level obsession with haunted antiques. You're the one collecting cursed heirlooms like trophies. I already gave you that key necklace. You're spoiled, and you know it."

The glow from her watch flickered—a soft teal, pulsing like a heartbeat—before settling again. Dani glanced down, but Mary was already speaking of other things, as if the light hadn't just responded to her touch.

Cleo had always been a woman you remembered. Mary's grandmother had a voice that pulled you into stories before you realized you'd stepped inside them. When Dani first met her, Cleo was still alive, still regal in her eccentric way—bold in spirit, with sharp eyes and a sharper wit. She lived in the old Mississippi district, nestled in a house brimming with plants, crooked clocks, and framed photographs that smiled from every wall.

When Dani visited, Cleo would light up like a lantern in a storm. There was always food—strange, fragrant, too much—and laughter that echoed down the narrow halls like magic.

One summer, when Mary was eight, she discovered the watch. It had been sleeping in the back of an old, velvet-lined case, tucked among a mess of brooches and timeworn lockets. Dani could still remember how Mary clutched it, like she'd found a portal to another world. And maybe she had.

After two years of relentless begging and bribes of housework, Cleo finally surrendered it on Mary's tenth birthday. From that day on, the watch became a fixture—scratched, scuffed, loyal. A relic worn like armor. It was the beginning of Mary's obsession with the Victorian and Edwardian eras, with all things strange and unlabeled.

Now Cleo was gone.

But her legacy lived on in three things: a watch, a box, and a key. A peculiar little trio, bound between Mary and Dani, like charms on a string.

Dani sometimes wondered if Cleo had planned it that way—knew exactly who would hold what in the end. And knew, too, which of them would never let go.

Mary pushed herself up with a sigh, brushing grass from her pants as if she were dusting off an entire evening. "Alright, Detective Barrington. Walk me to the light rail." Her voice curled into that half-commanding, half-sweet tone she wielded like a spell whenever she wanted something.

"Tomorrow—when you come over to help me pack—we'll crack this thing open." A beat. Then, a narrowed gaze. "You're still helping me, right? Right?"

The full force of her puppy-dog eyes hit wide and shining.

Dani exhaled slowly. *Not the pretty privilege voice again.* She smiled, tight around the edges, and forced it to reach her eyes. "Of course." But her throat ached because Mary was leaving.

It had always been inevitable—Mary, meant for bigger places, gilded halls, and impossible dreams. But the truth of it didn't feel any less sharp. Not as she watched her now, adjusting that ridiculous velvet jacket like it belonged on a stage, copper curls catching every scrap of light the sky had left.

A year in Newport. The Preservation Society. Studying sprawling estates and the ghosts of the Edwardian elite. Mary's dream.

Dani had tried to make her stay. Had offered logic, comfort, even silence—none of it had worked. Now, all that remained was this heavy hollow feeling carving space beneath her ribs. The slow rot of what-ifs.

"If I don't help you, you can't go," she muttered, the words lighter than they felt.

Mary grinned, teasing the moment. "Would you really deny me an entire year of playing a tragic Edwardian heroine? You know I've been training for this my whole life." She twirled once, absurd and beautiful in the same breath. "Besides—maybe I'll find a devastatingly handsome man in a waistcoat. One with a secret past and a crumbling estate."

And maybe, Dani thought bitterly, *I'll still be here, standing under a bridge, chasing lights no one else can see.* She forced a laugh. Of Course. Old-world charm has always attracted Mary. Velvet-draped drawing rooms. Faded letters, sealed with wax. Brooding well-mannered men. Dani never fits that mold.

"Well," she murmured, nudging her shoulder against Mary's, "at least I'll get a break from your surprise lectures on fork etiquette and how to curtsy without looking like you're about to collapse."

Mary grinned, a grin that stole the breath from Dani's lungs, and started walking again. The park path emptied. Twilight had gathered in earnest, sinking deep blues and purples through the canopy of trees. The breeze carried the scent of pine and river water.

Veering without missing a step, Mary sidestepped a man on a unicycle, wearing a unicorn onesie and playing the trumpet with alarming sincerity. They both froze.

Then, in tandem, utterly flat: "Only in Portland." They declared.

Their eyes met. Amusement flashed—brief and bright—a shared ember amid everything else Dani couldn't bring herself to say.

Dani watched her go.

The street swallowed her up, but the sound of her laughter lingered—ghostly, golden, trailing like a ribbon in the wind.

Mary will leave, but tonight Dani held the box against her hip. The ache blooming like a bruise behind her ribs. And the quiet, haunting aftertaste of lavender in the dark.

After riding the bus to the light rail, Dani rested her forehead against the window of the train, the cool press of glass a quiet relief against her skin. The city slipped past in blurs—neon signs bleeding into shadow, sharp edges softened by speed and distance. The steady clatter of the train beneath her was a kind of music, metal on metal, humming low in her bones. It lulled her—not to sleep, but into that in-between space where thoughts could stretch and tangle and time thinned out.

As the train eased toward Morrison Street and 3rd Ave, the rhythm softened, slowing into a gentle grind. Dani blinked, and her gaze caught on the familiar storefront just beyond the tracks—a sagging silhouette nestled between a shuttered bakery and a pawn shop still clinging to its last fluorescent buzz read: Dunwich & Sons.

The sign swung in the wind, its letters crooked and faded, as if time had tried to erase them and only half-succeeded. A single streetlamp buzzed weakly overhead, casting a pale light over the door's peeling trim. The building looked like it had exhaled and never drawn breath again—its paint curling away from the wood in tired spirals, glass fogged with grime, corners beaded with condensation.

She could barely make out the inside, but what little the murky windows revealed was a tangle of shadows and clutter—grandfather clocks with dark polished faces, cuckoo clocks stacked like gossiping old women, tarnished watches draped across hooks and velvet pillows, and shelves jammed with tiny, trinket boxes.

Not a display. A memory dump.

She'd meant to go in once. Just once. But something always kept her moving—school, practice, the next train pulling in. Still, every time they passed, her eyes found it. Not because it demanded her attention.

But because it waited.

A faded curtain hung behind the display window, stiff with age and stained the color of dried moss. Someone had tugged one side back with what looked like twine, the knot loose and fraying. The other side drooped low and shapeless, its hem unraveling like something forgotten in the attic.

The front door, warped and off-center, leaned in its frame as if bowing beneath years of weather. Its glass pane, once clear, was now cloudy and streaked from the inside, smudged by hands—or time.

The lettering on the door and window caught the eye next. Hand-painted in a once-regal Victorian script, every letter curved and adorned, with flourishes sweeping into the fogged edges of the pane like vines. It had been beautiful once, but the decades had taken their toll.

The paint had peeled in long, curling scars. Some letters were ghosts. Others clung on, proud and chipped and illegible.

It wasn't just a sign. It was a monument to itself.

DUNWICH & SONS
PURVE—— TIMEP——ES, HA——HERY, & ME——ICAL MARVELS
ESLISHED 18——

Specialis—— of Su——rior Cl——ks, Ge—— & A——ata R——s

Com——ons A——cepted

Like a puzzle halfway etched in a dream. Something there, and not. A business with its bones showing.

The train hissed as it came to a halt. Doors slid open with a tired breath, letting in the crisp bite of evening and the quiet shuffle of waiting commuters.

No one boarded. No one left.

Just the hush of the stop. The thrum of the city beyond. And that strange little shop, watching from the shadows.

As the doors sighed closed, Dani's gaze drifted one last time toward the clock shop—and caught.

In the window's reflection, something shifted.

Not outside. Inside.

A shimmer through the glass, like heat rising from asphalt. The world behind her bent at the edges; Someone had tugged the threads of reality just a little too far. A shadow slipped through the aisle—tall, narrow, wrong in ways. It moved behind her, slowly and silently, but when she turned—

Nothing.

Just rows of empty seats. Just her own warped reflection in the glass, staring back with wide eyes and a pulse fluttering too high in her throat.

Her neck prickled. A rush of static danced across her skin, buzzing under her collarbones, electric and directionless.

Then the train jolted. A metallic groan as the car rattled forward, snapping the moment like a twig underfoot.

Dani blinked. Hard. *Sleep. I need to sleep. Or sage. Maybe both.*

The unease coiled in her gut dissolved, drowned out by the familiar sway of the car and the low hum of the tracks beneath her. It was disquieting. But in its own strange way, it felt like a mercy. A lull.

She exhaled, let her body tilt with the rhythm, and closed her eyes.

But behind the lids, the image lingered. That impossible figure stitched into the dark.

Her stop trilled with a chime.

"Washington Park". A velvety pre-recorded voice announced.

The voice snapped her upright. She gasped and recoiled, pushing the box further into her coat pocket to hold it securely before getting off the light rail.

Outside, the night air bit clean through the remnants of her light sleep. Crisp and sharp, it cut through the fog in her head like glass—cool pavement beneath her boots, the faint tang of wood smoke curling from unseen chimneys. The usual city noise had softened into a low, distant hum.

She stood still for a moment, breathing it in. Damp asphalt. Wet leaves. A hint of ozone. Tiny insects danced around the haloed streetlamps like static, their wings humming in silence.

Then she moved.

The walk home carved upward through the hills, muscle memory guiding each step. Her strides were steady, efficient, built from years of conditioning. No part of this climb winded her—not the incline, nor the quiet. Not even the pull in her calves that most people would have cursed. This was nothing compared to soccer practice. The heat. The drills. The bruises. She'd earned every one—and caught the attention of the Portland Rose's scout more than once. But she wasn't ready. With her attention deficit disorder, splitting focus meant failure, and she couldn't afford that. College came first. She'd graduate that summer, and then she'd be all in.

She kept her pace, eyes ahead, the neighborhood closing in around her.

This part of the city didn't follow rules. The streets down below fit into a neat, grid logic—blocks and boulevards, and corner stores lined in repetition. But up here, the map forgot itself. The path wound through ancient trees and older homes—half-swallowed by ivy, their bones creaking with age.

Barrington Hill against Forest Park didn't care for order. It curled in on itself. Crooked and shadow-drenched, a place that had been forgotten by time and left to grow wild.

Overhead, the branches arched like cathedral ceilings, heavy with moss, swaying in slow conversation with the evening.

The road curved hard, dropping off as if some long forgotten hand had scooped the earth out. Shadows were pooling in the dip, so Dani quickened her pace.

The path went on—until it didn't.

Through the shroud of swaying firs and black-limbed trees, the mansion surfaced, rising like a ghost from the hillside. Barrington Mansion. Not just grand. Commanding. A relic with posture. It stood as if it had always been there, half in this world, half in another, its presence pressing against the bones of the hill.

The pale stone caught what little light remained, the surface etched in time and kissed with moss—nature creeping back, slow and patient. High above, the red shingles bled red as rust beneath the moonlight. Stained-glass windows pulsed, warm and fractured, casting shards of color over the grass.

From here, the house watched everything. The winding roads. The quiet sprawl of the city below. The sharp cut of Mount Hood slicing the horizon.

Cold bit at her cheeks, the wet cold that lived in your joints if you let it. Her breath curled in front of her, clouding the air. The view was the same as it had always been.

Home.

Inside, met her like an old friend. A dusty and familiar quiet that echoed. But the grand marble staircase that loomed in the foyer, in great condition, swept upward in a graceful arc that split the air in two. Its polished steps gleamed beneath the muted light, curving toward the second floor like a spine carved from stone. Behind it, a stained-glass window rose to the ceiling, spilling color across the pinewood floors in fractured ribbons of light—holy, in a way that made her skin feel too small. The air smelled the house's age. Warm wood, warped by time. Dust sharpened with a dry sting. Old metal and older pipes. And beneath it all, the barest whisper of rose perfume, clinging to the walls like a memory.

Somewhere under that rain. Damp and mineral, threading through unseen cracks, settling into plaster and floorboards. The entryway window, seeping with a water stain, signaling the dilapidation of the house. The dampness was always worse at night, wrapping around her skin like a second coat. A smell you only find in homes that have seen too much.

Her eyes drifted upward to the portrait that presided over the foyer—Alvie Barrington, captured in oil and time. The artist had been thorough. His dark suit, buttoned with precision, beard trimmed to strict lines, silvered hair swept back as if he had somewhere important to be. And the eyes—those were the problem. They followed you. Quiet, assessing. Like, even now, from his frame on the wall, he was keeping score. Keeping watch.

She tipped her chin up toward the painting. "Hey old man, got any ghost mail for me today?"

As always, silence. Regal and unmoved.

Turning to the side table beneath the frame, she sifted through the clutter—envelopes, flyers, bills that came thick with adult responsibility. The usual pile of quiet demands. Her fingers paused on a flash of orange peeking out from the middle. She didn't need to read the name. Mary.

That dramatic, looping script, fit for a Regency diary or tucked into a lace-trimmed invitation, proclaimed it all. Dani smiled as she turned the card over in her hands. "Happy Birthday" sprawled across the front, each letter with extra curls, as if penned with a feather quill dipped in sass. She slid a finger under the envelope flap and pulled free a $50 Coffee Haven gift card.

A soft laugh escaped her. "Keeping me caffeinated and socialized."

Same card. Same joke. Year after year. Some people build friendships on long talks and secrets. They built their friendship at corner tables—hands wrapped around lattes, laptops open, conversations winding from deadlines to dreams.

She held the card up like a tiny trophy and glanced at Alvie's portrait. "Guess what, Gramps? She's done it again." Her voice dropped to a murmur as she rifled through the mess on the table. "I should just set up direct deposit at this point."

A soft rustle pulled her attention. It came from the pantry hall just past the breakfast room—usually filled with the scent of bread and fresh coffee at dawn, but dead silent now. The sound stopped as suddenly as it had started. Then something shifted behind her. She whipped around, fists raised like a boxer, heart hammering—only to find her mother standing there, grocery bags cradled in her arms and an amused tilt to her lips.

"Jesus, Mom!" Dani gasped. "You can't just materialize like that—I almost ascended."

Teresa Barrington, all effortless mischief wrapped in poised grace, lifted an eyebrow. "I took off work early. Thought I'd surprise you with something home cooked for dinner." She set the grocery bag down and unwound her scarf, a slow smile tugging at her lips. "What's the matter? You look like you've seen a ghost."

Dani wiped the sudden sheen of sweat that had gathered on her brow. "I don't know how you do that."

"Well, if you want, I can teach you the ways of the stealthy housewife."

The absolute last thing I want to be.

Still juggling groceries, Teresa stepped closer and flicked her wrist, sending the rest of the mail spilling onto the side table—never one for a second trip outside. Among the usual clutter, another brightly colored envelope slipped free; Its beautiful script was also unmistakable, her grandmothers.

Tearing it open, Dani's chest lifted with a small burst of joy inside. Another Coffee Haven gift card. And tucked beneath it, a crisp hundred-dollar bill.

"Wow. Money this year? She must've run out of vintage dresses to send you. The closet must be empty," Teresa teased.

"Hey, those dresses are—"

"A lifeline," Teresa interrupted with a grin. "For Mary."

She tapped the edge of the envelope in Dani's hand. "Well, at least you two figured out a system. She gets the gowns; you get the mystery heirlooms."

"Yeah. Worked out better than either of us expected." Dani shook her head.

Like clockwork, Mary called every year, her voice buzzing through the phone. "So? What did you get? Anything with lace? Silk? Please tell me there's a bustle."

Mary lived for those hand-me-downs—silks, lace, impossibly tiny buttons. Some even belonged to their great-grandmother, Vivienne. Dani had zero use for any of it, but Mary wore them like she'd been born in the wrong century.

Some dresses were too delicate to wear. Those stayed at Dani's, tucked away upstairs in the dilapidated servant's quarters, carefully stored in a sealed box meant to protect their fragile history. They planned to have those pieces grace a museum exhibit someday, once the mansion is finished. Her parents dreamed of turning the old Barrington place into a museum, but that future felt tangled in layers of peeling paint and decades of bad remodels. The bathrooms still clung stubbornly to seventies wallpaper that screamed out of place.

Teresa set the grocery bag down by the side table, slipping off her shoes and shrugging out of her coat. "You doing, okay?"

Dani nodded, maybe a little too quickly. "Yeah. Just... a long day."

"Go rest. Unless you want to help me clean up before dinner. There are still some dishes from last night that someone forgot." Teresa's brow lifted.

Dani backed away. "Oh no, I was just heading upstairs. Those dishes are Dad's, anyway. You picked him—I just got born into this mess."

Gathering groceries again, Teresa huffed, spinning on her heel toward the kitchen. Her voice floated back down the hall, a teasing threat. "Yeah, well, next time I'm picking the quiet dishwasher-safe model."

Making her way to the stairs, Dani smiled softly. The cool marble chilled the soles of her bare feet, grounding her with each step toward the quiet refuge of her room. Halfway up, something pulled her gaze through the massive picture window framing the courtyard below. The last embers of daylight filtered through thick branches, scattering dappled patches of gold across the glass.

At the top, she passed the portrait of her great-grandmother, Vivienne. Regal and unyielding, golden-brown hair swept into a perfect bun, crimson gown spilling like rich wine across the canvas. The artist's hand had been precise—every fold, every shadow rendered with considered care. But it was Vivienne's eyes that held Dani's attention: piercing green, sharp, and unblinking, a challenge from across time.

"Still perfect after all these years," Dani muttered, catching her reflection in the frame's glass. "And here I am, looking like I survived the Oregon Trail."

Her room was a quiet contradiction—past and present woven together in a strange harmony. The vintage bed, dark wood posts heavy and carved with scratches from a hundred years, stood as the room's heart. The fireplace, the radiator, the faded wallpaper—all relics meticulously preserved, echoes of a century that refused to fade away.

Modern life had crept into her sanctuary. Clothes lay tossed over a plush velvet armchair; Textbooks piled in careless towers on the roll-top desk. The soft glow of a laptop screen flickered against the antique mirror, a quiet pulse of today nestled in yesterday's frame.

Her satchel slipped from her shoulder, the worn leather landing gently on the bed. From beneath the chair, Toaster stirred—a sleepy guardian in stripes of orange and black. Round and perpetually unimpressed, he blinked up with slow, golden eyes. A gravelly purr rumbled from his throat as he nudged her hand with his head, tail curling around her wrist.

She reached down, her fingers brushing the orange rings that caught the light as she scratched behind his ears. "The sweetest pea," Toaster answered with a contented rumble, settling beside her.

From her bag, she pulled the trinket box—gears still, frozen mid-turn. But when her palm pressed to the lid, a faint vibration thrummed beneath her skin, like something inside was quietly whirring.

And then, the thought pushed its way through—the one she'd been shoving down all day. Mary was leaving. No matter how much she'd tried to drown it beneath laughter, conversations, and distractions, now, in the quiet of her room, it pressed too loud to ignore. Her eyes rolled upward, chasing away the sticky weight of the feeling.

She set the box on the nightstand and shot it a skeptical glance. Her fingers found the familiar weight of the key hanging from her necklace—a small, solid anchor when her mind spun.

Pushing off the bed, she moved without thinking, drawn to the bathroom—a place that felt safe because it hadn't changed. The claw-foot tub sat where it always had, its porcelain curves softened by time. Subway tiles, a basin sink, brass fixtures—each a little piece of history. But even here, modern life had left its mark: a tangled hair straightener cord, a half-used bottle of skincare, and a laundry basket spilling over with more tossed outfits than actual dirty clothes.

She caught her reflection in the mirror.

Green eyes, tired and rimmed with faint shadows from a long day. Brown hair, chocolate-dark and wavy, tumbling past her shoulders in loose, unruly strands that caught gold in the light. Her skin held that warm, sun-kissed tone that suggested Mediterranean heritage, scattered with soft freckles across her nose and cheeks. Dark eyebrows framed her face with bold strokes, and her lashes were naturally thick with no help from mascara.

Taking a moment to study herself, she knew she was beautiful—but not in the delicate, feminine way magazines celebrated. Her beauty was something softer, more androgynous. Strong jawline, full lips, features that could make both men and women do a double-take without being able to explain exactly why. It was the face that transcended easy categories, magnetic in a way that had nothing to do with conventional prettiness.

Turning from the mirror, she peeled off her clothes and stepped into the shower. Toaster trailed behind lazily, curling into a tight ball on the bath mat. His quiet presence settled around her like a soft anchor. The hot water poured over her, sliding across the firm planes of her shoulders, tracing the lean muscles honed by years of sprints, sharp turns, and goal kicks. For a while, she let herself vanish into the gentle steam; The heat swallowed the edges of her restless thoughts.

When she stepped out, skin flushed, hair damp and tangled, the room seemed calmer—the night had tucked itself in around her. Wrapped in an oversized hoodie and soft sleeping pants, she fell onto the bed, surrendering to the pull of exhaustion.

Toaster, now a purring lump of fur, had settled back onto the pillows. Dani nudged him with a tired grin, fingers threading through his thick coat.

"How many squirrels did you yell at today? Be honest."

The tabby responded with a low, throaty meow, pressing his face into her knuckles.

For the first time that night, she truly smiled. His wide, soft eyes—dilated with trust and something fierce—always lifted her. They were proof of a love, steady and absolute, no matter the mood or the weight of the day. The tightness in her chest eased just enough to let her breathe.

But then, something shifted—not inside the room, but just beyond its edges. The air thinned—not from lack of oxygen, but as if sound itself had pulled away. A pressure pressed behind her ears, faint but unyielding. Her fingers stilled against Toaster's fur. The cat lifted its head, eyes wide, tail flicking once. A soft hum—more felt than heard—rippled through the room, feeling like the walls themselves had exhaled.

She glanced at the clock.

10:14 p.m.

She blinked.

11:14.

No—that couldn't be right. She could've sworn. She felt overtired. That is all.

Shaking her head, she switched off the lamp. Darkness pooled across the room like ink.

2

BE GOOD FOR ME

PRESENT DAY

Dani awoke so groggy she didn't even remember grabbing her keys. It was nearly 3 a.m., the house was still and quiet. One second, she was going to the bathroom, and the next she was pacing her room, staring at the ceiling like it had answers. Time folded, then she was shoving her feet into worn-out sneakers. She ran outside and got into the car.

I can't wait until tomorrow.

Not for this.

Not for her.

The streets were dead quiet, Portland curled up in that strange middle-of-the-night hush that made everything hit different. The freeway snaked, a ghost town with no cars, no cops, and no headlights in either direction. Just her. Speeding like she'd fallen straight out of Tron.

Fog clung low over the pavement, catching in the halos of streetlights soft, golden, almost retro looking. Portland at night could have that tinge, almost like the background of some old sci-fi movie. Eighties maybe. Blade Runner without the budget or Total Recall without the Mars part. The kind where the graphics were garbage, but the vibe? Untouchable.

Storefronts she knew never closed, sat dark. Neon signs unlit.

Bridges empty. No cyclists, no late-night weirdos, no tent cities tucked under over-passes. Just streets, wet and endless. Someone emptied the entire city for her emotional side quest.

She had to see her. Needed to feel her. Say it out loud or screw it up forever. It didn't matter. She'd figure it out once she was there.

The roads rolled by for what felt like hours until she rounded the last corner of Mary's Boise neighborhood in North Portland. The porch light glowed like it had been waiting for her. Nerves were flying out of control; she fought to calm them before stepping out of her car and towards the front door.

The door opened before she even knocked. Dani's brain stalled. Mary. Barefoot. Loose plaid pajama pants hanging low on her hips. Thin little lace bralette doing absolutely nothing to help Dani's grip on reality. *Who the hell opens a door like this?*

Mary didn't.

Mary never did.

Not for her or anyone.

Dani's heart did this stupid, traitorous lurch: half panic, half what-the-actual-hell, because this wasn't normal. This wasn't their dynamic. This wasn't how this night was supposed to go. Dani was supposed to be the one to confess.

And yet... here Mary was. Standing there like it was nothing, and it was fine. Dani was two seconds from completely losing her mind. Her throat felt dry and her brain was short-circuiting.

Say something. Say something. "...Hey." *Flawless Dani. Real smooth.*

Mary just smiled softly. She looked at Dani as if this was commonplace and permitted. Stepping back, she let Dani in. Dani barely made it a few feet inside. Oversized hoodie swallowing her frame. Cargo pants slung low. She wore her black puffer vest unzipped, as if it didn't matter. Ball cap pulled down low, shadowing her eyes just enough to make her look like trouble.

Apparently, that was all it took. Mary stared at her, with eyes wide and her lips pink. She was trying to suppress a smile, but it was losing the battle. Dani didn't even have time to speak. Because there it was — that little bite of Mary's teeth catching her bottom lip. The hungry kind, no the fuck me kind. Dani standing in her doorway looking so good, was the final straw.

Mary's hand came up like muscle memory. Tugged her in. Soft fingers against hoodie strings. Bare feet backing across the wood floor without looking.

Dani's brain went blank.

Mary's fingers slid beneath the hem of Dani's hoodie, palms splayed over bare skin, and paused.

"You always smell like this." she whispered, voice barely audible against Dani's throat.

Dani blinked, mind spiraling. "Like what?"

"Like you ran through a pine forest wrapped in Vetiver and never stopped."

Mary breathed deeper, eyes fluttering closed. "Mixed with Yuzu and sin. God, I've wanted to know if your skin tasted like your scent."

Soft hair brushed Dani's neck as Mary tipped her head back, lips finding the curve of her jaw. Warm breath against skin. Close. So stupidly close.

Dani turned into it, capturing Mary's mouth with her own. Those lips she'd dreamed about, soft and real under hers. She kissed her like she was starving.

The back of Mary's knees pressed into the edge of Dani's bed, or her bed. The hell if Dani could tell anymore. Nothing about this added up, but her brain didn't care.

Mary tugged her closer. No hesitation or awkwardness, just friends messing around in a gray area. Dani moved between her thighs like she'd done this a million times before. Her palms braced low on Mary's hips, guiding her exactly where she wanted her.

Mary's sigh punched straight through her like it had teeth. Softly feminine and delicate. Very sweet.

A fire burned instantly between Dani's legs, tightening her slick nub. She dipped her head, caught Mary's bottom lip between her teeth. Gentle, for someone this sweet. But the soft whimper it pulled from her hit low — a sound Dani wanted to swallow whole. Every part of her leaned in. She wasn't leaving or stopping.

Not when this pretty, flushed thing in a bralette was letting her take whatever she wanted.

And when Mary arched beneath her, trust-falling right into Dani's hands like she'd been waiting forever, something broke loose completely.

Hands slid lower.

Pajama pants peeled away.

Mary's bare hips. Soft skin. Lavender and heat and everything Dani had never let herself imagine, but had somehow known would be this stupidly perfect was laid out before her.

Mary shifted beneath her, allowing her legs to fall open in a quiet invitation. Dani sat back for half a beat. The view knocked the breath right out of her. Beautiful. Messy. Hers.

She gripped the curve of Mary's thighs, thumbs digging in just enough to leave a mark behind. She bent, mouth moving down, dragging sharply along her belly skin meant to be kissed raw. It wrecked Dani.

She bit Mary's thigh. Her left free hand floating up to graze Mary's breast and feel her hardened nipple. It's pointed bloom stabbing her palm like electric pulses. Mary tilted her head, cheeks flushed, lips pink and parted.

And for once in Dani's life, it felt like the universe finally quit screwing with her. She lowered her mouth, not being able to handle the whimpers any longer. She wanted to taste her and swallow her release. She looked up at Mary, eyes blazing.

Mary shook her head yes. "Please" was all she could muster.

Dani nudged her with her nose, Mary's hips rolled with anticipation. She loved her center; it was Dani's favorite kind. Blushed plump lips with a beautiful blooming nub barely peeking out, begging for attention.

It tasted like heaven. Like something she was never supposed to have, but now that she did, she wasn't giving it back. She savored it slowly. Mouth open, tongue pointed, dragging soft licks around her clit with just enough pressure to keep Mary straining beneath her. And yeah, the reaction was mutual. She could feel Mary hard and pulsing against her tongue. It didn't know whether to beg or break.

Mary's hands threaded into Dani's cap, tugging it off, yanking the ponytail, spilling brown waves loose against her hoodie.

"Naughty," Dani muttered against skin, voice rough. "Now I can't see what I'm doing."

She pulled back and sat up on her knees, attempting to shove her hair into a messy tie. Mary's hands coasted up her waist under her hoodie while she worked. Soft, tracing Dani's breasts to her ribs, down to her cut obliques.

"I want your pants off," Mary sweetly pleaded.

Dani's mouth curved confidently. "When I'm done with you, maybe." She caught Mary's wandering hand, kissed her fingers lazily before setting it aside. "Be good for me. Lay back."

Mary obeyed without a word. She laid back, eyes growing, and braced herself. Dani bent down and licked for what felt like hours. Her jaw never got tired, her tongue pulsed and swirled continuously.

She pushed her fingers inside slowly, deeply tasting everything that spilled for her. She pressed her mouth lower, tongue slipping inside to chase it, lips sealing around her entrance like she could drag her whole body closer through sheer want alone.

She couldn't get as deep as she wanted, but Mary moaned like it didn't matter, like she was close just from the effort. Her hands fisted in the shoulders of Dani's hoodie, holding her mouth tightly against her, desperate for more.

Hips rolled against Dani's mouth, shaking, riding that edge like she didn't care how long it took because she never wanted it to stop.

"I want to feel yours against mine, get on top." Mary whispered again, sweeter now. She pulled Dani up off her knees and to her face. She placed the softest kiss on Dani's lips.

Dani interrupted through her teeth. "I came here to say something," she whispered back between kisses.

Mary's smile tilted. "That you love me?"

Everything in Dani's body froze. Her eyes snapped open, her heart pounding. "I… what."

She uttered barely any words. Her mouth kept moving, but nothing came out. She repeatedly moved her lips, but no words formed. She knew what she wanted to say, but it felt like she was stuck in a loop, unable to move forward.

Breaking through the never-ending circle of doom was that sound.

Sharp. Real. Rude.

Glass rattling on the nightstand. The buzz of a phone notification, dragging her out by the throat.

Mary's body vanished.

The bed was cold and wide beneath her.

Figures.

She silenced the phone and let her hand fall back onto the mattress. Sheets twisted around her legs.

Skin damp. Still alone.

The ceiling stared back at her, all innocent and dark. *Of course, it was a dream.* She let out a flat laugh too loud for the quiet. Her brain was out here directing full-length fantasies starring her best friend, and she couldn't even claim it meant anything.

Not really.

It wasn't love.

Her heart couldn't be involved. Right?

Tomorrow, she'd go help pack up Mary's sweaters and books like a totally normal friend.

Fantastic for me.

She jolted upright, breath gasping as the bed frame thudded hard against the wall. Sheets and pillows spilled to the floor in a heap, her heart pounding loud in her ears. Blinking, she took in the room.

"Shit, what time is it?"

Morning light poured through the wide picture window, casting long golden streaks across the floor. The downtown skyline rose in the distance, its pink skyscraper catching the sun's first rays with glass glowing like fire against the city's waking hum.

Across the room, Toaster remained entirely unfazed. Lazily grooming an extended paw with the slow accuracy of someone unrattled, he perched on the dressing table.

Dani glared at him. "Really? Not even a Saturday courtesy meow? At least knock something off the counter like a real cat!"

He flitted his tail in indifference with his usual blank stare.

No time to argue with a cat.

She pulled on light-wash jeans and a vintage tee that might've passed for clean, tucking the hem into her waistband while shaking out her half-damp brown hair. A hat kept it corralled around her shoulders. The corduroy jacket made it look like a choice, not a scramble. So did the Converse—retro, scuffed, but still holding on.

Bounding to the grand staircase, she saw her father already stepped into the entryway, adjusting the strap of his weathered messenger bag. He had the effortless charm that made him impossible to stay mad at—lean, broad-shouldered, with warm green eyes and a smile that never quite faded. He'd just run a hand through his dark hair, peppered with the first hints of gray, leaving it slightly tousled.

"Rise and grind, noodle!" He yelled up.

The nickname had stuck since she was five and tried to cook dinner by dumping an entire box of spaghetti into the toilet—because, apparently, it "looked like a big enough pot." She swore it would "soften, eventually." He hadn't let it go since.

"Are you taking the car today?" She yelled down as she descended the staircase.

"I'm going to bike to the Saturday Market," he gestured towards the kitchen. "She's having another episode, so I don't mind the long ride home."

"You sure? I can give you a ride."

He waved a hand. "I'm good. I love the exercise." The door closed, leaving a hush in his wake.

She moved toward the kitchen.

Her mother, lost in thought, stood by the window as a bagel smoldered in the toaster. Dark tendrils of smoke rose upward. Dani rushed to yank it out, waving away the burn before the smell lingered on everything.

"Yo, Earth to Mom! Are we just summoning the fire department for fun now?"

Something startled Teresa; her eyes momentarily unfocused before she shook her head. "Oh my goodness, I'm so sorry. I was... lost in thought."

Dani pressed her fingers to her forehead. "Mom, respectfully, you need a new hobby that isn't spiraling about my life. I'm twenty-one. I can't even stick to a meal prep plan, let alone manage your anxiety, too."

"Sweetheart, you're a Cancer. Overthinking and self-sabotage basically are your full-time jobs."

Dani crossed her arms. "Okay—ouch. That was uncalled for."

The corner of Teresa's mouth twitched, but her focus drifted, fingertips grazing the edge of the counter.

"It's just your tuition for next year," she mumbled. "I don't know if we're going to have enough."

"Mom." Her tone softened. She reached out, squeezing her arm. "So far, we've succeeded. We'll figure it out. We always do."

"I know. It's just frustrating. All that wealth locked up in Alvie's properties, and we can't touch a cent without drowning in legal fees."

Dani forced a laugh. "Great-Grandfather Alvie: business legend, estate planning disaster. Generous beyond the grave but still micromanaging from the afterlife."

"He always said, 'Land is power.' Just wish we had a bit more money to go with it." Teresa replied with sadness in her voice.

"How about you focus on breakfast first?" Dani offered a crooked smile, trying to lighten the mood.

Teresa's eyes widened in surprise as she turned to the toaster. "Oh, honey, I've burned your bagel..."

"I'll just grab something quick on the way, probably something questionable." She kissed her mom's cheek and grabbed her keys. "Love you. Don't sign up for any credit cards while I'm gone."

Teresa rolled her eyes while fussing over the toaster.

Outside, the morning air hit her like a splash in the face. She's late—and completely unprepared for what the day would bring.

3

STOP-AND-GO HEARTS

PRESENT DAY

Brake lights flared up ahead, casting an angry red glow inside her car. Dani drummed her fingers impatiently on the steering wheel as traffic inched forward in a stop-and-go crawl on the 405. It was just another typical day in Portland. She flicked on the radio, then off again two seconds later. Nothing helped. No song could override the noise in her head.

The woman in the car next to hers caught her eye—a black Subaru with a rainbow sticker on the bumper and a "Save the Trees" decal on the rear window. Two women sat up front, laughing about something. Windows cracked low enough for the music to spill out. They were the people Dani used to watch from a distance when she was younger, imagining what it might feel like to be that comfortable with herself.

The driver, a black-haired woman with piercing blue eyes, glanced over and smiled. Her bold smile caught Dani's attention. The sunlight glinted off her nose ring. Dani offered a polite nod and quickly looked away, feeling a strange flutter in her stomach for no apparent reason.

Well. Maybe for one reason.

Out of the corner of her eye, she noticed movement. The passenger was gesturing wildly and mouthing something. Then the driver leaned over and rolled down the window further. They must have noticed the rainbow sticker her dad had quietly added to the back of the car after their awkward but heartfelt conversation about her sexuality—his sweet, wordless way of saying "I love you exactly as you are."

"My friend wants to know if you have a girlfriend and what your number is!" she called across the two feet of traffic separating them with a wink.

Dani scratched the back of her neck, suddenly hyper-aware of her own face. "No girlfriend," she called back, her voice catching a bit. "But definitely on the roster."

The passenger groaned and sank lower in her seat, burying her face in her hands. "Oh my God, please stop! I'm so embarrassed, I can't even" she laughed, muffled and mortified.

The driver motioned her hand to Dani. "You spotted her, just say hi. It's not that difficult."

The girl hesitated.

The driver didn't miss a beat. She leaned over the console, her eyes meeting Dani's for a split second. "Her loss!" she exclaimed, grinning.

Dani let out a surprised huff of laughter. Feeling a mix of flattered and off balance emotions, she raised a hand in a vague wave, then immediately regretted it. Her fingers hovered in the air, unsure of what they had just committed to.

The light turned green.

The Subaru rolled forward with a chirp of tires, their arguing echoing behind them, lingering in the air. Dani sat there too long, that weird half-wave still hanging in the space between thought and instinct.

She dropped her hand slowly, shoved it into her jacket pocket, and exhaled through her nose.

She could've really flirted back. Could've enjoyed feeling wanted. But all she could think about was one person.

Mary.

Was that even a thing? Or was it just a deep friendship complicated by the length of their friendship, the extent of their shared experiences, and the closeness they shared? She had never lived such a situation with anyone else. No one else made her mind feel like a scratched record. Skipping, repeating, and looping through an unanswerable question.

By the time she turned onto Mary's block near Mississippi Avenue, she still lacked clarity—only more confusion.

Then she noticed the boxes stacked outside.

Her stomach dropped.

It was undeniable now.

She pulled up to the curb and killed the engine. The street was quiet, just the sound of birds and the distant low hum of a lawn mower somewhere down the block. She stayed in the car longer than necessary, staring at the crooked stack of packing tape and permanent marker.

She could still feel the ghost of that dream. The way Mary had opened the door. Barefoot, bralette, eyes soft and heavy with wanting. It wasn't just the heat of it still lingering; it was the ease. That version of Mary had been waiting for her all along. As if none of this confusion had ever existed.

Dani shook her head, hard. She needed to lock it down. That hadn't been real. This was.

She opened the door and stepped out.

As she rounded the sidewalk, Mary appeared on the porch, hair pulled up into a loose twist, curly locks catching the light. She wore a fitted black top tucked into high-waisted jeans and a cinched wrap sweater, cream-colored and dramatic in that vintage way.

"Well, well," Mary called, leaning against the railing. "If it isn't my favorite indentured servant."

Dani raised an eyebrow. "I'm not lifting a single box until I see a signed contract, and a catered lunch."

Mary smiled in that way she did when she knew she was being just charming enough to get away with it.

"Oh, don't worry. I pay in emotional damage and vintage collectables. Get in here."

She didn't wait—just turned, heading back inside.

And for a second, Dani paused again.

The wrap sweater, the sweetly high voice, the way Mary's hips swayed effortlessly as she walked—all of it was too close, too much, too soon after the dream. Dani followed, her grip on the inside of her pants pocket tightening, hoping it would anchor her. She stepped into the house and the dream crashed into her full force.

The floorboards were the same. The scent of lavender and laundry was the same. There was no bralette, no bare skin, but the emotional static was identical. She swallowed hard. Time to pack boxes and pretend she hadn't mentally undressed her best friend for eight straight hours of deep sleep.

This is going to be fantastic.

Mary sat for a second, watching Dani dart in and out of the house like a machine. Arms full of books, sleeves pushed to her elbows, hair in a messy bun that somehow still looked planned.

Mary didn't miss a beat. "Yo! Can you also grab anything labeled 'fragile.' I don't trust myself not to drop it."

They fell into rhythm easily, packing, lifting, sorting the clutter of Mary's life like it was one last shared project. Nostalgia softened the edges. At one point, Mary groaned, trying to muscle a box labeled Books Heavy! toward the front door.

"Ugh. Why do I own so many books?"

"Because you're a nerd." Dani stepped in and lifted it clean onto her shoulder.

"Okay, show-off. Since when are you this strong?" Mary narrowed her eyes.

Dani bit the inside of her cheek. *Since I dreamed about pinning you down and wrecking you six ways to sunrise. Yeah. Not saying that out loud.*

"Ten years of soccer drills and strength training," she said instead. "You think all that running was just for fun?"

"I knew there was a reason I kept you around," Mary smirked.

They reached the last box. Everything else was packed. Dani's grip tightened—not to steady it, but to stall, to keep from sealing the moment that would send Mary away.

With a sigh, Mary dropped onto the couch—the only piece of furniture stubborn enough to stay put.

"Thank God Cleo left this place to me," she muttered, patting the cushion beside her. "Renting in Portland is a joke."

The room felt hollow, packed and echoing. Dani looked around, unsure where to rest her hands.

"At least I only have to move my personal crap," Mary added. "If I had to haul all this furniture too, I'd be on the floor sobbing." She popped up and crossed to the fridge. "Want a kombucha? They're still cold."

Dani took the bottle and dropped it onto the couch beside her. "So the tenant's just... using everything?"

"Yeah, my cousin's friend. She's moving in next week. I told her it's all hers if she waters the plants and doesn't summon demons or whatever."

She took a sip, then paused. "It's weird though. Leaving it all. Feels like pressing pause on my life here." They sat in silence for a beat. Just the clink of glass. The faint hum of neighborhood noise.

Mary tilted her head, and her eyes were sharp. Something had just dawned on her, and it was clear in her expression... "So..." she started slowly. "So... are you gonna be okay while I'm gone?" Mary asked, trying for breezy. "You were finally making headway in the 'seducing the tea party wife' chapter of your coming-out memoir. Not that I've been... paying attention or anything."

Dani's mouth opened, but nothing came out.

"You know I'm right," Mary wagged her finger.

Dani smirked, but it didn't fully land. She rubbed the edge of the bottle lip with her thumb. "Yeah, well. The freedom to remain confused is sacred, right?"

Mary didn't look away.

Shoulders tightened before Dani caught herself. It was just Mary. The one person she didn't need to run qualifiers with. Still, something about the way she said it twisted like a hook behind her ribs.

She picked at the kombucha label. "Depends on the day. Some days, I think I've figured my life out. Other days it's like wait, am I just tired? Hungry? Bi? Lesbian? All the above?"

"Classic identity crisis combo meal." Mary joked.

"I seriously need a punch card."

Mary held up a hand, counting off fingers. "So... Questioning? Emotionally allergic to commitment?"

"Can I get a 'none of the above'? It's been a wild few years. Nothing has worked out for me, and I'm sure I'm just defective." Dani groaned.

"I mean, it's your identity crisis. You can do whatever the hell you want with it."

"I just—ugh. I hate how different it feels. With girls, it's like gravity. Like I've always been orbiting them, even before I realize it. With guys, it's like... spinning a wheel. Total chaos. Sometimes, it lands on something bearable. Sometimes it's just noise."

"You're twenty-one, Dani. You're allowed to not have an answer yet." Mary leaned her head back against the couch.

"Tell that to the rest of the world," Dani muttered. "Everyone's ready to hit me with their label printer."

The silence that followed wasn't awkward; it was simply tense. It wasn't just about orientation or labels. Mary had been her sounding board, her lifeline. And now, at the very moment, Dani needed her support the most, she was leaving. And everyone knows that, regardless of the circumstances, when there's a gap between two individuals, the relationship naturally weakens. It becomes more challenging to maintain consistency without the physical proximity.

Mary's hand landed lightly on Dani's arm. A small, familiar gesture—but there was something about it now that felt sweeter, softer.

Dani's heart fluttered.

"Hey," Mary said, her voice a little quieter than usual. "For real... thank you. For all of it. You've been the best friend I could ask for. I don't say that lightly. I'm lucky to have you, dude."

"Okay, gross. Shut up. I was literally late and just did the heavy lifting." Dani let out a strained laugh, the sound scraping at her throat.

"You're like a sister to me," she said—and then, after a beat too long, "At least, most days."

The words landed with a soft thud between them. *Sister. Right.* That really drove the knife in. *Dream me? Absolutely unwell. Real me? Absolutely friend-zoned.*

Dani sensed Mary's piercing gaze, searching, waiting, and yearning for her approval. However, she lacked the agreement. Was this merely a platonic friendship, or was there something more? Her own emotions were uncertain. Despite this, she compelled herself to meet Mary's eyes and mustered a weak smile.

"It's just a year. We got this."

Tucking her bangs behind her ear, Mary tried to find words. "I hope you're still here in Portland when I come back," a frayed laugh followed, as if it weren't even her own voice. "Please don't run off with some incredibly handsome man while I'm away."

Mary, uncomfortable with the silence, began rambling to fill the void.

"Or... a girl." She spat out, the implication loud. "Or get recruited by some out-of-state soccer team."

Dani offered her a reassuring smile. "I'll be here. If I know, you'll come back with your ridiculous hats and corsets."

Mary's fingers curled around the strap of her bag. "Don't say that like it's easy," she said, voice low. "I don't want to come back and find everything's different."

"Not you turning this into a Hallmark goodbye! Disgusting. I love it." Mary's eyes filled with tears, but she swiftly blinked them away. She stood up, slapped her hands on her knees, and exclaimed, "Welp!" She took a step forward and tossed her kombucha bottle into the trash. "Are you done?" she asked, holding out her empty bottle to Dani.

"Yeah," Dani lazily point-shot the bottle from the couch with a perfectly arched, clean shot.

"Okay, wow," Mary tilted her head, bit her lip, before her brain caught up. Dani didn't breathe.

They froze for a moment, staring at each other. Mary looked at Dani's mouth, and Dani looked at hers. And then—nothing.

Mary turned, adjusted the strap of her bag as if she hadn't just rewired Dani's entire central nervous system.

"Welp, I've signed the contract. There's no turning back now."

"I don't think you packed enough," Dani replied, forcing a playful grin.

"How dare you imply I travel light? I am deeply wounded."

Clutching her imaginary pearls, Mary gasped as if attacked.

They stepped out of the house, Mary turning and locking the front door. She gave the outside a quick glance, then turned to look at the overstuffed trunk, giving it a final theatrical flourish. A sigh escaped her lips, and she shifted her weight, unsure of what to do next. Her fingers tapped a restless rhythm against the strap of her bag.

"This is it, huh?" Dani swallowed, a hint of apprehension in her voice. "Yep."

Another tense pause ensued. Mary fidgeted with her bag once more, her hands clutched tightly. "You'll write, right? Like actual letters, not those lazy text messages?"

Dani huffed, a playful scoff escaping her lips. "Handwritten notes? What century do you think we're living in?"

Mary's smile softened, a gentle glint in her eyes. Her fingers traced the frayed edge of her sleeve. "I cherish old things far more than you'd expect."

Those words.

Old things.

Dani was older. Not by much. But enough. Enough that it might have meant something. *Say it now, Dani.* But a lump climbed her throat, thick and immovable. She knew if she opened her mouth, the wrong truth would fall out, maybe something irreversible.

So she reached for her shield. Humor.

"Don't forget about us peasants back home."

"Impossible. I'd miss my favorite peasant too much," Mary teased.

Another dreadful pause, dripping with meaning and shadowed by the inevitable risk.

Mary's lips parted like she was about to say something. Her gaze dropped—Dani's mouth, then her hand. But her phone buzzed in her pocket, and she flinched like the sound had struck her. She glanced at the screen, sighing.

"It's that time. I should go."

Dani nodded, the tense air inside her cracking like glass. "Yeah." Then she felt Mary's arms envelop her. The hug was stronger than it should have been. Mary held her tightly, as if unwilling to let go.

"Don't replace me, okay?"

She squeezed her eyes shut. "Not a chance."

When Mary finally closed her car door, Dani felt like she had been unmoored, left standing on unfamiliar ground. And when the car disappeared down the street—Dani let the tears fall.

In the car, Mary gripped the steering wheel tighter than necessary. Her knuckles paled. She didn't cry. But she didn't turn on the radio either.

At the first red light, she touched her necklace—then her lips—and shook her head like she could shake the feeling loose.

4

HOME RENOVATION, MENTAL DETERIORATION

PRESENT DAY

She swung open the front door, and the overwhelming scent of sawdust and freshly cut carpet hit her like a tidal wave. Dani groaned, "Dad." Sure enough, the guest room renovation project—the one he had promised to put off until summer—had begun.

Dani barely made it up the stairs before spotting Toaster, in a frenzied attack on a dangling thread from a roll of carpet over the banister. His tail thrashed wildly as he batted at it with his paws and gnawed on it with determination, engaged in a life-or-death struggle. Dani swiftly scooped him up, chuckling, "Fear not, citizens—I have vanquished the mighty beast! Who knew my fiercest opponent would be so fuzzy?" as Toaster let out an indignant meow, still tenaciously holding the thread.

A sharp bap! Bap! Echoed from upstairs.

The stapler clacked again.

Grumbling under her breath, Dani trudged toward the noise, her patience already thinning. She threw open the guest room door. Her dad was on the floor, elbows deep in a losing battle with the carpet. Tools and fabric scraps littered the room, and someone had shoved the antique furniture into the hallway in a mess.

Arms folded, she leaned against the doorframe. "Okay, correct me if I'm wrong, but last I checked, it's not summer yet, and we definitely didn't win the lottery."

He wiped his forehead with his sleeve, still struggling against the fabric. "Your mother wanted this done," he said, still adjusting the carpet as if it had offended him. "I figured if I start now, we might have time to go somewhere interesting this summer."

Dani raised an eyebrow. "With what money? And, where exactly were you thinking? Everything exciting is on the other side of the country or world."

That elicited a chuckle from him. "I worked overtime. Thank you. Unless you want another thrilling staycation. And there are only so many times we can take the Shanghai Tunnel ghost tour before the ghosts recognize us."

She laughed. "Yeah, we reached our limit when the tour guide started referring to us as regulars."

"Your mom is out with Lavinia at the spa. She'll be home in an hour. If I complete this task before then, I'm officially a legend." He grinned. This was his usual style; he would start projects with boundless optimism and disregard for the timeline.

"Ah, yes, nothing quite like home improvement to conclude an already hectic day," she remarked, retreating toward the hallway. "No one will coerce me into this."

"Well, to each their own." He snorted, returning to his struggle.

She turned and headed towards the sanctuary of her room. Jeans and a hoodie hit the floor first, clinging slightly as exhaustion finally settled into her bones. The room hadn't changed. It was still that peculiar blend of antique elegance and modern chaos. Across the bed, Toaster had already claimed his throne, elongating languidly like a miniature king in his castle. She had barely dropped onto the mattress before a nagging sensation tugged at the back of her mind.

She reached for the box covered in cogs and beautiful woodwork designs. The small stones on the lid cast shifting hues of violet, teal, and orange across the ceiling. Toaster's ears twitched at the mesmerizing light show, and his paw lazily swatted at the air. With a quiet breath, she ran her thumb over the carvings, getting to the lid seam. She attempted to lift it.

Nothing.

Shit, she said she would help me open it. Forgot.

Flipping the box over, she traced its edges with her fingertips, searching for a clasp or any other mechanism that might open it. However, she found nothing except a tiny keyhole in the front. A glimmer of hope ignited in her mind as she glanced towards the bedroom door.

Slipping out of bed, she approached the original Edwardian door lock, skillfully rolling the skeleton key between her fingers. The cat watched her movements with deep attention, its tail flickering with annoyance at the way she shifted on the bed. She tried to insert the key into the lock, but it was a tad too large.

"Alright," she muttered, flipping the key over and trying again. Still doesn't fit. Frustration crept in. "Seriously?" Setting the box down, she grabbed a letter opener from her desk, wedging the blade along the seam. No shift. No give. She tried the butt of her palm. Nothing. Her frustration boiled over. With a dramatic groan, she spun on her heel and stalked down the hall toward her dad's construction zone.

"Dad, do you have a tiny screwdriver?"

"Depends—what for?"

"This ridiculous thing Mary gave me. It won't open."

"Maybe it's not meant to be." George delivered the line like it was ancient wisdom.

She shot him a dry look. "It'wise forest elder."

Spotting what she needed, she reached across a roll of carpet and snatched up the screwdriver. "Thanks," she said, holding it up like a trophy.

"Always a pleasure," he called back, already half-buried in wall trim.

She hurried back to the box. Five minutes passed. Still nothing. Dani slumped back in her chair, pushing the tools aside. As she looked in the mirror, something silver glinted, catching the bedside lamp's glow. A small key dangled from the chain around her neck, brushing lightly against her skin as she shifted. She'd forgotten it was there, but now, as her eyes dropped to the box in her lap, a thought struck. The key also came from Mary's grandma, Cleo. Could it belong to this box?

She lifted the key to the box's keyhole and slid it in. It fit smoothly. She paused, took a slow breath, then turned it with care.

Click.

The box gave a small shudder. Inside, tiny brass gears rotated—some clockwise, some counterclockwise, and some in strange, impossible directions that made her eyes ache to follow.

"What in the?" she whispered, leaning closer.

The gears aligned, clicking into place with a satisfying sound like a combination lock unraveling. Beneath them, barely visible, she glimpsed etched numbers—dates carved into the metal. Its gears were stuck on 1905 and wouldn't budge. A low hum vibrated through the box, seeping up her fingers and into her arms. It wasn't just a mechanical sound; it was a bad feeling, the air in the room stuttering and distorting around her.

Toaster arched his back, his fur standing on end. He let out a warning growl that Dani had never heard from him before. The cat fixed its yellow eyes on the box, its pupils dilated to black circles.

A small, blue arc of light crackled from the keyhole. The lid flapped open, showing all of its gears inside. Dani flinched, jerking back. The inside flashed brilliantly, blinding them.

The box snapped shut with a sharp clack, its light vanishing instantly. Then silence fell. Once alive beneath her hands, the metal was cold again. The air tingled. A faint static charge crackled over her skin, humming through the metal in steady, unnatural throbs.

The cat was now watching her, fully alert and unblinking.

Her ears were ringing with adrenaline as she slowly withdrew the key. There was no jolt, no spark, nothing. She pressed the key necklace back against her chest. Turning the box over in her hands, she inspected every side. *If it's closed, it can't start a fire, right?* It was far easier to joke about it than to panic. It was simpler to dismiss it as a mechanical malfunction, like an old wiring issue, a magnetized lock, or even a trick of the light. There always had to be some explanation.

The thing had to be over a hundred years old. Probably some elaborate novelty from another era. She'd been to the Musée Mécanique in San Francisco—one of her dad's quirky vacation stops. Wall-to-wall automata, player pianos, coin-operated fortune tellers. Weird stuff that moved and blinked and made noise, all built with springs and gears. This box? It wasn't so different. Just older. More... dramatic.

She shook it off and set the box gently on her nightstand, the key still warm in her hand. Answers could wait. The adrenaline was ebbing fast, leaving behind a deep, physical fatigue. Her shoulders ached. Her brain felt like static. She was finished for the night.

Laying back onto her pillow, she twirled the tiny key on her necklace between her fingers, exhaustion tugging at the edges of her mind. Toaster nudged her hand, pawing curiously at the dangling metal. His purr rippled through the quiet, coaxing her closer to unconsciousness.

As the last threads of wakefulness unraveled, the key necklace slipped from her grasp, landing softly on her shirt. Outside, the wind stirred. The house groaned. The box sat untouched, its edges emitting a faint hum—barely audible but undeniably there.

Teresa sat at the large wooden desk, red pen in hand, flipping through a stack of essays. The sharp scratch of ink against paper was rhythmic, steady. Across the room, George sat at his desk, the glow of his laptop casting a soft hue over his face. The soft rustle of papers and the faint glow of lamplight filled the Barrington library. But his fingers had stilled on the keyboard. She looked up at him. He had been silent, his thoughts clearly elsewhere.

"Dani and Mary went to see the lights again."

A chuckle escaped him, and his lips curved in amusement. "That time of year already?" He swiveled in his chair. "What's missing from my storage this time?"

Her eyes softened, though they didn't quite laugh. "George..." She set her pen down and rubbed her thumb over the bridge of her nose. "She cares about that girl. We know it. She knows it."

He leaned back in his chair and exhaled slowly. "Tess, we live in Portland, and in a world where kids have entire coming-out playlists on Spotify. This isn't an issue."

She tilted her head, searching his face. "Then why do we never talk about it?"

He sighed, frustration showing as he ran a hand through his hair. "She's smart. She knows how we feel, stickers included. Do we really need to say it out loud?"

Teresa leaned forward, elbows resting on the desk. "Maybe she doesn't know that." Her voice softened. "Maybe she worries. She'll disappoint us."

That hit its mark.

George's jaw locked. He turned toward the window, staring at the dark silhouette of trees outside.

It was never about whether Dani liked boys, girls, or both—her parents didn't care about that. What they cared about was the silence. The way she kept orbiting the same question without landing. Even when she was younger, crush talk was something she dodged, brushing it off like it didn't apply to her. There had always been that quiet draw toward Mary, heavier than she let herself admit. And maybe her parents noticed. Maybe that's why Teresa sometimes hesitated before asking about boyfriends, like she didn't want to spook her.

They were never the problem. They wondered—had they done something that made her feel like she couldn't share? Had they missed a moment where they should've said, Whoever you love, we just want you happy?

Because that was the truth. It always had been. Dani just hadn't completely said it out loud.

"She's an adult now," George said after a beat. "She'll figure it out. We just need to let her be... her. And we'll be here when she's ready."

Teresa studied him, then nodded slowly.

He pushed back from his desk and crossed the room, kneeling beside her chair. Resting his head in her lap, he traced slow, absentminded circles on the back of her hand.

"Everything is okay," she murmured, threading her fingers through his hair.

"I know," he smiled. "But you know who might not be okay?"

She tilted her head, amused.

"Me," he said flatly. "Because I might've already started the upstairs carpet."

Dani stood barefoot in the kitchen, staring into the open fridge like it might offer ideas. Her hand rested on the door, unmoving, long past the point of actually looking.

"You're going to let all the cold out," her mom called gently from the pantry.

"I guess I'm not hungry," Dani replied, grabbing a single grape anyway and popping it into her mouth like it might prove otherwise.

She shut the door slowly, then grabbed a bagel from the counter and a book from the living room side table. Without another word, she padded quietly back upstairs. The trinket box, untouched for a week, sat on her nightstand.

She tossed the book onto her bed, climbed in beside it, and then realized she was avoiding other things. "Oh, Shit. I have a test soon." She groaned. A slow stretch rolled through her limbs, muscles aching from yesterday's soccer match. Her body wanted to stay tangled in the blankets with this book. But now, her brain was already ticking through the day ahead, midterms and errands.

With a quiet sigh, she swung her legs back over the bed. The wooden floor met her feet with a soft, extraordinary shock. Ugh, Time to move. Toes and ankle joints popped as she shuffled through her room, searching for her keys, a semi-clean pair of jeans, and whatever semblance of preparedness she could muster.

She needed to lock in, but everything like her desk, the scattered notebooks, even the air, felt cluttered. With a small huff, she rifled through her papers, then froze. The bag. Still hanging from the back handle of the door, packed and ready. She rolled her eyes at herself, grabbed her smart tablet, and stuffed it into the front pocket.

Toaster hadn't moved from his cozy nook on the bed, his tail wafting lazily, even though he knew she was about to leave.

Leaning down, she pressed a quick kiss between his ears. "Try not to stage a coup before dinner," she said, scratching under his chin.

Grabbing her bike from the garage, she adjusted her green coat and threw on a helmet. The morning air hit her like a brisk wave, thick with fog and damp earth. As she coasted down the steep hill, the gears clicked with the rubber hum of tires weaving through the silence.

Two older buildings nestled her favorite coffee shop, its paint-chipped antique teal sign barely visible through the mist: 'Coffee Haven'. Inside, the rich aroma of espresso mingled with the warmth of freshly baked croissants wrapping around her like a familiar comfort, woven with the soft scent of well-loved books.

She pulled her gift card from her pocket, pretending to study the menu even though she already knew what she wanted. It was just a habit. She placed her order, fall in a cup, and some semblance of control in a morning she hadn't even been awake enough to assess.

She scanned the crowded cafe while waiting for her drink. Portland types everywhere. Laptops, flannel, battered copies of obscure novels, and heated discussions about screenplays no one would finish. A barista with a nose ring poured oat milk into a latte while someone in the corner argued whether farm-to-table ethics applied to coffee beans. This was her city, yet somehow, she felt like she was watching it from the outside lately.

"Extra-hot, oat milk, mushroom-infused chai with a hint of smoked sea salt for Dani!" the barista announced unenthusiastically. Stepping forward, she nodded her thanks as she took the warm cup, the heat seeping through the cardboard sleeve and into her chilled fingers.

Finding a seat was always nearly impossible, but fortunately today one was open. A small two-person table near the back sat empty, a napkin draped over the surface like a half-hearted claim.

Dani pulled out her smart tablet and pen as she settled into a chair. The seat across from her was vacant, which felt unusual. It was silly; she had sat there alone countless times before, but today, the absence felt more significant. The coffee tasted bitter, and the music overhead seemed too loud. Everything just felt... off.

The fog outside thickened, curling around the streetlamps, and her gaze drifted to the window beside her, where soft blue lights flickered—bouncing, pulsing, almost playful—darting through the mist like restless fireflies in the center of the busy street. She blinked, leaned closer, but the lights vanished, swallowed by the fog as if they'd never been there at all. She rubbed her eyes, *should have stopped doom scrolling earlier and went to sleep.*

Her pen hovered over the tablet, but no thoughts came to mind. Questions swirled restlessly in her head: *Full ride scholarship for soccer. Am I good at anything else? Why am I majoring in business? It's boring as hell. Why do I feel like I'm drifting?* She absentmindedly tapped her pen against the table, trying to keep her focus. However, a sudden voice cut through her mind-numbing rambling.

"Excuse me, may I have this seat?"

She looked up.

A tall, dark-haired man stood at the table. Sharp features, calm expression, quiet confidence. His piercing green eyes focused on the vacant chair. She paused. The urge to refuse clashed with the fact that she had no reason to.

"No one's coming," she muttered, pointing her pen toward the chair.

"Ah, thank you." He pulled the chair out smoothly, but as he sat, his hand brushed the table's edge, sending her smart pen rolling across the surface.

She rolled her shoulders and reached for the pen. He settled into the chair, movements rigid. She could sense she was being studied—not like a stranger stealing a passing glance, but like he was cataloging details, piecing something together. Then she noticed his eyes weren't on her face. They were on her necklace.

When he realized she was watching him, he looked up. "Is that homework?"

She lifted a brow. "Yeah. English." Then she looked him up and down. "And you're a big fan of dressing like a Titanic extra, huh? Bold choice."

"A—" He adjusted his cuffs. "I'm a history major, actually. Hence the attire." He settled back slightly. "My focus is on the ecological shifts of the Edwardian era. More precisely, introducing European skylarks to the Pacific Northwest."

I didn't ask, but okay. The last thing she wanted was some verbose stranger interrupting her already fragile morning concentration. Her pen hovered over her tablet—a silent protest against the impending conversation. But he wasn't taking the hint.

He leaned in. "And yourself?" His voice changed, sharpening. Each look felt slightly overwhelming; he was mapping out her face. "You're fond of antiques, I take it? Tell me, where did you get that necklace?"

The question wasn't casual. It wasn't a pickup line. It was something else. *Sir, I will throw hands.* Her fingers curled around her cup, heat pressing into her palm. His good looks and neat appearance doesn't indicate he's totally crazy.

He seemed to sense the shift in her demeanor. His composure softened. "I apologize," he said, his voice dropping. "I'm afraid that came across as extremely forward."

She arched an eyebrow. Forward? Who says that? His clothing caught her attention again—impossibly period-accurate, down to the shoes. Who wore such uncomfortable, meticulously crafted footwear while walking around downtown Portland? The shoes looked like they belonged in a museum.

A cosplayer, ok sir, I see you.

If Mary were here, she would have dissected every peculiar detail—known exactly what to say, how to unravel this kind of puzzle. Dani watched him scan the coffee shop, then glance down at his wristwatch.

A faint blue glow pulsed against his coat, flickering in rhythm—his hand hanging off the far side of the table where she couldn't see its source. He adjusted his coat as the glow intensified, and then, almost mechanically, like a marionette yanked by invisible strings, he shot up from his seat.

"I must leave," he announced abruptly, urgency cutting through the cafe's warmth. No explanation followed—only those words and a long, soft stare. He wasn't even her guest, yet his declaration felt rehearsed.

She sat there, mouth open. He was already moving, chair scraping against the floor. In three precise steps, he was halfway to the front, weaving between tables with mechanical grace. The bell chimed, and then—he was gone.

With her chai growing cold, she stared at the empty doorway.

Well, that was uncomfortably cinematic.

5

INTO THE LIGHT

PRESENT DAY

She spent the day hanging out too long at the coffee shop, helping her mom pull weeds and deadhead roses, and hauling furniture back into the freshly carpeted bedroom. Her dad had looked at the room like he'd just finished building a cathedral. She was exhausted.

Finally, finding a moment to breathe, she let the day settle around her. Stretched flat on her bed, she traced the ceiling cracks with her eyes, but all she could see was him. The way he'd studied her. The precise cadence of his words. That suit, those sharp eyes. The whole encounter had been magnetic. She never reacted to men like this. At the moment, she'd felt nothing but mild irritation, but now that she had space to think... Something about him had struck like a match against dry kindling, and she could still feel the heat.

She released a slow breath, forcing herself to let it go. It was nothing. It had to be.

Outside, the city hummed with traffic, voices, and life moving on. She rolled onto her side, pulling the blanket tighter around herself. Sleep found her slowly. Her fingers twitched, and her breathing came fast and uneven, chasing something elusive with the tiny key hanging from her necklace clutched in her fist.

The words slipped from her lips, barely audible amidst the haze of forest blurring in and out, lights dancing at the roots. The dream pulled her under like an unseen tide.

"I can't do it without you... I need..."

A thud shattered the silence.

Her eyes snapped open just as Toaster landed heavily at the foot of the bed, paws sinking into the mattress. She sucked in a sharp breath, the remnants of the dream clawing at the edges of her consciousness.

"You—" she gasped, the last word of her dream conversation ringing out.

Damp chill clung to her skin. Sweat beaded at her temples, strands of hair plastered to her neck. Her fingers, clenched tight around the sheets, slowly released. A faint indent creased her palm. She frowned, running her thumb over a small, unmistakable imprint. A little key. She must have held onto it during sleep.

Toaster let out a sharp, insistent meow. His tail was still, his ears pinned back.

"Alright, alright," she muttered, rubbing her face as she slid out of bed. "Are you having a full-blown exorcism?"

The cat hopped down and padded toward the door. His whiskers twitched, and he let out another piercing meow when she didn't move fast enough.

It's too late for this. "Let's go pee."

She grabbed a robe, slipping her arms into the soft fabric before sliding into her Birkenstocks. Toaster darted ahead, tail puffed like a bottlebrush, his eyes fixed on something beyond the stairs.

Something shimmered faintly in the reflection of the two-story picture window. The colors were purple and teal, moving like they breathed. Her heart raced. The glow wasn't coming from inside the house—it was coming from outside.

She paused at the mansion's front door, her fingers hovering over the handle. Deep instinct warned her to turn back. Instead, she made a sharp turn and slipped through the kitchen's servant entrance.

Outside, dense fog enveloped the estate. The ground beneath her feet was damp, and the usual scent of pine and earth felt suffocating. Her footsteps barely registered as she passed the buggy house, drawn toward the flickering light at the woods' entrance. She pushed past the first ferns, their branches snagging at her robe as she stepped into a small clearing beyond the tree line.

A trinket box hovered above the ground. Its lid slowly creaked open, releasing a mesmerizing glow of liquid fire. Dani's heart pounded as she reached for the key around her neck. To her astonishment, the key was also glowing. Teal light emanated from its edges, pulsing in sync with the box's rhythm. As the box dropped from its suspension, it landed gently amidst the pine needles. Curiosity propelled her to pick it up.

The light illuminated her skin, making her fingers feel hot as they clutched the key. An electric charge buzzed beneath her skin, and the box shook in her hands, its metal surface vibrating with increasing intensity. Tiny gears embedded in its surface rotated—some clockwise, others counterclockwise, and a few seemed to spin in directions that made her eyes hurt to follow.

She tried to set the box down, but her fingers refused to release it—as if the metal had fused to her skin. A small key, similar to Dani's, still partially turned in the lock, grew hot enough to burn, yet she couldn't let go.

The box's lid creaked open wider, exposing more of the intricate mechanism within. The year wheel spun so fast the numbers blurred into streaks, then suddenly jolted to a stop, its pointer settling decisively on "1905."

The humming grew louder, and Dani felt a sudden surge of dizziness, as if the ground beneath her head tilted. The towering trees appeared to sway, their edges becoming translucent, revealing glimpses of a different place with wooden walls and darkness.

"What the—" Dani gasped, her heart pounding. "Shit, stop—"

But the mechanism only sped up, the blue light intensifying as the box's metal heated to where she should be in excruciating pain. Surprisingly, she felt none—only an unusual spreading numbness that began in her fingers and crept up her arms.

A sharp crack reverberated through the yard, like ice shattering over a frozen lake. Toaster yowled from the grand staircase window.

She recalled Mary's words about her box, initially dismissed as playful nonsense. "Found this buried under her stuff, wrapped like she really didn't want anyone to see it. Great-grandma Cleo, in her delusional stages, was always on about the box, said it was important but never why. Something about people getting lost and it being, like, a tether. Macabre as hell, but I never bought into her superstitions."

The memory faded as quickly as it had surfaced.

The blue light was everywhere now, filling her vision, her lungs, pressing against her skin like a physical force. The surrounding forest shattered like glass, fragmenting into a thousand shimmering pieces that swirled around her in a vortex of color and sound. She tried to scream, but the roaring in her ears consumed the sound.

The glow shifted, revealing someone standing in the light. A figure emerged from the other side. He was tall, his dark suit and top hat casting an enigmatic shadow over his features. The unnatural teal glow from his hand partially obscured his face, sending pure, unfiltered fear through Dani's veins.

"Little lark?" The name, barely audible, pierced the air like a thread, summoning something long forgotten. Their eyes met through the dark shadow of his hat, and recognition washed over him. Instinctively, she wanted to run, yet he drew nearer. His gloved hand extended, fingers brushing hers softly. Her body didn't move, but inside, she was screaming.

"After all this time," he whispered.

Dani's head spun. She tried to pull back, to resist, but his hand grabbed her and pulled her into the light. And then she was falling. Not downward, not sideways, but through. Through layers of what felt like fabric, then water, and finally, nothingness. Her body was weightless, suspended in a void that pressed against her from all sides.

Fragments of places flashed before her eyes. A city street with people dressed in old-fashioned clothing. The wail of an air-raid siren in the distance. A forest clearing bathed in moonlight, scented with pine. A dusty workshop where a man bent over a workbench, surrounded by clockwork pieces and half-finished trinket boxes identical to the one in her hands.

Is this what it feels like to be dead? The thought struck her with horrifying clarity. Would she keep falling forever? Terror clawed at her throat. If she couldn't stop, couldn't find any anchor in time or place, this endless free fall would trap her for eternity. The thought was so devastating that something primal within her rebelled, reaching out with desperate mental fingers, searching for anything to cling to.

And then, she felt it—a tug, a connection, something familiar drawing her toward a specific point amidst the kaleidoscopic chaos. She reached for it, straining against the disintegrating fabric of reality. She felt it as home, belonging, a missing piece of herself that had waited all along.

With a final, wrenching effort, Dani channeled all her willpower into that connection, envisioning herself clutching it with both hands. The falling sensation transformed. Instead of an endless, aimless tumble, she was now being pulled, drawn toward something tangible.

The last thing she saw before consciousness slipped away was a familiar yet strange face. A man with piercing green eyes, gazing down at her with shock and recognition as her body materialized in a bed of straw.

Darkness enveloped her completely.

The grand front door swung open with a groan of old hinges, sending a gust of crisp autumn air inside. George Barrington stepped in, shaking off the chilly breeze and tucking a folded newspaper under his arm. From the grand staircase, Teresa was already in motion, her dark hair elegantly twisted into a perfect bun with a bobby pin clenched between her teeth. Her tailored suit was crisp, her computer bag slung over one shoulder.

She reached for her keys on the entryway table, but her fingers brushed the empty space. A frown creased her forehead. Near the window, Toaster's tail flicked once, then twice. His yellow eyes narrowed and locked onto something outside.

"Dani!" she called out, her voice echoing through the house. "I'm leaving! Do you have my keys?"

She waited. The house remained silent—an unsettling stillness far from typical for a morning in their home. A sharp breath escaped her lungs. She dropped her bag and headed toward the staircase.

"Dani, I know you're awake. It's nine in the morning!"

Still no answer. Her heels clicked softly against the polished wood as she ascended the old stairs, the creaking adding weight to the hushed atmosphere. At the top landing, she spotted a glimmer of silver. Her keys. They sat neatly on the hallway table, tucked beneath Grandmother Vivienne's stoic portrait.

She chuckled, shaking her head as she picked them up. Of course. Dani had a habit of moving things absentmindedly—one of those endearing yet exasperating quirks.

Even as she chuckled, something about the house's silence felt off. Her smile faltered, and she turned toward Dani's room. The door was slightly ajar, allowing the hallway light to spill inside. She pushed it open fully. Toaster darted past her, paws barely making a sound as he leaped onto the bed and settled into the familiar indent where Dani usually slept.

The comforter lay thrown back, but the sheets remained untouched—not the usual messy sprawl of someone who had just woken up. Her fingers tightened around her keys. She stepped deeper into the room, scanning for any sign of movement. A backpack and clothes tossed over a chair. The nightstand, where Dani's cell phone, watch, and trinket box rested, was undisturbed in a way that suggested she had just set them down.

Teresa heard a low, drawn-out meow from Toaster. The room appeared untouched, as if Dani had never returned to it. A knot formed in her stomach.

Maybe she had left early?

No—her bike is still outside.

Maybe she was in the shower?

No—the bathroom door is wide open, and the towels are untouched.

Teresa felt a wave of unease, the first actual pang of worry. Something was not right.

"Where are you, Dani?"

6

Veil between Hours

Edwardian Era

A sharp gasp escaped Dani's lips as her eyelids opened against the unforgiving glare of morning. Squinting, she found the light too intense, nausea rising within her. The air felt wrong. Too cold, too clean, too quiet.

Dani's heartbeat jackknifed. Her skin prickled with that primal wrongness usually reserved for horror movies and lucid dreams. Her fingers twitched toward her neck for the key—still there. But everything else was off.

The smells, the textures, the heaviness of the clothes clinging to her body. Even the silence felt older—like it had settled in long before she arrived.

"Okay," she whispered, gripping the edge of her robe. "This is fine. Totally fine. You hallucinated yourself into an Amish Airbnb. Happens all the time."

She tried to sit up, her head throbbing and muscles aching as if someone had violently thrown her from a moving car. Her limbs felt heavy with strain, and her lungs burned with dull pressure, as if she'd swallowed water but never emerged for air. She coughed, the sound dry and foreign in her throat as the scent of hay filled her nostrils. The soft rustling of straw brushed against her skin, accompanied by a deep, rhythmic breath—not her own. Dani turned her head to find dark, large, unblinking eyes staring back at her. A horse. It huffed, stirring loose strands of her hair with warm breath.

She jerked upright, her robe tangling around her as the hay beneath her shifted, sending a wave of dizziness crashing into her and forcing her to sprawl against the stall wall. Her breath came in shallow bursts as she took in the wooden beams overhead, the polished tack lining the walls, and the muted sounds of a barn waking up for the day. This wasn't her bedroom or the yard.

Footsteps crunched against the hay-dusted floor. Dani pressed her back against the wooden planks as they grew closer. She leaned forward, peeking through the slats and nearly choked on air. A man approached, his clothing straight from a film set: a tweed cap, a curled handlebar mustache, brown trousers tucked into polished riding boots, and a vest buttoned snugly over a pressed linen shirt. He looked like he belonged to this place.

She pressed her hand against her forehead, wondering if this was a dream, if she had a fever, or if she'd hit her head. The man stopped just outside the stall, holding a carrot to the horse's nose and scratching the animal while speaking in a voice low and familiar.

"I think we'll have rain today, Maggie." The horse nickered, nudging his shoulder in lazy agreement while she held her breath; he hadn't seen her yet.

Her mind raced with possibilities, each fighting for dominance. If this was a staged scenario, where were the cameras? If it was a dream, why did it feel so authentic? And if neither of those applied—if it was something entirely different—she urgently needed to escape. As he exited, Dani inched forward, rising slowly and stepping out of the stall with each step echoing through her, urging her to remain silent and move undetected.

The stables stirred with shifting horses, creaking leather, and cheerful birds outside greeting the day. This left her feeling exposed as she passed the polished brass fittings and beautifully crafted wooden doors, all too well-maintained and perfect. Her eyes adjusted when she reached an open window, the crisp morning air rushing through, and she paused, squinting into the sunlight at a sight that made her stomach drop.

The Barrington Mansion stood beyond the stables, its stone walls gleaming pristinely, its towering windows untouched by time. It wasn't her house, not truly; it appeared brand new.

The climbing rose bushes were vibrant and untouched by age, the landscaping immaculate rather than overgrown as she remembered, and the people outside—landscapers, maids, and workers bustling about the courtyard—all dressed like they belonged to a different century.

Her hands gripped the windowsill as her legs suddenly felt unsteady beneath her. This wasn't just a period drama being filmed on the property; this was—What the hell is happening?

As she stepped away from the window, she heard voices from just outside the stable: "—another vagrant, sir. Shall we call the authorities?" "Immediately. Can't have strange women wandering the grounds..." She froze. *Authorities. Vagrant.* When footsteps approached, panic took over. She stumbled back and collided with something solid: a pair of polished leather shoes that hadn't just appeared but had been there, waiting. Dani's lungs seized as she looked up.

The man before her stood tall and broad-shouldered, his rosy cheeks framed by a well-groomed brown beard just beginning to gray. A fresh flower adorned his crisp tweed suit lapel, and peculiar brass-rimmed spectacles with dark lenses perched on his nose. As he assessed her, he seemed to be trying to place her—almost as if she were familiar yet somehow out of place. His pipe rested between two fingers, the faint scent of clover smoke drifting lazily around them. His brows knitted together, and his grip on the pipe tightened.

"Good Heavens..." His voice came out hushed, as if the words had escaped before he could grasp them. He took a deep breath, anchoring himself, his gaze never leaving hers. "You resemble—" He paused, correcting himself. "No... that can't be accurate?" His lips curled slightly, and he muttered to himself.

Dani stared, unable to respond.

He tipped his head, his curiosity sharpening. "To whom do I owe the honor of this visit?"

She backed away; her heel catching on a horse brush. Her arms flailed wildly, but she landed flat on her back with an ungraceful thud. The man gave a long-suffering sigh, took a slow drag from his pipe, and extended a gloved hand.

"Are you injured, miss?" he asked.

She paused, her mind urging caution, but her hand moved before she could stop it. His grip was firm, lifting her to her feet. She brushed hay from her robe, trying to compose herself. She needed to think clearly. Her mouth moved before her mind could fully process the situation.

"Dani—" She paused, then, "Barrington."

The air shifted, and his expression darkened as if upset. "Barrington, you say?" He quickly masked it, offering a polite nod.

Her throat went dry. "Oh, uh—no, I meant Wood. Miss Danielle Wood." *Shit. Why did that feel like a mistake?*

A slow smile curved across his lips. "Well, Miss Wood," he said carefully, tapping ash from his pipe, "perhaps you can explain why you're hiding in my stable, dressed for bed, and... speaking most peculiarly?"

"What? I... I..." Her words didn't come.

"Are you going to tell me how you came upon my stables?" he prompted, watching her expectantly.

Think. Think. "I—uh—I got robbed," she blurted out.

His face turned pale with shock. "Robbed?"

"Yes," she rushed. "Left with nothing but these—uh—nightclothes." She gestured vaguely. "I needed shelter for the night before finding my... family."

He sighed, shaking his head. "What despicable scoundrels would abandon a lady in such a state?"

She nodded swiftly, scanning his face for any signs of doubt in her story. She couldn't find any, or he was great at concealing them.

He hummed in thought, then gave a decisive nod, gesturing toward the house. "You cannot stay in the stables, Miss Wood. Come—let's get you out of this dreadful chill before you catch your death."

As he guided her out of the stable doors, every fiber of her being was on high alert. The house before her seemed off. She stumbled slightly; her gaze lifting to take in details that weren't usually present. The lingering ache in her body was palpable. With each step toward the imposing stately home, past the staff members in the yard who stared in wide-eyed astonishment, the man remained composed, gracefully smoothing his coat.

"Ah, but where are my manners? I seem to have gotten ahead of myself." He offered a smile, his voice perfectly poised and removed his sunglasses. "Barrington. Alvie Barrington. A pleasure to make your acquaintance."

The name struck her like a physical blow, stripping her of breath. The portrait above the grand staircase, that stern, unsmiling face she had passed a thousand times growing up, now stood before her, alive and breathing. Without the handlebar mustache, but still the calculating eyes that appeared to follow her from the painting. Her great-grandfather.

"Th—" she stammered, her mind racing wildly, connecting impossible dots.

Her throat tightened as realization washed over her. Her fingers trembled; she clutched them together to conceal her fear. The family stories of Alvie Barrington, the shrewd businessman who had amassed the Barrington fortune, owned half of downtown Portland,

and the eccentric who had designed the mansion in all its splendor was standing in front of her.

"Miss Wood?" His voice cut through her panic. "Are you quite well? You've gone rather pale. Let's get you inside."

With a keen eye, he looped his arm in hers and escorted her the rest of the way. They approached the buggy's side entrance, while Dani shuffled beside him, her mind spinning with one overwhelming thought: *How the hell do I get back home?*

The soles of her feet touched the cool, veined, expensive marble floor. It was the kind of floor you didn't walk on—you glided across it. Dani stared, then stared again. Her hand gripped the edge of the doorframe as if the outside might vanish behind her. This wasn't some charming, fixer-upper version of the Barrington house. This was the real deal—untouched, new, and brimming with life. Tapestries towered above her, their colors vibrant and alive. The banister gleamed, without a single chip, and richer scents—beeswax, lavender, and old money—filled the air.

Her mind searched for logical reasoning. She stood motionless, not because she lacked the will to move, but because she couldn't. Alvie held the door open, patiently waiting as she shuffled inside.

Dani stood at the base of the grand staircase, its three-story sweep dominating the foyer. Marble steps gleamed under the chandelier's soft glow, and wrought-iron railings, capped with polished wood, framed the ascent. A large window on the first landing bathed the space in golden light—a testament to Gilded Age wealth.

But something was off. That peculiar water stain on the wallpaper—gone. She remembered leaving the entryway window open during a storm in her sophomore year; the rain seeping in, leaving its mark. But sophomore year hadn't happened yet. Her knees buckled slightly.

This staircase, where she had broken her arm at nine, where her parents had taken prom photos, and where she had slid down the banister in socks when no one was watching, became a vortex of memories colliding with the present. Reality slipped away as she spiraled internally.

"Miss Wood?" Alvie's voice cut through her thoughts, firmer this time. "You appear rather overwhelmed. Perhaps a seat and some tea might be in order?"

She looked down at herself. *Oh, my.* Robe, sleep shorts, and a tank top. *Girl, you are way underdressed for this situation.* Feeling even more embarrassed, she mustered the courage to press on. She turned to Alvie, choosing her words carefully to blend in: "Thank you for inviting me in."

He gestured toward the nearby library.

The room unfolded before her—gold ceiling tiles glistening under the chandelier's light, walls adorned with dark wood panels, and shelves lined with leather-bound books. Heavy drapes framed tall windows, casting a warm glow. A carved desk stood majestically in the center, resembling an intellectual throne, flanked by high-backed chairs and plush velvet settees. She perched at the edge of one, trying not to fidget. Stepping into the room felt like entering a painting you couldn't touch.

"Would you care for some tea?" he asked, already moving toward a small side table with a brass kettle. "It's the least I can do for a lady in such a state."

Think, Dani. Stay calm.

"Tea sounds wonderful," she said, trying to sound like someone who didn't just time travel out of a Wi-Fi zone.

"It is my favourite, Darjeeling," he noted, settling into the chair opposite her.

She reached for the teacup, her fingers closing around the delicate porcelain handle. It was a subtle gesture; he did the same, maintaining the exact grip, their fingers curving identically around the handle. She remained oblivious to it, but he was aware. His eyes shifted to her hand, pausing before his expression settled.

"You hold it strange," he noted, amusement in his voice.

Dani went still. "Do I?"

"Yes." He studied her over the rim of his cup. "One might think you've never held a teacup before."

She forced a laugh. "Oh, quite so—I am... regrettably inelegant."

Alvie's lips quirked. "Or unfamiliar with the customs." He took a slow sip, his eyes lingering a fraction longer than necessary, filing away the observation.

She bit the inside of her cheek. *Oof, inelegant? Is that a word?*

Dani's vision blurred for a heartbeat—not from blows but from the memory of that other place, her bedroom back home, the trinket box's dial frozen on "1905" as the portal shimmered around her. And now she was seeing faint lights outside the library doors, though no one else seemed to notice. Was she still reeling from the jump?

She looked up at Alvie. "What year is it?"

He gave a small, amused tilt of his head. "Those thieves gave you quite a knock—let's see if it left you dazed. What year do you think this is, Miss Wood?"

Her throat tightened as she recalled the box's glowing numbers. "1905?" she offered, keeping her tone steady, though her accent slipped.

Alvie's lips curved in a teasing half-smile. "Indeed—1905. Lucky for you, your fall was gentle. Had you of hit your head, one might slip through time itself. We should be grateful the rogues spared you any real harm."

Dani's heart skipped. *Time?*

He leaned forward, elbows on his knees. "You're a peculiar young lady, Miss Wood—" He paused, as if weighing another name. "It's almost as if you were raised somewhere... else."

She forced a smile, brushing a stray lock of hair from her face. "No need for the formalities; you can just call me Dani. Keeps things simple."

Alvie raised an eyebrow and took a sip of his drink. "Very well, Dani. After all, we all have our little mysteries."

Lifting the cup to her lips, she felt the warmth seep into her fingers. The floral notes were more potent than expected, grounding her in the atmosphere. She took a slow sip, allowing herself a moment of comfort before reminding herself: *Something is off.*

"So, tell me, Miss Wood—I mean, Dani," he continued in a polite yet probing tone, "you simply couldn't have ventured all the way here to Portland on the mere pretense of finding your family with no resources, could you? I dare inquire, what indeed is the true purpose behind your arrival?"

"I..." She cleared her throat, tried again. "They sent me to visit a distant relative in Portland." But after being robbed, I couldn't find their address. I thought maybe I'd run into them downtown or ask around."

"Oh dear, I must inquire. From where did you travel? Must be far, considering that accent," he asked, his voice smooth and clipped, with just a trace of skepticism.

Dani forced a smile.

Where was she from? Portland? Too easy.

What if he asked more? Troutdale? Did that even exist yet?

Gresham? Possibly. But what neighborhood? What landmarks? What year was the train line finished?

Her brain scrambled, chasing facts she didn't have.

"I'm definitely from Oregon—Salem," she blurted. "Never been to this part of the countryside before. The accent, um... My parents homeschooled me."

Wait. Was that even a thing back then? *God, Mary, where's your random fact generator brain when I need it?* The words already felt flimsy, vague, and modern. Do people even show up unannounced in this time?

He sipped his tea for a minute; the silence was deafening. "Salem, indeed. A fair journey. Still, I imagine one might find it worth the trouble, as it is not the East Coast you are braving. I trust you're not feeling too out of sorts?"

"Not at all," she replied, "just tired." Her eyes dropped to the teacup in her hands, grateful for something to focus on that wasn't his stare.

Time dragged on as they sipped their drinks. She prayed for no more inquiries about her character because she simply didn't know what else to say. Telling too many lies would be insane to maintain.

"Miss Wood—"

"Please, call me Dani."

"Dani," he said, his tone careful. "Forgive the forwardness, but there's something familiar about you. Not just the name—though that too. It's your face. The way you carry yourself. It reminds me of someone." He studied her like he was trying to put a memory back together.

There was a shift—not dramatic, but enough to make her skin tighten. Her heart sped up. She needed to find her way home, a trinket box. Now.

She forced a smile. "Guess I've got a long-lost twin out there. Let me know if she owes me money." That got a genuine laugh out of him, the kind that surprised even him. He leaned back slightly, nodding.

"You're funny, Miss Wood." His eyes crinkled into crescents—the biggest smile she'd seen from this familiar stranger. "I like that," he said simply.

He was still smiling as he set his teacup down with a soft clink. Rising, he adjusted his waistcoat before turning toward her. "Miss Wood, if you'd be so kind as to follow me."

She paused for a moment before standing up and pulling her robe tighter as he guided her away from the library. The hallway seemed to blur around her, yet here she was—barefoot—in a mansion that shouldn't still appear in such a state.

Wait... barefoot? Where the hell were her Birkenstocks? She had them when she ran outside to check out the lights. She'd been breaking those things in for a damn year. Were they just... gone? Vaporized by the space-time continuum? Does time travel have a strict no-sandals policy? *Fantastic. I'm trapped in the past and apparently must be barefoot to do it.*

A movement to her left caught Dani's eye. A young man emerged from the coatroom, straightening the lapel of his waistcoat as he crossed toward the open doors of the library.

"Edmund, this is Miss Cleo," Alvie said, his clipped vowels carrying that slight Oxford drawl.

Cleo? Dani's stomach flipped. "I—I didn't tell you my name was Cleo."

Alvie paused as if waking from a reverie. "Oh, dear, forgive me—I'm rather fatigued after back-to-back meetings this week." He cleared his throat. "Edmund, this is Miss Wood."

Edmund stopped in the foyer, golden blond hair in a perfect side part, steel-blue eyes alight with polite curiosity.

"Good day, madam," he intoned, the soft tone of Edwardian courtesy in every syllable.

"This young lady has had the great misfortune of encountering some rather dishonourable transients. She was travelling when they absconded with her belongings, her luggage, her funds, even the clothes from her back. She shall be a guest of the house until proper arrangements can be made. Kindly see to it that she is treated with care," Alvie ordered.

Edmund's eyes dipped, briefly, to her bare legs before snapping politely back to her face with a smirk. "Yes, sir," he replied smoothly. "Shall I make any further arrangements, or wait for instruction?"

Alvie waved a hand, casual but commanding. "Ring Jacques in the stables. Have him prepare a second buggy. Laurel will accompany Miss Wood into town to see her properly outfitted."

Dani barely kept her face from reacting. *Why is he suddenly being so accommodating?*

Edmund moved to a recessed alcove in the wall where, to Dani's shock, a sleek wood and gold telephone sat like it had no business existing in this century.

She stared, and before she could stop herself, the words tumbled out. "Will it teleport me to Salem? Or just connect me with some guy named Reginald who speaks in riddles and has a monocle?" Humor, her best defense when she was nervous.

"Reginald is dreadfully overbooked this week. You'd be stuck with his brother—the one who only speaks in railway timetables." Alvie let out a loud and genuine laugh, startling Edmund mid-dial.

Dani smiled back. Guess I know where my quick wit came from. That wasn't the reaction of a man who believed she was a deranged, barefoot runaway. Unlike a half-dressed stray who'd stumbled from a hayloft, he treated her with respect. He showed no suspicion, made no further inquiries, and didn't call the police. He was just... amused. He regarded her as if she belonged there, as if the decision to take her in was already made and unquestioned. Was he just incredibly trusting?

Crossing over to Dani, Edmund's eyes darted to her legs once more, just for a moment. A single eyebrow raised before he averted his gaze. Not quickly enough. She tightened the robe around her hips, her eyes burning a hole in his face. Being stared at in gym shorts was one thing; being stared at barefoot and partially undressed for this decade was an entirely different matter.

Before Dani could think of anything clever to say, the sharp click of heels echoed from the servants' hallway. A tall woman entered, composed, mid-forties, and instantly intimidating. She pinned her copper hair into a flawless bun and stood with a posture straight enough to shame a soldier. Nothing about her suggested softness. Everything suggested control.

Her emerald eyes swept the room like a ledger being meticulously tallied, revealing a woman of power. The navy gown, adorned with shimmering gold embroidery, accentuated her frame with quiet opulence. Dani didn't need to be brilliant to discern the woman's authority. Their eyes met, and Dani felt a sweeping gaze over her. It wasn't a look of mere attention; it was an assessment. Then the woman's face went cold. Whatever she'd been thinking, she clearly didn't like it.

"And what, precisely, have you dragged home this time, Mister Barrington?" she asked, voice cool and sharp.

Awesome, a hater.

Alvie just smiled. "Laurel. Impeccable timing, as always. This is Miss Danielle Wood."

Her eyes cut through Dani like a knife. "Where in God's name did you find such a floozy? She's made a holy show of herself."

Dani's mouth fell open.

Edmund leaned in just enough for only Dani to hear, "Mister Barrington grants Miss Laurel a rather generous liberty of opinion." A smile played on his face.

"Apparently," Dani responded.

Alvie explained he found her staggering out of the stables, as if it were an ordinary occurrence. Thieves had robbed her blind, leaving her only with her dignity and an oddly persistent streak of luck. He turned his eyes sweetly to Laurel and asked, "I trust you'll see that she's dressed appropriately?"

Laurel inhaled through her nose. Her spine straightened, jaw tight. After a pause, she gave a reluctant nod. "Very well. But it will take more than a gown to tidy up this mess."

Wow. Okay. Damn.

Dani, momentarily surprised, opened her mouth to respond, but the phone in the alcove rang, breaking the tension. Alvie, evidently satisfied with his win, turned on his heel and sauntered over to answer it.

"Vivienne," he said into the receiver. "Yes. I'll meet you at the clock. Ten-thirty sharp." A pause, then the quiet click of the phone returning to its cradle. He returned, adjusting his coat, all business. "Laurel," he said, already heading for the door, "make sure Miss Wood is appropriately dressed before you take her into town. I'm due to endure a few painfully dull acquaintances."

Before Dani could react, he turned, took her hand, and pressed a fleeting, familiar kiss to her knuckles.

"Miss Wood," he said with a smile, "do try not to get yourself robbed again while I'm away." With that, he vanished. Dani watched after him.

Laurel let out a sharp huff and grabbed Dani's wrist, pulling her like a weary mother yanking a toddler out of a checkout line. "Come on," she ordered, already dragging her toward the kitchen. "I have no time to play nursemaid today." A single glance from him had made her fold. And for a servant? She wore impeccable clothing. Strange.

Marching ahead, Laurel's heels struck the marble floor like punctuation. Dani stumbled to keep up, still clutching the robe tighter around herself. As they rounded the corner toward the kitchen, a female staff member nearly collided with them.

"Miss Laurel," she said with a quick bow of her head, then looked over at Dani with a wince. "Are you in need of assistance?"

Laurel didn't break stride. "Not unless you have learned how to sew a full young ladies' wardrobe within the hour."

The servant arched a brow, her eyes floating from Laurel to Dani's bare legs with quiet amusement.

Dani broke the silence. "If I end up in a corset, send help."

"You'll end up in far worse if you don't keep moving, Miss Wood," Laurel replied.

As the hallway engulfed them, Dani shook her head with a tired smile. *Time travel. Woke up in a horse stable. Drank tea with Grandpa Sherlock. Now being dragged to breakfast by the human embodiment of a thundercloud.*

Sure. Why not?

QUESTIONS WITHOUT ANSWERS

PRESENT DAY

Mary was halfway through unpacking a small box of books when her phone buzzed against the wooden floor. She glanced at the screen. Teresa Barrington.

She answered quickly. "Hello?"

"Mary..." Teresa's voice wavered. "How are you, honey?"

Something was wrong. This wasn't a check-in.

"I'm fine... just unpacking. Why?"

"It's Dani." The words tumbled out in a rush. "She's missing."

Mary's stomach dropped. "What?" The word came out strangled. "What do you mean, missing? I just saw her. She was fine."

"She never came home two nights ago. We've looked everywhere. Talked to everyone. No one's seen her."

Mary gripped the edge of the desk. The room tilted. *Missing.* The word didn't fit. "This doesn't happen," she said, her voice climbing. "She wouldn't just disappear."

"I know. But she's not here."

Mary started pacing, phone pressed to her ear. "Does she have her phone? Did you try tracking it?"

"She left it on her nightstand. Still there when I went to wake her up."

Mary's hand flew to her hair. Dani *never* left her phone behind. "What about her laptop? Social media?"

"We checked everything. No posts. No messages. Nothing."

The silence stretched.

"Mary..." Teresa's voice dropped. "Do you think she could've run away?"

"No." The word came out sharp. "If something was wrong, she would've told me. She tells me everything."

"The police aren't doing anything. They think she just wandered off. Told me to wait 48 hours. *Wait.* Like I can just sit here while my daughter is—" Her voice cracked. "We've posted everywhere. Social media, the college, friends..."

"If she's not home by tonight, I'm coming back. I don't care about this program."

"No. You just got there. Don't drop everything. Not yet."

Mary wanted to argue, but Teresa was right. *For now.* "Fine. But if I don't hear from you by the end of the week, I'm coming home."

"I just need her to come home." Teresa's voice broke into quiet sobs.

"She will," Mary said. The words felt hollow.

The line went dead. Mary stared at the phone. The surrounding room—books, unpacked bags, the promise of a new beginning—dissolved into background noise.

8

ANGEL OF MY DREAMS

EDWARDIAN ERA

The kitchen was a controlled storm of movement. Near the far counter, a young girl, no older than eighteen, stirred a pot, steam curling up to the high smoke-stained white ceilings. Laurel stood nearby, directing the cook. Her tone was stern, but calm. She glanced back over her shoulder.

"Shannon, watch that broth girl. Don't let it stick."

The girl, Shannon, nodded obediently. Partially pinned back, her long, wavy auburn hair revealed a few curls framing her delicate, heart-shaped face. She resembled Laurel closely, sharing the same sharp cheekbones and striking blue eyes. However, there was something else about her that Dani couldn't quite place.

A heavy wooden spoon landed with a loud thud in the center of the prep table.

"Sheesh!" Dani flinched.

"Sit." Laurel didn't look up. She focused on the plate she was placing with terrifying precision. "You're probably half-starved."

Dani hovered. "Uh, weren't we going to dress?"

"You won't be trying on a single dress until there's food in your belly. I don't dress corpses."

Dani bit back her retort and took a seat on one of the wooden stools. The legs wobbled slightly against the uneven tile. The heat from the stove warmed her legs. Somewhere behind her, something else sizzled. She glanced around.

The Barrington kitchen was a stark contrast to the ones she was familiar with. There was no hum of electricity, no polished stainless steel, and no clock glowing on a microwave. Instead, firewood, cast iron, and long wooden counters, worn smooth by years of use, surrounded her. The black-and-white tile flooring tugged at a memory within her. She recognized this pattern. Her father had spent months obsessing over restoring something similar back home, ranting about the lost craftsmanship of "real tile work." *So, this was what he had been chasing*, Dani mused, tracing a small crack on the floor with the toe of her boot. It looked incredibly perfect here. She hadn't realized how long she had been staring until Laurel spoke again.

"Silly girl, have you taken an unusual interest in the flooring?"

"Uh—yeah," Dani admitted, the words tumbling awkwardly from her lips. "They're gorgeous. My dad—" She paused, correcting herself. "My family's really into...flooring. He'd absolutely lose his mind over this work."

Laurel let out a dry chuckle and set her knife down. "Certainly. They are simply floors, though. Naturally, Alvie was adamant about sparing no expense, even for a well-staffed area. I dare say Vivienne does pop in here occasionally to try her hand at cooking."

Another girl worked silently in the corner, her elbows deeply plunged in the dough. She rolled up her sleeves to her elbows, and flour covered her arms. Across from her, Shannon kept stirring the pot, her eyes fixed on it. Laurel moved gracefully among them, as if she had always been a part of their circle, despite her position as the boss, not the cook.

This wasn't some typical Portland cafe with oat milk and tofu scrambles. Everything around her—the clothes, the house, and the way people carried themselves—screamed either Victorian or Edwardian. However, phones suggested a more likely Edwardian-era. And she was pretty certain it was the latter, thanks to Mary's incessant ramblings about Victorian culture.

Laurel placed a heavy plate in front of her. It held a sandwich, thick with ham, sandwiched between two crusty slices of bread. There was no garnish, and no small talk. *The people here eat like they've prepared for a famine.* She stared at the sandwich, biting her inner cheek to hold back a sigh. She wrestled with whether to refuse politely or risk sounding crazy. Glancing towards the pantry door, she had an idea: *maybe I could quickly grab an apple or something before anyone notices.*

A figure stepped through the kitchen doorway, and the thought that had been in her mind suddenly vanished. The man was older, his beige slacks held up by suspenders, and a worn cap comfortably perched on his head. He walked with a steady gait and an unbothered expression. She recognized him, the face of the first man from the stables who had an eerily similar resemblance to someone else. Jacques, Mary's great-grandfather and Cleo's husband.

The man whose great-grandson still worked for her family and lived in the workman's cottage below the mansion. She had seen photos of him. Just weeks ago, she had sat across from his aged son in her parents' kitchen, sipping coffee while he told her stories about the Barrington Estate. He had mentioned generations of service, born into it and never leaving. At the time, she hadn't given it much thought.

"Your payment is next to the stove, Jacques. And bring more milk next time, will you?" Laurel called out.

Jacques gave a slight nod, already moving toward the counter.

Laurel shot Dani a look. "Eat."

She hesitated, glancing at the sandwich as if it might suddenly lunge at her. However, her stomach eventually made the choice for her. With a resigned sigh, she grasped it and pushed herself to take a bite. Then another. Surprisingly, it wasn't bad. The bread was fresh; the ham was thick-cut, and the saltiness was just right. *Time travel and carnivorism, love that for me.* She mechanically chewed, attempting to convince herself that it was merely a salad or a cucumber side dish from her beloved Korean restaurant.

Laurel's hand suddenly clamped around Dani's wrist—firm and without warning. "Come now."

Dani didn't argue. Laurel, already in motion, guided her towards the kitchen's back and up a narrow servant's staircase. Dani reluctantly followed, her feet dragging slightly behind. The air grew cooler as they ascended. There were no fires here, only stone, draft, and Laurel's unwavering pace.

Laurel said, "We have designated these rooms for the staff," as they walked down the corridor. "For the time being, you shall live in one of the vacant staff quarters. However, do refrain from settling in too comfortably. Your departure is imminent."

"Is that a threat or a promise?" Dani grumbled under her breath.

They stepped into a small common room. Modest, but lived in. A low fire snapped in the hearth. A few chairs sat around it, cushions sunken and worn. By the window, a writing desk leaned under the weight of papers and ink bottles. In the middle of the room, a round tea table stood with four mismatched chairs. She'd seen this room before—but only as ruins. In her time, it was bare plaster and rotted beams.

Laurel tipped her head toward a nearby door, eyeing her with thin patience. "Go on, then—see to freshening yourself up. Something dragged you unceremoniously through a thicket. I will find something appropriate for you to wear—though, truthfully, I doubt I can improve your current state much."

Emotional Damage. Dani thought.

Laurel pointed, already turning away. "The powder room is in that direction—make use of it while the offer still stands."

Dani tightened the belt of her robe and stepped through the door. The staff bath was cleaner than she had expected. A white porcelain sink stood under a framed mirror, its edges just beginning to tarnish. A steel claw-foot tub caught the low light, gleaming. Along the far wall, a high-mounted toilet rested under a polished chain pull. The air smelled of soap and old wood. She ran a hand over the sink. Smooth porcelain, not rough or neglected. This wasn't just functional; it was comfortable and maintained with intention.

She kept waiting for the glitch. For her bedroom ceiling to reappear. For her phone to buzz and pull her out of whatever Victorian escape room her brain had conjured. But it never came.

Leaning forward, she gazed into the mirror. Tangled hair framed her face, with bits of hay stuck in it. Dirt streaked across one cheek. Her reflection didn't lie; she had experienced something real. This wasn't merely a bizarre fever dream or an elaborate prank. She had traveled back in time, and her great-grandfather—who should have been long deceased—was downstairs, casually existing as if none of this was utterly insane. A sharp knock at the door startled her.

"Miss Wood," came Laurel's sharp voice, laced with impatience. "I have left a dress for you at the door—boots, too. Be properly dressed in fifteen minutes, or I'll dress you myself—and you won't enjoy it."

She cracked the door and snatched the fabric like it might bite. The dress was heavy as hell and the exact color of regret—somewhere between dirt, despair, and full-on fecal brown. Puffed sleeves, high collar, zero mercy.

It took her twenty full minutes just to figure out where her arms were supposed to go. The corset laces stretched like they were mocking her. No zipper in sight—just a web of complications. She tried yanking it over her head, then stepping into it, then pulling it halfway up before getting stuck with one arm pinned like a haunted scarecrow.

"Nope. Nope. Absolutely not," she muttered, flailing like a spider in a sink.

Eventually, she spotted the side seam—hidden hook closures, front-lacing after all. Still a nightmare. She braced her foot against the bedframe and pulled until the bodice snapped closed with an ominous click. Victory, sort of.

The boots were just as tragic: knee high, laced to death, with stubby little heels designed by someone who clearly hated women.

This is a cringe fest.

She stared at the stranger in the mirror; the transformation was instant. The corset forced her spine straight, her shoulders back—a physical correction of everything natural and comfortable. She'd play along and wear this little costume. Follow the script. But she was still Dani Barrington, and she'd figure a way out. She stepped into the common room, the dress heavy, half-fastened in the back, and dragging her limbs like a weight.

Edmund looked up as she entered. "Miss Wood, how excellent you look."

"Yeah, dude, I had no options." Dani kept her hands stiff at her sides, trying not to squirm under the weight of his attention. *Shit, I said dude.*

He blinked. "'Dude'..." The word rolled off his tongue with hesitation, like it might break if he said it wrong. "Is that some sort of title?"

Laurel's voice sliced in before Dani could respond. "Sir, I believe your presence is urgently required downstairs." She didn't wait for his reply—just stared him down until he obeyed.

The moment he was gone, Dani exhaled. "Shit. That was—"

"You might want to workshop your vocabulary," Laurel said, adjusting a vase on the mantel like she hadn't just saved Dani's ass. "Unless you're hoping to get tossed into a sanatorium."

Dani narrowed her eyes. "You didn't even blink at 'dude.'"

Laurel smiled faintly. "I've heard worse."

A beat of silence passed, and Dani felt something tighten in her chest.

She somehow *knew* that word.

No one here should know that word, I think. Crap, I don't even have a phone to check. Double shit.

If she didn't start talking like they did—and soon—she was going to blow her cover.

"Miss Wood," she said, with a pointed scoff, "surely you were not intending to parade through the house with your fasteners in such a state? Good heavens, it appears as though you've been toiling in the fields! And what is this? Presenting the figure of a farmhand than a lady of distinction?"

Laurel spun her around and pulled the dress tightly. "You may look an absolute spectacle in this ensemble," she muttered, fingers flying across the fabric, "but at the very least, you shall no longer be scandalizing the entire household."

Dani scowled. *Where's the matching paper bag for my face?*

With brisk, purposeful steps, she turned and led Dani through the winding servant halls. The soft patter of approaching footsteps brought their journey to a brief halt.

A maid stepped forward, an air of urgency in her manner as she addressed Laurel about some stubborn stain ruining the surface of an expensive rug. Laurel, her attention diverted, began issuing sharp, precise instructions.

Dani drifted. The hallway ahead, quiet and dim.

She rounded a corner—and stopped in her tracks.

Shannon and Edmund stood tucked into an alcove just off the main hallway, closely. His hand rested on the wall beside her head, his body angled forward.

Not touching, but almost.

Shannon looked up at him, eyes locked on his mouth. Waiting. Dani didn't move. Didn't breathe. Then a sound, some small creak or distant voice, and Edmund pulled back. He straightened his waistcoat like nothing had happened, but his eyes snapped down the hall, scanning.

Shannon's cheeks burned pink. Her hands worked nervously at the edge of her apron, smoothing fabric that didn't need it. Dani pressed herself against the wall, hoping she was out of sight. Edmund's crisp footsteps approached. Dani ducked into the nearest doorway, adrenaline coursing through her veins. A stolen, breathy meeting in the stairwells of the Barrington house? It was more than a simple conversation.

Oh. Okay. *Miss Shannon and Mr. Edmund.* Dani raised an eyebrow at no one. *I see you.*

Laurel's voice cut through the quiet. "Where are you, girl? You've wandered off. We must be on our way!"

"I'm here," Dani called back, slightly breathless. She just stepped out of the doorway in time to catch Shannon smoothing her apron and Edmund fixing his collar. Neither looked at each other. Laurel appeared around the corner and didn't slow down. Dani fell into step beside her, casting one last glance over her shoulder as they descended the stairs towards the servant's entrance for the buggy.

The late morning air hit Dani like a cold slap, carrying with it the scent of pine, damp earth, and chimney smoke.

As they crossed the gravel path toward the buggy house, the buggy awaited them—wood polished to a gleaming shine, brass fittings catching the light. A bay horse stood hitched and ready, its pawing at the ground and rising breath forming soft white clouds. Its ears flicked forward, impatiently waiting for their arrival.

Edmund stood beside the buggy, his posture impeccable as he prepared to assist the ladies with a smile. Laurel was already engaged in conversation with the driver and distracted.

Now or never.

Her heart pounded as she slipped behind the buggy and darted into the stable. The crunching straw beneath her boots sent shakes down her spine as she dropped to her knees.

The enticing aroma of hay, leather, and horses filled the air. With trembling hands, she began digging. Her fingers tore through the straw, sweeping aside handfuls, desperately searching the space where she had awakened.

But there was nothing.

No trinket box.

Just straw, dust, and the steady fart of a horse in the nearby stalls. Dani winced at the amount of air being released.

Laurel's voice rang loud and close.

"Miss Wood! What in heaven's name are you doing?"

Shit, shit, shit. Busted.

"Uh—just, uh—conducting... stable morale checks?" she blurted, smacking a hand on the nearest stall like it was a time clock. "You know. Making sure the horses are emotionally supported. Happy horses, quiet stables."

A loud horse's snort echoed from the stall.

Shut up, traitor.

Laurel stood in the large stable doors, hands on her hips, head tilted slightly to the side, eyes narrowed in skepticism at what Dani was doing. "Ah, well, unless you plan to sprout hooves and gallop off yourself, I suggest you come along now."

Dani scrambled up, brushing hay off the borrowed dress as best she could. She looped around the buggy and climbed in, settling into her seat, Laurel joined her.

Edmund entered the buggy last. "I see you've developed an interest in animal husbandry, Miss Wood," he chuckled quietly as he took his seat.

Dani shot him a sly smile. Okay, you can be funny too. This is friend language now.

The buggy lurched forward. Icy wind brushed her cheeks. The air felt fresh here, and it was great. It felt like you were actually going camping. The wheels clattered over the uneven road. Dani shifted, trying to get comfortable. Layers of stiff fabric bunched under her legs. The corset pinched her ribs with every breath. She tugged at the high collar, swallowing a sigh. *I miss sweatpants like oxygen.*

Laurel sat stiff and straight. Her attention stayed locked on the passing landscape. Beside her, Edmund stared out the window, smiling and cheerful. Occasionally, his eyes shifted towards Dani, quietly observing her before darting back to the passing scenery.

Laurel clearly wasn't into small talk, and Edmund followed her lead, but Dani couldn't handle this much awkward silence.

"So," she said, finally giving in, "have you worked for the Barringtons long?"

Laurel turned her head. Her look was sharp, not unkind. "Long enough."

Cool. Conversation over. Dani flushed and looked away. She wasn't great at talking to people with that much spine. Then—barely audible—a breath of laughter. Edmund cleared his throat into his gloved hand. He was holding back a smile. Laurel didn't notice or care.

"Why Alvie brought took you in is beyond me," she said briskly. "Whatever the reason, he cannot have you wandering about looking as though you've crawled from a haystack. He has a reputation in society to uphold." She must have been finishing a conversation in her head out loud, because neither Dani nor Edmund knew where that came from.

Dani swallowed the urge to snap back. She needed allies, not enemies. "I appreciate his kindness," she said carefully, striving for diplomacy. The city came into view. She leaned toward the window, breath fogging the glass.

This absolutely wasn't her Portland.

No food carts. No baristas with sleeve tattoos. Just cobblestone streets, and stray animals. The sound of wheels, hooves, and muffled voices filled the air. She was watching history play out from the wrong side of the glass.

The buildings looked brand new—brick facades bright in the morning light, like they'd just gone up yesterday. The streets buzzed with movement. Men in sharp suits and stiff collars moved with purpose. Women glided past in long skirts, parasols tilted just to block the sun. Kids darted between them, chasing balls and hoops, their laughter mixing with the clatter of buggys and the hiss of a steam trolley rolling by. Dani twisted in her seat, trying to take in everything at once.

Where the Victoriana Apartments stood in her time, there was now a ho-tel—massive, pristine, flanked by tall stone columns. Uniformed butlers ushered guests up the marble steps.

They passed a large sign: Grand Ringler Hall.

She blinked. *The Celeste Ballroom*—before it was the Celeste Ballroom. It was nothing like the venue she knew back home. No bright ass neon signs. No grunge band posters peeling off brick walls. Instead, the building stood tall and polished, its massive front windows framed in dark wood. A pair of grand double doors flanked the entrance, with a flyer for an evening orchestra performance posted in crisp, looping calligraphy.

A soft laugh of disbelief escaped her lips. She'd danced here before. Jumped in packed crowds, screamed lyrics with strangers, clutched Mary's hand while weaving through the chaos. *Unreal.*

She squinted at a structure in the distance. "Is that...?"

"Pioneer Courthouse," Edmund said. "Completed in 1875."

She stared at its spotless sharp edges and clean lines, framed by a city that barely resembled the one she knew. Another jolt of cold clarity hit her. She'd stood right there during poetry nights. She'd watched people cheer, protest, speak, sing. But this version? It didn't welcome crowds. It commanded them. The doors weren't backdrops for activism—they were entrances for judges and politicians.

A low rumble passed by the corner, Dani's head reeled around to eye it. "Wait, is that a car?" It was. Sleek, boxy, absurdly loud. *You're telling me we had to ride a horse-drawn Uber? but those guys get a motorcar?*

She turned toward Laurel. "Doesn't Alvie own, like, everything? Where's his?"

"Oh, indeed, he has one on order. But Mr. Barrington rather insists on keeping one foot in the past and one in the present, as he says. Believes it keeps him properly tethered to both sensibility and tradition."

Dani drummed her fingers against her knees, watching Laurel's composed smile. *One foot in the past and one in the present?* She echoed, tilting her head. *He called me Cleo earlier.*

"Speaking of the present," Laurel trilled, "motorcars remain something of a novelty—you'll still see more hooves than horns on most days."

The buggy passed a row of shops. A wooden sign swung gently from an iron bracket: *ST. JAMES & CO. Fine Soaps, Tonics & Grooming Provisions Best of 1905 Hand-cut soaps, bespoke beard tonics, and gentlemen's hair restoratives.* The window display was surgical, with its glass bottles lined up like lab samples, soaps wrapped in waxed paper with perfect corners. A far cry from the drugstore body wash aisle.

The buggy turned onto a wider street, slowly approaching a grand white stone building about eight stories high. Above the entrance, an ornate awning proudly displayed: *LIP-MAN WOLFE & CO.* The beautiful, swirling Victorian lettering led her eyes down to the entrance, where well-dressed women moved in and out, their gloved hands clutching parcels and shopping bags.

"The most distinguished clothing establishment in Portland," Laurel announced as the buggy rolled to a stop. She gathered her skirts. "If you are to remain in the company of the Barringtons, you shall get to know every attendant in this store personally."

Edmund stepped down first and offered a hand. Dani stepped down, her borrowed boots scraped against the sidewalk. She tilted her head back, attempting to get a full view of the department store that stood across the street from what would be the site of today's Pioneer Place.

Inside, the scent hit her first. Perfume, pressed wool, and something sweet under it all, maybe soap or silk. Crystal chandeliers cast a warm light on the glassy marble floors. Wax mannequins in extravagant gowns stood frozen in place, like museum pieces.

Laurel moved through the crowd like she belonged there with her head high, steps sharp, eyes scanning. Her usual edge softened, replaced by something close to... joy. She was in her element. No question.

Dani tried not to gawk at the endless rows of gloves, hats, and lace-trimmed everything. Edmund trailed a few steps behind, accidentally pulling a mannequin hand off and pressing it back on.

"Mrs. Barrington usually favors the fourth floor for her personal shopping," Laurel explained. "The ready-made section upstairs should suffice for you."

Reaching the heart of the store and Dani reveled in awe.

Two sweeping marble staircases curved inward from opposite ends of the massive room, meeting like an embrace on each level, rising in perfect symmetry through the entire eleven-story atrium. Each landing held towering arched windows, flooding the space with natural light and offering panoramic views of the city on every floor.

The effect was dizzying and theatrical, like a cathedral of commerce. But it wasn't the staircases that stole her breath. It was the elevator at the center.

The brass frame gleamed as if someone had polished it that morning, every curve and corner catching the light. Heavy iron gates opened, revealing an interior lined with beveled mirrors and lush velvet paneling. Patterned tile inlaid the floor, and above, a filigree dome resembled a gilded cage. Dani had seen antique elevators before, usually tucked in the corners of historic hotels or half-working in museums, but never anything like this. This wasn't just a way to move between floors. It was a statement.

"This," Laurel proclaimed with a graceful sweep of her hand, "is the first lift in town. A marvel of modern ingenuity, wouldn't you agree? Like ascending to the heavens without so much as lifting a virtuous finger!"

She pressed the elevator call button, letting her tone shift into something more conversational. "Vivienne, of course, won't set foot near the thing. She claims it's utterly unnatural for maintaining the female figure. But as for myself? Oh, I quite relish the experience."

Laurel's voice blurred as Dani stared, consumed. Her dad would've lost his mind—pacing, gesturing, launching into lectures on cables and counterweights. She pictured the look on his face when they'd found the old elevator in their own house, hidden behind a false wall during the remodel. Pure wonder. Like he'd struck gold. Dani swallowed hard. *They must be freaking out,* she realized.

The elevator arrived and opened. A group of young women floated off in a cloud of perfume and passive aggression. Silk skirts shifted with every step. Pearls clinked. Laughter sparkled just loud enough to sting. They clocked Dani immediately, sweeping over her like she was a smudge on the glass. Gloved hands adjusted necklaces. Lips curled.

One woman, tall, blonde, and practically dripping with generational wealth and disdain, let her stare linger a little too long. "Well," she sniffed, voice like spun sugar and venom, "they are simply letting in anyone now, aren't they? Standards seem to be... slipping."

Heat flared across Dani's cheeks. She hesitated for a moment before opening her mouth, then let the grin come slow and sharp. "Wow," she said, voice syrupy sweet. "It must be exhausting carrying all that self-importance. Does your neck ever ache from the weight?"

The blonde inhaled sharply, stunned. One of her friends stifled a laugh, pivoting it into a cough. Another looked pointedly at a glove button, shoulders trembling.

"Beatrice," one of them said, laying a gentle hand on her arm, "a lady doesn't engage in street brawls no matter how well-phrased." Her voice was polished, but her eyes gleamed.

Beatrice drew herself up with a prim little sniff, eyes still locked on Dani. "Of course. Some of us possess decorum." They turned, skirts flaring, and swept off toward the perfume counter like they hadn't just been verbally body-checked.

The elevator attendant motioned them forward. Dani stepped in, anticipating the ride. Laurel and Edmund followed, with Laurel mouthing something dangerously close to a damn as the doors slid shut.

"Careful now, that would be Miss Beatrice Ashdown. Daughter of Lord Ashdown. Alvie's acquaintance, though I daresay 'friend', might be too generous a term. A very wealthy and powerful man." Laurel warned.

The attendant, a young man with a perfectly parted haircut and the dead-eyed look of someone who'd rather be anywhere else, cleared his throat. "Which floor, Ma'am?"

"Fifth," Laurel answered gracefully.

As the lift rose, Dani's attention shifted to the street outside, framed in the massive display windows. The world below buzzed with movement. A chimney sweep wobbled across a roof. Her eyes landed on a storefront across the street. The sign swung gently in the breeze: **DUNWICH & SONS.** Something about it snagged in her memory. She'd seen a similar crusty sign from the light rail. Same name. Same lettering.

"The Clockery!" Dani exclaimed abruptly, realizing her mistake. Laurel and Edmund turned to look out the window, to see Dani fixated.

"Ah, yes—the Clockery," Edmund said with a nod. "Old Mr. Dunwich crafts some of the finest timepieces in Portland. Alvie owns several, in fact. Though it's mostly the son at work now. What a peculiar fellow. Always muttering to himself. Quite the eccentric lot, really."

Dani huffed. "Sounds like my people."

The elevator chimed. "Fifth," the attendant announced.

A rush of silk and lace hit Dani like a wall.

Gowns in deep blues draped over wax mannequins with blank, glassy stares. In the summer heat, some had melted—one eye drooping like it was sliding off the face. The effect was unsettling, as if the mannequins were slowly dissolving into grotesque parodies of themselves.

Feathered hats perched at awkward angles, while glass cases displayed lace fans, silk gloves, and delicate perfume bottles. At the center, a velvet settee sat like a throne, waiting for someone rich and bored to sink into it.

They reached the women's department. Laurel signaled a salesgirl with a flick of her fingers. "We shall require several day dresses, appropriate undergarments, and at least one pair of shoes," she declared.

The girl nodded, eyes darting to Dani with barely concealed curiosity. "Of course. If you'll follow me?"

But Laurel shook her head. "I have other things to shop for. Have Mr. Quinn assist her. He knows Mrs. Barrington's preferences better than I do." She turned to Edmund. "Edmund shall remain to ensure all is in order in my quick absence."

The salesgirl's smile faltered. "Mr. Quinn is with another customer at present, but—"

"Then Miss Wood shall wait." Laurel spoke firmly and decisively, and with that, she swiftly swept away, her copper hair glistening in the light as she vanished into another section of the store. Dani exhaled slowly, allowing her shoulders to relax as Laurel's presence gradually faded.

"If you would like to wait here, miss," the salesgirl said, motioning to the velvet settee, "Mr. Quinn will be with you shortly."

Beside a column, Edmund assumed a quiet, supervisory stance with his hands clasped behind his back, imitating the way Dani's dad used to stand—pretending not to care about the TV until he suddenly became very invested in whatever teen drama she was watching.

Her heart ached. *God, I miss Dad. I hope they are okay.*

Dani sank into the plush seat and watched the shoppers. Women moved from table to table, browsing gloves and accessories. Their posture, their voices, gosh everything felt different.

"Would madame care for refreshment while she waits?"

Dani looked up. A woman stood before her with a silver tray, offering tea, coffee, lemonade, and small cakes. She took a coffee. It wasn't great, but it was something. "Thanks. I'm waiting for Mr. Quinn?"

The server nodded. "He'll be along presently. He's our most sought-after tailor, especially among the younger ladies." She said it with a smug little smirk, like she was in on some joke Dani hadn't been told.

"Is that so?" Dani took a sip. "And what makes Mr. Quinn so special?"

Before the server could reply, a commotion drew their attention. A group of women, probably about Dani's age, had gathered around someone, their laughter high and forced. When the crowd parted, Dani nearly choked on her drink. The person at the center of their attention was the most striking individual she'd ever seen, a young man no older than twenty-five.

This is not the time to get heart-eyed over someone who looks like they belong on a currency note. She warned herself. *And it's a guy! This isn't your thing!*

He moved with a grace that felt almost otherworldly, an ultra-androgynous charm that sent her stomach flipping. Blonde hair tousled into a curtain cut framed his high cheekbones, softening the sharp angles of his face and drawing her to those warm, stunning blue-gray eyes. He could've stepped straight off the Titanic in that uniform. He wore a deep red and navy vest, tailored so precisely that it seemed stitched directly onto him. Being taller than the other women, he must have been 5'9" or 5'10".

He's becoming my thing. Her mouth hung open.

She was now painfully aware of her uncombed hair and the fact that she probably smelled of horse and desperation.

Then his eyes found hers.

A strange recognition washed over his face, mirroring the jolt she felt in her chest as if they had known each other in a past life and were only now recalling that connection. The store's noise faded away, replaced by the laughter, the rustling of silk, and even her own breathing—all of it became background noise.

Time stretched out like taffy, expanding far beyond the mere few heartbeats it actually lasted.

There you are.

She couldn't tell if the thought was hers or somehow his, transmitted across the crowded room.

His lips parted slightly. He almost spoke, but then hesitated. The world around Dani sucked back into focus as he turned back to the surrounding crowd. She noticed how his shoulders tensed and his smile didn't quite reach his eyes anymore. He glanced back in her direction when he thought no one was watching.

"Mr. Quinn," the server interjected in her stupor, "is quite popular."

Dani swallowed, setting her glass down with fingers that weren't relatively steady. "Yeah. I see that."

"Been that way since he started Miss," the server continued, seeming not to notice Dani's dazed state. "Some ladies buy dresses they don't require just for a fitting with him." She leaned in conspiratorially. "Though I can't say I blame them."

Dani nodded absently; her eyes still drawn to him like magnets while he navigated through his admirers. The perfect professional.

"Would you like another refreshment, Miss?" the server asked, following Dani's stare.

"I'm suddenly very thirsty," she managed, fumbling for another glass and one last shot of hydration.

As if summoned by sheer cosmic cruelty, Mr. Quinn excused himself from the group of women and began walking straight toward her.

9

HIGH DEMAND MEASUREMENTS

EDWARDIAN ERA

She reached blindly for the teacup and tried to hand it off to the server, but missed the tray by a solid inch. Her fingers trembled as she corrected, the porcelain clinking awkwardly against silver. *Don't drop it. Don't embarrass yourself. Be cool. Be a person.* Rowen was almost there, his expression filled with interest and eyes locked on hers.

Then Laurel's backside swept directly into view. A blocking wall of satin bustle and unapologetic timing.

Dani blinked, face full of pleats and perfume.

Laurel glided effortlessly into the space, her smile bright, her tone syrupy sweet. "Ah, good morning to you, my handsome friend." She brushed gloved fingers along the polished display. "Back again, I find myself. Not on Mrs. Barrington's errand today, but Mr. Barrington's. Had I known you'd be working this week..." Her head tilted, lashes fluttering. "Well, I might've found an excuse to visit much sooner."

Rowen's expression didn't shift. He inclined his head with trained ease. "Miss Laurel, always a pleasure." Not a hint of interest. Not even a grin.

Bothered by the lack of response, Laurel redirected. "Allow me to present Miss Danielle Wood, a... visiting... relative."

"Miss Wood." His voice curled around her name warmly.

The effect was immediate. He was unrealistically beautiful. Not rugged or tradi-tional, but ethereal like a K-pop idol stepped out of another dimension. Soft lips, flawless smooth skin, the kind of face that made people forget what they were saying mid-sentence.

No. No. Nope. Absolutely not. She isn't planning on staying in 1905.

He extended his hand, looking her dead in the eyes, then stopped short, recon-sidered, then withdrew the offered hand. Pulling off his glove, he extended his bare hand to her again.

Dani reeled, caught fast in his stare. Only one thought surfaced: Mary's voice matter-of-factly explaining how, in the Victorian era, a man removing his glove before shaking a woman's hand was a subtle sign of interest.

"Oh, for goodness' sake," Laurel snapped, annoyance clear as she broke the spell between them. "Mr. Quinn, we are on quite a schedule."

Heat crept up Dani's neck. She placed her hand on his bare one, noticing his fingers were long and elegant, the nails neatly trimmed.

"Rowen Quinn. Pleasure to make your acquaintance."

"Dani—um, Danielle, actually, but Dani works too. Or, well, you can call me whatever you can remember—definitely not saying you can't remember my name, but, I mean, with all the other names floating around, like, I wouldn't blame you if I'm just one of many, right? Not that I'm... one of many. Oh god, I'm totally one of many. Wow, okay, let's just start over—Dani is fine. Totally fine." Her face flared bright red. "I swear I'm normal."

Rowen stood still, his expression softening as he watched her ramble. His lips curled into a gentle smile, eyes filled with a warmth that made it clear her nervous-ness did not bother him.

He didn't interrupt, just let her words tumble out, as if fascinated by every strange syllable.

"We require a few dresses and undergarments for Miss Wood, naturally." Laurel's voice cut through their moment. "Mr. Barrington has instructed that no expense be spared—kindly charge it to Mrs. Barrington's account."

Rowen's eyes hadn't left Dani's. His eyebrow lifted slightly. "Spare no expense?" He tilted his head in contemplation. "Then only the finest shall suffice. I've a fair selection of ready-made dresses, though if none should suit, we might take your measure and have one properly fashioned."

"Please, nothing too... I don't know, Bougie. Just something practical." Dani suggested.

"'Bougie?'" He savored the unfamiliar syllable with a thoughtful air.

Her face felt hot, but she plowed ahead, deciding to lean into the awkwardness. "Yeah. Bougie." She gestured at some of the overly exquisite mannequins. "Look, just something practical would be amazing. This thing I'm wearing is basically a very itchy, very mud-colored wool prison."

It lit up his face, erasing traces of formal propriety. "A wool prison." His eyes swept over her with fresh, open interest. "A preference many ladies might share, but few would dare express in such... colorful terms. You have a rather unique way with words, Miss Wood."

"So I've been told. A lot. Today."

He leaned in slightly, placing a hand on the counter. "Well then, let us see what we can do to secure your release from this woolen penitentiary. Be so good as to turn for me."

Confusion spread across her face. "I'm sorry—what now?"

"'What now'?" He studied her for a beat, amused. "The absolute strangest way of speaking, Miss Wood. You are most decidedly not from Portland."

"Well, I'm... from Salem." The words landed with a thud.

"Salem?" His brow furrowed. "Curious. You don't sound as though you're from Salem, either."

"And what exactly does someone from Salem sound like?"

"Your manner is, shall we say, rather... singular?"

Dani grinned. "Well, I guess I'm a limited edition. Straight from the capital."

His blue eyes crinkled as he chuckled—the sweetest, softest sound cracking through his professional mask. She'd gotten to him. *Yes.* That genuine Rowen smile was proof. Then, just as quickly, he cleared his throat and returned to business.

"I shall need to assess your measurements."

Her sight fogged as she met his eyes. Though accustomed to admiration, the intensity of her gaze ignited a reciprocal response in him.

God overachieved with you. She thought.

He reached for the tape measure, his hand brushing against her side as he positioned it carefully around her. The sensation of his fingers so near her skin sent heat rushing through her, her heart threatening to beat out of her chest. He caught the way her breathing stuttered, the subtle shift in her posture. He smelled good, like cedar and bergamot. *I love bergamot.*

Rowen's eyes never left hers as he measured, his face mere inches from hers as he reached around her waist to circle the measuring tape. The way his curtain bangs cascaded down his temples when he looked down. The dark eyebrows, the blonde hair, and the warm skin—all these details captivated her. They held each other's eyes for a moment too long before he pulled back, his posture instantly straightening.

"Ahem, let's see what you'll require." He murmured, more to himself. "I am confident I have just the thing. Please—" He gestured toward the display area.

She looked around the showroom. No racks, but a hushed presentation of high fashion, like art for the privileged. A salesgirl in uniform dress retrieved a bodice from a top shelf. Dani caught their reflection in a nearby mirror—the mess standing next to a masterpiece. Her shit-brown dress, frizzy hair, smudged everything... and Rowen, polished like he'd stepped out of a painting. *Oh, hell.*

"How long will you be staying in Portland, Miss?" He asked, attempting small talk.

"As of twenty minutes ago, not long enough." Her sarcasm shield was in full swing.

A commotion from the street below drew their attention. A crowd had gathered outside, voices raised in what appeared to be some kind of demonstration. She moved to the window, peering down at the scene below. Men and women marched in a tight group, carrying signs demanding "Fair Wages" and "Safe Working Conditions." Their clothes were simple and practical, the attire of people who worked with their hands. Leading them was a tall figure in a neat but modest suit, his face obscured by the angle.

"What's happening?"

He joined her at the window. "Textile workers protesting. Again." His tone was dismissive.

"You don't approve?"

"I concur they should be heard," he said calmly. "Lord Ashdown ought to address their concerns promptly to prevent the situation from worsening."

"Ashdown?" The name rang familiar.

"He is the proprietor of the textile mill, as well as several other substantial enterprises." His voice remained even, but his eyes were taut. "Tragically, three women perished there last month, their garments becoming entangled in the machinery. A regrettable incident, perhaps, entirely avoidable with the installation of proper safeguards."

"That's awful." The matter-of-fact way he stated this, contrasted with the horror of what he described, made her stomach turn.

"Indeed." He turned from the window, pushing back whatever thought had crept in. His chin lifted, voice returning to business. "Now then, your wardrobe."

His fingers gently caressed fabrics and delicate materials, casually pointing out designs and styles. With incredible knowledge of materials, cuts, and sewing techniques, he described each piece with easy expertise.

His gravity field is strong, she thought, because she couldn't seem to focus on anything else. Her eyes tracked his movements like a heat-seeking missile—specifically, his hands. Long, veined, stupidly elegant hands. He was saying something. She nodded vaguely, completely unaware of the actual words. Her mouth opened before her brain caught up.

"Yes," she breathed, eyes still glued to his hands. "Mm-hmm. Quite... handy."

Rowen realized she wasn't listening and stopped mid-sentence. His gaze lingered on her, soft and unblinking, and then—God help her—he smiled. Just a slow, amused curl of his mouth, like he knew exactly what she'd been thinking.

His top lip was a touch thinner, the bottom one full and soft, and when he smiled, it revealed slightly crooked incisors—barely noticeable, but enough to make her heart lurch. It was unfair. Devastating, even.

Her brain short-circuited. *Abort mission. Abort.* Everything inside her screamed in sirens and blinking red lights. *He has cute teeth. You're going to die here.*

"I meant—the handiwork! Of the, um—the seamstresses! Their hands. Very... skilled." She winced, internally kicking herself into next week.

His amusement was clear. She felt humiliated and spiraled—it's what she did best. She walked away, because why not? Panic looked best from far away. Upon her exit, she caught the edge of the floorboard with her toe.

Gravity took over.

Dani's arms flailed to catch herself, but she over-corrected. Badly.

Rowen's eyes widened, his reflexes kicking in as he lunged to catch her.

Too late.

One hand caught the edge of a dress on a rack. The other grazed his pant leg. Neither offered salvation. She twisted mid-fall, still locking eyes with him as she slid—slowly, mortifyingly—down the length of his leg like a melting popsicle. Dignity evaporating with every inch.

With perfect deadpan, she muttered, "Don't... let... go... Jack," her eyes locked on his while she sank lower.

When she hit the floor, she didn't bounce. She flopped. One leg tangled in the dress's hem, one hand still clutching his shin.

Silence.

Rowen looked down at her, visibly struggling to keep a straight face. His mouth opened, then shut. Tried again.

"My name is Rowen," he said finally, voice catching slightly. "Are you quite alright?"

He cleared his throat, the corners of his mouth twitching with barely contained laughter. "You seemed to have taken quite the... theatrical descent."

He ran a hand through his hair, as if the motion might restore some composure. It didn't. Not even close.

"Apologies," he said, still fighting a smile. "It was just remarkably impressive, that's all."

Still sprawled on the floor, she brushed herself off like that would fix anything. "I'm totally fine. Just... casually hurling myself at you." *There's that awkward word vomit we all know and love. Shit.*

He extended a hand. "You certainly are agile, Miss Wood."

She let him pull her up. "You have no idea how agile I can be."

"You are a strange lady," he said, the smile too smug to hide. "But strangely charming."

A pause.

He looked at her mouth.

She looked at his.

"I do hope this isn't how you treat all gentlemen," he added, voice low. "I'd hate to think I'm not special."

Dani blinked, then grinned. "I rarely go for the leg grab on the first try, but hey! If it works, it works."

Their hands stayed gently clasped, fingers softly intertwined, as they stood too close—close enough to count each other's eyelashes. In this time, people rarely stood so near. A strand of her hair had slipped across her temple, catching the light as it grazed her cheek. Her skin glowed, warm-colored from the sun, and her green eyes met his without wavering. He didn't look away.

Crunch.

From across the room, Laurel took a loud, perfectly timed bite into something. Rowen blinked, focus snapping back to reality.

"Now that you're upright," he said, cooler and more official, "let's try on some dresses, shall we?"

Laurel lounged on the velvet settee, popping sugared fruits and nuts into her mouth. She sifted through a stack of gloves, slipping one fine pair into her satchel—then paused, frowned, and returned them with exaggerated care.

Rowen strolled around, selecting dresses. When he returned, he carried a deep purple and teal day dress draped over one arm, among several others.

"It's beautiful," Dani said.

He held it up. "Square neckline, fitted waist. Bit of flair in the back. Not a poor choice."

She swallowed. "Is this where I say thank you, or do I curtsy?"

"Let's not go to such extremes just yet. First, let's see if it fits, shall we?"

He motioned her toward the dressing room and flagged down an attendant. Laurel rose to watch the action. After a few muffled grunts and huffs behind the curtain, Dani stepped out. Even she had to admit, it was a look. The plum and teal tones lit up her skin, the fit hugged just right, and the fabric carried weight without feeling stiff. She felt... oddly regal. A muscular Mary Poppins.

Rowen's mouth parted before he caught himself. "Well, well. There is a young lady, after all. That brown dress—my great-grandmother had curtains finer. Quite the rage, if I recall... in 1812."

"That was my dress, sir," Laurel cut in, offended. "And a fine one at that."

He shot her a playful wink. "Of course. A fine tapestry, indeed."

When Rowen turned back to Dani, he noticed something. His eyes dropped to the necklace just visible at her neckline. The softness in his face vanished, replaced by curiosity. He lifted his hand, fingers brushing beneath the tiny key. His knuckles grazed the base of her throat. She froze, her breath catching. He didn't quite touch her, just his knuckles. The brief skin-to-skin contact sent little lightning bolts through her.

"Interesting necklace." His voice was lower now. Dark lashes fanned up to hers, close enough that she could see the thin ring of orange around his blue irises.

Her mouth went dry. "It was a gift."

"Hmm." His hand fell away softly.

Dear god, put him in women's clothes, and I'd still die.

For the next two hours, they moved through fabric and color. Rowen pulled dresses from the walls with uncanny accuracy, each one more suited to her than the last. Dani tried them on, stepping out with flair—sometimes twirling, sometimes making dramatic model faces in the mirror just to make him laugh.

She didn't take herself too seriously. When a hat sat too high or a bodice refused to cooperate, she turned it into a bit, complete with commentary. And Rowen, polished and composed as he was, couldn't hide how much he enjoyed it. They laughed often. Fell into silences just as easily. Shared glances with no need to explain them. The connection felt natural, not forced or awkward.

Edmund remained posted near a column, now bored half to death. He stayed there until they chose the last dress and boxed the last pair of shoes.

"Right then, so we have four dresses, along with shoes and all the trimmings," Laurel commanded. "This should suffice—one for the evening, one for sleep, one for daytime affairs, and one for tea."

She paused, turned to Rowen, and leaned in slightly. Her voice dropped. Meant only for him. "And that fifth dress for my Shannon—you know her size."

Rowen's pen paused for a beat; he gave a nod. "Of course, Miss Laurel. And perhaps shoes to match the ensemble."

"Careful—she's got an eye for brown," Dani joked.

The shared connection and laughter between them snapped Laurel's last thread of sanity. Her hand instinctively wrapped around Dani's arm.

"Thank you, Mr. Quinn. You've been most gracious. I do hope it won't be too long before I have the pleasure of seeing your handsome face again. Edmund, please grab the boxes." She tugged Dani firmly away. "Come along, Miss Wood."

All warmth vanished, replaced by the rustling of skirts and the sharp click of heels on tile as Dani hurried to keep pace. As they reached the elevator doors, Dani glanced back. Rowen stood behind the counter, his pen resting idle on a small notepad. His eyes, fixed on hers, winked and smirked quickly. The elevator doors swung shut, cutting him off from view, but the image lingered in her mind.

Outside, Edmund trailed behind, arms stacked with packages containing the rest of her reluctant transformation. "Careful with that hem, Miss Wood," he said gently, noticing her struggle. "These cobblestones are treacherous for ladies' skirts."

Someone had plucked Dani from one world and awkwardly sewn her into another. Her current mint-green dress, a softer style than previous choices, featured a modest cut and delicate white polka dots. Rowen had said the dress made Dani's eyes stand out, but Dani was only aware of the collar's tightness. As she walked, she concentrated on not tripping on her hem or adjusting her sleeves.

Laurel had already vanished into the neighboring millinery, declaring a need for "proper hats for proper ladies" before disappearing among the shop ladies, chatting and carrying on.

The afternoon was warmer; people bustled across the cobbled street as they waited for the Barrington buggy to arrive.

And just like that, she remembered—Mary. Her mother. The weight of that unfinished life pressing on her chest like a stone.

A year of plans. Soccer. Graduation. That dumb cardigan her dad kept promising to fix.

She'd been chasing lights and found herself in someone else's century—and now she couldn't even see the road back.

Edmund set the mountain of packages down on the uneven sidewalk with relief, resting his elbow atop the precarious tower while flexing his fingers to restore circulation. His eyes kept drifting to a small, wrapped box tucked discretely among the purchases, and Dani caught the hint of a nervous smile tugging at his lips.

"You know, Alvie didn't have to buy all this for me," Dani said, folding her arms. "Who knows how long I'll even be here?"

"It's not the first time he's done this, miss. Likely won't be the last," Edmund replied briskly, adjusting a package beneath his arm.

She eyed him. *Not the first time?*

"He takes in a lot of strays, then?"

"Not my place to say."

That kind of response created an uncomfortable silence, which she hated.

"Someone's getting a present." She nodded to the parcel.

His ears went pink. "It's... well, it's nothing elaborate. Just some sweets from the second-floor confectionery. I grabbed them when you were struggling into your fourth dress."

"For Shannon?"

His blush deepened. "Miss Shannon works very hard. She deserves something nice."

She leaned against a nearby lamppost. Her attention drifted to the Clockery across the way, and Edmund followed her gaze.

"Interesting establishment," he said thoughtfully. "Been there longer than anyone can remember. The old gentleman who runs it... he's not quite himself these days."

"What do you mean?"

"Gets confused. Sometimes thinks it's twenty years ago, sometimes thinks people are someone else entirely." Edmund's eyes narrowed. "The son manages most business operations now."

"You know all the town's secrets."

"Not I. Everyone knows Laurel is a busybody. She's probably conducting reconnaissance as we speak."

She leaned against the lamppost as well. "You know, there are lots of pretty ladies on this street."

"And yet, here I am. Managing just fine without them," he replied while checking his nails, but there was humor in his voice now.

"So... Shannon's great, isn't she?"

Edmund's hand went to the wrapped sweets without him realizing it. "She serves the family well," he replied stiffly, then softened. "She's... she's kind. Diligent. Makes the best tea in the house."

"Ah, I see."

"Miss Wood would do well to acquaint herself with all the staff," he added, but his tone suggested he was specifically implying Shannon.

Oh-ho—he's definitely smitten.

Satisfied, she let the conversation drop. "Edmund, do we have time to cross the street before the buggy arrives?"

He looked at the sun's position, then consulted his pocket watch. "The buggy is not due for another quarter hour. However, Mrs. Barrington was quite specific about returning directly—"

"It'll just take a minute," Dani interrupted. "I want to look at the clocks."

He pulled up, clearly torn between following Laurel's instructions and accommodating the Barrington's mysterious guest. He looked at the Clockery, a shadow of concern crossing his features.

"Very well, miss. But we must be brief." He glanced at the shop again. "And perhaps... stay close to the front of the store?"

They crossed the busy street, Edmund keeping a protective pace beside her. Landing in front of the shop, Dani's eyes locked onto the golden lettering painted on the large window and door glass. For the first time, she could actually read the whole sign:

DUNWICH & SONS

PURVEYORS OF FINE TIMEPIECES, HABERDASHERY, & MECHANI-CAL MARVELS

ESTABLISHED 1812

Specialists in the Craft of Superior Clocks, Gents' Furnishings, & Automata Repairs

Commissions Accepted

The Clockery's front window displayed an assortment of timepieces, each one more intricate than the last. She peered through the glass and spotted a shelf with trinket boxes. Nearly identical boxes to the one she'd arrived with.

"Edmund, I need to go inside."

Edmund shifted, clearly uncomfortable, eyeing the packages stacked along the sidewalk. "Miss Wood, the buggy will arrive shortly. Perhaps another day would be more appropriate for shopping excursions." His tone was careful. "And I really shouldn't leave these packages unattended—"

Dani shoved the shop door open with a little more force than necessary.

Edmund sighed and retreated to stand guard over the parcels like a weary footman.

"I'll just be a moment," she called over her shoulder as the bell jingled overhead. "Keep an eye out for Laurel?"

Edmund nodded reluctantly, positioning himself where he could watch both the packages and the shop entrance.

The interior was dim and fragrant with brass polish; the air filled with a soft ticking that didn't quite match any one clock. It sounded... layered.

She paused at the threshold. Clocks lined every surface. Some were massive sentinels against the walls, others no bigger than her palm—delicate pocket watches resting in neat glass cases. Trinket boxes sat among them, some small and simple, others so meticulously carved they looked like they belonged in a museum.

Behind the counter stood an elderly man, his thin white hair wisping over his deeply lined face. His spectacles sat crooked on his nose, having long since given up the fight to stay in place. He stood with a slight hunch, his bony fingers resting lightly against the counter's surface.

Beside him hovered a young apprentice, no older than sixteen, watching like an attentive shadow.

The old man's attention floated past her shoulder, tracking something invisible. His fingers—weathered and spotted with age—drummed an erratic rhythm on the countertop.

"Something for the young miss?" he asked, then frowned and looked at the space beside her. "Misses? Are there—was it today or yesterday you came?"

His confused eyes suddenly sharpened, focusing directly on her face with startling clarity. He leaned forward, studying her features with an intensity that made her skin crawl.

"Those eyes..." he whispered, his voice barely audible. "I remember those eyes. You've touched it, haven't you?" His weathered hand reached toward her face, trembling.

Clarity vanished; his smile returned, eyes unfocused, seeming to see past her. "Ah... a visitor. Good day to you, miss."

The abrupt shift left Dani reeling.

She cleared her throat, trying to shake off the unsettled feeling. "I was wondering if I could speak to the person who makes your trinket boxes."

He hesitated.

The pause dragged.

Seconds felt like hours. Dani could feel the tension building in her chest, her mind already racing ahead while the silence dug its claws in. Stillness was unbearable—like sitting in wet clothes or waiting for a sneeze that wouldn't come.

Her patience snapped.

She reached beneath her collar and tugged out the tiny key. The chain caught slightly before slipping free, and the metal glinted in the dim shop light.

"I think this belongs to one."

He leaned in, adjusting his glasses. His brow furrowed as he studied the key, floating his gaze between it and Dani, until his expression shut down completely—blank.

"Trinket box, you say?" His bony hand lifted vaguely toward the display cases behind him. "What you see here... is what we have."

Before Dani could press further, the door behind the counter swung open. A man stepped through; the late afternoon light softened his sharp features somewhat.

Standing tall, with ebony hair swept neatly back, a firm jaw, and eyes the color of emerald and aged whiskey. He looked familiar, but she couldn't place where she'd seen him.

He reached across the counter delicately and wrapped his fingers around the key hanging from her neck.

"That is quite an interesting piece you have there," he said, voice low and smooth as silk.

A soft, quick gasp escaped her lips as he raised the object higher and observed it. She studied him intently.

Yikes, he's gorgeous. What the hell is in the food in this era?

"My name is Gabriel Dunwich," he continued, "though, if you prefer, you may call me Gabe. Miss...?"

"Wood," she supplied awkwardly. "Danielle Wood."

He moved with meticulous precision; each step placed as though the floor were a chessboard and he was calculating three moves ahead. His hands clasped behind his back, spine straight as a ruler.

"I couldn't help but overhear your inquiry about our trinket boxes," he said, his eyes never leaving her face. "Perhaps we might discuss this more comfortably in my office?" He gestured toward the back room. "I may provide some... insight."

The old man stiffened, his hand on the counter. "I don't think that's necessary. Unaccompanied, I mean," he muttered, positioning himself between them. His fingers shook.

"It's merely a conversation, Father," Gabe replied. "I believe I may be of greater help than the shop floor allows."

This was her chance, but something about his calculated politeness set her on edge. Still, she had to try.

"Fine, let's go." She tucked the key back beneath her collar, resolute.

The old man looked up at his son, confusion flickering across his features. "Lunch?" he asked, as if the word was foreign.

The apprentice stepped forward gently. "Yes, sir. Time for your meal. I've prepared it in the back."

"Ah, yes." The old man nodded slowly, allowing himself to be guided toward the back room. "Mustn't forget to eat, mustn't forget..."

As they disappeared behind the counter door, Gabe moved to a small side table near the window where a tea service sat. The afternoon light caught the delicate porcelain as he poured.

"Please," he said, offering her a cup. "I was about to have tea before you arrived. I find conversation flows more easily with proper refreshment."

Accepting the tea, she observed a shift—the shop felt cozier, intimate, just the two of them amongst the clocks' ticking. He leaned casually against the counter, but she could sense the calculation behind his relaxed posture.

"Thank you." When their fingers touched, an unwanted, primal heat surged beneath her skin.

"How can I help you, Miss Wood?" His lips curved into what might have been a smile.

Taking a sip to steady herself, she set the cup down. "You recognized the key."

He leaned back against the chair, arms crossed. "Your key is quite beautiful. Anyone would notice it." A pause. "But I make clocks, not keys."

"I just got into town, and I'm looking for a trinket box that glows blue. Do you have one of those? Preferably takes a key like this." She showed her necklace again.

He choked on his tea and set the cup down.

A wait. Direct eye contact.

This was no idle question.

A parley, then.

He stood, crossed to one of the display cases, and unlocked it. From inside, he withdrew a trinket box—similar to Mary's, but not quite. He placed it on the counter between them like a chess piece.

"Miss Wood, if I made glowing trinket boxes, do you think I would work in this dusty shop?" He kept his gaze fixed on her. "Besides, the sort of... illumination you're describing would require innovations far beyond our current capabilities. We've only just mastered the incandescent bulb, and those require considerable apparatus." A pause, his eyes studying her reaction. "Dangerous business, meddling with forces we don't yet understand."

"What's that supposed to mean?"

"Precisely what I said." He moved closer to the counter, afternoon light catching the angles of his face. "Though I do keep correspondence with several forward-thinking gentlemen in the sciences, theoretical physics scholars. Fascinating theories about electrical phenomena, the nature of light itself..." He trailed off, as if catching himself. "We have not produced any new trinket boxes in three years."

"Tell me, where are you staying?"

The question seemed casual enough, but random, and something in his tone made her wary. "With the Barringtons."

His eyebrows rose slightly. "Ah, the Barringtons. Lovely family." He paused, as if considering. "And how long will you be enjoying their hospitality?"

"I'm not sure yet."

"Mm." He moved closer to the counter, the afternoon light from the window casting sharp angles across his face. From somewhere in his waistcoat, he produced a tiny cog, rolling it between his fingers as he spoke. "You have the strangest way of speaking, Miss Wood. It's... rather unconventional."

"Unconventional. That's one way to put it."

"Another would be theatrical," he mused. "Are you quite certain you're not some rogue actress fallen out of a traveling company?"

She snorted. "Not unless they let soccer players join Equity these days."

That earned the faintest spark of amusement. "Soccer," he repeated, like he was collecting rare specimens. "Another curious phrase for the collection."

His attention momentarily fell to her hands clasped around the teacup. Not flirtatious, exactly. Just... cataloging.

"Not a seamstress. Not a lady of leisure," he said thoughtfully. "Tell me, Miss Wood, what brings you to our little town? Business? Family?"

She felt him collecting information; each question looked harmless, yet built toward a point. "Just visiting."

"And your family? Are they expecting you back soon?"

"My family..." She paused, choosing partial truth. "They're not expecting me back soon."

Something changed in his eyes—satisfaction, maybe? "How fortunate for us, then. Tell me, do all young women from your corner of the world question strange men so extensively before the tea's gone cold? Or is that charming boldness entirely your own invention?"

Dani eyed him. "Wouldn't you like to know?"

His smile widened—not quite arrogant. Just very aware of the game they were playing.

"Aside from the stimulating dynamics," she said, "if you can't make the type of box I need, do you know anyone who can?" Are there other clockmakers in town?"

"Are you being serious right now, Miss Wood? Why would you ask a business owner to send you to a competitor?"

He adjusted the cuff of his sleeve, brushing his fingers along the fabric before flicking open a cufflink. As his wrist turned, the edge of a watch caught the light.

Dani's head cocked to the side. The design was unmistakable. Mary's watch. Or something *impossibly* close to it.

She leaned forward without thinking, and as she did, a strange sensation washed over her—like standing too close to something electrically charged.

"Where did you get that watch?" Her voice came out sharper than intended.

Gabe followed her gaze to his wrist. "This old thing?" He made no move to hide it. "It's been in my family for some time."

"How long?"

"Long enough." His eyes never left her face. "Why do you ask?"

Before she shaped the words, his expression changed. Something almost predatory passed behind those green-gold eyes.

"You've seen one like it before, have you?"

"Maybe," she said carefully. "Why don't you tell me where exactly you got it?"

The back room door unexpectedly burst open.

The old man stumbled out, the young apprentice close behind, trying to steady him. His wild eyes darted around the shop, his hands trembling as he twisted against the gentle grip on his arm.

"I've lost my love, Little Lark!" his voice cracked, raw with decades-old grief. "Have you seen her, sir? She has the most beautiful eyes..."

His eyes fell on Dani once again, and he became motionless.

"There," he whispered, pointing a shaking finger at her. "There she is. Those are her eyes."

Gabe stepped forward, placing himself between his father and Dani. "Father—"

But the old fellow's eyes remained fixed on Dani's face. "Don't leave again Little Lark. Please don't leave again."

"I'm sorry, miss," the apprentice said, guiding the old man toward a chair behind the counter. "He gets confused sometimes. The afternoon can be difficult for him."

The old man allowed himself to be seated, but his gaze never left Dani's face, his lips moving as if trying to remember something just out of reach.

Gabe's mouth was a thin line, irritation and something else—embarrassment? shame?—shadowing his features.

"I'm sorry you had to witness that," Gabe said. "There are days when the world slips from his grasp."

Dani felt the old man's eyes upon her and heard soft muttering from him. "Don't leave again?"

"He says many things." Gabe's voice was carefully neutral. "Losing his wife... it broke something in him. He's been stuck in that moment ever since."

"Who was Little Lark?"

"His wife. She died many years ago." Gabe turned away, busying himself with straightening papers on the counter. "He sometimes thinks he sees her in other women."

She glanced toward the old man, still seated behind the counter, his whispered words creating an unsettling backdrop to their conversation. The apprentice hovered nearby, uncomfortable with the situation.

She rose quickly, setting her teacup down on the counter with a soft clink. "I should go. Edmund will be worried."

Gabe straightened, his composure restored. "Of course. I wouldn't want to keep you from your... companion."

There was something in the way he said 'companion' that made her pause.

"Edmund works for the Barringtons," she clarified. "He's making certain I don't get lost."

"Ah." Another piece of information filed away. "How considerate of them."

He walked with her toward the shop entrance, the old man's eyes tracking their movement. At the door, Dani's gaze caught on a small brass placard: ALL SALES FINAL. NO EXCHANGES, NO RETURNS. WHAT IS DONE IS DONE.

The Barrington buggy was just rolling into view, drawing to a stop near the curb with impeccable timing. Edmund looked visibly relieved to see her emerge from the shop.

"Miss Wood," he called, "we must go. Mrs. Barrington has a dinner party to prepare for."

Gabe's eyes narrowed slightly, his attention shifting from Edmund's armload of packages to Dani with renewed calculation.

"May I call on you?" he asked quickly, just as she stepped toward the buggy.

She should've said no. Every part of her said no.

But he had that stupid jaw, and those sleeves rolled just enough showing those muscular forearms.

"Yes," she said, faster than she meant to.

Damn it.

"Excellent." His smile was warm, genuine—or at least, it looked genuine. "It's been a pleasure, Dani."

She stopped dead. "Wait, what?"

But Edmund was already helping her into the buggy, the door closing with a decisive click. As the wheels rolled, she pressed her face to the window.

Gabe stood in the Clockery's doorway, watching her leave. Even at this distance, she could see something satisfied in his posture.

He'd called her Dani. Not Danielle—Dani.

A name she'd never given him.

"Miss Wood?" Edmund's voice was gentle but concerned. "Are you alright? You look rather pale."

"Edmund," she said slowly, "what do you know about the Dunwich family?"

He considered the question. "Old family. Been in the clockmaking business for generations." He paused. "There are... stories."

"What stories?"

"The kind people don't like to talk about, girl." Laurel's voice dropped, eyeing Edmund.

That was all she was going to get out of them, it seemed as they rolled through the narrow streets of town, dirt roads rattling beneath the wheels.

How was she supposed to get back? Back to the present day. Back to normal. Back to the version of herself who didn't feel like her heart buzzed every time Rowen looked at her. *Ugh, Rowen. A MAN.* Was it possible for someone to be that enigmatic and still be real? Or was that the time travel'esque jet lag talking to? And why—why—were both men making her feel this way? She wanted women. She preferred women. Women make her heart sing.

So what the hell was going on? *Definitely something in the food here, or the water. Definitely.*

The buggy turned onto the tree-lined road. The sun was moving behind the hills, washing the sky in pink and copper. She leaned her head back against the cushion, mind spiraling.

Getting home might be trickier than she thought.

10

BOUND BY BLOOD

EDWARDIAN ERA

The kitchen door swung open as Dani slipped inside from the servant's entrance. The thick scent of roasting meat hit her—*gross*.

Servants moved in rhythm around dinner preparations. The clang of pots, steady chopping, and bursts of laughter wrapped the lower halls in bustling energy.

She climbed the narrow servant's stairs, each step a struggle. The dress was suffocating—laced so tight she felt like a sausage stuffed into expensive silk. The previous gown had been uncomfortable; this one was actively hostile.

Reaching the tiny powder room, her chest heaved with each breath. She slammed her palms against the old porcelain sink before attacking the dress fastenings. Her fingers fumbled with the buttons.

"Come on, come on. Release me, you foul beast!" A growl slipped through gritted teeth as she twisted at an awkward angle.

With a final, desperate tug, her foot slipped on the smooth tiles. She crashed against the sink, catching herself just in time, pressing her forehead to the cool porcelain.

A soft voice emerged from behind the door.

"Miss, you sound as though you're in quite a predicament."

Yeah, I'm a human pretzel in Edwardian drag.

"I am very much NOT alright," she snapped. "This straitjacket of a dress is holding me hostage."

Relief flooded her as a hand appeared through the crack, deftly working the buttons she'd been struggling with. "Allow me to assist you," the voice continued, and the pressure lifted as small fingers skillfully undid the stubborn fastenings.

"I've had a great deal of experience helping ladies out of difficult gowns," the girl chuckled, warm amusement coloring her tone.

Dani looked up at her savior.

"I'm Shannon. I noticed you in the kitchen earlier. My mother, Laurel, thought you might need some help."

Shannon.

Dani squinted in the dim light. There it was—that same easy warmth, the same playful glint that felt achingly familiar. Just like Alvie. Her huge blue eyes gave her away.

The kitchen glimpse hadn't been enough—too much noise, too many faces. But here, up close, it was obvious.

Alvie had invited Dani in without hesitation. He'd looked at her, really looked, and seen something familiar. Something that made him trust her without question. Had someone else shown up at his doorstep once? Another mysterious stranger, lost and alone?

Shannon's fingers worked at the back of Dani's gown, unbuttoning layers.

"You speak most extraordinarily, Miss Wood." Her voice was gentle, more curious than critical.

"Funny? I keep hearing that lately."

Dani caught the soft smile tugging at Shannon's mouth and the glint of something small at her throat—a locket, half-tucked beneath her collar.

The dress popped loose. Relief hit hard. Dani groaned, rolling her shoulders. "Holy moly! You're officially my savior in this house."

"A rather low bar for sainthood, I daresay," Shannon joked, gathering scattered pieces of Dani's dress.

Her attention drifted to Dani's hair, twisted in a messy ponytail held by a simple elastic band. She hesitated, brow furrowing.

"I beg your pardon, miss, but what curious contraption is that?" She pointed delicately.

Dani blinked. "Uh... my hair?"

"No, no—the arrangement in your hair. How remarkable! It keeps everything so neatly styled without a single pin!"

"Oh. This? It's just a hair tie. Elastic. Holds your hair without stabbing your scalp fifty times." She tugged it loose and held it out like forbidden technology. "Revolutionary, right? Go on—take it."

Shannon's eyes widened like Dani had handed her a diamond. "Oh, Miss, I couldn't possibly..." Though her expression absolutely betrayed her. "How singularly clever! And no pins whatsoever?"

"Nope," Dani grinned. "Modern miracle. But I'm thinking... fair trade." She twirled the band between her fingers. "I give you this little life-changer if you help me with something."

Shannon's curiosity sharpened. "And what sort of help would you require?"

"Pretty sure I'm about to get hauled downstairs for dinner like some reluctant debutante." Dani gave her a look. "Can you do hair? Like... fancy hair?"

"I am rather accomplished, if I may be so bold. Mother has taught me many fashionable arrangements." Shannon visibly perked up, quiet pride mixed with mischief.

"Perfect," Dani said, dangling the hair tie like bait. "This is for your styling skills. Deal?"

Without thinking, she held out her hand for a high five.

Shannon stared at it, entirely baffled. After a beat too long, she reached out and lightly patted Dani's hand like approaching a skittish kitten.

Dani wheezed, doubled over, clutching her stomach. "Love this!"

"Was that not the proper response?" Shannon stammered, ears turning pink. "I thought perhaps it was a genteel greeting I had not yet encountered."

"Not even close," Dani choked out. "But honestly? Great. From now on, we'll seal deals with a palm pat. That's law."

Shannon giggled despite herself. "How utterly improper. And yet... I find I rather like it, Miss Wood."

"Dani," she corrected, smile softening. "You can just call me Dani when it's just us."

Her attention caught on the delicate chain at Shannon's neck again. "That's a pretty locket."

Shannon's fingers rose to touch it, the light in her expression shining.

"It was a gift from Mr. Barrington. On my sixteenth birthday." She hesitated, then slowly opened the locket, revealing a tiny pressed flower.

Another puzzle piece sliding into place.

As the last layer came loose, Dani collapsed onto the nearby stool. Shannon folded the abandoned gown with far more respect than it deserved.

"You know," Shannon mused, "you are not what I expected."

"Oh? What's that supposed to mean?"

"My mother said you were exceedingly peculiar and that I ought to maintain proper distance."

Dani snorted. "And yet here you are, ruining your reputation in the servant's quarters with a known menace."

Shannon smiled. "But you're..." She searched for words. "Simply unlike anyone I have ever encountered. You speak your mind with such freedom. Sometimes, I wish to do the same. The constraints of propriety can be most... suffocating."

"Well, that makes two of us," Dani nudged her playfully. "You can be yourself around me." She held out her palm again. "Palm pat on it?"

Shannon's eyes sparkled with mischief as she delicately patted Dani's palm with exaggerated formality. "Palm pat, indeed."

She had worked quickly but carefully, sculpting Dani's hair into an elegant updo with twists and pins. Far more effort than she normally spent on her head.

Dani smiled, but it didn't quite reach her eyes. Something about this moment—soft hands, old air, corset creases in her skin—it made her ache.

She missed her room. Toaster. The squeak of her mother's shoes on the wood floor.

She was getting used to this life too fast. And that scared her more than anything.

Afterward, Dani slipped to the small servant's quarters prepared for her. The narrow bed creaked as she flopped onto it, staring out the tiny window.

A day hadn't passed, but the hours dragged. No scroll holes to disappear into. No text notifications to save her from her thoughts. Just questions, exhaustion, and quiet. How was she supposed to get home with what she thought was a lead, to possibly no leads now?

Eventually, she forced herself up and dug through the boxes Edmund had delivered. The dinner gown shimmered in low light—gold embroidery and delicate beaded florals with a tulle overlay that floated like a warning sign. Delicate. Expensive. Clearly meant to dazzle or distract.

Her reflection was almost unrecognizable. Shannon had cinched her waist to an unreasonable degree. The high collar sat like a polite chokehold, and the sleeves itched like sandpaper. She tugged at the bodice, searching for comfort. Corsets didn't negotiate.

All this for dinner. What happens when someone gets married—fireworks? Parade? Blood sacrifice?

She followed the murmur of voices down the grand staircase, her shoes clicking awkwardly on polished wood. Shannon had briefed her on the Barringtons—their wealth, their rules, their taste for elegance and control.

But as she neared the dining room, it wasn't the opulence that struck her. The candlelight bounced off crystal glasses and silverware in perfect rows. Classic Barrington overkill.

She noticed the pause. The entire room held its breath, waiting for her to step in. When she finally did, the grand dining hall erupted in whispers.

Nobody had expected her. Nobody but Alvie and the staff.

Alvie sat rigidly at the table's head, his usual effortless charm just slightly out of reach. To his right sat Vivienne's family—well-dressed, sharp-eyed, people aware of their elevated status. Their conversations hummed like annoying bees.

Across from them, Laurel stood by the sideboard, overseeing dinner preparations. She wasn't looking at the table. She was waiting.

Then Vivienne entered mid-laugh, flanked by two equally polished women. Her voice carried—she was used to ruling every room. She glided forward until she saw Dani.

The air in the dining room changed.

Vivienne's eyes locked onto her, the laugh dying mid-breath. One woman gasped. A man near Alvie lowered his glass. Even the servants hesitated.

For one long beat, no one moved.

Smash.

Glass hit the floor at Vivienne's feet, a wine glass sparkling across the tile like scattered diamonds. The dining hall went still.

Yep. She sees it.

Vivienne's face drained of color. Her lips parted like she meant to speak, but couldn't. Then the shock drained away, replaced by something colder. The mask slammed into place.

"Good evening," Dani managed, barely above a whisper.

The word rippled through the space. Every pair of eyes bounced between her and Alvie. The resemblance was undeniable. Alvie looked like a version of Dani just a decade older. His regal posture contrasted starkly with her casual existence.

Before the room could tip into awkwardness, Alvie interjected. "Ladies and gentlemen, allow me to introduce Miss Danielle Wood." He smiled, but his eyes rolled toward Vivienne. "Our long-lost relation. Miraculously, she found us."

The whispers started instantly. A well-dressed woman near the table's end covered her mouth with a gloved hand. "It appears history repeats itself, then. There's always another."

The man beside her swirled his wine with quiet satisfaction. Under his breath: "You cunning old fox." He tipped his glass toward Alvie.

When Shannon entered with a plate of food, their similarity became even clearer. Same eyes. Same cheekbones. Rich, powerful men with too many "distant relatives" raised eyebrows, and Alvie had already been the subject of whispered speculation.

She'd probably just handed these people their new favorite dinner party scandal.

Vivienne was still staring, studying her like a riddle that shouldn't exist.

"Might I ask for your family name, kindly, miss...?" Her voice was calm, but the edges wavered.

"Barr—eh, Wood. Danielle Wood," Dani stumbled from nervousness.

"You look..." Vivienne trailed off. "Familiar."

Alvie chuckled softly, stepping into the tension. "I found her, Vivienne. But for now, let's enjoy dinner. There will be time enough for conversation afterward."

"Plenty of time, indeed." Vivienne returned to her seat. Dani followed, settling stiffly into the only open chair.

The guests hesitated before resuming conversations. Silverware clinked against porcelain, crystal glasses lifted to lips, and high society life resumed. But a strange undercurrent ran beneath it all.

Dani sank into her seat and picked up the correct fork carefully. Thank God for Mary and her history obsessions—all those rants about Victorian dinner etiquette and that summer of forced Downton Abbey rewatches had, against all odds, paid off.

She kept her posture straight, took small bites, and resisted the urge to shovel food. By some miracle, she made it through dinner without committing a social crime.

As guests drifted toward the grand music room, Dani hung back. She hadn't said a word since dinner started—success by her own low bar. Quietly, she slipped toward the servant's stairs, plotting her escape before anyone noticed.

She had nearly reached the landing when Alvie's voice cut through the air.

"Miss Wood."

She froze.

"Come with me, if you please. I would like to have a word."

Her anxiety ticked up. A dozen possibilities spun through her mind, none particularly reassuring. Still, she nodded, swallowing whatever sarcastic remark threatened to escape, and followed him down the dimly lit corridor.

Dark-paneled walls and rich carpets lined the hallway, muffling their steps. Dani recognized the space immediately—in her time. This was a dusty hall with peeling wallpaper stacked with old boxes and forgotten furniture.

Alvie reached the door at the corridor's end and pushed it open. Warm, golden light spilled into the hall as she entered. Quiet luxury steeped the room—plush leather chairs, opulent rugs, and the glow of a Turkish lamp casting intricate patterns across the blue and gold ceiling. But here, in 1905, it was a gentleman's retreat. A sanctuary of privilege.

Alvie crossed to a crystal decanter. Without a word, he poured two glasses of amber liquid, setting one on the small table beside an empty chair before lowering himself into his seat. He gestured toward the other.

"Sit, if you will."

She hesitated, then sank into the chair, watching Alvie lean back and roll the glass between his fingers.

"When you first arrived, I could not shake the notion that you were familiar to me, given our extraordinary resemblance." His eyes turned toward the fire.

He swirled the whiskey, taking a long sip.

"At dinner, I said you were family because, in truth, I had no better explanation. The resemblance to my own is striking and unavoidable. But beyond that?" He shook his head slightly. "I simply did not know what else to say. The family you seek...one might venture to suggest the family you seek may be here."

They spoke for what felt like hours. Dani chose her words carefully, navigating the conversation like treacherous waters, careful not to reveal too much. Despite his simple charm, Alvie was sharp—a natural student of people. His eyes missed nothing, and she could tell he sensed the gaps in her story.

At one point, she leaned back in her chair, extending her legs slightly, and released a long, thoughtful hum while her fingers drummed against the wooden armrest. A tell she couldn't suppress.

Simultaneously, Alvie did the same.

Their eyes met.

The tap of their fingers had been in perfect rhythm, the same absentminded habit, like a quiet thought rolling around at the same pace.

What are the odds?

Alvie stilled, his lips parting slightly before curling into something between amusement and disbelief. "Well, now... that's rather curious." His voice was softer, like he was turning something over in his mind.

Dani forced a laugh, shifting in her seat. "Total coincidence. Probably."

Alvie raised an eyebrow. "Hmm."

No words, but you could feel the tension change. Dani was no longer just a guest in his home. Alvie was processing behind his sharp blue eyes—recognition, curiosity, a thought he wasn't ready to speak aloud. The resemblance, mannerisms, and instinctive way they moved was too much to ignore.

He leaned back slightly, exhaling through his nose, his fingers idly brushing his waistcoat pocket. His expression tensed briefly, but just as quickly, his effortless charm slipped back into place. Whatever storm had passed through his mind, he tucked it away, buried beneath a decision already made.

At last, he reached into his coat pocket, pulling out a delicate brass key. The metal gleamed in the candlelight—a replica of the one Dani had on her bedroom door at home.

Alvie studied it briefly before turning her hand over and placing the key into her palm.

"You shall stay in a guest suite upstairs," he said, his tone softer now. Something in him had changed. "We'll talk more tomorrow. But for now, you need rest."

Dani blinked at the key, her fingers curling around the cool metal. This was odd. If she was just some girl he'd found in his stables, wouldn't the servants' quarters be more appropriate? Even Shannon lived among the staff. What had elevated Dani so quickly?

This wasn't just hospitality. Alvie must have sensed something. And this key wasn't just to a room—it was to whatever game he was playing.

When they reached the door at the hall's end, Dani hesitated. She knew this door. She had studied it in house plans, walked past it countless times at home. In her time, this space was different. But here it was, untouched. Restored. Alive!

Alvie pushed the door open. The interior almost exactly replicated her room at home, only without age. The huge canopy bed and windows were still there, but the bathroom was all shiny copper pipes and a fancy shower—like something from an old photo.

As Alvie bid her goodnight and shut the door behind her, Dani stood still, staring at her reflection in the large standing mirror.

Well Noodle, you're definitely on your own now.

She collapsed onto the bed, her limbs sinking into the mattress. This had been the longest day of human history. A buggy ride into town, where she met someone who embodied that impossible, magnetic pull—the presence that left her completely unhinged after one meeting.

Dani pressed her palms against her face.

Rowen. Oh, hell.

How could she see him again without making it weird? Her thoughts raced ahead, already plotting ridiculous excuses to return to the shop, but she forced herself to slow down. *I can't get ahead of myself. Finding a damn trinket box should be my priority. I can't stay here forever.* But even as she reminded herself, Rowen's stupidly perfect face burned in her mind.

So instead, she lay awake in her borrowed-but-not-borrowed bed, staring at the familiar-but-unfamiliar ceiling. The day's events tumbled through her mind—Alvie's scrutiny, the strange way he looked at her hands, her face. She couldn't shake the feeling that behind his polite smiles lay sharper insight than she'd given him credit for.

Somewhere else in this house, the Barringtons were likely doing the same—lying awake, piecing together the puzzle of her arrival. The thought should have terrified her. Instead, it felt strangely like coming home.

A sharp knock at the door jolted Dani from sleep. For a split second, she thought she was home. "Dad, it's too fucking early, c'mon!"

Her eyes barely opened to the soft morning light spilling through the curtains. The distinct click-clack of heels against wooden floors shattered any last illusion of waking up in the 21st century.

She groaned, dragging a pillow over her face. *God, mornings exist here, too?*

"Miss Wood, morning has come," Shannon's voice rang out, bright and far too cheerful for someone who had likely been up for hours. "I have brought your tea and toast."

Dani squinted at the doorway, contemplating selling her soul to remain cocooned in these blankets forever. But there Shannon was, radiating saintly governess energy, effortlessly balancing a tray. The air filled with the rich scent of warm butter and tea leaves.

"Aren't you just the sweetest thing?" Dani flopped dramatically against the pillows. "I believe I shall stay in bed for eternity."

Shannon's light laughter filled the room as she placed the tray on the nightstand. "If only, miss. But I fear Mr. Barrington has made other arrangements for you this day."

"Oh?" One suspicious eye cracked open. "You mean the whole 'find my family' thing?"

"Indeed, miss." Shannon folded her hands neatly. "And I think he would not take kindly to finding you sprawled about like some indolent house cat."

A groan escaped as Dani rubbed her hands down her face. "If I knock things off shelves, then he can worry."

"Whatever that may mean," Shannon replied, moving to the window and drawing back heavy curtains. Beyond the glass, gardens lined in perfectly manicured rows, treetops swaying gently in the breeze.

"Mr. Barrington holds a firm belief that you and he are possibly related, miss." A pause. "Yet he is not a man given to impulsive actions. He trusts that, in time, the truth shall reveal itself."

Dani lowered her hands, blinking against the sunlight.

"And he told you this because...?"

"Mr. Barrington and I occasionally discuss such matters, but we don't share all our words with curious ears."

Dani frowned, studying her, then pushing herself upright. She swung her legs over the side of the bed. "I wouldn't mind going back into town. Perhaps the dress shop," she added sneakily.

"Ah, yes, Lipman Wolfe & Co." A small, conspiratorial smile spread across Shannon's face. "A most reputable establishment, to be sure. They have exquisite tailoring." She folded the duvet's edges before adding, "And, of course, there's that certain gentleman who commands the attention of half the young ladies in Portland."

Dani leaned forward. "So, you're saying it's a revolving door of ladies?" Perfect. Not only am I time-traveling, but I'm also competing in the Edwardian-era thirst games.

"Should you return, miss, best steel yourself. Some ladies visit for the gowns—most return for his measurements."

Dani couldn't help but shake her head as warmth spread through her chest. Shannon was so relatable in this moment, offering no judgment, just girl talk.

She gently placed a hand on Dani's shoulder. "I'll help you get dressed now. Mr. Barrington is waiting for you."

Steam curled lazily from Alvie's coffee cup as he sat at the head of the breakfast room table, one arm draped along the chair's back. He looked up at the soft shuffle of footsteps, his gaze catching Dani and Shannon as they entered. A smile played at his mouth's corners before he lifted his cup for an unhurried sip.

"Ah, Miss Wood," he said, voice as smooth as sunlight pooling through tall windows. "I trust you found your accommodations satisfactory?"

Dani flopped into the nearest chair, snagging a croissant and tearing into it with bleary determination. "Like a baby," she mumbled, scattering crumbs across her plate. Her gaze drifted across the room until it snagged on something inside a glass built-in cabinet. Tucked between gleaming silver and delicate antiques sat a small wooden trinket box. Her fingers stiffened, croissant forgotten. The metalwork was absolutely familiar.

She took another bite, feigning interest in her surroundings. "This place is... very nice." She gestured vaguely before nodding toward the cabinet. "And that little wooden box—it's kinda beautiful."

His eyes followed hers, lips curving in quiet amusement. "Ah. That one." He leaned back, swirling his coffee absentmindedly. "A gift from an acquaintance."

Dani's grip tightened around her teacup. She fought to keep her face neutral.

After a few minutes of simple conversation, she hesitated. "Mr. Barrington, I'm very thankful you've taken me in."

He looked up from his coffee, intrigued. "Oh?"

"I don't know what I would have done with no money or belongings." She wrinkled her nose. "You've been my savior."

"Ah, yes. A rather dramatic way of putting it, but I shall accept the title all the same." He took a slow sip before continuing, "I think we shall find something to occupy your time this week—perhaps an introduction into society. If that aids in your search for your family, all the better."

"Truly, you are a saint among men. I would appreciate that."

Cue freeze-frame.

Narrator (with that classic, over-the-top 80s voiceover): "Yep. This is Dani. She thinks everything's going great. But here's the thing—she does not know she just royally screwed up. Like epic proportions. And Mary? Oh, sweet Mary. All that 'wisdom' she dished out? Turns out, it didn't cover what an 'introduction to society' really means. But don't worry... Dani's about to find out. Hard."

Cue record scratch, synth-pop music kicks in, and the scene unfreezes.

Alvie gave a hearty laugh over his cup's rim. "I do what I must, young lady."

A moment of kindness and warmth was all she needed today. She hesitated for half a second, a thought skimming just beneath her mind's surface. *Thanks, Grandpa.* She swallowed it back before it could take root.

After breakfast, Dani wandered the halls, drawn to Alvie's study by the door's slight parting—just enough to suggest an invitation. She had never been one to ignore an open door.

Dust danced in the sunlit air, and the room filled with the scent of leather-bound books. Her fingers trailed along book spines lining the shelves—titles about astronomy, mechanics, and philosophy catching her eye.

Movement from the hallway caught her attention. She held her breath, noticing footsteps approaching, then passing by. Exhaling softly, Dani ventured deeper into the study.

That's when she spotted the open file folder on Alvie's desk. Beneath a sketch, he had written: 'The theory of temporal frequencies suggests each plane resonates at a specific pitch.'

Another book and funding proposals obscured the rest, but numbers filled the margins. Dates? Coordinates? As her fingers brushed the page, she scanned curiously.

Footsteps approached. Dani quickly stepped away from the desk.

Alvie entered with a pipe in hand, his expression guarded as he took in her presence in his private sanctuary.

"Forgive me for startling you," Alvie said, his voice carrying that refined cadence that spoke of drawing rooms and proper education. "I hadn't realised you'd taken such a keen interest in... administrative matters."

Dani straightened abruptly, tucking a stray paper back onto the desk. "Oh, yeah. I love... office work."

"Is that so?" He arched a brow, strolling toward her with measured steps. "How peculiar. Most young ladies of my acquaintance avoid ledgers and correspondence as though they were carriers of some dreadful plague."

"Well," Dani shrugged, recovering, "maybe I'm not like most girls."

Alvie's lips curved slightly, but his eyes remained sharp. "Indeed, you are rather... unique." He gestured to the neatly stacked papers and opened volumes spread across the desk. "Tell me, Miss Wood, do you truly find such matters engaging? Business ventures, financial projections, partnership agreements?"

Dani felt herself on steadier ground now. "Actually, yeah. Back ho—" She caught herself. "I mean, I've always been interested in how businesses work. The strategy behind it all, you know? Like, how do you know which investments will pay off? What makes one partnership succeed where another fails?"

Alvie's eyebrows rose considerably. "My word. That's rather... sophisticated thinking for a young lady. Might I ask where you've acquired such knowledge? Surely not from the usual finishing school curriculum?"

"I'm studying Business Administration," Dani said without thinking, then immediately realized her mistake.

The silence that followed was deafening. Alvie's pipe froze halfway to his lips.

"I beg your pardon?" His voice was barely above a whisper. "You're... studying? At university?"

Dani's mind raced. "I... well, it's complicated."

"Complicated?" Alvie set down his pipe with trembling hands. "Miss Wood, women do not attend university. They cannot attend university. The very notion is..." He stared at her as though she'd claimed to have sprouted wings. "Wherever did you come by such an extraordinary idea?"

"Um…" Dani scrambled for an explanation. "It's a… special program. Very progressive. My family has connections with some forward-thinking educators who believe women should have more… opportunities."

Alvie sank into his chair, looking genuinely shaken. "Business Administration. Good heavens. And they're teaching you about investments? Financial management? Corporate structure?"

"Yeah, all of it. I'm actually pretty good at it, too."

"I dare say you must be." He studied her with newfound intensity. "This explains a great deal about your… unconventional observations. Tell me, what other pursuits occupy your time? Surely you have the traditional feminine accomplishments as well? Needlepoint, perhaps? Watercolours? Piano?"

Dani almost laughed. "Not really my thing. I'm more into soccer."

"Soccer?" Alvie tilted his head like a confused spaniel.

"Yeah, I'm actually kind of a sought after player back home. I play forward, and I'm hoping to sign with a professional team at the end of—" She stopped herself again. *Too much, Dani, shut it.*

"I'm afraid I'm not familiar with this… soccer. Is it some sort of parlour game?"

"No, it's a sport. You know, you kick a ball around a field, try to get it into the other team's goal. Two teams, eleven players each, you can't use your hands except for the goalkeeper…"

Alvie's face lit up with recognition. "Oh! You mean football!"

"Well, we call it soccer, but yeah, basically."

"Good gracious," Alvie breathed, leaning back in his chair. "A young lady who plays football. Competitively. And studies business at university." He shook his head in wonder. "Miss Wood, you are quite possibly the most extraordinary person I have ever encountered. Your family must be remarkably progressive indeed."

"They're… unique," Dani said carefully.

"I should say so." Alvie picked up his pipe again, but didn't light it, just turned it over in his hands thoughtfully. "Tell me, in your business studies, have you learned about investment portfolios? Asset management? The principles of compound interest?"

"Yeah, all of that. Why?"

Alvie was quiet for a long moment, his gaze drifting to the closed file on his desk. "No particular reason. Simply… fascinating to meet someone with such capabilities." He looked up at her again. "I suspect you have a rather remarkable future ahead of you, Miss Wood. Whatever path you choose to take."

His pride in her was clear, even if he didn't say it, the impact of his words lingered. And that meant everything to her.

"I was searching for a book to read," Dani said finally, breaking the silence. "Everything in the library seemed a bit... heavy."

Alvie smiled, and this time it reached his eyes. "Ah yes, Father's collection runs toward the philosophical. Rather dry stuff, I'm afraid. You're welcome to browse here anytime, though I suspect you might find my technical journals more to your taste than most young ladies would."

She recognized the subtle shift, the polite dismissal wrapped in invitation. As she moved toward the door, Alvie's voice stopped her.

"Miss Wood? This conversation... perhaps it would be best if it remained between us. Some ideas are rather ahead of their time."

"Of course," she said, understanding completely.

She stepped back and pulled the pocket doors shut, the latch clicking sharply in the stillness, both of them left to contemplate just how extraordinary—and impossible—their exchange had truly been.

11

ROLLERSKATE CONFESSIONAL

EDWARDIAN ERA

The air reeked of roasted peanuts and frying oil, and screams from the small wooden roller coaster looped overhead like banshee calls.

Dani hadn't expected to be here, but now she was nodding politely through another long-winded story from Alvie about Portland's timber tariffs. Vivienne had declared her need for socialization and insisted they take the day at Groves Amusement Park.

Three weeks into this strange new life, Dani still didn't know where she fit. But as she took in the vendor stalls, carousel, and blinking electric lights overhead, it was hard not to admit the simplicity was growing on her.

And so were the Barringtons.

Vivienne kept her distance—or pretended to. But Dani could feel her subtle warmth and curiosity. She liked her energy, maybe even saw something familiar about how Dani moved. Something that reminded her of Alvie. Whatever the truth was, it felt like family.

Alvie had brought her here thinking a public outing might increase her chances of meeting someone from her supposed family. But now both he and Vivienne were meeting with acquaintances, leaving Dani to fend for herself.

She had just begun wandering toward the bustling midway when her gaze snagged on something unexpected—Shannon and Edmund, together. It was Sunday; they should have been at church or elsewhere with the rest of the staff who had the day off. But there they stood beside one of the brightly colored game booths, Shannon's laughter floating through the air in response to something Edmund had whispered. His arm curled around her waist with an ease that felt too natural.

Oh shit.

Just beyond them, Alvie and Vivienne approached, completely unaware. If they saw Shannon and Edmund together, questions would follow. Acting on instinct, Dani pivoted sharply, stepping in front of them with a sudden, overly bright smile.

"Oh, look at that!" Dani exclaimed, pointing dramatically toward a nearby performer juggling flaming torches. "Now that's something you don't see every day."

Alvie watched happily. "Most impressive."

Vivienne pursed her lips. "I suppose, if you enjoy such spectacles."

Dani let out an exaggerated laugh, stepping sideways just enough to ensure Shannon and Edmund had time to slip away unnoticed. When she dared to glance back, they were gone.

Dani walked beside Alvie and Vivienne down the bustling midway, sounds of bells and laughter mixing with the scent of horses and sawdust. They passed rows of carnival games and brightly painted rides, Alvie explaining each with pride, Vivienne gliding effortlessly at his side.

But Dani's attention snagged on movement near an old oak tree.

Rowen stood with one shoulder pressed against the bark, arms crossed, watching the crowd flow past him like he was studying a particularly fascinating species. A little smile touched his lips—not quite a grin, more like something gentle. Two women had slowed their pace as they passed, stealing glances and whispering behind gloved hands. He didn't seem to notice. Or pretended not to.

Dani's chest loosened, like she'd been holding her breath for hours without realizing it. Her fingers uncurled from the fists she hadn't known she was making.

Then his eyes found hers across the promenade of booths and people.

Heat shot up her neck. Her stomach dropped clean through the cobblestones.

Yep. That's it, she thought, even as her feet started moving toward him without permission. *That's the face of someone you should absolutely run from.*

It wasn't just his appearance—it was his very existence. Even amidst the chaos of an amusement park, Rowen exuded elegance, like he'd stepped out of a tailor's shop. An expert cut dark navy suit, perfectly fitted, and neatly buttoned over a muted pinstriped vest.

As he passed, he captivated the ladies, holding their gaze. They covered their faces with gloved hands, smiling, tipping their eyes and hats. A small group of younger girls had gathered near him, giggling and staring in awe. *competition seems fierce.*

He looked up just as Dani approached.

Rowen smiled. "Miss Wood. I must confess, I did not expect to encounter you at a place of such... spirited entertainment. Then again,"—his eyes gleamed—"after your rather memorable performance at the store, perhaps I should not be so surprised."

And...he remembers my flop.

She shrugged, casual, like falling into an entire display of dresses was no big deal. (Except it totally was.)

From his breast pocket, he produced a slim, leather-bound notebook. With a flick of his wrist, he jotted something down in a brisk, neat script, then tucked it away as if it had never left his hand.

Dani crossed her arms, trying to look cooler than she felt. "It was this or an embroidery circle. I made the reckless choice."

Rowen's mouth curved, just barely. "Fortunate for me, then. I'm happy to have your company." As he spoke, he absently tugged at the fingertips of his gloves, the fine leather slipping slightly before he adjusted them with simple grace. His movements were effortless, but there was something delicate about the way his fingers worked the fabric.

Dani glanced down at her outfit—a high-collared ivory blouse tucked into a deep blue walking skirt, the fabric heavy and stiff. A matching jacket cinched at her waist, and beneath it, layers of petticoats made movement oddly restrictive. "God, I miss jeans," she muttered.

"Pardon?" Rowen tilted his head, his voice smooth but pitched in a register Dani hadn't heard yet.

She rubbed the back of her neck, then quickly dropped her hand, feeling self-conscious. "Oof. Nothing. Forget it." She shifted her weight. "So, what's your plans? Just standing around collecting admirers?"

"My... plans?" he asked.

"Yeah. What are you doing here today?"

"I am merely observing the revelry, making sure everyone is properly attired, and considering whether I should join the festivities."

"So... people-watching and being judgy?"

"I prefer to call it maintaining standards." He joined her in step, matching her quick wit.

"And is that notebook full of judgmental poetry about people's hats, or are you secretly writing a murder mystery?"

Rowen looked mildly amused. "I assure you; the contents are far less dramatic."

"Mmm. That's exactly what someone writing a murder mystery would say."

He opened his mouth like he might correct her, then closed it again and made a tiny mark in the book.

"Oh my god," she said. "Are you writing right now? What did I just inspire?"

Leaning forward, he clicked his tongue. "A single word," said calmly. "Interruption."

Dani laughed. "Wow. Brutal."

Rowen offered a faint, not unkind smile. "I consider it a fair trade."

"For what?"

"Your chaos. My calm. The dynamic is oddly... efficient."

Dani tilted her head. "You mean I'm fun and you're uptight."

"I was trying to be diplomatic."

"And I was trying not to call you stuffy."

They grinned at the same time, and for a moment, the space between them felt like it bent closer. Dani's pulse kicked up. She took a step sideways, playing it off.

"So, what exactly does it take to convince you to 'lower yourself' to some actual fun?" The challenge was flirtation disguised as mockery.

Rowen tapped his gloved fingers against his pocket watch. "That depends. Are you willing to risk your dignity?"

"Always," she replied. "Dignity's for people who don't fall into dress racks."

Rowen laughed heartily then gestured toward the roller-skating pavilion, where couples glided across polished wooden floors beneath soft electric lights. The air inside buzzed with laughter, the faint scuff of wheels, and the distant strains of a string quartet struggling to keep up with the upbeat organ tempo.

"Roller skating. I assume you have done it before?" he asked.

"Please." Dani grinned. "I could skate circles around you."

"We shall see, Miss Wood." With an exaggerated bow, Rowen swept his arm toward the entrance.

Dani completely abandoned Alvie and Vivienne, who had gotten distracted by a chattering group near the concession stands. They didn't even notice her slip away, and she wasn't about to miss the opportunity to get to know Rowen better.

At the ticket counter, a sharp-eyed woman peered at them over thin wire glasses.

"Entry for two, please," Rowen said.

The woman raised an eyebrow. "Couple's ticket? It's priced more modestly."

Rowen glanced sideways at Dani, who shrugged helplessly.

"Yes," he said after a pause. "A couple's ticket."

Behind them, a gaggle of girls let out a collective disappointed "Aw" and slowly dispersed, whispering among themselves.

Inside the pavilion, they selected skates and found a bench along the wall. Dani laced up with quick, practiced motions, feeling more at ease despite the strange twist her afternoon had taken.

When she glanced up, Rowen was watching her with a mischievous glint.

"Miss Wood," he said, leaning conspiratorially, "while it was absolutely entertaining to see you slither down my leg like a snake the other day, I must warn you—this will be riskier. And these pants are quite expensive. Please try to stay upright."

Dani snorted, but as she pushed off the bench and rolled tentatively onto the floor, humor drained from her face.

She had played ice hockey when she was younger—aggressive, fast-paced, brutal skating. But roller skating on this old, highly polished wooden floor was different. The wheels felt heavier, clunkier, and the surface was slicker than any rink she'd known. Her skates slid awkwardly, the grip inconsistent.

She wobbled, arms pinwheeling slightly.

Rowen laughed and skated backward ahead of her; hands tucked casually behind his back.

"Careful," he called, teasing lilt in his voice. "I'd hate to carry you off the battlefield."

He moved far too gracefully for someone who had claimed to be equally unprepared.

"You've done this before," Dani accused, wobbling.

Rowen tilted his head with feigned innocence. "Perhaps."

"Yeah, okay. Now I really don't trust you."

Rowen laughed softly, reaching out just as Dani's balance betrayed her. His fingers curled around her wrist, steadying her with ease. "That's probably wise."

They skated together, and Dani realized something fundamental was happening. It wasn't just about learning to balance—it was about finding rhythm with someone. With Rowen. Each near fall, each steadying touch, felt like a conversation without words.

Her brain still categorized his sex as 'not her type,' but her body hadn't gotten the memo.

"I see how it is," Dani muttered after a near fall. "You're letting me struggle just enough to be entertained."

Rowen's eyes sparkled. "Would I do such a thing?"

"Absolutely."

"Oh, you wound me."

The music from the piano organ melted into a soft background beneath chatter and occasional bursts of laughter from passing couples. For the first time in forever, Dani let herself stop thinking and just enjoy it.

They found a bench near the rink, catching their breath. Rowen sat closer than before, their legs almost touching. Not quite, but close enough that she could feel his warmth radiating between them.

They talked about books—mostly older ones, obviously. When Pride and Prejudice came up, Dani lit up just enough to catch Rowen's attention.

"A classic," he said casually, "though perhaps a touch… romantic for some tastes."

"Oh, sure," she said. "All that slow-burn eye contact and emotional repression. Super boring."

He raised an eyebrow. "You're teasing."

"A little."

Rowen tapped a finger against his knee, watching her closely. "So, which did you prefer? Mr. Darcy… or Elizabeth Bennet?"

Dani hesitated because that question felt loaded.

She allowed the silence to linger just long enough to be noticeable, then smirked, tilting her head.

"Honestly? I always thought Elizabeth had the better lines." Her tone wasn't joking, but her posture said *catch me if you can.*

Rowen didn't speak at first. His expression remained composed, but she could see that hint of computation.

"Ah," he said finally. "Sharp tongue and clearer thinking. A worthy combination."

"Exactly," Dani replied. "Yeah, I love a sharp tongue." *And not just in conversation.*

He stifled a laugh that turned into more of a splutter. "Tragic. And here I was, hoping my conversational skills might suffice. How will I ever live up to Miss Bennet's skill set?"

"Oh, you're doing fine. We've already survived our first argument."

"Was that an argument?"

"Well," she said, nudging his leg with hers, "I did just reject your entire gender through a simple character preference." *My loaded answer.*

"Yes, and... I'm recovering remarkably well, thank you." A slow, tight smile tried to break free.

The silence that followed wasn't awkward—it was simply a lack of knowing what to say next. Dani wasn't sure if he truly understood the meaning behind his question or her answer, or what the dynamic between them would be if he did.

She glanced toward the rink, giving herself a moment, fingers tugging absently at the laces of her skates.

"You ready to roll again?" she asked, bending to tighten the knot, her hair spilling forward across her cheek.

Then, almost without thinking, Rowen reached out and brushed the stray strands behind her ear so she could see.

It was nothing.

And it was *everything*.

Dani felt her heart bloom outward like wildfire creeping through dry grass. She looked up at him, his fingers warm against her cheek, his eyes drinking her in. She wanted to brush it off, turn it into a joke, make a sarcastic remark. But damn it, she couldn't.

It wasn't like anything she'd felt before. Rowen was something else entirely—perfect balance of sharp angles and soft edges, effortless grace and quiet strength. The best of both worlds, blurring every line she thought she understood. Not even with Mary. What she'd felt for Mary was nothing compared to this. She wasn't supposed to feel anything. Not for a boy. Not like this.

Dani inhaled. "Rowen, I need to tell you something. Something crazy."

Rowen leaned back slightly, observing her. "I'm all ears, Miss Wood."

"Dani. You can call me Dani now—I think we're past the formalities."

No response. Just that small, infuriating smile.

You're still going to call me Miss Wood, aren't you?

She hesitated. If there was anyone in this world who might believe her—or at least not immediately label her a lunatic—it might be him.

She wet her lips and forced the words out before she could lose her nerve.

"I'm not... from here."

Rowen's brow barely lifted. "Portland?"

Dani huffed. "No. Not here-here. Not from this... time."

Rowen paused. Then let out a soft, disbelieving laugh. "Miss Wood, you've read one too many novels. Though I must admit, you are good at being dramatic."

Little shit. It's Dani now.

"I'm serious," she insisted, hands curling into fists beneath her dress folds. "I was born in the twenty-first century. I don't know how, but I ended up here."

His smile held, but his eyes sharpened. Something had shifted—a flicker of unease, maybe even curiosity.

"A time traveler, are you? How... convenient?"

Dani groaned, pressing her palm to her temple. "It was a gamble telling you, but I had to tell someone, and I feel you wouldn't call me a witch and burn me at the stake. Or is that a different century?"

Rowen tilted his head, still studying her. "I do enjoy a good fiction, Miss Wood. But if that's your best effort, I'd recommend another draft."

DANI.

This was pointless.

She stood up and rolled onto the rink, chest tight with embarrassment and stupidity.

But then he glided up beside her, skating backward, facing her again. Maybe he didn't believe her. But maybe she'd planted a seed.

A familiar voice cracked through the rink's laughter and music.

"Danielle."

She jumped.

Alvie stood at the edge of the rink, arms folded.

Rowen, for the first time, looked the slightest bit uneasy.

Dani skated toward Alvie, sighing as she slowed to a stop. "You wanted me to socialize—"

"It is time to leave." His tone was casual, but his eyes stayed on Rowen, assessing.

Dani looked back. Rowen had already tucked his hands into his coat, that familiar curl at his lips just a touch sharper than before.

"Until next time, Miss Wood," he offered with a slight tip of his head.

Dani smirked, eyes glinting with challenge. "I've spared my dignity for today, but next time? We're kicking balls, and you'll be the one on the defensive."

Alvie sighed, placing a hand on her shoulder. "You do realize who he is, don't you?"

"I do," she said, not looking back. "And?"

"He has a reputation."

"So do I."

Alvie muttered something under his breath, urging Dani to remove her skates as the music swelled behind them. Vivienne was waiting at the entrance with more friends than she'd found. And all Rowen could do was watch her go.

"Higher! The drapes must be at least six inches above the floor. Mrs. Barrington will notice if they're not." Laurel clapped her hands sharply, sending a maid scurrying up the ladder. "And mind, you don't leave fingerprints on the brass rods."

The head housekeeper pivoted, catching Shannon trying to slip past with a half-empty bucket. "Shannon! Where do you think you're going with that water? The east wing floors still need washing."

"Yes, Mother," Shannon muttered, changing direction with a sigh.

"What?" Laurel called after her, hands planted firmly on her hips.

"Yes, Ma'am!" she repeated, louder this time.

The charity ball was just two weeks away, and Vivienne was demanding perfection. Everyone who mattered in Portland would be there, and then some.

Laurel snatched a list from her apron pocket and scanned it with narrowed eyes. "Where are those new candles? And who's attending to the guest rooms?"

The front doors swung open, bringing autumn air, loose leaves, and approaching footsteps. Laurel straightened as she turned to face the newcomers.

"You're late and you've brought the leaves in," she scowled. "Shannon! Bring the broom!"

"Ma'am," Edmund greeted, panting heavily. "I do believe I may not recover from that ascent."

Dani stood beside him, barely winded. The climb home had been her kind of work-out—steep, fast, and just enough to leave her pleasantly sore. Edmund had dragged behind her like a sulking child, sweating and complaining with every step. She'd needed the exercise after weeks of inactivity, but Edmund had clearly been unaware of what he was signing up for when he offered to escort her.

She had meant to use the walk to sneak off and visit the Clockery again—to interrogate Gabriel about other clockmakers in town, anyone who might know about trinket boxes or a woman named Cleo. The nightmare from three nights ago still haunted her: Cleo's voice echoing through the darkness, calling for her box, demanding its return. Dani had woken in a cold sweat, finally understanding that this wasn't just about finding *any* box—it was about finding whomever made *Cleo's* box. But where did you even start looking for someone who might not exist in Portland in 1905? If the box transports, she could be anywhere. Downtown seemed as good a place as any.

Edmund, who had initially attempted to wander downtown, whimpered like a baby as soon as they reached the outer limits, expressing a strong desire to return home. It seemed as if the Barrington household was deliberately thwarting every attempt to escape. Whether it was a coincidence or a planned strategy, someone was determined to keep her close.

"We might have taken the cable car," Edmund continued, dabbing his forehead with a handkerchief, "but Miss Wood here insisted on the scenic route."

Dani shot him a look, then grinned and nudged his elbow playfully. "Oh, come on. You loved hearing my theory about horses having regional accents."

Edmund's lips twitched despite himself. "I must admit, your assertion that Portland ponies sound more refined than Salem steeds was... illuminating."

"See? Educational!" Dani bumped his shoulder, and he actually chuckled.

Laurel's eyes narrowed at their easy camaraderie. "Is that so?" she asked, stepping closer, arms folded tightly. "Did you find it necessary to promenade the heights?"

Dani slipped her arm through Edmund's in an exaggerated gesture of solidarity. "Oh yes. Edmund was the perfect escort—so patient, so accommodating."

Edmund straightened slightly at the contact, a hint of color in his cheeks. "Indeed, we partook of this most invigorating climb, adorned in our finest footwear."

Sir. You absolute narc.

Laurel's disapproval was palpable. "Miss Wood, I'm uncertain what customs you follow in Salem, but we do not wear our good boots to climb dirt roads. And we certainly don't link arms with the help."

Dani caught a short laugh in her throat, masking it with a cough. She unhooked her arm from Edmund's and shoved her hands into her pockets.

"That's better." Laurel's attention had already moved elsewhere. "Dinner is in two hours, so please be punctual. Also, clean your boots."

Their dismissal was clear.

With an exaggerated pat to Edmund's shoulder—part sympathy, part defiance—Dani turned toward the grand staircase. Behind her, Edmund dipped his head politely before heading toward the kitchen, still dabbing sweat from his brow.

The quiet of the upstairs hallway was a relief after the bustle below. When Dani entered her suite, the familiar scent wrapped around her like it was feeling like home. The scattering of her things made the room look like her old one—messy, but comfortable.

Then she noticed it. A small package wrapped in brown paper and twine sat on the bed.

Who would send me something? She didn't really know anyone here well enough for gifts.

The thick paper unfolded easily, revealing neat handwriting:

Miss Wood,

It is with sincerest regret that I must inform you that the second pair of ladies' shoes ordered some weeks ago did not arrive as intended. In their stead, I have enclosed a set of walking flats, which I suspect may be more suited to a lady untethered by time.

Given your admirable indifference to convention, and your truly perilous relation-ship with roller skates, I trust these will offer greater practicality (and fewer bruises).

Should these shoes prove unsatisfactory, I shall endeavor to secure another pair with all due haste. If you require anything else—be it shoes, an ear to call upon, or otherwise—you need only say the word.

Ever at your service,

Rowen Quinn

84 Haversham Rd., Portland

P.S. They will also prove quite useful should you decide to play football (the proper kind) when I inevitably trounce you. We've a decent little club forming here in Port-land, and I've already been recruited. Prepare accordingly.

She traced the signature with her eyes, captivated by his elegant handwriting and clever words. A smile spread across her face, warmth returning to her chest like ink in water. *Of course, he plays soccer. That smug little nod when I mentioned kicking a ball around. He probably thinks he's some kind of pro, too.*

She wasted no time untying the twine and peeling back the paper. Inside, Oxfords gleamed up at her—low-heeled, lace-up shoes, practical for walking and far simpler than the elaborate boots with heels she'd tried on at the store. Flat and perfect.

Fine, then. Game on.

She kicked off her boots and slipped her feet into the comfortable flats. The soft leather molded to her feet, a delightful contrast to the restrictive shoes she'd worn since her arrival.

A thrill bubbled in her chest. She pressed the note between her fingers, glancing at it again, trying and failing not to smile. "Rowen Quinn," she mouthed, shaking her head.

It was a crazy mix of exciting, nervous, and maddening. She couldn't decide if they were always vibing or always flirting. Probably both.

The letter made no room for doubt—cheerful, clever, not a hint of the friction from ther abrupt departure at the roller rink. Maybe he hadn't taken Alvie's anger to heart. Maybe he'd already decided she was worth the chaos. Or maybe, just maybe, he'd believed her time travel confession, even if he made a joke of it.

The shoes clacked quietly on the hardwood as she paced, restless energy alive in her limbs. If he could make her feel all this after barely knowing her, then what the hell was happening to her?

Dani paused mid-step. Then what had she been feeling for Mary? She sank onto the edge of the bed, running a hand through her hair. Had she ever felt this kind of thrill with Mary? This heart-pounding, head-spinning rush?

No.

The answer pressed down like a paperweight. She had always assumed her feelings for Mary were romantic, had convinced herself of it. But now, with space between them, doubt crept in. Maybe it wasn't love. Maybe it was just Mary—the best friend she couldn't live without.

Regardless of his tempting nature, I still need to get home, she reminded herself, even as her fingers traced the edge of Rowen's note. *I need to find a box, possibly find Cleo if she exists here, figure out how this all works.*

She glanced toward the window, where the afternoon light was already beginning to fade. Tomorrow, she decided. Tomorrow she'd slip away from Alvie's watchful eye and get back to the Clockery. She'd ask Gabriel about other clockmakers, about his boxes, about anything that might help her understand how she'd gotten here.

And after that? Her eyes drifted back to Rowen's letter. Well, after that, maybe it was time to see if he was as good at football as he thought he was.

12

LETTERS THE WORLD FORGOT

PRESENT DAY

"She's not coming back."

The words left Mary's mouth before she could stop them as she petted the Toaster, softly. Was she saying it for him or for her? It really didn't matter anymore.

She sat nestled beneath a thick blanket on Dani's bed, her eyes fixed on the sleeping porch beyond the window. The wind rattled the wooden frame, the late autumn chill creeping in through those elusive damp cracks. Outside, skeletal branches stood motionless in the light wind.

The freshly carpeted guest room door remained open, untouched since Dani disappeared. And in the yard, trapped in an endless cycle, George Barrington raked leaves in slow, mechanical sweeps.

He didn't look up. He never did anymore.

Gone was the warmth and the quiet hum of family life. What remained was silence, the kind that sunk into your bones, making it impossible to breathe without feeling the loss.

She drew the blanket tighter around her shoulders, holding the phone in her lap, hoping she could will it to ring. She had made calls every day, traced Dani's last known steps, scoured every corner of the Portland looking for any sign of her.

She had promised not to call again, but she did. The phone rang twice before a familiar, low voice, sounding exhausted, answered.

"Detective Grayson."

Mary steadied herself. "Any news?"

A sigh. "Hello Mary, Nothing yet. I wish I had more for you."

Her grip on the phone squeezed tighter. "There has to be something. A neighbor's doorbell camera, a traffic camera, someone's driving recorder! Someone has to of seen her."

Grayson hesitated, the silence dreadful. "We're pursuing a few leads," he admitted, though his tone was cautious. "There's a case we're working that might be linked to her...and many others."

She sat up, shocked. "What kind of case?"

"Can't say yet, it's an open investigation Mary, I've told you this. But if something comes up I can share, I'll absolutely let you know."

"Please call the second you find anything." She insisted.

Grayson sighed again, softer this time. "We're doing everything we can. You don't need to keep going into those woods alone. We've covered them."

She swallowed the lump in her throat. "I'll stop when she's home."

Another pause. Then, a quiet, resigned, "I'll be in touch."

The call ended.

Mary lowered the phone, staring blankly at the screen as though her insides were screaming. The helplessness curdling in her gut pissed her off more than anything.

She usually styled her coppery red curls perfectly and pinned them beneath something theatrical, but now they lay flat and slept on, frizzing slightly at the ends. She hadn't bothered fixing them since Dani disappeared.

Gone were the layered Edwardian jackets, the lace gloves, the corseted waistlines. In their place was a muted gray t-shirt and a pair of black workout pants she hadn't worked out in. She wore them like armor, something easy to throw on while her thoughts spiraled. The watch still sat on her wrist, its gears dark and unmoving.

She looked like a girl who hadn't slept. Like someone who was supposed to be preparing for a life she no longer cared to live.

Toaster, perched atop the rocking chair, his thick tail waving in steady rhythm. His green eyes met Mary's and lit up. He let out a soft, throaty purr, the only comfort in a house that felt too big and empty without Dani.

Wiping her hand down her face, she forced down the exhaustion clawing at her. She had put her entire life on hold just to come back.

Despite that, nothing.

The Barringtons had let her stay in Dani's room without hesitation. Her own condo was still under lease, with a tenant mid-contract and no way to boot them out, not without notice. And truthfully, she didn't want to go back. Not yet. Dani's house had become her refuge, surrounded by Dani's books, Dani's notes, the faintest trace of her still clinging to the air. But the longer Dani was gone, the more the house changed and for the worse.

George was unraveling in silence. He went to work. He came home. He sat in the library, staring at open books without reading a word. His grief was suffocating.

Teresa, though still managing the household, was cracking. Mary had found her crying in the pantry more than once, shoulders shaking, fingers pressed to her lips to stifle the sound.

Exhausted and strung out from no sleep, she decided it was best to hydrate. Heading downstairs for a glass of water, she wandered through the home aimlessly as she always did, staring at the artifacts and antiques. Her attention drifted toward the small bookshelf by the library window. Among the dusty first editions, a single book stood slightly apart from the rest shoved at the way bottom shelf. A small, blue leather-bound diary.

It had been half sealed in a paper sleeve, labeled with estate inventory stamps, and marked Alvie Barrington. Distribution: Grandchildren.

She had assumed it was just another old family relic they had collected. However, when she pulled it from the shelf and carefully opened its crisp old pages, she discovered it belonged to her great-grandmother, Cleo. How did Alvie have this?

At first, she had flipped through the pages absently, expecting stories of dances and proper courtships. But as she skimmed, her fingers hesitated over something unusual. Small slips of paper, delicate and aged, glued carefully onto the pages.

Notes. Letters. Love letters.

Alvie wrote a message on each page, then pressed letters into the paper. Some folded and some lay flat; someone had carefully preserved remnants of a love. The handwriting on the letters was Cleo's.

She traced the inked words, and dates scrawled in the margins. These weren't just diary entries; they were a conversation and a story unfolding.

Her great-grandmother's words bled with longing—how deeply she had felt for him, how wonderful their love had been, the future they had once dreamed of. Letter after letter, Cleo had poured her heart into the pages, believing in the life they shared.

Until the final one.

Mary smoothed the brittle paper with a quiet carefulness, afraid it might crumble beneath her touch.

> *Alvie,*
>
> *I have read your letter repeatedly, searching for even the faintest hint that you still love me or that you regret and might fight for what we were. But there is nothing.*
>
> *You have made your choice, and it is not I.*
>
> *I was never enough for you. I was never of sufficient means or proper standing. Your father made that plain, but I had thought you would rise above such trifles. That love, in its purest form, would prevail. Yet love, it seems, is feeble when set against lineage, against duty, against expectation.*
>
> *I implored you not to turn me away. Yet you did so coldly, without pause, without so much as a backward glance.*
>
> *Very well, then. I shall not look back either.*
>
> *You have chosen your path. Now, I shall choose mine.*
>
> *Dearest,*
>
> *Cleo*

Mary's vision shook as she reached the last lines. He had rejected her. The secret her grandmother had buried for decades wasn't just a lost love story; it was a betrayal. She pressed the diary shut, her stomach sick.

This wasn't just another relic of the past. Cleo's truth was a secret she had kept hidden, just like the trinket box. Mary had dismissed it as a meaningless heirloom, oblivious to its significance. Dani then received the same trinket box. Mary had never opened it, even to peek inside. And then Dani vanished.

Clutching the diary tightly, a wave of nausea rose in her stomach. She felt a deep sense of regret, first for parting with something that held major meaning for her grandmother, and second for passing on an item that might carry negative energy to Dani.

Her frayed nerves needed relief, so she rose. Craving the fresh air, she grabbed her water and returned to Dani's room. Stepping onto the sleeping porch, she felt the wind nip at her skin. Below, the sky had transformed into a dull gray and George was still raking leaves.

She turned back towards the room, her eyes landing on the nightstand. The trinket box sat there, just where she had left it.

She had kept it beside the bed ever since Dani disappeared. Initially, it was merely an old, insignificant box, but because Dani cherished it, putting it away felt wrong. But now, with a deeper understanding of its past, the box takes on a new significance.

Her fingers traced the wood. Dani must have never opened it. Instantly, she felt regret. She remembered she wanted to show Dani how to open it before she left. They had joked about it not having a key, just a weird puzzle on the side. But time passed quickly, and then Dani was gone.

She curled her fingers into a fist.

Her grandmother had warned her once. She could still hear the words, spoken offhandedly like some old wives' tale, passed down too many times to be taken seriously. "Keep it shut. Keep it safe. That's what my mother always said."

She had never put much stock in it. Her family had plenty of superstitions like salt over the shoulder, mirrors covered at night, never whistling indoors.

Her exhaustion was making her sentimental. The box had nothing to do with Dani's absence. Or did it?

The watch pulsed softly against her wrist.

She froze.

A slow, rhythmic beat that was barely noticeable.

She had ignored it at first, dismissing it as some kind of malfunction or maybe a trick of the light.

But deep down, she knew better.

Her eyes drifted back to the trinket box.

No way.

She was not about to sit here and convince herself that an old family heirloom had anything to do with Dani's disappearance. That was ridiculous. She rubbed her temple, exhaling sharply. She was tired. That was all. Tired and missing her best friend, grasping at anything for answers.

The watch lit up again.

A distant memory surfaced.

"It pulsed whenever he was coming or going, like a signal."

More family sayings.

She frowned, shaking her head.

It couldn't mean anything.

And yet—

Staring down at the watch, at the box, at the space where Dani used to be.

The watch was responding, and the box was humming.

To something.

She just didn't know what, but now she's on a path to figure it out.

13

REVELATIONS AND INVITES

EDWARDIAN ERA

"You missed a spot," Dani called down, pointing at the wood. "Right there—no, left. Your left. My right."

She stood at the top of the grand staircase, watching Edmund polish the banister with surgical precision.

Edmund didn't look up. "Miss Wood, I assure you, I have not 'missed a spot.' I have been polishing this staircase since before you were in nappies."

Dani grinned. "That sounds weirdly confusing, considering how old that would make you."

Edmund straightened, adjusting his gloves with mock dignity. "Not every mark upon this banister is removable, particularly those made by your dirty boot soles."

"So bold, Edmund. You're getting spicy in your old age."

"I am twenty-seven," he replied, affronted. "Hardly ancient."

"Sure, sure. For a tree."

He looked up with a slow, theatrical blink. "Miss Wood, were you placed upon this Earth solely to test my intelligence, or is it merely a delightful byproduct of your presence?"

"Honestly? It's my side hustle."

Edmund gave a long, suffering sigh but couldn't hide his amusement. "Might I suggest a less destructive pastime? Needlepoint, perhaps. Or silent reflection."

"You'd miss me if I suddenly went full Jane Austen." She clasped her hands dramatically. "Edmund, I daresay the weather is most agreeable—"

"I beg you," he cut in, laughing, "do not weaponize Regency diction."

"I should start a YouTube channel if I ever get home. 'Polishing with Edmund: A Meditative Series.'"

Edmund paused, genuinely puzzled. "You... tube? What manner of contraption is that?"

"Moving pictures. Episode One: 'Varnish Vengeance.'"

"Do not attempt to capture me in moving pictures, Miss Wood."

"No promises."

The front door's heavy brass knocker echoed through the foyer. Edmund straightened, smoothing his waistcoat.

"Expecting someone?" Dani asked.

"Indeed. Mr. Quinn mentioned he might call this afternoon."

Rowen. Her pulse quickened despite herself.

Edmund opened the door to reveal Rowen, impeccably dressed as always—navy waistcoat, pressed shirt, polished shoes reflecting the afternoon light. But there was something different today, something looser in his posture.

"Miss Wood," he greeted with that familiar half-smile. "I trust you're prepared for defeat?"

"Defeat?" She raised an eyebrow. "Those are bold words from someone who probably thinks you play soccer with your hands."

"Football," he corrected smoothly. "And I believe you'll find I'm full of surprises."

Edmund cleared his throat. "Shall I inform Mr. Barrington of your departure, Miss Wood?"

"Tell him I'm going to Groves Park," Dani said, already heading for her coat. "Educational purposes."

"Educational?" Rowen's eyes sparkled with mischief.

"I'm teaching you how to lose gracefully."

"But don't you need an escort..." Edmund called out as the door shut in his face.

Groves Park sprawled before them, all manicured lawns and carefully pruned trees. But Rowen led her past the main paths, through a copse of overgrown oaks, to a hidden clearing where the grass grew wild and thick.

"Here," he said, shrugging off his jacket and rolling up his sleeves. "Away from prying eyes."

Dani's breath caught at the sight of his forearms—lean muscle shifting beneath pale skin, a thin sheen of sweat already glistening at his temples despite the cool air.

Focus. It's just a game.

But as he moved, there was something almost graceful about him, something that made her stomach tighten in ways she didn't want to examine.

"You sure you want to do this?" she asked, kicking off her heavy boots in favor of the flat Oxfords he'd sent. "They didn't design these clothes for sports."

"I'll manage," he said, loosening his collar. "Though I think you're about to discover that Edwardian gentlemen are more resilient than you assume."

"We'll see about that."

She'd grabbed a worn leather ball from the park's equipment shed, and now she dropped it between them. "First to three goals wins."

"And the stakes?"

Dani grinned. "Winner gets to gloat. Loser buys ice cream."

"Acceptable terms."

The moment the ball touched the ground, everything changed. Rowen was fast—faster than she'd expected—but his technique was all wrong. Too much finesse, not enough aggression. She slipped past his guard easily, the ball dancing at her feet. It was a little muddy, but nothing a good bath and clean clothes could fix.

"Too slow," she called, scoring the first goal against a makeshift target of stacked stones.

"Merely warming up," he replied, but she caught the competitive edge creeping into his voice.

The second goal came just as easily. But by the third attempt, Rowen had adapted. When she tried to slip past him again, he was there, solid and warm as their bodies collided.

"Not bad," she admitted, breathless.

"I'm a quick study."

They were standing close now, closer than necessary. She could smell his cologne—the bergamot and cedar that made her want to lean in. He fixed his blue, unreadable eyes on hers.

This is dangerous, she thought. *The way I want this man doesn't make sense.*

"Your move," he breathed.

She feinted left, then darted right, but Rowen expected it. He blocked her path with a swift movement of his arm, and suddenly they tangled together, fighting for control of the ball. His chest pressed against her back, his breath warm against her ear.

"Cheating," she gasped.

"Strategy," he corrected.

She twisted in his arms, trying to break free, and for a moment they were face to face, his hands on her waist, her pulse hammering against her throat.

Then the ball squirted loose, and they both lunged for it.

They went down hard—Rowen hit first with a sharp breath, Dani collapsing over him in a tangle of limbs and laughter. The world spun for a second. Then everything stilled.

"Rowen," she gasped, bracing her hands on either side of him, trying not to laugh, trying to breathe. "You absolute menace—"

His mouth curved, teeth white against the smear of mud across his cheek. He looked wild like that—flushed, breathless, beautiful in a way that made her chest tighten.

She reached out, unthinking. Just to wipe the mud away.

Her thumb touched his skin.

The rest of her forgot how to move.

His smile faded. Not gone, just... quiet now. Watching her. Breathing her in.

Dani hovered above him, still caught in the fall's aftershock, but something else was blooming beneath her ribs—slow, thick, unrelenting. She could feel every place they touched: the way his hip pressed up against her thigh, the solid weight of his shoulder under her palm, the faint tremble that passed through him when she didn't pull her hand back right away.

The sun filtered through the trees in sharp, golden stripes, catching in his hair. His eyes never left hers.

Neither of them spoke.

And yet, there it was—that terrible, exquisite closeness that seemed to hum in her bones. Not desire. Not yet. Something quieter. Something making her heart sing.

Her thumb slipped over, brushing just beneath his bottom lip.

His breath caught.

So did hers.

The world around them narrowed. Just this moment. Just the soft press of skin. Just the sound of the wind dragging its fingers through the grass beside them.

She should move. She knew she should.

But she didn't.

Then Dani's gaze drifted lower, and the words died in her throat entirely.

Rowen's white shirt had taken the worst of their fall, soaked through with muddy water and clinging to every line of his torso. And there, clearly visible through the transparent fabric, was the unmistakable curve of bound breasts.

Oh.

Oh, shit.

Time seemed delayed. Dani stared, her mind struggling to process what she was seeing. The careful way Rowen moved, the androgynous beauty, the voice that could slip either way—it all suddenly made perfect, impossible sense.

Rowen's eyes widened as she followed Dani's gaze, her face draining of color. In one swift movement, she pushed her off and scrambled to her feet, crossing her arms over her chest.

"You're—" Dani started softly.

"Don't." Rowen's voice cracked, all pretense of masculine bravado stripped away. She reached for her jacket with trembling hands. "Please don't say it."

Dani rose slowly, her heart hammering. "Rowen—"

"You do not understand." Rowen's eyes darted around the empty park, wild with panic. "If anyone knew... if anyone even suspected..." She pulled the jacket tight around herself. "They would destroy me. Or worse."

The raw terror in her voice made Dani's chest ache. She took a careful step closer. "I would never—"

"Wouldn't you?" Rowen's laugh was bitter, broken. "When the novelty wears off? When you realize what I am, what this makes you?"

What this makes you. The words were questionable, filled with implication, maybe? Is she implying it makes her a lesbian or an ally? Does Rowen truly understand the extent of Dani's attraction to her even more now that she knows?

Dani replied. "You think I'd hurt you."

"Everyone hurts people like me. It is safer that way."

"I'm not everyone." Dani's voice was quiet but firm. She held out her hand, palm up—an offering, not a demand. "And you're not alone in this."

Rowen stared at the outstretched hand, her breathing shallow. "You do not know what you're saying."

"Don't I?" Dani's pulse thundered in her ears, but her voice remained steady.

The unsaid attraction, dangerous and true.

Rowen's eyes widened, searching Dani's face for deception, for mockery. Finding neither, her shoulders sagged with something like relief.

"This is madness," Rowen whispered.

"Maybe," Dani said, her hand still extended. "But you're not alone." She didn't say the other thing—not yet. This wasn't the moment to center herself, to risk making it heavier or more complicated. Rowen didn't need a confession; she needed a friend. Dani would hold that space for her. The rest could come later—when it felt safe.

After a long moment, Rowen's fingers brushed against hers—testing. When Dani didn't pull away, she took the offered hand properly, her grip firm despite the tremor.

"Ice cream?" Rowen asked, her voice still shaky but touched with something that might have been hope.

"Ice cream," Dani agreed, and this time when she smiled, Rowen smiled back—small and uncertain, but real.

They walked from the park, arms linked, neither speaking of the electricity that sparked between their joined arms or the way their shoulders bumped with each step. The silence wasn't empty now—it thrummed with possibility, with secrets shared and trust tentatively offered.

Everything had changed, Dani thought, stealing glances at Rowen's profile. And somehow, that felt exactly right.

Dani sat curled in the window seat of her room, staring out at the gardens without really seeing them. Three days had passed since the soccer game, and she hadn't been able to stop thinking about it. About her.

The revelation had turned everything upside down. All those moments of her own confusion, of attraction that made little sense, suddenly clicked into place like puzzle pieces finding their proper positions. The way her pulse quickened when Rowen smiled. The way she found excuses to sit closer on park benches. The way she was drawn to someone she considered entirely unsuitable.

Because she wasn't wrong at all.

A commotion from downstairs pulled her from her brooding. She could hear Edmund's voice, more animated than usual, and what sounded like... bickering?

Curious, she padded barefoot to the top of the grand staircase and peered down.

"—absolutely not tracking mud through Mrs. Barrington's foyer!" Edmund was saying, but his voice carried a different heat than usual.

"It's barely a speck," Shannon protested, stepping closer to him with a coy smile. "And I've been working in the east garden all morning while you've been playing with your precious banister."

"Playing?" Edmund's voice dropped lower, more intimate. "I'll have you know this banister requires very... careful attention."

"Oh, I'm sure it does," Shannon murmured, reaching out to straighten his already-perfect collar. "You have such skilled hands, Edmund."

Dani's eyebrows shot up. *Oh.* The tension crackling between them wasn't annoyance—it was something else entirely.

Edmund caught Shannon's wrist gently, his thumb brushing over her pulse point. "Perhaps you'd like me to show my technique later?"

"Perhaps I would," Shannon whispered back, her cheeks flushed.

Jeez, Dani thought, feeling like an intruder on something private. That's what she wanted—that spark, that electricity, the way they looked at each other as if sharing delicious secrets.

Before Edmund could respond, a sharp knock echoed through the foyer. Both servants froze, their playful argument forgotten.

He straightened his waistcoat and moved toward the door. "Were we expecting anyone, Miss Shannon?"

"Not that I'm aware of." Shannon quickly smoothed her skirts and tucked a loose strand of hair behind her ear.

Edmund peered through the glass pane beside the door, and his expression immediately shifted. "Oh, not him again."

"Who is it?" Shannon whispered, moving closer.

Despite his apparent reluctance, Edmund unlocked the door and pulled it open. The man who stepped inside made the very air seem to tighten with presence.

Someone carved Gabriel Dunwich from marble and brought him to life. His perfectly styled dark hair, his burgundy waistcoat fitted to showcase his broad shoulders, and his polished shoes, all caught the light from the chandelier. He curated everything about himself with precision.

Holy shit, Dani thought, her body responding before her mind could catch up. *The man I've been avoiding.*

But even as her pulse quickened, she compared him to Rowen. Where Rowen was elegant and understated, Gabriel was commanding. Where Rowen made her think and laugh, Gabriel made her body forget how to function properly.

Shannon, who was usually the picture of composure, looked like she'd forgotten how to breathe.

"Mr. Dunwich," Edmund announced flatly, his entire presence radiating deeply unamused butler energy.

Gabriel smiled with serene confidence. "Good afternoon. I wish to speak with Miss Wood."

Edmund didn't budge, keeping his expression carefully neutral. "She isn't expecting visitors, and calling hours are nearly concluded."

Shannon continued staring at Gabriel with slightly parted lips, and Dani had to resist the urge to throw something at her, to snap her out of it.

"That voice sounds familiar," Dani called, making her way down the staircase with practiced casualness.

"Miss Wood," Edmund announced with obvious reluctance, "Mr. Dunwich is here to speak with you. I informed him you weren't expecting anyone."

Dani shrugged as she reached the bottom of the stairs, deliberately not looking at Edmund. "Unexpected, yes, but not unwelcome." She turned her attention to Gabriel and immediately felt that familiar flutter of awareness. "Mr. Dunwich, would you like to join me in the library?"

"Unaccompanied, miss?" Edmund interrupted, though his tone suggested he was asking out of duty rather than genuine concern.

Dani dismissed him with a nervous laugh. "Well, if decorum collapses and no one tweets about it, did it really happen?"

Edmund blinked in confusion. "Tweets? What manner of... tweets?"

Before he could puzzle it out further, Dani pushed open the library's pocket doors and gestured for Gabriel to follow. As she did, she caught Shannon still gawking and shot her a look that clearly said, Control yourself.

Shannon's response was an expression that clearly said, Have you seen him?

Fair point, but Dani motioned for her to leave them alone.

The library held them, quiet and filled with the scent of leather-bound books. Gabriel settled into the chair across from her with fluid grace, and Dani studied him despite her best intentions.

He was undeniably attractive in the most conventional sense—all sharp jawlines and confident masculinity. But as she watched him, she couldn't help but think of Rowen's softer beauty, the way her eyes crinkled when she laughed.

Shannon entered to serve tea, hovering near the table longer than was strictly necessary. She watched Gabriel with obvious fascination, tracking his every movement as she poured.

"Thank you, Shannon," Dani said pointedly.

Shannon startled, nearly dropping the teapot. "Oh! Yes, miss. Of course." But she continued to steal glances as she retreated, practically walking backward to keep Gabriel in sight.

Dani waited until Shannon had reluctantly closed the door behind her before speaking. "You mentioned scholars the other day. People who study temporal mechanics."

Gabriel set down his teacup, his expression sharpening with interest. "Indeed. There are several gentlemen in the city who dabble in such theories."

"And other clockmakers? Besides yourself?"

"Ah." Gabriel leaned back, studying her face with new curiosity. "Might I ask what has sparked this sudden fascination with horology, Miss Wood?"

Because I need to find a way home. But she couldn't say that. Instead, she tried for casual interest. "I find the craftsmanship fascinating. The precision required."

"Precision, indeed." Gabriel's smile was enigmatic. "There are other artisans in the city who share your appreciation for fine workmanship. Some specialize in rather unique pieces—music boxes with intricate mechanisms, timepieces with... shall we say, remarkable properties?"

Dani's pulse quickened. "Could you introduce me to them?"

"I could," he drawled. "Though such introductions require... proper circumstances. These gentlemen are quite particular about their circles."

Of course they are. "What circumstances?"

Gabriel leaned forward, and she caught that familiar pull—something purely masculine in his presence that made her body respond despite her best efforts. "The kind that develops naturally between... compatible individuals. Perhaps you might accompany me to the Lewis and Clark Exposition this Saturday? There's a fascinating exhibit on temporal mechanics, and several of these scholars will be in attendance."

Perfect. Dani's mind raced. An exposition would mean other craftsmen, other clockmakers, direct access to the people who might have answers. And Gabriel was offering to be her introduction.

"I'd like that," she said, surprised by how easily the words came.

Gabriel's smile widened with satisfaction. "Excellent. I shall collect you at nine o'clock on Saturday morning." He leaned forward, ostensibly to set his teacup on the small table between them, but the movement brought him much closer. "I hope you're prepared for... enlightening company Miss Wood." His proximity triggered that familiar pull—something purely masculine in his presence.

His dark eyes met hers with obvious intent, and warmth crept up Dani's neck despite her best efforts to remain unaffected. His fingers brushed the chain, curling around it with surprising gentleness. A light tug pulled her forward.

Their faces were close now, his dark eyes meeting hers before trailing down to her lips. Warmth crept up Dani's neck, blooming across her cheeks despite her best efforts to remain unaffected.

This is just biology, she told herself even as her heart stuttered. *Pheromones and proximity and whatever evolutionary nonsense that makes women respond to masculine voices and broad shoulders.*

But with Rowen, it had been different. Deeper. Less about biology and more about... connection. Understanding. The way she could make Dani laugh, even when she was trying to be serious.

Gabriel tilted his head, coming closer. His voice dropped to a lower register. "I find myself quite... eager to show you things you have never seen, Miss Wood."

No. Absolutely not. Dani's thoughts scrambled. *I like women. I like women.* But apparently her body hadn't gotten that memo either, because her face was on fire and her pulse was doing things that had nothing to do with fear.

This is just nerves. Just proximity. Just — Her gaze dropped involuntarily to his mouth, and she felt a stab of frustration at her own traitorous biology. With Rowen, it felt like a choice. Like want. *This feels like... being hijacked by my own hormones.*

The parlor door burst open.

Shannon stumbled backward, caught red-handed with her ear practically pressed to the door. Behind her, Edmund stood on his tiptoes, craning his neck to peer over her shoulder into the library.

Dani and Gabriel jolted apart, straightening in their chairs like guilty schoolchildren.

"Shannon!" Edmund hissed. "I told you we shouldn't—"

"You were listening too!" Shannon whispered back fiercely.

Laurel appeared in the doorway like an avenging angel, arms crossed and eyes blazing. Both Shannon and Edmund scattered like startled birds.

"Miss Wood," Laurel said, her voice carrying enough ice to freeze the Thames, "Mrs. Barrington is inquiring after you." Her gaze shifted to Gabriel, assessing him with the efficiency of a general surveying a battlefield. "Mr. Dunwich, I assume you're finished here?"

Gabriel set his tea down with unhurried care, his composure intact despite being caught in what must have looked like a compromising position. "Quite concluded."

He rose smoothly, one hand adjusting his waistcoat. There was something tighter in the set of his jaw now, like he'd tasted something bitter.

As he moved toward the door, he leaned down just enough that his voice could fall into her ear alone.

"Miss Wood," he murmured, "I shall have a carriage sent for you at nine o'clock, three Saturdays hence, to take you to the Exposition."

Did I black out and agree to something? Dani thought, but before she could protest, Gabriel straightened with that crooked grin and disappeared into the foyer.

She sat back in her chair, feeling like she'd just survived a small tornado. Her body was still humming with unwanted awareness, but her mind kept drifting back to Rowen. To the way she'd looked in that muddy field, vulnerable and real and nothing like the carefully constructed masculinity she usually wore.

Two different kinds of want.

14

WE MOVED IN SHADOWS

EDWARDIAN ERA

Lord Ashdown stood near the tall parlor window, his eyes fixed on the hazy stretch of city in the distance. Beyond the hills and rooftops, his factory's outlines were just visible, tiny figures spilling from its doors like ants as the day's work ended. His posture was formal, rigid, hands clasped behind his back in the same austere manner his father had once adopted.

It wasn't his first visit to the Barrington home. He occasionally requested use of the study to discuss matters concerning the southern timber tract—a parcel jointly invested in with Alvie. These conversations, he insisted, were best kept from drawing rooms and certainly from his daughter's ears.

Alvie joined him, settling into his chair with effortless grace. "Beautiful weather today, wouldn't you say?"

Ashdown barely glanced at him. "Progress has its price, Barrington."

"Indeed. Though some might argue about who should pay it."

A muscle twitched in Ashdown's jaw. "My father arrived in this country with nothing but determination. He built our first mill with his own hands, working alongside his employees. Do you know what he paid them?"

"I imagine it was generous for the time," Alvie replied diplomatically.

"He paid them in shares. Every worker owned a piece of that first mill." A shadow passed over Ashdown's face. "Then, in '73, when the financial panic hit, they sold for pennies. To speculators and vultures. My father bought back what he could, but by the time he died, we only controlled sixty percent."

His knuckles whitened. "I've spent my life reclaiming what should have been ours. These workers, these unions—they see only today's comforts, not tomorrow's security."

"And your interest in young Quinn?" Alvie asked, though his tone suggested gentle concern rather than curiosity.

"Quinn has the ear of the workers. They trust him." Ashdown's voice hardened. "His writing carries considerable weight—the man has a gift for moving hearts and minds. Those same persuasive pieces that currently champion the workers could become powerful weapons for our cause if properly redirected. With him in the family, aligned with our interests, we could turn his very talent against the unions' inflammatory rhetoric."

Alvie's brow furrowed slightly. "Forgive me, but is it altogether wise to force such an arrangement? Young people can be... unpredictable when pressured."

"Force?" Ashdown's laugh was sharp. "My dear Barrington, I've observed my daughter's fascination with Quinn for months. She practically swoons when someone mentions his name. Now is simply the time to... encourage that natural inclination."

"Beatrice has expressed such feelings?"

"She needn't express them. A father notices these things." Ashdown straightened his waistcoat. "Quinn's mother is gravely ill and requires care beyond what his writing income can provide. A generous marriage settlement, along with provisions for his mother's medical expenses... what reasonable son would refuse such an opportunity?"

Alvie's pipe paused halfway to his lips. "And if he proves unreasonable?"

"Then we shall discover what motivates him beyond idealism." Ashdown's smile didn't reach his eyes. "Every man has his price, Barrington. It's simply a matter of finding the correct currency."

The conversation settled into an uncomfortable silence. Alvie drew thoughtfully on his pipe, watching the smoke curl toward the ceiling.

"Well then," Ashdown said, collecting his hat and gloves. "I must depart for dinner. Other matters require my attention." He paused at the door. "Do give my regards to your... houseguest, won't you? Miss Wood, I believe? Quite the remarkable resemblance she bears to the family."

After Ashdown's departure, Alvie remained at the window, watching Dani cross the garden below. She walked with purpose unlike the women he knew—shoulders squared, strides sure, untouched by the era's expected delicacy. Even from this distance, there was something unsettlingly familiar about her.

He tapped his pipe against the windowsill. The resemblance was undeniable.

When he'd first spotted her in the stables six weeks ago, disheveled and disoriented, wearing the strangest garments he'd ever seen, his initial instinct had been caution. But then she'd lifted her head, and Alvie had felt the air leave his lungs.

Those eyes. The sharp angle of her jaw. The way her brow furrowed when confused—all of it reflected something he saw daily in his own mirror.

"Barrington," she'd said, before catching herself. A peculiar slip for a stranger.

Alvie moved to his desk and drew open the lower drawer, retrieving a well-worn folder thick with notations. He flipped through precise sketches of clockwork interiors, neatly typed funding ledgers, and newspaper clippings chronicling Gabriel Dunwich's "scientific marvels."

He paused at an article describing a presentation Gabriel had given years ago, long before the public dismissed his ideas as eccentric parlor tricks. The headline read: "Local Craftsman Claims Temporal Manipulation Possible Through Mechanical Resonance."

With a sharp snap, he closed the folder.

His fingers drifted along the desk's edge, mind quietly sorting through a timeline that no longer felt hypothetical. A girl appearing out of nowhere. The little key she wore bearing all the hallmarks of Dunwich's handiwork. His own features reflected in her face.

The implications were... astonishing.

He needed her close. Needed to understand what this curious Miss "Wood" might reveal about paths yet taken. And most importantly, he had to ensure no one else uncovered what she truly represented.

"Edmund," he called.

The footman appeared instantly, as though he'd been waiting just outside the door. "Sir?"

"Please see that this reaches town with all haste." Alvie sealed a hastily written letter. "And Edmund? Discretion, as always."

"Of course, sir."

As Edmund departed, Alvie returned to the window. Below, Dani had paused near the rose garden, her head tilted toward the sky with an expression of such profound longing that it made his chest tighten.

What future are you running from, my dear? He wondered. And what past have you come to change?

"Brilliant," Rowen muttered as she tried to balance the dress box and the book in her arms. The book slipped from her grasp and thudded against the marble floor. The sound echoed through the foyer. Edmund pushed the heavy door shut with a solid click as Rowen straightened, adjusting her grip on the box while retrieving the book, now clutched tighter against her chest.

"Will that be all, Mr. Quinn?" Edmund asked.

"Yes, thank you," Rowen replied, and Edmund's footsteps faded down the corridor.

Upstairs, Dani paused mid-step. That voice—quiet, but unmistakably her. Finally. Rowen had ghosted her for nearly two weeks, and part of her wondered if she was nervous about Dani knowing her true identity. But now, with her standing below like no time had passed, something inside Dani unclenched.

She didn't hesitate. Her steps were confident as she descended the stairs halfway, a faint smile playing at her lips.

"Ball-kicker, vanishing act, and now book-tosser?" she called. "What's next on the list?"

She glimpsed the book's cover before Rowen tucked it away—dark leather, unmarked. Whatever it was, it mattered.

Rowen's shoulders tensed at the sound of Dani's voice. She kept her eyes fixed on the dress box, anywhere but up those stairs. Dani was certain Rowen had spent two weeks freaking out and worrying about when the hammer would fall. Sure, Dani had said Rowen was not alone when she glimpsed Rowen's bound chest, but was she just saying that? Did she have nefarious reasons to ruin Rowen's life with this vital information? Rowen was obviously visibly nervous about it all—the careful way she held herself, the way she'd been avoiding eye contact since the moment she walked in.

"For Mr. Barrington," she said quickly, almost too quickly. "Something he requested."

"What is it?"

"A book." The words came out clipped, professional. Safe.

"No kidding." Dani's voice held that familiar edge of amusement, and Rowen's pulse betrayed her with its immediate response. "You know, for someone who seemed so... at ease with me before, you're acting like I might bite."

The heat that crept up Rowen's neck had nothing to do with embarrassment and everything to do with the memory of that day tumbled upon the wet grass with her body against Dani's. She shifted the dress box higher, using it like armor against her own traitorous body. "I'm not—"

"You're not what?" Dani took another step down, close enough now that her voice carried easily. "Not nervous? Because you look like you're about to bolt."

"I suppose I'm just... tired."

"Tired." Dani repeated the word like she was testing it. "From all that avoiding me, I'd imagine."

Rowen's breath caught. She could feel her carefully constructed walls beginning to crack, but she still couldn't bring herself to look up.

Dani could see the cover of the book Rowen had brought. In clear lettering it stated "The Balance of Iron – A Manifesto for Preservation Through Revolution."

"Oh, Mr. Quinn," Shannon interrupted, stepping into the hall. "How kind of you to bring the gown yourself? I'd thought Madam Laurel would collect it."

"Preparations for the ball occupied her," Rowen replied, grateful for the reprieve. "I am, if nothing else, accommodating."

"How thoughtful," Shannon said. "Mrs. Barrington will be so pleased."

Dani watched the exchange with poorly concealed impatience, her fingers drumming against the banister. When Shannon finally excused herself and disappeared back down the hall, the silence suspended between them like a taut wire.

"Well," Dani said, her voice dropping to something softer, more intimate. "Now that we're alone..."

Rowen's grip on the dress box tightened.

"I have to say," Dani continued, and there was something almost vulnerable in her tone now, "I've missed you."

The words hit Rowen unexpectedly. All her fears—about being exposed, about being found disgusting, about Dani knowing exactly what she was—warred with something else entirely. Her head snapped up before she could stop herself.

The impact was immediate and ruinous. Dani's expression shifted the moment their eyes met, her lips parting slightly as if she'd just walked into a cloud. Whatever teasing confidence she'd carried dissolved. And she saw everything in return: the want, the hunger, the desperate desire that Rowen had been trying so hard to bury.

For a heartbeat, neither of them moved. Softness in Rowen's eyes, longing in Dani's, as their gazes met. Rowen inhaled sharply, her breathing uneven.

Then Dani seemed to catch herself, that familiar smirk returning like armor, though it didn't quite reach her eyes. "There," she said, though her voice was slightly breathless. "Hi."

The dress box slipped from Rowen's suddenly nerveless fingers. Regardless of Dani assuring her during ice cream that she was not alone, it was clear Rowen had been waiting for mutiny, for the shoe to drop. And instead—this.

"Miss Wood, excuse me," she whispered, and fled.

Even more entertaining was the absence of her usual bravado. Another glimpse of the Rowen beneath—soft, a little flustered, unexpectedly sweet. She must know she's safe now. I'll see soon enough if she lets it stay that way.

Shannon returned from the kitchen and let out a thoughtful hum, looking between Dani and the empty hallway.

"What?" Dani asked, crossing her arms. "Were you watching?"

Shannon didn't acknowledge her question, but it was all over her face. Yes, yes she was.

"It is simply... peculiar."

"How so?"

"Mr. Quinn is not ordinarily so... informal with clients. There is something quite different in the manner in which he interacts with you."

"So, this isn't just him being charismatic?"

Shannon gave her a pointed look. "He does not look at his admirers the way he looks at you, miss."

Dani grinned. "Well, that's excellent news."

The sound of approaching footsteps made them turn as Rowen re-entered the foyer. But something had shifted. The nerves in her expression had cooled, replaced by something restrained. She barely glanced at Dani, instead adjusting her coat cuffs with precise movements.

"Is something amiss?" Shannon asked.

Rowen checked her pocket watch. "I must be going. Good evening, Miss Wood. Shannon."

She turned toward the door, pace brisk.

"What was that about?" Dani asked.

"That, Miss Wood, was someone whose mind has just turned elsewhere," Shannon replied.

What changed between delivering the dress and now?

Dani's curiosity overruled her caution. She slipped down the hall toward Alvie's study, where she could hear voices through the partially open door.

"Edmund," Alvie said, "I need you to deliver a message to Mr. Aimsbury." Tell him the meeting is at seven o'clock sharp—entrance through the warehouse hatch behind Morrison's dock, third building from the wharf. He will unlock the iron handle after six-thirty.

"Very good, sir. And shall I inform him that Mr. Quinn will expect him?"

"Indeed. Though I confess, the situation grows more precarious each week. If Lord Ashdown continues his pressure tactics on the workers..."

"Quite so, sir. Shall I depart immediately?"

"Yes, but Edmund—discretion, as always."

"Of course, Sir."

Footsteps approached the door. Dani quickly retreated, her mind racing.

Morrison's dock. Nine o'clock. Third building.

By the time Edmund emerged from the study, Dani was already planning her next move.

"Jacques," Dani said breathlessly as she burst into the stables, "I need to get downtown. Quickly."

He looked up from brushing a horse. "Now, miss?"

"Something for the ball. I forgot." Not entirely a lie. "Just drop me at the cable tram station and head back. No questions."

His brow lifted, but he nodded. "The mare's quick."

Fifteen minutes later, Dani stood at the base of the steep incline, staring up at the Portland Cable Tram station. The wooden structure looked precarious, all creaking timber and questionable engineering, but it was her fastest route downtown.

She fished coins from her pocket—just enough for a ticket. The evening air carried the scent of coal smoke and river water as she waited for the next car.

What am I even doing? The rational part of her mind protested. *Following someone to a secret meeting based on overheard instructions? This is insane.*

But the other part—the part that had been wondering about Rowen for two weeks, the part that had seen her vulnerability in that muddy field and that foyer—needed answers.

The tram car lurched forward with a mechanical groan, climbing steadily down the steep track. Below her, Portland spread out in a beautiful pattern of gaslit streets and river lights. The Willamette glistened, dotted with boats and barges. From this height, the city looked peaceful, orderly. Nothing like the undercurrent of tension she'd sensed in Alvie's voice.

If I can survive time travel, I can survive this death trap.

Halfway down the incline, she spotted a familiar figure on the street below. Edmund, walking briskly along a tree-lined avenue, his distinctive formal posture unmistakable even from this distance. He paused in front of an elegant townhouse—three stories of pristine brick with ornate ironwork balconies. Lamps glowed in the windows, and even from the tram, she could tell it was the place that spoke of serious money.

Edmund climbed the front steps and disappeared inside. He emerged a minute later, walking just as briskly back the way he'd come.

Mr. Aimsbury's, I presume.

Dani pressed closer to the tram window, memorizing the house's location. Whoever lived there was important enough for Alvie to send his most trusted servant with hand-delivered messages about secret meetings.

The tram reached the street level and began its descent toward downtown. Front porch lights glowed as dusk settled over the city, casting long shadows between buildings. The business district gave way to the industrial waterfront, where the sounds of the working day were winding down—whistles, shouts, the clang of metal on metal.

By the time she reached the bottom, full darkness had settled. The rougher streets near the docks, vibrant with a unique energy, one that differed from her manicured, familiar neighborhoods. Men in work clothes headed home or toward the taverns. Women hurried past with shawls pulled tight against the river chill.

This is Rowen's world, she realized. Not the drawing rooms and tea services, but this.

She checked her pocket watch—nearly eight-thirty. *Time to find Morrison's dock.*

Her thoughts weren't on the grand existential crisis of being stuck in 1905, but on the far more pressing mystery unfolding. She knew Rowen's secret—knew she was a woman living as a man. But this? This was something else entirely.

Labor meetings. Dangerous waters. Workers with no one else to speak for them.

Who are you really, Rowen Quinn?

The warehouse district near Morrison's dock was a maze of brick buildings and narrow alleys. The smell of tar, fish, and coal smoke hung heavy in the air. Dani found the third building from the wharf easily enough—a weathered structure with loading bays that faced the river. Paint peeled from its sides, and someone had stacked wooden crates haphazardly near the entrance.

She strolled past the front, then circled around to the back, trying to look casual. A few dock workers passed by, but none paid her any attention. Just another person in the evening crowd.

The back alley was dimmer, lit only by a single gas lamp at the far end. She found the heavy wooden hatch exactly as described, its iron handle dark with age and wear. It was slightly ajar, and voices drifted up from below—muffled but urgent.

Eight-thirty. Right on time.

Dani hesitated at the edge of the hatch. Once she went down there, there was no pretending. This was casual curiosity. She'd be deliberately spying on people who had every reason to keep their business secret.

She lifted the hatch carefully, wincing as the hinges gave a soft creak. The wooden steps disappeared into the darkness below. The voices grew clearer as she descended—at least a dozen men, maybe more.

The air cooled the moment she stepped underground. It was damp down here, heavy with coal dust, sweat, and the lingering scent of pipe smoke. The walls were rough brick, stained with decades of moisture and soot. The ceiling was low enough that she had to duck in places, and ahead of her, lanterns cast flickering shadows that danced across the tunnel walls.

The Shanghai tunnels. *Dad would be so jealous.* They visited the tourist version so often the tour guides knew them by name.

She'd heard whispers—how men vanished from waterfront saloons and awoke on ships bound for China, how these tunnels connected every major building in the district, how people made and lost fortunes in the darkness below the city. But this wasn't about kidnapping or smuggling. She crept forward, staying close to the wall, moving toward the sound of voices.

The tunnel opened into a wider chamber, and there, in the circle of lantern light, stood Rowen. And Rowen was clearly leading them.

"The dockworkers are already on edge," one man muttered. "Let these barons have their way, and the mill workers will be next."

Another voice, rougher: "We're still nothing but hands to these men. You think Ashdown will let a tailor's son dictate wages?" He gestured with scarred palms, fingers stiff from years bent over cloth and steel.

The others muttered in agreement, low and bitter.

Then came Rowen's level voice. A blade dressed as civility. "You're mistaken if you believe the wealthy will keep building their empires unchecked. Every brick, every beam, every dock and rail line exists because of you—because you've given your backs and blood to it. I may not know your days firsthand, but I do know what it is to labor beneath someone who sees you as disposable."

That earned a pause.

Rowen continued, steady as stone. "All I know how to do is write the truth in ways that move people. My observations—my words—have found their way into the hands of those who listen. Who read. Who remember. It's what I can offer."

Dani shifted where she stood, watching the way the men leaned in—how they didn't know who they were listening to, not really. And how it didn't matter, because they felt it.

"You think that'll change things?" the scarred man challenged. "You think your pretty words'll keep Ashdown from cracking down the minute we talk union?"

"Not alone," Rowen said. "But if we stand together—every dockworker, every seamstress, every railway man and machinist—if we move as one, there are more of us than there are of him."

Dani's breath caught at that. Seamstress. Her mother had worked under men like Ashdown. Always bent, always silent. Never expecting more.

But Rowen stood in a room full of men who didn't know they were speaking with a woman—and still, they listened. Still, they leaned closer.

And Dani, watching from the edge, understood exactly what kind of power that was.

Dani pressed closer, fascination overriding caution. This wasn't just a discussion—it was a battle plan. And Rowen wasn't some neutral figure in high society. She was fighting for something much bigger than herself.

Through the tunnel opening, she caught sight of the sky in its blackness and remembered. The ball. *Vivienne will have my head.*

She should stay, keep listening, figure out what exactly Rowen was planning. But there were only so many things she could get away with in one day before someone started asking questions.

Carefully, she retraced her steps through the dimly lit tunnels until she emerged into the open air. The city had transformed while she was underground—evening in full swing, the hum of nightlife beginning..

She boarded the creaking tram, gripping the wooden railing as it climbed steadily upward. Below, the docks spread out like a living map, boats bobbing in the harbor, the warehouse where she'd just been now just another shadow among many.

Her thoughts weren't on Gabriel or the ball or even the existential crisis of time travel. They were on Rowen Quinn—who wasn't just the elegant, mysterious woman she'd fallen for, but an activist risking everything for workers' rights. Two secrets now. The gender revelation from the soccer field, and this. A woman living as a man, fighting for the powerless in underground tunnels.

The tram gave another ominous creak as it reached the top. Time to get dolled up for the ball and figure out how to navigate this minefield of secrets and desire.

One thing was certain: tonight, she would experience a proper party.

15

LADY OF NO PROPRIETY

EDWARDIAN ERA

"Like hell I'm sticking around long enough to be married off," Dani jeered.

"Hopefully for you, miss, it won't go that far," Shannon replied.

"Shannon, did you know what an introduction into society is?" Dani winced. "Vivienne just told me—it's not where I meet people, it's where they declare I'm able to marry." She growled. "This was NOT on my bingo card for this year. I must have fallen asleep when Mary was explaining this during Pride and Prejudice movie night."

"Pride and Prejudice! I love that book!" Shannon exclaimed brightly.

"Shannon, this is about my forthcoming doom," Dani said dramatically.

Shannon giggled despite herself. "Well, if it were a certain handsome tailor doing the declaring, I do not think you would mind."

Dani leaned against the cool glass of her bedroom window, observing the scene unfolding below. Tables, chairs, food tables, lights, and flowers adorned the backyard and patio.

So much time had passed since she'd landed in this world, and she was still stumbling through it. Her presence smudged like a perfectly painted portrait, and tonight, they will parade her like a prize filly. Vivienne had orchestrated everything—including Dani's attire, her presence, even the dreaded potential for matchmaking.

Of course, she'd scoffed at the suggestion. Back home, at twenty-one, marriage was something people swiped left on. Here, she was dangerously close to spinsterdom.

It wasn't the idea of suitors that made her stomach turn. It was the way Vivienne wanted to press her into a mold, smooth down her edges and shape her into something delicate.

On the vanity, a dainty bottle of lavender-scented soap sat, probably from Vivienne. The label boasted in swooping script: *Ladies' Castile Soap for the Hair - Nothing so adds to the charm of an individual, especially a lady, as a good head of hair.*

Charming, she thought *Let's take you to the bath.*

Twenty minutes later she emerged fully dressed from the bath in an evening gown from her first visit to the dress shop, Shannon waited, practically vibrating with excitement.

"Oh, you'll be the finest in the room tonight," Shannon gushed, clasping her hands together. "I only wish I could attend."

Dani stared at her reflection. "Believe me, I wish I could hide in the kitchen with you."

Shannon giggled, stepping behind her to twist the damp strands of Dani's hair. "Nonsense. This is a grand affair, miss. You might even enjoy yourself."

Her answer came as a dry stare.

The knock at the door was sharp and unexpected.

Shannon ran to open it while Dani fussed with the bustline of her dress.

Then came the voice.

"Miss Wood, I see fate insists on bringing us together again so soon."

Smooth. Effortless.

Dani shot up so fast she nearly knocked over the vanity stool. She turned, finding Rowen lounging in the doorway, carefully keeping the door wide open—proper decorum for a gentleman visiting a lady's room.

"Shannon held me in the hall," Rowen explained with amusement. "She kept me waiting until you were properly dressed before letting me enter. Quite the fierce guardian you have there."

The boldness was back—Rowen, composed and unapologetically sharp, no longer wary of Dani. Which meant that the flirtation on the stairs had landed. Her evening wear didn't help: a black coat that cut clean along her shoulders, a waistcoat that hinted at lean lines beneath. A silver watch chain winked in the light as she pulled her gloves taut over long, graceful fingers.

Dani swallowed hard.

"Rowen." Her voice came out more breathless than she liked. "I wasn't expecting you to be back here for the event."

Rowen tilted her head, amused. "Should I have sent a raven with word?"

"No. I mean—" She cleared her throat. "Are you about to duel someone for their inheritance?"

Rowen gave a rich, unguarded laugh in return.

Behind her, Shannon stilled amid twisting hair. She fought from smiling out loud, but it was a losing battle before she bent slightly, her voice a murmur against Dani's ear.

"You see, miss? Did I not say he laughs heartily but rarely for others?"

Dani's heart picked up like it had somewhere important to be.

"I am escorting someone as a date. I hope this does not displease you." Rowen teased while pulling a thread from her lapel.

"A date?!" Dani blurted, then winced at how fast she'd said it. "I just—didn't expect you."

Her eyes caught on the large white box in Rowen's hands. "What's in the box?"

"Mrs. Barrington requested a last-minute evening gown for you. I felt compelled to deliver it personally."

Compelled. A dramatic word for fabric delivery. Unless, of course, she meant her.

The curve of Rowen's cheekbones, the slope of her nose, the way her upper lip was just a little thinner than the bottom.

In this light, she's smoking hot.

The long column of her neck, the relaxed edge of her jaw, the elegant line of her throat where Dani could see the delicate veins beneath pale skin—so damn sexy. A beauty mark near her chin, and lashes so thick they looked smudged with ink.

And then the cleft in her chin. Had she ever noticed that before? No. And now she was in the weeds. Lost. Staring at Rowen like her brain had hit the loading screen, her mind wandered as it usually does.

Oh no. This isn't just in the weeds. This is the whole damn forest. Someone throw me a map.

I'm intoxicated.

How do I kiss those lips?

No. Bad timing for that thought. Delete. Undo. Gay Panic! Abort mission.

Rowen's smile spread slowly, like honey dripping from a spoon. "Something on my face, Miss Wood?"

"I was just thinking—" she hesitated. "Your...suit is very nice."

"Oh? I do hope so." Rowen's smile turned slightly wicked. "Though I must say, I look better without it."

The way she said it made Dani's cheeks flush. *All the layers off please,* she thought, then immediately felt her face burn hotter.

"Well, yeah, that's... you definitely succeeded in the... the looking good department. Mission very much accomplished. Top marks for... for looking," Dani stammered, then immediately thought, *Shut up.*

Behind them, Shannon made a small, barely audible sound—half sigh, half swoon. When Dani glanced back, Shannon was watching them with the expression of someone witnessing the world's most obvious mutual pining.

Clearing her throat, Rowen stepped forward to place the package on the bed. Lifting the lid, she peeled back the delicate tissue paper to reveal the most exquisite gown Dani had ever seen.

It was a vision in amethyst—deep, regal violet silk that shimmered in the light. Delicate patterns of gold embroidery cascaded down the bodice, and elegant beadwork, glittering like stars, edged the neckline. It was luxurious, ethereal, and utterly breathtaking.

She gasped out loud before she could stop herself. She hated dresses, but far from making her gag like the others, anyone would have thought this the most beautiful thing they'd seen, male or female.

"Does it suit your liking?"

"How did you know I would like it? You picked this out?"

"Naturally, Miss Wood. This is my vocation." Her expression screamed pride.

Dani folded her arms. "So that makes you an expert on my taste?"

"I am not at liberty to say, however—" Rowen gave a witty little look. "One could surmise that your tastes are... quite particular. And by that gasp, I would conclude that it meets them."

Dani traced the dress with such care, as if it were something sacred. Her smile was brighter than anything Rowen had expected—and it undid her.

Something inside her shifted.

So this is what it feels like...

She cleared her throat, composed her face. "I must leave you now."

Dani bit her lip, struggling to suppress the heat bubbling under her cheeks.

It took twenty minutes to get into the dress. She twisted, adjusting the gown's bodice as she stared at herself in the mirror. The fabric hugged every inch of her; The corset cinching just enough to highlight her curves but still letting her breathe.

Her reflection was elegant, dramatic, and—she had to admit—kind of hot.

Shannon gave her a slow, approving once-over. "You look a vision, Miss Wood."

"I've never worn a proper dress in my life until I got here."

Shannon paused in her work, eyebrows raised. "Never, miss? How very... unusual. What did you wear to church? Or formal occasions?"

"Uh..." Dani scrambled for an explanation. "Very... practical clothing. Where I'm from, women dress more... practically."

"If you should need some quiet amidst the chaos downstairs," Shannon whispered, "the servants' stairs beyond the east hall..."

"Oh, I remember well." Dani raised an eyebrow.

"I know a thing or two about finding quiet space with a lover," Shannon whispered.

Dani choked on absolutely nothing.

"Enjoy your evening." Shannon patted her arm and stepped back.

Then she was gone.

"Senator, you're incorrigible," someone teased, followed by polished flirtation.

Laughter, low and lacquered with champagne, spilled up the stairwell. Below, a string quartet played a waltz, crystal wine glasses clinked, and silk swished in perfect harmony.

Dani blew out a slow breath. She wasn't ready, but stepped toward the landing, anyway.

The hem of her gown trailed against the marble floor as she reached the top of the grand staircase. She paused, fingers tightening on the polished banister, and looked down.

Every head turned.

The music faltered. A beat of silence pulsed through the glittering crowd.

Dani scanned the ballroom, her posture dignified, almost regal. The gown clung in all the right ways, showcasing her athletic frame—lean muscle and toned curves that spoke of strength rather than delicacy. Her body was striking in a way these men had never seen before, hotter than any soft, corseted woman in their usual circles. Not soft. Not dainty. But undeniably powerful.

She spotted Rowen at the bottom of the stairs. Her face utterly wrecked, jaw slack with admiration and disbelief. Standing beside her was Beatrice Ashdown, who radiated pure murder. Rowen wasn't even trying to be subtle.

Fucking Beatrice. Of anyone Rowen could have come with, it's HER.

Dani felt Rowen's eyes shift and melt like little moons with unabashed want. Beatrice caught sight of it—oh, she caught sight of it. Her expression could've shattered glass.

Barely holding back a laugh, Dani placed one gloved hand on the banister and slowly began her descent.

Rowen didn't move, breathe, or blink. Then, just as Dani reached the bottom step, she leaned in slightly, eyes never leaving hers, and winked.

Dani's grin bloomed, electric and irrepressible. *Self-respect? Never heard of her. I'm about to make some choices tonight.*

The evening was full of overpriced food, forced laughter, and old-money gossip. Unfortunately, she had zero chance of getting near Rowen since Beatrice was clinging to her like a barnacle on a shipwreck. So she drifted toward the edge of the ballroom, slipping between conversations and wine glasses, trying to stay out of Vivienne's line of sight.

As she rounded one of the arched columns, she nearly bumped into Rowen, alone now, standing just far enough from the crowd to look like she wasn't part of it. She stood partially tucked into the shadow of the corridor, a small leather-bound notebook balanced in one hand, a pencil poised in the other. Quickly and neatly, she wrote across the page, fully engrossed.

Dani stopped short, arching a brow. "Seriously? You brought your little notebook to a ball?"

Rowen kept writing. "I find the periphery more honest, Miss Wood. One sees more when no one expects them to speak." She glanced up to return a wink from earlier, closing the notebook and tucking it into her pocket.

Dani leaned in slightly, lowering her voice. "Don't tempt me with looks like that. Because if I'm not stuck dancing with some stranger all night, I'm definitely getting you alone."

Something shifted in Rowen's expression—a flash of determination, almost possessive.

"Might you indeed?" she whispered, her voice carrying an edge that made Dani's pulse quicken.

"Now, my dear guests, the highlight of the evening—our charity auction! The winning gentleman will have the honor of the lady's entire dance card and her company for the rest of the evening!" Vivienne's voice rang out near the small orchestra.

Oh damn, she'll be stuck with some stranger the whole night. Dani realized with growing dread that Vivienne had absolutely seen her talking with Rowen and was orchestrating this to keep them apart. She wouldn't dare say it outright, but the timing was too convenient to be coincidental.

Before she could retreat, she heard the familiar rustle of skirts. Vivienne materialized at her side, one hand brushing Dani's elbow in a gesture that looked gentle but gripped just a shade too tightly.

"Don't wander off, Miss Wood," she said, voice sweet as her eyes flitted across the ballroom. Her smile was pleasantly fake. "You'll be auctioned soon."

She turned slowly. "You never mentioned I'd be auctioned." She scowled, brow lifting.

"It's for charity, darling. A bit of fun."

Her lip curled. "Do I have to? I've got two left feet and the rhythm of a dying metronome."

"If you've any heart for charity, you'll make the sacrifice. Even if it means stomping a gentleman's toes clean off," Vivienne replied, her tone light but her eyes tight with warning.

Fine. But if I take someone down, it's on you.

The bidding rose like a tide—quiet at first, then swift, almost frantic. Gloves lifted. Numbers murmured. Men who had barely looked her way before now vied for her hand. Dani stood still, flushed and disoriented. One moment she was invisible, and the next she'd become the room's most coveted prize.

The auctioneer cleared his throat.

"For Miss Danielle Wood—kin to the Barrington family, we begin at ten dollars."

Vivienne. That scheming snake. No one had ever called her kin until tonight, but it made her more desirable—more legitimate. More expensive.

"Fifty," called Mr. Aldridge, his mustache twitching.

The dramatic jump from ten to fifty sent a ripple through the crowd. This would not be a polite charity bid anymore.

A pause. Then another voice: "One hundred."

"One-fifty," called another man with a cigar.

"Two hundred."

The numbers rose like a fever. Gentlemen shifted, their posture tightening. The light tone had vanished; this was no longer sport.

"Two-fifty," said a short fat banker, breathless.

Silence followed.

And then—

"Three hundred," said Rowen.

Calm. Steady. Like stating the weather.

The room didn't erupt. It recoiled.

The number rang out too clearly, too plainly, without embellishment or grin. It was a flat declaration, as though someone had already settled the matter.

A few heads turned. Beatrice went utterly still.

Dani stilled.

These men were wealthy, yes, but not stupid. They played for prestige, for show. Rowen? She had made a move with no expected return. No strategy. Just certainty.

But Dani felt it crack through her ribs like lightning.

She hadn't just won the bid.

She'd marked her—with nothing loud, nothing crude. Just a quiet, relentless force. The kind that said: She is already mine. I'm only waiting for the rest of you to understand it.

A hush moved through the crowd, followed by whispers. Speculation, scandal, envy.

Beatrice's jaw was tight.

The crowd shifted, the heat of the moment cooling into laughter and gossip.

But Dani still felt the brand of three hundred dollars, steady and searing.

Vivienne's smile tightened as she watched Rowen approach the platform. She'd orchestrated this evening to attract wealthy suitors, men with titles and fortunes who could elevate Dani's standing. A tailor—however charming, sought after by all the town's ladies, and well connected—wasn't exactly what she'd had in mind.

Dani hurried toward the edge of the ballroom, her heart still racing from the auction. She needed a moment to process what had just happened—Rowen had claimed her for the entire evening in front of everyone. The whispers and stares were overwhelming, and she could feel Beatrice's eyes burning into her from across the room. If she could just find a quiet spot to catch her breath before Rowen found her.

She ducked behind a pillar, pressing her back to the cool stone.

Just blend in. Fade. Become marble.

"Miss Wood." The voice came sweetly, but aggressively.

Damn it.

She turned to find Beatrice standing just a few feet away; her smile half-parted like a guillotine.

"Oh," Dani said, not making eye contact. "Hi."

Beatrice smiled thinly. "I must say, you wear borrowed gowns convincingly."

"Oh, thanks," Dani said vaguely, not really looking at her. "It's lovely, isn't it? I should probably find—"

"Such a generous benefactor you have," Beatrice continued, stepping closer. "Though I wonder how long such... charity will last."

Dani forced a polite smile, still trying to edge away. "Well, it's been nice chatting, but I should really—"

Beatrice stepped directly into her path, her gloved fingers clutching a crystal champagne glass with surgical precision.

"Quite the spectacle this evening," she said. "How very bold of you to monopolize a gentleman who escorted another lady—for the entire evening, no less."

"I didn't monopolize anyone. The auction was open to everyone."

Beatrice's eyes narrowed. "How refreshing to see someone so... unburdened by the constraints of proper society. Most ladies would never dream of such a public display."

Okay bitch, I'm about to go full feral.

"Stealing? I'm sorry. Are you seriously accusing me of stealing?"

Beatrice sipped her champagne delicately. "I merely offer an observation, Miss Wood. Mr. Quinn has ever been a rather... peculiar soul. He's so easily charmed by the allure of novelty. But novelty, I assure you, is ever-fleeting. Your peculiar manner of speech and muscular strength may initially strike some as intriguing, but it shall wear thin... and begin to feel rather commonplace. Even vulgar."

Dani lifted her chin, her smile razor-sharp. "Funny. Because from where I'm standing, it really sounds like you're worried about being replaced. And considering he just spent serious money to have my company for the entire evening instead of dancing with his you, his actual date..." She let the words evaporate.

"Oh, darling," Beatrice said, stepping closer, voice low like a serpent. "I know him far better than you ever will. His obligation lies elsewhere."

"You know what's actually confusing?" Dani said, leveling her gaze. "You talk like he's yours, but I'm the one he chose to spend the entire evening in front of everyone here."

She let her eyes drop to Beatrice's hand. "I don't see a ring. So, what exactly are you to him?"

The malice in Beatrice's eyes was brief but satisfying.

"Enjoy your dance, Miss Wood," she said sweetly, turning away. "Do take care not to overstep your place."

A voice from behind rang out proudly.

"May I?"

Dani turned slowly. Rowen stood before her, eyes burning with happiness.

"I believe I'm owed this dance, Miss Wood," she murmured, offering her hand.

"I hope you have steel-toe boots on."

Rowen chuckled. "Steel-toe what?" as she escorted her to the dance floor.

As they moved through the crowd, Dani caught the reactions rippling around them. The men who'd bid against Rowen watched with barely concealed envy, their wives whispering behind gloved hands.

Near the back of the room, Lord Ashdown's face had gone ashen. His carefully laid plans hinged on Rowen's remaining unattached, pliable. A man in love has priorities that are unbuyable.

But it was Alvie's expression that caught her attention—a proud, almost paternal smile as he raised his glass in a subtle toast. Go get 'em, champ, his eyes seemed to say.

The music swelled, and suddenly they were moving. She wasn't sure how, but Rowen made it effortless. Her steps were smooth, her grip assured, her palm resting lightly at the small of Dani's back.

"So," Dani started, then caught her heel on Rowen's boot and stumbled. Heat flooded her cheeks as she found her footing. "Earlier, when I said that thing about stealing you away..." She bit her lip. "That was kind of a bluff. I talk a big game, but honestly? I'm entirely too nervous around you to follow through on half the things I say."

Rowen's eyes softened. "And yet here we are."

"Here we are," Dani repeated, looking down at their joined hands. "Which is amazing."

Rowen's lips curved slowly. "Careful, I may think you didn't want this."

"No no no, I do. Very much, thank you." She glanced away, then back again. "I think we can both admit there's something happening here."

Rowen's hand tightened slightly against hers. "Oh?" she said.

"Yeah. I mean—this." She exhaled, shoulders dropping slightly. "I've been trying to play it cool and failing miserably."

Rowen said nothing, but the look she gave her was all attention.

"Either you're attracted to me, or you are one hell of a player."

"Player," Rowen repeated thoughtfully, letting the silence drag. Her grip on Dani's waist tightened slightly, her thumb brushing against the fabric just below her ribs.

"So," Dani said, a little too brightly, "we should probably acknowledge what this is. If anything at all."

Rowen's steps faltered almost imperceptibly. "Should we?"

"Yes." Dani's voice dropped lower. "But also, I'd like to know why you disappeared for a few weeks."

Dani stumbled again, almost bringing them both down, but Rowen steadied them, steering back into the perfect swirling line of dancers. Her grip on Dani's hand tightened.

"Well, I wasn't entirely certain if I could trust you. I had to wait and see if my world would come crashing down. When the parade of doom failed to materialize, I gathered rather more respect for you."

"I had a feeling." Dani met her eyes steadily.

A muscle worked in Rowen's jaw. "Once certain truths are acknowledged, there's no returning to the safety of pretense."

"For you," Dani said softly, her lips curving into something fierce, "I would let all my truths be acknowledged a hundred times over."

Something shifted in Rowen's expression—vulnerability breaking through her careful composure. Her voice dropped to barely above a whisper.

"Tell me honestly, Miss Wood," she said, her breath warm against Dani's ear. "If I had not bid for you tonight, if we had met as ourselves, without masks or games... would you have let me have you?"

Dani's stomach clenched. Everything inside her braced.

She didn't breathe, didn't blink.

Because suddenly, nothing else existed.

Rowen's words weren't just a confession. They were a challenge.

And God, the way she said it—proper and filthy all at once.

She was already falling, fast.

Let's speed-run these bad decisions, Dani. This is it.

She leaned in; her lashes lowering just enough to be enticing. With warmth that softened the edges of her voice, she whispered, "I have a very urgent and completely suspicious reason to drag you away before I step on your foot again. Interested?"

Rowen stiffened. Her eyes widened, just slightly.

For the first time, Dani saw hesitation.

But then her grip on Dani's waist firmed.

The song ended. The applause started.

Her steps faltered just slightly.

With a quick grin, she grabbed Rowen's forearm and pulled her along.

Rowen nearly stumbled.

Dani's grip was firm, far stronger than she had expected. Her fingers wrapped around her wrist with confidence that sent a jolt through her.

Women didn't move like this. Their hands were soft, their steps careful, their personalities hidden beneath layers of etiquette.

But Dani?

She handled her like she'd done this before.

Rowen's brows shot upward. "Should I be concerned?"

Dani didn't break stride. "Not yet, but give me five minutes."

With no protest, Rowen watched Dani and mirrored her steps. The thought struck her harder than she liked—perhaps Dani's story about being from another time was true. She wasn't quite ready to say she believed it, but for the first time, she wasn't so sure she didn't.

A waiter stepped into their path, silver tray glinting with champagne flutes. Without missing a beat, Dani plucked one from the tray and pressed it into Rowen's free hand like it had always belonged there.

"Which way to the food table?" she asked, smiling as if she had all the time in the world.

The waiter pointed toward the foyer.

"Perfect," she chirped. "Thank you so kindly." Her laugh was light and effortless as she guided Rowen forward by the elbow.

Rowen turned back just long enough to lift the glass in a silent, amused toast before disappearing past the ballroom's columns and into the dim hallway beyond.

As Dani spotted her escape route to the servants' stairs—thank you, Shannon—a familiar, annoying voice cut through the air.

"Miss Wood!"

They halted. Dani's eyes rolled. *Oh, for the love of—*

Beatrice glided forward, all grace and barely concealed desperation.

"Rowen," she said, her voice softer now, almost pleading. "Surely you could spare just one dance? I know the evening's spoken for, but perhaps... just a few minutes?"

There was something vulnerable in her tone, a crack in her usual composure that made even Dani feel a flicker of sympathy.

Rowen's expression remained polite but firm. "I'm afraid not, Miss Ashdown. As you said, the evening is quite spoken for."

Beatrice's smile faltered for just a moment before snapping back into place. "But we had an understanding—"

"I escorted you to the ball, as promised," Rowen said gently. "Nothing more was arranged."

"Tactfully handled," Dani murmured under her breath, impressed despite herself.

Beatrice's composure cracked further. "Surely you can spare five minutes for your—"

"I really must insist," Rowen interrupted smoothly. "Miss Wood requires my attention."

The rejection was polite but absolute. Beatrice's face flushed, and Dani could see her scrambling for another angle of attack.

Time for a rescue mission.

Then—she did the only logical thing: faked a swoon.

One moment, she stood upright. The next, she dropped into Rowen's arms with all the grace of a concussed deer.

Rowen barely caught her, snapping up instinctively to steady her, nearly dropping the wine glass.

"Ah—apologies, Beatrice," Dani said, voice fragile and breathy. "I'm afraid I'm feeling rather faint."

Beatrice skeptically narrowed her eyes, but Mrs. Morwood's sharp voice nearby cut in. "Oh dear! Is she unwell?"

The distraction was perfect. All eyes turned to them. Beatrice visibly tensed, her social instincts kicking in—too many eyes for her to continue pressing.

"Get well soon, Miss Wood," she said in a voice that carried to the onlookers, her defeat complete.

Dani offered her a sugary-sweet smile. "So thoughtful of you."

They slipped away, Rowen guiding her with exaggerated gentleness around the corridor toward the staff staircase.

As soon as they were out of earshot, Dani dropped the act. "Tell me I deserve an award for that performance."

"You deserve something," Rowen said, laughing under her breath.

"God, I love making her angry." Dani threw a few punches in the air like a boxer.

Rowen laughed, her eyes crinkling at the corners.

They half-fell into the narrow stairwell. The door clicked shut behind them with a hollow echo. Dani stumbled first, catching her balance with a muffled laugh as Rowen nearly collided with her.

"Well," she said, breathless, "so much for being subtle."

Rowen grinned, adjusting her jacket. "You call that subtle?"

"I saw it in a movie once," Dani said, then winced.

Rowen tilted her head. "A what?"

"Oh—uh, never mind. Future talk."

Rowen gave a soft, incredulous laugh. "What are you?"

The sound echoed in the cramped stairwell, quiet and intimate. Their bodies nearly touched in the narrow, dim space of bare wood and cold drafts.

"I think this is a better place for acknowledgements," Dani said nervously.

"Ah, yes," Rowen looked around the tight quarters with a wry smile, "this dark empty stairwell is certainly the ideal place."

She shifted, brushing a hand through her hair and tucking it behind her ears—casual, effortless, devastating.

And that was exactly the problem.

Dani wasn't usually the shy one. She'd always known how to lead, how to make the first move, how to laugh off the nerves. But Rowen was undoing her.

There was something about her—in the way she looked at Dani, the way she made her laugh, the sharp spark of connection that had hit fast and burned ever since.

Whatever bravado she usually carried had quietly left the building. And from the look on Rowen's face, with her flushed cheeks and soft grin, it seemed like she'd forgotten hers, too. That cute vulnerability was back.

Dani swallowed hard. She needed to say something. Do something. Anything.

Her mouth opened before her brain could catch up.

"If you keep looking at me like that, I'm going to forget how my feet work." The ridiculous words spilled out in the quiet like a brick through glass.

"I'm already well acquainted with your roller skating and dance floor footwork, Miss Wood. After that dance, I'm astonished you play football at all."

Dani's fingers twitched at her side, slowly lifting as if unsure whether to fidget or reach for Rowen—because she wanted to. Desperately. But then alarm bells went off: *Don't rush it.* She drew her hand back.

Rowen noticed. Her eyes tracked the aborted motion, quiet and watchful as Dani's nerves betrayed her.

"I had thought someone hailing from the future would possess a better grasp on being alone with someone," she mused. "Perhaps you are not the grand time traveler you so claim to be."

Dani crossed her arms. "Oh, I'm sorry. Do you think there's a school for this in the future? Awkward Moment Navigation for the Chronologically Misplaced? Because I totally missed that class."

Rowen tilted her head slightly, chuckling. The corners of her mouth still curled with amusement, but her eyes had softened. They were no longer teasing.

Angel of my dreams, Dani thought. *Breathe, you idiot—like a normal person.*

She looked down at Rowen's perfectly pouty lips. And when she looked back up, Rowen was already watching her mouth, too.

Her heart pounded. Her cheeks flushed hotly. *Say something before your face combusts.*

The kitchen-to-stairwell door creaked open.

They jolted backward from each other like guilty teenagers. Shannon stood in the doorway, a tray of clean cutlery balanced in her arms, one brow arched to high heaven. She blinked once, her gaze bouncing between them, then cleared her throat.

With practiced grace, she stepped between them, brushed past Dani, and disappeared down the corridor, the door clicking gently shut behind her.

One beat passed.

Then the door cracked open again.

Shannon peeked in, locked eyes with Dani, and gave her a sly wink.

"I'll keep watch," she whispered, then slipped back out.

Dani winced.

"A most faithful ally," Rowen suggested.

"You people always seem to have perfect timing."

"Near-miss encounters and hallway interruptions are our specialty, I fear."

A loose tendril of Rowen's hair had slipped into her eyes, and without thinking, Dani moved forward, closing the distance. Her hand rose gently, brushing the loose strand away, tucking it behind Rowen's ear.

Rowen shivered.

Dani's fingers hovered near her ear, the warmth of Rowen's skin still blooming against her knuckles. She didn't move. Couldn't. Her eyes dropped to Rowen's mouth.

This is it.

Slowly, breathlessly, she leaned in, each inch forward loaded with hesitation and hunger.

Then something wavered behind Rowen's eyes. A familiar wariness.

She pulled back.

Just a few inches, but it might as well have been miles. The spell broke as her nervous smile dissolved, replaced by something more careful, more distant.

Her shoulders squared, posture straightening into perfect propriety.

Another step back. Ever the gentleman.

"Forgive me, Miss Wood," she said, her voice taking on its proper cadence. "A gentleman should not presume liberties after a single dance, nor does he compromise a lady's reputation by allowing her to remain unescorted in such circumstances."

The walls were up—polished, impenetrable. This must be her practiced defense, honed by years of experience with women who pursued "him" without knowing the truth. Women who thought they wanted adventure, rebellion, something different from their usual suitors. Women who ultimately wanted men.

And even now, she was still nervous Dani would hurt her.

"I have spent years resisting advances," Rowen said, raising her arm and placing her hand behind her neck, speaking almost to herself. "From ever so many women in this town who fancied they knew what they desired—women who saw me as a gentleman."

She shook her head rather delicately. "I have turned away every single one when it reached the point of contact, never permitted myself even the briefest kiss, quite terrified they should discover who I truly am, make use of me and then cast me aside when the novelty had quite worn off." She shifted on her feet. "Even at the underground establishment for people like me, surrounded by persons who truly comprehend such matters, I have held myself back. Made friends, indeed—many most dear friends—but never allowed myself to venture further. My fear of trusting anyone completely leaves me feeling exposed. And tonight, I have ventured the furthest I have ever dared. Most remarkable."

Dani found herself caught completely off-guard by the sudden shift from summer to winter in a heartbeat. Biting her lip, Dani tried to pull her thoughts together, but nerves betrayed her and she rambled.

"I'm sorry. Maybe I misread the situation. This is... completely uncharted territory for me." Dani bit her lip, rambling now. "I dated one guy once—complete disaster doesn't even cover it. Honestly? I usually only date beautiful, emotionally unavailable women who have this uncanny ability to disappear the moment I actually start catching feelings. It's practically my specialty at this point."

Something shifted in Rowen's demeanor the moment she spoke.

No surprise—she'd already suspected. But relief. Pure, overwhelming relief. Dani wasn't curious. She'd been with women, and not just one.

Her hands opened and closed at her sides as if trying to ground herself. A strange clarity overtook her features—a thousand locked doors inside her had just flung open.

She stepped forward, slow and careful, lips drawn in a tight line.

Dani's stomach dropped. *Oh god, did I just assume too much? Maybe she's not—*

But then Rowen spoke, voice stripped of all pretenses.

"You did not misread the situation," she said timidly. "I've imagined your lips on mine so many times I fear I've conjured this into waking life. So please... end this torment. Let me have the real thing—just once, before I go mad."

Dani's jaw parted in shock. Her response couldn't find its way out.

When Rowen finally pressed her lips to hers, everything shifted. The kiss was achingly gentle, tentative in a way that caught Dani completely off guard. Rowen's nervousness radiated through every touch, including the slight tremor in her breath.

This confidence isn't practiced. This is something else entirely.

Dani's mind went blank, every coherent thought dissolving. People who knew exactly what they were doing had kissed her before. But this—this felt like discovery. Like Rowen was learning her in real time, and she was learning herself through Rowen's wonder.

She pulled back just enough to meet Rowen's eyes.

Rowen's gaze swirled with fear—wide and unguarded—already bracing for rejection.

Dani's voice softened. "You're safe with me."

Rowen's breath shuddered out in something between a laugh and a sob. "I—" She swallowed hard, voice barely above a whisper. "You're not... you're not running." Her eyes searched Dani's face desperately. "I've been so tired of pretending. So tired."

"I'm not running," Dani replied. "I've been trying to breathe without you since the moment we met because it has taken everything in my power not to orbit you like a lost star. And now, I understand why."

At that, Rowen exhaled shakily. Her eyes fluttered shut. Those perfectly poetic words undid something vital inside her. She leaned forward and dropped her head to Dani's shoulder, her body finally giving in.

"Look at me," Dani requested.

Rowen looked up, her face lighting up with a smile as she reveled in the sheer disbelief of it all.

The next kiss was different—deeper, but still achingly careful. Dani moved slowly, savoring each moment, each soft sound Rowen made. This wasn't about rushing toward anything; it was about this moment, this discovery, this perfect first.

When they finally broke apart, both were breathing hard, foreheads pressed together.

"Still worried about propriety?" Dani murmured softly.

Rowen's laugh was breathless. "No."

Then Vivienne's voice rang out in the distance, announcing the next act of the evening. The sound sliced through the moment.

Dani blinked, trying to refocus. "We should probably..."

"Slow down," Rowen declared, a smirk tugging at her lips as she clicked her tongue softly. "That was my first kiss," she added. "Let me have one more moment to savor it."

Dani paused, heart stumbling.

Her first.

An unfamiliar feeling bloomed in her chest, making her feel thrilled and protective all at once. She smiled, forehead dropping gently to Rowen's.

"Well," she said with a shaky smile, "better than my first."

Rowen tipped her head up in curiosity.

Dani grinned. "Mine was behind a—uh—really unfortunate shed situation. There was a frog. And panic. I don't think we ever spoke again."

That earned a genuine laugh, and Rowen tucked her face briefly against Dani's shoulder.

"But this one?" Dani said, tilting Rowen's chin up gently. "This one is worth remembering."

She kissed her again—softly this time. As if truly giving something back.

16

THROUGH THE GLASS

PRESENT DAY

The wind clawed at the bare branches outside the Barrington mansion, scraping the windows like fingernails. Mary barely noticed. She sat at the edge of Dani's bed, knees tucked to her chest, watching the soft glow of her watch pulse in the dark.

Again.

A heartbeat glow that was faint, steady, and wrong.

The first time it happened, she chalked it up to a glitch. Maybe the battery was dying again, or maybe it was picking up interference. Watches didn't do this. But it kept happening. And now, it was all she could think about.

She glanced at the bedroom door. Still closed. Still quiet. Dani's parents had gone out for the night. They'd said something about a chef's tasting menu in the Pearl District and a bottle of Pinot Noir that was "just divine."

Mary had barely listened. All she'd heard was *we'll be back late*, and that was good enough. She was alone.

Which was fine. Really.

Except it wasn't.

She looked toward the window, where fog had crept across the glass in hazy spirals. Outside, the yard stretched into shadow. A strip of landscape lighting at the edge of the drive cast long, crooked silhouettes across the cold lawn. Everything looked empty.

But it wasn't. She knew that now.

Because she'd seen him.

Her fingers clenched around the blanket as the memory snapped through her again—sharp, sudden, and impossible to shake. It was two nights ago. She'd been brushing her hair, zoned out, half-awake. Something moved—not in the mirror, but just beyond it. At first, she thought it was her reflection shifting. But when she turned—

He was there.

A figure. Walking out of the woods.

She couldn't make out his face, just the shape of him: tall, broad shouldered, too solid to be a trick of the eye.

And then he was gone.

Vanished like a glitch in reality.

Mary had bolted. No hesitation. No overthinking. She'd flown down the stairs, heart slamming, lungs burning, and yanked open the front door. Cold air slapped her in the face. But the yard?

Empty.

Silent.

The streetlamp buzzed faintly above the trees, its glow stretching across the grass like a spotlight on a lie.

She'd called the cops. What else was she supposed to do? Dollar Store Slenderman shows up in your home, you call 911.

The officers arrived quickly. Flashlights slicing the dark. Voices low. Professional.

They found nothing. No prints. No tracks. No broken locks. Just wind and shadows.

"Maybe a shadow from a deer," one of them had said, closing his notebook with a soft snap. "You've been under a lot of stress."

Mary had nodded. Swallowed her disbelief. Pretended to agree.

But she wasn't imagining things. And it wasn't a deer.

The glow from her watch reflected faintly off the corner of Dani's grandfather's journal. The rhythm of the light pulsed—unsettlingly calm. She turned her wrist again, staring down at the soft, steady glow. It came from beneath the gears, deep in the bones of the thing.

Mary's skin prickled.

She couldn't stay in this room any longer. The air felt thinner with each breath, heavy with memory and something else—something waiting. She grabbed her phone and slipped down the hallway, socked feet quiet against the hardwood. Her breath clouded faintly in front of her. The old house never really held heat.

She climbed the back stairs toward the servants' quarters—a half-rotted narrow stairwell behind the linen closet. Dani's dad had said it was unlivable, probably full of rats, but Mary didn't care. She needed to move.

The top floor smelled like dust and pine and time. Wallpaper peeled in long curls, the kind you could unravel like ribbon. Old furniture covered in moth-eaten sheets hunched in the corners like ghosts.

She swept her phone's flashlight across a stack of books on a crooked bookshelf. Ledgers. Gardening journals. An embossed leather spine caught her eye—thick, dark, gold-lettered:

"The Balance of Iron — A Manifesto for Preservation Through Revolution."

Her pulse kicked.

She opened the book carefully; the spine crackling. Inside tight, controlled handwriting—not modern. Alvie's.

Notes scribbled in margins. Dates circled. Diagrams annotated. Entire sections underlined. It wasn't passive reading—he'd devoured it, used it, maybe built something from it.

She turned another page. A yellowed scrap of paper fluttered free.

It was a list—just names.

Someone crossed out most of them.

But one wasn't.

Danielle Wood — disappeared 1905

Mary clutched the page. Her hands shook. Danielle? Dani?

She looked toward the window at the end of the hall—its glass warped with age. Frost crept along the corners like veins.

And that's when she saw him again.

Not a shadow.

Not a dream.

That man.

Standing at the edge of the treeline where the yard met the woods. Dressed in dark wool, posture perfectly straight, his hands tucked neatly behind his back.

He looked like a ghost out of a museum exhibit—or a painting that had stepped out of its frame.

She gasped. Before she could think, she was running down the gritty stairs.

The cold bit hard as she tore across the lawn, heart hammering.

"Hey!" she shouted. "Hey! Wait!"

The man turned as she approached—his face calm, indecipherable. He was absurdly handsome, in that old-world kind of way that shouldn't exist anymore. Like he'd stepped out of a daguerreotype and landed here by accident.

Mary stumbled to a stop, suddenly breathless for reasons that had nothing to do with running.

"Who... who are you?" she asked.

He tilted his head, studying her. His eyes were green and strange—like they'd seen more than they should. A beat of silence passed.

"I'm looking for someone," he said finally. His voice was soft. Polished. Edwardian.

Mary blinked. "Are you... a re-enactor? Is this... a cosplay thing?"

He smiled faintly. "I think I may have arrived at the wrong house."

She took a step forward. "Did you come through the woods? Are you lost? We're you hiking the trail in that?" She pointed at his clothes.

But his gaze had already turned distant. Sad, almost. He dipped his head in a subtle, formal nod—so out of place in the modern world it felt like a glitch.

"Forgive me," he said. "I shouldn't have lingered."

Then he stepped backward—not fleeing, just... receding—and vanished into the trees.

Mary stood frozen. The wind cut through her coat. Somewhere inside her watch, the light pulsed again.

17

TERRITORIAL HEARTS

EDWARDIAN ERA

Morning came faster than anyone wanted.

Dani stirred in the dim room, golden slivers of light spilling between the curtains. The memory of her time with Rowen clung to her skin like silk, her dress still crumpled at the foot of the bed where she'd carelessly thrown it hours ago.

The remnants of last night's perfume and the fading warmth of Rowen's presence lingered in the air.

She shifted, fingers tracing the comforter, remembering.

Rowen's lips on hers. The quiet confession in the dark. The way their bodies had moved together. The revelation that had changed everything.

It played on repeat, looping between thrill and utter disbelief.

A soft knock cut through the haze.

"Sleeping in, miss?"

Shannon's voice was bright and entirely too awake.

"Shall I draw you a bath?"

"No bath. Just food," Dani groaned, grabbing a pillow and pressing it over her face.

Shannon's footsteps moved across the room, setting down a tray. "You must have had a splendid evening if you're this exhausted."

Dani snorts, sitting up to grab a slice of toast. "Splendid. That's one word for it."

She chews absentmindedly, her mind drifting back to the sleeping porch...

The night air is cool against her skin, a stark contrast to the warmth radiating from Rowen beside her on the chaise. Moonlight catches in Rowen's hair as she sits with her hands folded, lost in thought.

"Women have always attracted me," Rowen explains. "But I dress as a man, not out of deceit, but necessity."

"What kind of necessity?"

Rowen's smile doesn't reach her eyes. "My mother was a seamstress. She possessed the most beautiful hands—delicate, skilled. She could stitch three hundred perfect stitches within the hour."

Dani watches her, sensing this is just the beginning.

"When my father died, those beautiful hands shook. From grief, at first. Then hunger." Rowen meets her eyes. "Do you know what becomes of a widow with no means in this world?"

"I can't imagine."

"Nothing good." Rowen turns toward the window. "The cough started that winter. Every night, I would lie awake, listening to her struggle for breath, thinking: tomorrow I shall find a way."

"What did you do?"

"I cut my hair first. Bound my chest. Spent hours lowering my voice, altering my gait. My father had left behind his finest suit—it hung off me dreadfully, but a kind tailor helped with adjustments." Her gaze drifts. "Leaving our home as Rowen, no longer Rowena, felt rather like leaving a piece of myself behind."

She pauses, collecting herself. "But it worked. I secured a position at a tailor's shop. Once the proprietor noted my skill with a needle—an aptitude I owe entirely to my mother—he entrusted me with greater responsibility. Within the year, I was overseeing operations."

"And your mother?"

"She recovered, eventually." Rowen's expression softens with pride. "She never questioned why her daughter would only visit after dark, dressed as herself again. I am quite certain she knew, but we never spoke of it."

"So you just... became someone else. For her."

"For us both. If I were to survive, to keep her in this world, there remained but one course. I had to become someone the world might see fit to employ."

Rowen's fingers reach for Dani's hand in the darkness. "Tomorrow shall prove difficult. The mill workers mean to stage a walkout."

"Is that why you brought Alvie a book?"

Determination flashes in Rowen's eyes. "He's interested in my writings. Someone must speak for those who cannot speak for themselves. The women at the textile mill work fourteen-hour days for barely enough to feed their children. Two perished last month when their skirts caught in the machinery."

"That's horrible," Dani whispers, inching closer.

"What's worse is how easily someone could have prevented it," Rowen says, voice hardening. "Safety guards cost pennies compared to human lives, yet the owners refuse. They call us agitators, but what we seek is simply dignity."

She squeezes Dani's hand. "If I, with my education and position, say nothing... who shall?"

"So you really are Rowen."

"Indeed."

"Damn," is all Dani can manage. It isn't eloquent, but what else is there to say?

Rowen releases a sigh. "Indeed. Damn."

"Do you ever tire of remembering all the lies?"

Rowen's eyes widen slightly. "Perpetually."

"Yeah. I get that." Dani's voice softens. "You said that was your first kiss? You've never been with anyone?"

"No," Rowen replies, her formal cadence carrying raw resignation. "My circumstances have been... rather complicated. I have learned to navigate society's expectations with skill—to flirt, to create the illusion of possible intimacy." She looks up at the ceiling. "But to follow through? To risk everything? My livelihood, my safety, my very existence? It would invite utter destruction. There was a woman once, before you, disappeared. I never had the chance."

She meets Dani's eyes directly. "Finding someone of like mind is rather like finding a needle in a haystack."

Dani understands. In this society, exposure would mean ruin. Imprisonment. Complete social annihilation.

"Finding another woman who shares such inclinations that I'm actually attracted to," Rowen continues, "is an art form more complex than any language. A lingering glance could be friendship. A touch could be nothing. Or everything. The margins are treacherously thin."

She searches Dani's face. "And yet, it felt as though you saw me somehow, before I ever spoke the truth. You made me feel safe before I ever asked for it."

Dani's heart does something strange. "So all this kissing means you're attracted to me?" She winks. "I knew something was different from the moment I saw you."

Silence fills the space between them.

Rowen's thumb traces across Dani's knuckles, such a simple touch that sends electricity up her arm. "I've been trying to maintain my composure," she whispers, her voice fragile with desire. "But goodness, Dani... you're so different. A ray of sunshine in my otherwise dreary existence. And beautiful. Those green eyes, the way you move... your body drives me quite wild."

Dani's heart jumps. She lifts their joined hands, pressing a soft kiss to Rowen's palm.

Rowen breaks the conversation with action—her lips meet Dani's in a soft, careful kiss. Not rushed this time, but full of emotion. Dani responds instantly, though she stops short of full surrender. She has to play it cool, take it slow. Slower than all those other women who disappeared the minute she got serious. She has to be careful. She doesn't want to lose this one.

The night air is cool, but Rowen's mouth is warm.

Rowen's kiss deepens, less shy. It feels like a dam bursting after prolonged waiting. She isn't smooth, but she means every second.

Dani lets her lead—for a moment. But then Rowen's pace quickens, turning eager, almost desperate.

"Now it's my turn to savor," Dani whispers, cradling Rowen's chin as she places sweet, small kisses across her face. One on her nose, her cheek, her dimpled chin.

Rowen nods, eyes wide, chest rising and plunging.

"Is this alright?" Dani murmurs against Rowen's ear.

"Yes," Rowen breathes, the word barely audible.

They lose themselves in kisses and sighs. Rowen's careful control unravels completely, replaced by a raw need that matches Dani's own.

When they finally break apart, both are breathing hard, foreheads pressed together in the moonlight.

"I cannot seem to quench my thirst," Rowen confesses, voice shaky with wonder.

"Then kiss me again," Dani replies.

They hold each other in the cool night air, hearts still racing, both knowing this moment has changed everything between them. Even though Dani keeps it to just kissing—being so careful not to push too far, not to scare Rowen away.

The memory sends warmth flooding through her again, even hours later.

Then reality crashes back.

"Oh, shit."

Shannon turned, startled. "Miss?"

Dani bolted upright, throwing off the blankets. "What time is it?"

"A quarter past eight. Why?"

"I was going to meet Rowen at the park.

There were entire days Dani forgot to breathe.

Monday, it was the way Rowen's hand curled around her waist to steady her as she mounted the mare, the heat of her palm through wool and whalebone. Dani lasted ten seconds side-saddle before tumbling into a clumsy heap in the grass, laughing too hard to care. Rowen laughed too—genuine and full-bellied—and didn't let go of her hand for the rest of the afternoon.

Tuesday, they slipped through the back door of the Natural History Museum, Rowen flashing a sly smile at the curator who owed her a favor. They wandered the shuttered halls, whispering among taxidermized lions and ancient stone gods. In a sunlit atrium, Rowen pulled her behind a statue of Apollo and kissed her like it was a secret. When Dani gasped, Rowen said softly, "You look rather like marble when you're still."

Wednesday smelled like warm cinnamon and coal smoke. They ate sticky buns from a bakery that opened before dawn, hiding in a delivery alley to avoid being seen. Rowen dabbed sugar from the corner of Dani's mouth with her thumb and then paused—just long enough to make Dani burn—before brushing her lips to Dani's cheek.

Thursday brought piano music and poetry. Rowen played Chopin in a friend's parlor, fingers light and exact, brow furrowed in concentration. Dani sat on the chaise with her knees hugged to her chest, spellbound. Later, they shared a tattered book of verse beneath a blanket on the drawing room rug. Dani read aloud while Rowen traced the bones of her wrist, word by word.

And Friday, they climbed the hill to an abandoned observatory, a ruin Rowen had stumbled upon as a girl. Ivy curled through the cracked dome. Through the telescope, Rowen showed her the belt of Orion.

"He's a hunter," she says, voice hushed.

"So am I," Dani whispers, though she doesn't say what for.

Their hands meet between constellations. A long kiss follows. Careful. Starved. Like neither of them wants to be the one to break it.

Dani didn't push. She let everything evolve naturally, let Rowen come into her own, and she absolutely adored it. Every second, Rowen leaned in for a kiss on her own. Watching Rowen experience what it was like to want someone, to savor someone, was more intoxicating than any relationship she'd ever had. Being present for the wonder of first love was precious, and she treasured every minute.

She was falling so hard that she almost forgot she was trying to find a way home. Rowen was so intoxicating, she wasn't even certain she wanted to leave. But she must.

It could wait, though. Right now, her heart was here with Rowen.

Dani kicked off her boots just inside the door and unpinned her hat, setting it on the dresser with a sigh. Her cheeks were wind-bitten, and her hair was coming loose from its braid, but she didn't care. Alvie would forgive her for being late. He always did.

She crossed to the wardrobe, already rehearsing what she might say to feign interest in the lumber mill he wanted to show her in Oregon City. Something about water power and stacked fortunes and timber rights. She liked Alvie well enough—but it wasn't him she was thinking about. Unlike Vivienne, Dani enjoyed the outings and Alvie loved having company who didn't interrupt or ask questions.

Her fingers hovered over a wool skirt before stilling.

It came back all at once. That week. A tide of memory she didn't know she'd been holding back.

Rowen, reaching for her reins as she laughed herself breathless in the grass. Rowen, brushing sugar from her mouth like she belonged to her. By firelight, Rowen read Keats, steadying her voice, then faltered slightly when Dani touched her knee.

They had crossed no lines. Not the ones they could name, anyway. But Dani felt the change like a pressure in the air before rain. It wasn't just heat anymore. It was hope.

She unbuttoned her blouse slowly, the fabric stiff from the cold. A shiver ran through her—not from the air, but from memory. Her lips still tingled from last night's kiss beneath the observatory dome, long and lingering, chased by starlight.

She reached for her corset—

And froze.

A folded scrap of paper sat on the edge of the washbasin. It hadn't been there this morning. Shannon must have brought it in.

She opened it with careful fingers.

"Tonight. Trust me, if you would. Dress prettily for me—we shall visit a rather illicit establishment."

No signature. None needed.

Dani didn't smile. Not exactly. But something in her expression softened—like a flame curling low and steady between her legs.

She pressed the note flat against her palm and whispered to the room, "Whatever you're planning... I'm in."

The velvet hush of the club hit Dani like a bruise made of silk and smoke. Music coiled through the underground space in the Shanghai Tunnels, slow and lush, a woman's voice dragging her vowels like syrup over warm skin.

Dani didn't know where to look. It was too much—color, motion, bodies pressed close, laughter like falling water. A woman in a tailcoat twirled another woman with bare feet, their mouths meeting in a kiss that drew appreciative murmurs from nearby dancers. Two men sat entwined on a velvet settee, one's hand resting possessively on the other's thigh while his companion traced lazy circles along his neck. A person in elegant evening wear had their arms wrapped around someone shorter, fingers boldly exploring the curve of an exposed collarbone, eliciting soft sighs of pleasure. In a shadowy alcove, two women embraced each other with desperate tenderness, their hands roaming freely over each other's bodies, only touchable in this hidden sanctuary. Candles flickered, dripping onto the stone floor like wax had always belonged there.

She'd never seen so many kinds of want in one place—not whispered or hidden, but named and celebrated and utterly unashamed. Of course, they were still technically in hiding. This wasn't socially acceptable above ground. But down here, in these tunnels, they could finally be free. Free to touch the way lovers should. Fearless to hold. Free to steal precious moments of intimacy that the outside world denied them completely.

Rowen stayed close but didn't crowd her, one hand resting at the small of Dani's back, guiding her gently through the space. But Dani felt the tension in that touch—something coiled and watchful.

"They will no stare," Rowen murmured in her ear, though her voice carried a distinct quality than usual. Sharper. "Not unless they're rather hoping to be stared at in return."

As they moved deeper into the club, faces turned toward them. A woman with short-cropped hair raised her glass in greeting. A person in an elegant waistcoat nodded to Rowen with familiar warmth. These were Rowen's people—artists, poets, and rebels, those who lived in the spaces between what society allowed.

"Rowen!" a melodious voice called out. A slight figure in an emerald silk evening dress approached, moving with dancer's grace, though the broader shoulders and stronger jawline beneath carefully applied cosmetics hinted at the person beneath the feminine presentation. "You did not tell us you'd found someone."

Rowen's smile was genuine but brief. "Jamie, do meet Dani. Dani, this is Jamie—he runs this most scandalous speakeasy." Her voice carried warmth and respect as she gestured to the elegant figure before them, whose masculine frame was draped in exquisite emerald silk that flowed like water over broad shoulders.

Jamie took Dani's hand with theatrical gallantry. His voice pitched higher and more melodious than his natural register. "We treasure any friend of our dear Rowen. Though I must say—" He glanced between them with knowing eyes, then paused as he took in Rowen's protective stance, the way her hand lingered at Dani's waist. A slow smile spread across his painted features. "Well, well. Our Rowen, displaying affection rather openly. That's... delightfully unexpected after all these years." His eyes sparkled with genuine warmth behind long, darkened lashes. "She's been keeping you rather the secret, but I can see why she's finally decided to... stake her claim, as it were."

But Rowen's attention had already shifted, her body going still in that way that meant trouble. Dani followed her gaze across the smoky room.

There, leaning against the far end of the bar like she owned it, stood a woman who made the candlelight seem dim. Lean and poised, draped in black silk that moved like liquid shadow. Her hair was dark gold, swept up to reveal the elegant line of her neck. She held a cigar between gloved fingers, her eyes—green or gray, it was hard to tell in the low light—fixed first on Rowen with unmistakable longing, drinking in her familiar form with the desperate hunger of someone who had lost something precious. But then her gaze raked over to Dani, and the longing transformed into something hungrier, more predatory.

The woman didn't smile. Didn't look away from Dani. Just watched with the focused intensity of a cat that had spotted something it intended to claim.

"Who is that?" Dani asked, though something in Rowen's stillness made her voice come out quieter than intended.

Rowen's jaw tightened almost imperceptibly. "Someone who ought to know better."

The name came like a sigh from Jamie: "Clarissa."

Clarissa's face comprised high cheekbones, a straight Roman nose, and a mouth that rarely offered softness unless earned; it was all sharp lines and sculpted defiance. Her brows were thick and elegantly sloped, arched just enough to give her resting expression a quality of amused judgment.

Her eyes were a deep, unreadable brown—so dark they caught candlelight like mirrors, and just as unyielding. When she looked at you, it felt like she was measuring your usefulness, your secrets, your pulse. She wore her long, dark brown hair in an elegant Edwardian twist, although several strands artfully fell around her face. Clarissa looked like a woman who didn't just walk through time—she wrote it down afterward and then lit the page on fire.

"I see." Rowen's voice had gone flat, professional. "Well. She always did have rather impeccable stalking methods."

Jamie glanced between them, clearly sensing undercurrents, then melted away with a murmured excuse about checking on other guests, his silk skirts rustling as he moved with practiced feminine grace.

"Come," Rowen said, her hand sliding more possessively around Dani's waist. "Before someone else decides they're rather braver than is wise."

They reached a shadowy side wall booth carved out of brick and red velvet. Rowen dropped onto the bench with fluid grace, legs spread, coat open—every inch the confident gentleman. She took Dani's wrist and pulled her down across her lap, one arm guiding Dani's legs to drape over her thighs. Her skirt flew up and bunched at her thigh crease with all the motion, accidentally baring her legs to the dim candlelight.

Dani found herself seated sideways across Rowen's lap, her legs draped over one of Rowen's thighs, her heart skipping with surprise at the intimate positioning, this was far bolder than anything they'd done yet. The heat of Rowen's coat pooled beneath her, velvet catching at the sides of her exposed thighs.

Rowen's gaze dropped to Dani's bare legs—and froze. She'd never seen them fully before, had only caught glimpses through fabric and movement. But now, with the skirt bunched high on her thighs, she could see the elegant curve of muscle, the firm definition that spoke of years of soccer drills. The candlelight played across skin that was smooth but strong, thighs that weren't delicate but powerful and utterly mesmerizing. Rowen's breath caught audibly, her pupils dilating as heat flooded through her. These weren't the scrawny, pampered legs of a society lady—these were the legs of a woman who knew her own strength, and the sight sent a bolt of pure desire straight through Rowen's chest.

Dani opened her mouth to speak, but she gestured to suggest Rowen should pull her skirt back down. Rowen leaned in and pulled some of the skirt down to Dani's knees. The warm brush of her fingers down Dani's thighs was excruciatingly sensual.

"Now, do sit still. You're far too pretty this evening for me not to savor." She whispered into Dani's ear.

It wasn't a suggestion.

A waiter materialized beside their booth—a lean man with sparkling eyes and a serene smile. "Evening, Rowen. The usual?" His gaze flickered curiously to Dani, taking in her position across Rowen's lap with practiced discretion. "And who might this lovely creature be?"

"Whiskey for me and the lady," Rowen said smoothly, her hand tightening possessively on Dani's waist. "And Thomas, do meet my lover." The word rolled off her tongue like honey and steel. "You may tell anyone who asks—including certain unwelcome observers—that she's thoroughly spoken for."

Thomas's eyebrows rose with delighted surprise. "Well, I'll be damned. Our Rowen's finally claimed someone properly." He winked at Dani. "You must be something special, miss. She's called no one that before."

In the booth next to them, a lesbian couple sat with bodies intertwined, hands exploring with the desperate hunger of those who could only meet here, only touch here. One woman's fingers traced her lover's throat while the other's hand disappeared beneath layers of silk and cotton. The music drowned out their soft murmurs and quiet gasps, but their faces revealed precious stolen intimacy. This might be the only place outside of hurried, fearful encounters where they could meet and touch and talk freely. Where they could be lovers instead of just "dear friends."

The club's purpose wasn't vulgarity—it was sanctuary. A place where people who lived cramped in family houses or under the watchful eyes of society could finally breathe, finally touch the person they loved without shame or fear.

Across the room, Clarissa was still watching. Head tilted. One eyebrow raised in what might have been amusement or challenge.

Rowen saw it. Of course she did.

"You know her," Dani said. It wasn't a question.

"I did." Rowen's voice carried years of complications. "We were... quite close. Before she decided we ought to be closer than I will allow."

"And now?"

"Now she's a problem that won't stay solved." Rowen's thumb traced a slow circle against Dani's knee. "Clarissa has rather a talent for wanting what she cannot have. And for making everyone around her pay for it."

As if summoned by her name, Clarissa straightened from the bar. She moved through the crowd like smoke, never seeming to hurry but somehow covering the ground with unsettling speed. She didn't approach their booth—that would have been too obvious. Instead, she claimed a small table with perfect sight lines, settling into her chair like a queen taking her throne.

She ordered something amber and expensive. She crossed her legs with precision. And she watched.

"She's seriously eyeballing me," Dani muttered.

But Rowen's response was to reach for her gloves—black leather, worn soft—and peel one off slowly between her teeth. Finger by finger. Though barely audible over the music, the sound stimulated Dani, who watched Rowen's teeth and lips work the leather.

Rowen folded the glove in half, then slid it into Dani's palm. "Do hold this," she said, voice pitched low enough that it seemed to bypass Dani's ears entirely and settle somewhere much deeper. "Behave for me."

"Why?" Dani asked, though her fingers were already closing around it.

Rowen didn't answer immediately. Instead, she shifted slightly, bringing Dani more fully into her lap, Dani's bottom hitting the booth seat between Rowen's spread legs, Dani's legs still over the left one. The movement was subtle but unmistakable—a clear statement of possession for anyone watching.

"Because," Rowen murmured, her bare hand settling on the curve of Dani's neck, "that one's been looking at you as though she's quite ready to bare her teeth. And I don't feel rather inclined to share."

Dani's breath hitched. Across the room, Clarissa raised her glass in what might have been a toast—or a declaration of war.

Rowen's response was to let her hand drift lower, bare fingers splaying across the outside of Dani's dress where her breasts sat with unmistakable ownership. "Do let her look," she said, loud enough for her voice to carry in their immediate vicinity.

The club continued its sultry rhythm around them, but Dani felt as though they existed in a bubble of charged air. Rowen's hand was warm through the fabric of her dress, and when her thumb began tracing lazy patterns against Dani's raised nipples, logical thought became increasingly difficult.

"Rowen," Dani whispered, though she wasn't sure if it was a warning or a plea.

"Hmm?" Rowen's other hand came up to rest against stomach, fingers spread across it. The position drew them closer together, tighter, close enough that Dani could feel the rise and fall of Rowen's breathing. Her breasts against Dani's back felt tight and hard.

"She's still watching." Dani panted between heart murmurs; her pulse was wildly out of control.

"Splendid." Rowen's smile was all sharp edges. "Then she'll see precisely how I'm no longer available, and you're nothing to pursue."

The word sent heat spiraling through Dani's chest, pooling low between her legs creating a soaked gap. She was acutely aware of every point of contact between them—Rowen's thigh beneath her, the solid warmth of her peaked chest, the way her hands seemed to burn through the fabric.

Rowen leaned in, her lips brushing the sensitive spot on the back of Dani's neck. Not quite a kiss, but close enough that Dani shivered. "You're trembling," Rowen observed, and there was something rather predatory in her satisfaction.

"I'm not—" But Dani's protest died as Rowen's mouth pressed more firmly against her neck, a proper kiss this time, slow and raking lower.

A soft sound escaped Dani's lips—half gasp, half moan—and she felt Rowen's smile against her skin.

"That's my dear girl," Rowen murmured, and the possessive endearment sent another wave of heat through Dani's body.

Rowen was a virgin—she'd had her first kiss barely a week ago. Where had she learned such expressions? Such practiced seduction? Enough to put on this full display?

Then Dani understood. Here. This place had taught her. All those evenings watching lovers claim each other openly, witnessing the bold touches and possessive gestures that the outside world forbade. This sanctuary had been Rowen's education in desire, her school for learning how to be confidently masculine, how to take up space, how to claim what was hers. Every theatrical gesture she'd seen, every bold caress between other couples, had become part of her repertoire. She learned the practiced bravado she used to charm Portland's ladies, and her confident way of moving through the world like a gentleman, here in these tunnels, watching love's free expression.

And now she put that education into action, and Dani was burning under every sensitive caress, caught between the innocence beneath Rowen's steely sexual claim and the knowledge that this boldness was born from making a statement.

Across the room, Clarissa's glass had stopped halfway to her lips. Her expression was no longer amused. She watched Dani like she already knew her. Not just from across the room—but from somewhere further. Her eyes glittered under the low lamplight, sharp as garnet and just as dangerous. She raised the glass to her lips—something dark and old-world—and smiled as she sipped. It wasn't seductive. It was... amused.

As if Dani had just walked into the middle of a joke she hadn't been told yet.

Rowen noticed, too. Her hand on Dani's stomach shifted, fingers pressing more firmly, and when she spoke, her voice carried a dangerous edge: "We've got her."

But instead of pulling away, she did something that made Dani's world tilt sideways—she took Dani's free hand and guided it to rest between her own thighs, high up where the fabric of her trousers was warm from her body heat.

"Do you feel that?" Rowen asked, her voice rough with something that made Dani's pulse stutter. Dani, who had always been in control, felt a surge of nervousness when someone else took charge. This new experience was exhilarating. And she could feel the tension in Rowen's muscles, the way her breathing had changed. Could feel the evidence of how this display was affecting her, too.

"Rowen," Dani breathed, her fingers stroking involuntarily against dampness.

The line between performance and reality was blurring. Dani could feel the heat building between them, could see the way Rowen's pupils had dilated. What had started as a territorial display was becoming something else entirely—something that had nothing to do with Clarissa and everything to do with the way Rowen's hands felt on her body.

"I think—" Dani started, then lost her train of thought entirely as Rowen's thumb traced from her knee up to the inside of her bare thigh.

"What do you think, darling?" Rowen asked, and her voice was pure silk and invitation.

Dani's hand pressed in harder on Rowen's center, almost of its own accord. The response was immediate—Rowen's breath caught, her grip on Dani's thigh tightening.

"I think we're getting carried away," Dani managed, though she made no move to stop.

"Are we indeed?" Rowen's smile was wicked. "I rather thought we were simply making certain everyone understands the situation."

But when they both looked toward Clarissa's table, the chair was empty. She had vanished as quietly as smoke, leaving only a half-finished drink and the lingering scent of expensive perfume.

"Well," Rowen said, her voice carrying a note of dark satisfaction. "I'd say the message was rather thoroughly received."

But she didn't let go of Dani. If anything, her hold became more tender, less performative, and more genuine.

"Do dance with me," she said, and it was a request this time, not a command.

Dani nodded, not trusting her voice. Rowen helped her stand as they moved together onto the small dance floor where other couples swayed to the languid music.

Rowen pulled her close—closer than propriety strictly allowed, even in this unconventional space. Dani could feel the line of her body, could smell the scent that was becoming dangerously familiar. When Rowen's hand settled at the small of her back, fingers spread possessively, Dani had to bite her lip to keep from making an embarrassing sound.

They moved together as if they had been doing this for years, their bodies perfectly matched. The music wrapped around them, slow and sweet, and for a while there was nothing but the gentle sway of their movement and the feeling of being held. Around them, other couples danced with the same desperate tenderness.

"She's truly gone?" Dani asked, her lips close to Rowen's ear.

"Mmm." Rowen's hand moved lower over Dani's rear. "Clarissa was never one to fight a battle she couldn't win."

"And this was a battle?"

Rowen pulled back just enough to meet her eyes. "Everything with Clarissa is rather a battle. But you..." Her voice softened. "You're mine."

The words sent warmth spreading through Dani's chest, different from the heat of desire—something deeper and more dangerous as Rowen squeezed her bottom.

They danced through two more songs, occasionally chatting with Rowen's friends, to sample the excellent whiskey and simply exist in this pocket of freedom and possibility. But underneath it all was the constant awareness of each other—the way Rowen's eyes tracked Dani's movements, the way Dani gravitated toward Rowen's warmth.

When they finally left the club, the night air was crisp and sharp after the smoky intimacy inside. Rowen offered her arm like a proper gentleman, and they walked through the quiet streets with easy familiarity to Rowen's buggy.

"Thank you," Dani said as they reached the Mansion. "For this evening. For… all of it."

"I thank you," Rowen replied, "for trusting me with it."

They stood facing each other on the servant's entrance steps, neither quite ready to say goodbye. The space between them hummed with unfinished business, with words neither was quite ready to voice.

"Dani," Rowen said finally, her voice serious. "What happened this evening—with our hands?"

"Was perfect," Dani finished. "All of it."

Rowen's smile was soft, almost shy. "Even the rather dramatic territorial display?"

"Especially that." Dani stepped closer, close enough to reach up and touch Rowen's face. "I've had no one so innocent change so dark before."

"Possibly, I'll surprise you," Rowen said, and the quiet certainty in her voice made Dani's heart skip.

The kiss was inevitable. Soft at first, then deeper than Dani's hands fisted in the lapels of Rowen's coat. She was still on fire from Rowen's hand on her bottom from earlier. SO intoxicated.

When they finally broke apart, both were breathing hard.

"I rather ought to go," Rowen said, though she made no move to step away.

"You should," Dani agreed, though she still held Rowen's coat.

Another moment passed. Another kiss, brief but burning.

"Good evening, Dani," Rowen said finally, her voice rough.

"Goodnight."

Dani watched from the servant's entrance window as Rowen disappeared into the night, her heart still racing from the kiss, from the whole impossible evening. She pressed her fingers to her lips, already expecting the next time she would feel Rowen's mouth on hers. She felt like a giddy teenager again.

Soon, she thought. Soon they would stop pretending that stolen kisses and careful touches were enough.

Soon.

18

WHEN WORLDS COLLIDE

EDWARDIAN ERA

The Saturday came where Dani had to stop lying to herself that she didn't want to go home yet. The past weeks with Rowen had been a revelation—discovering parts of herself she'd never known existed, experiencing a kind of connection that felt both thrilling and terrifyingly real. Every stolen moment, every heated glance, every touch that left her breathless had shown her what it meant to truly want someone to be wanted in return. For the first time in her life, she understood what all the fuss was about.

But underneath the intoxication of new love was a growing certainty she couldn't ignore: she didn't belong here. No matter how charming the gaslight and carriages, how romantic the stolen kisses in shadowy corners, this was still 1905. A world where women like her had no actual choices, where love like theirs had to hide in underground tunnels and behind closed doors. Even in that beautiful, forbidden club, they were still criminals in the eyes of the law, sinners in the eyes of society.

She knew she needed to focus on finding a way home, regardless of the Rowen obsession that had swept every waking moment of her thoughts. But now she had a plan—one that made her heart race with possibility. If she could find a way home, maybe she could bring Rowen with her? The thought was exhilarating. If she could identify the scholars and see how she can find a box, she could return home and build an accepted life with Rowen. Where they could hold hands on the street, where Rowen could be herself without the constant performance, where they could build something real without fear.

Bringing someone from 1905 to the present day would be incredibly difficult. But if anyone could adapt, it would be Rowen. And the alternative—staying here, watching the woman she was falling for live a lie for the rest of her life, never being able to truly be together—was unthinkable.

The crisp autumn air tugged at Dani's coat sleeves as she approached the figure waiting at the end of the drive. Gabriel leaned against the electric buggy, one boot crossed casually over the other, like he belonged in some cigarette ad. Even dressed in a waistcoat and tweed, he looked... chewable.

That used to mean something. Before Rowen.

He straightened as she approached, eyes lighting with a familiar gleam.

"Miss Wood," he said, tipping his hat, "I was fearing you'd left me to wander the fairgrounds alone."

"And miss the spectacle?" She injected brightness into her voice. "Not a chance."

He offered his hand, but she bypassed it, grabbing the side rail and stepping in herself. The seats were narrow—either that or he sat too close on purpose.

He settled beside her, their coats brushing at the elbow. She kept her hands locked in her lap, trying not to notice the scent curling off him. Clean, fresh, and Cedar. Of course he wears cedar.

The buggy hummed to life, wheels clacking over gravel. Her knee brushed his, and she pretended it hadn't happened.

"Eager, are we?" Gabriel turned slightly toward her. "The exposition promises wonders, I've heard. Fireworks. Flying machines. Possibly even dancing bears, though I suspect they're merely metaphorical."

"Where I come from, we don't do events this big anymore." The smile came easily enough.

He tilted his head. "And where exactly is 'where you come from,' Miss Wood?"

Crap. "Oh, you know... Salem."

"Ah. So, you are not city folk."

"Didn't say that."

"Nor did you deny it." He leaned in slightly; voice dipped in amusement. "Let me surmise—you've come all this way in pursuit of some grand opportunity, haven't you?"

"Something like that." She turned, forcing a bolder smile. "And what about you? Always this charming, or do you save it for the rideshare?"

That sparked something new in his expression. "Miss Wood, if you compliment me this early in the day, I may start believing we're friends."

"Depends on how well you behave."

Gabriel chuckled, settling back against the seat. "Tell me, what drew you to our little corner of the world?"

She almost said it—that she was here to manipulate him, find information, and leave. Instead, she shrugged. "Curiosity, I guess. Something told me I'd find answers here."

"To what?"

"Still figuring that out."

She caught his profile—jaw too sharp, nose straight, eyes that missed little. The kind of face that made girls rethink things. She had, once. Before Rowen made it harder to lie about what she preferred.

She shifted in her seat, angling toward him. "Do you always dress like you're about to negotiate a treaty?"

That earned a low laugh. "And here I thought you admired my efforts."

"I do. Most men I know barely manage matching socks."

"A tragedy," he murmured, eyes flicking to hers.

"You're full of surprises, Mr. Dunwich."

"So I've been told. Not all of them flattering."

"Now I'm curious."

He leaned in. "And here I thought I was the curious one."

Something stupid fluttered in her stomach, and she hated how easy it was to want attention even when her heart was somewhere else.

The fairgrounds sprawled before them as they stepped from the buggy. The Lewis and Clark Exposition arched high overhead—columns, flags, carved flourishes bathed in golden afternoon light. Electric bulbs blinked beneath sculpted eaves, and the air thrummed with invention. Children darted between vendor carts, steam hissed from strange machines, and somewhere to the left, a mechanical bird squawked into the sky.

"This is... unreal," she breathed, struck by the towering spires and crackling wires.

"As well, it ought to be," Gabriel replied, coming to stand beside her. "These grounds are intended to astonish. A celebration of man's mastery over nature, of vision made manifest. Nothing here exists by accident."

"Alright, Nikola Tesla. Dial it back."

She turned back to the chaos ahead, trying to drink it all in. The chime of music boxes, the scent of roasting nuts and hot brass voices mingling in half a dozen languages. And yet—her thoughts drifted unwillingly to the man standing beside her.

Gabriel was still, as always. Perfect posture, polished tone, too calm. People fell into orbit around him without realizing it. But under the charm, she felt something quiet and careful, coiled like a spring.

He extended his arm with that old-fashioned grace. "If you would permit me the honor, Miss Wood?"

Her hand moved before her mind did, sliding into the crook of his elbow. The fabric was warm against her skin. Her stomach reacted—not fireworks like with Rowen, but still something. Not overwhelming, but enough to annoy her.

His arm shifted, anchoring her as the crowd thickened and jostled. She didn't pull away. Hours passed as they wandered from pavilion to pavilion—through the Agriculture Hall with its towering grain displays, past the Forestry Building where massive tree trunks stood like ancient pillars, into the Arts and Crafts exhibits where local artisans showed their trades.

Sunlight caught on the curl behind his ear, the subtle flex of his jaw as he scanned each new exhibit, the low drop of his voice when he leaned in close to explain some mechanism or historical detail. Things she shouldn't notice—but did.

He's messing with my wiring. Time to change the pace.

"Let's check the quiet stuff," she said, steering them away from the shrieking children and brightly painted food carts. The exhibit halls offered cooler, echoing spaces filled with brass and wood. Steam engines thudded rhythmically behind red velvet ropes. Hydroelectric models whirred in glass tanks.

One wing honored the original Lewis and Clark expedition, showcasing worn journals with spidery ink nearly faded, and a stuffed grizzly that loomed like it had thoughts about everyone passing by.

She was halfway through making a snide comment about the bear's taxidermy snarl when they stepped into the Machinery Hall and she stopped cold.

At the center stood an intricate clock tower, every gear polished, each arm moving with mathematical grace. Beside it, a brass automaton dressed like a servant announced the hour in a clear voice, then poured tea with unsettling elegance.

"That's..." she started.

"Magnificent," Gabriel finished, stepping forward. His fingers rested on the display's edge.

"You're looking at this thing like it left you at the altar."

He didn't laugh. "It is art, Miss Wood. Precision and vision brought into harmony. Just brilliance, perfectly executed."

For the first time, he sounded like he felt something beyond mild amusement. He rambled about escapements, balance wheels, hand-forged cams. This wasn't performance—it was real.

Her eyes drifted to the plaque: Clock and Automaton by Gabriel S. Dunwich, Sr. She expected a reaction. Pride, acknowledgment, something. Gabriel said nothing, didn't even glance at the nameplate. He touched the brass once and stepped back. Why wouldn't he claim it? She gave herself a slow breath. Stretch the day. Keep the door open.

"You mentioned scholars yesterday," she said casually as they moved to the next exhibit. "The ones who study temporal mechanics? I'd love to meet them."

Gabriel's step faltered almost imperceptibly. "Scholars?"

"You said there were several gentlemen in the city who dabble in such theories." She kept her voice light, curious.

"Ah, yes." His tone grew careful. "I'm afraid they are... quite exclusive in their associations. Not readily available for introductions."

"But they're here? At the exposition?"

"Unfortunately, no. They rarely attend such public gatherings." He guided her toward another display. "Perhaps another time."

Liar. The ease with which he deflected set off every alarm bell she had. There were no scholars, were there? The whole thing had been a setup.

She filed the information away, letting him think she'd accepted his excuse.

Gabriel was too smart to trip over obvious questions. Every time she nudged at the edges, he stepped around it, answering with charm instead of truth. But one thing was clear: he was attracted to her. Really attracted. He looked at her too long and didn't bother hiding it.

If she wanted answers, she'd have to use that. Disrupt the smooth veneer.

They spent the entire afternoon weaving through exhibits, feet aching, stomachs growing empty. The Patent Office pavilion showcased everything from improved corsets to mechanical calculators. In the Transportation Hall, a gleaming automobile sat beside a

                        AMANDA LUPER

primitive flying machine that looked like it might kill whoever was brave enough to pilot it.

Gabriel proved to be an informed guide, explaining the mechanics of steam turbines and the principles behind Edison's latest phonograph. But every technical discussion felt like a deflection, every charming anecdote a way to avoid saying anything real about himself.

She caught him watching her when he thought she wasn't looking—the way her skirt moved when she walked, how she leaned in to examine the exhibits. His attention felt like heat against her skin, and she hated that she noticed.

This is just biology, she reminded herself. Pheromones and proximity.

But when he steadied her elbow as they climbed the steps to the Electricity Building, when his voice dropped to explain how the massive generators worked, when he smiled at her questions with genuine warmth rather than practiced charm—she felt that unwanted flutter again.

Focus. The box. Getting home. That's what matters. And maybe I can take Rowen.

As evening settled, and shadows lengthened across the grounds, she made her move. Leaning in just enough for her shoulder to press into his arm, she sighed quietly.

He stiffened almost imperceptibly. "Are you feeling unwell? Shall I escort you home?"

She tilted her head, lips curving with practiced innocence. "No. I just need some air. This place is packed. And the people are..." She made a face. "Aggressively fragrant."

He almost smiled. "That does tend to happen where the public gathers en masse."

She let her gaze drift lazily over the crowd, as if distracted. The whole day had been perfectly polite conversation and deflection. Time to change tactics. "Maybe I just need food. Can you take me somewhere to eat? Somewhere... normal."

His expression shifted. "Normal, Miss Wood?"

"You know. Real food. With real people. Not caviar on silver spoons. Something where I don't feel underdressed."

"I may know a place," he said carefully. "But you mustn't tell a soul I brought you there. It's hardly the sort of establishment a reputable young lady should frequent unescorted."

"Why not?"

"Because, Miss Wood, if word reached the wrong ears, your virtue and my judgment might be subject to unkind speculation."

She gave a solemn nod. "Utmost secrecy."

Gabriel whispered something to the footman nearby. The man's eyes widened, brows jumping.

Wherever they were going, it would not be respectable.

As they traveled deeper into the city, the landscape changed around them. Clean brick buildings and manicured sidewalks gave way to narrower roads where the architecture grew older, more weathered. The orderly street lighting became sparser, casting deeper pools of shadow between the lampposts.

Here, the air itself felt different—thicker, more alive. Electric lamps cast pools of gold over couples tucked into shadowed doorways and men moving through the dark with quiet purpose. The scent shifted dramatically—less lavender soap and fresh bread, more coal smoke, damp stone, and the briny tang of salt from the nearby docks.

They passed a corner where women in worn shawls gathered around a street vendor selling hot chestnuts, their voices mixing with the distant sound of ship bells and creaking rope. A man in a newsboy cap stumbled from a tavern doorway, cackling, a bottle swinging loose from his fingers. Nearby, dockworkers clustered against a brick wall, their voices low and urgent, the ends of their cigars glowing like fireflies in the gathering dusk.

The buildings pressed closer together here, leaning over the streets like old friends sharing secrets. Laundry lines stretched between tenements, and the warm yellow squares of lit windows revealed glimpses of families gathered around dinner tables, children playing on floors, women bent over sewing.

"So this is where the normal people go?" she asked, taking in the bustling life around them.

"Normal, Miss Wood, is often defined by the cost of your dinner," Gabriel replied, his tone suggesting this wasn't his usual territory, either.

The buggy slowed toward a whitewashed building wedged between its neighbors. The sign above read: *O'Driscoll's.*

With its faded paint, O'Driscoll's was a workingman's pub—no pretense, no polish. Outside, men leaned against the rail with cigars and red faces, laughter pouring off them in waves. Horses shifted and snorted at the hitching posts, steam rising from their nostrils into the cold air. No motorcars here. No parasols. Just whiskey, smoke, and noise.

The buggy came to a stop just shy of the pub.

"Wait," Dani said, frowning, "we're not pulling up to the door?"

Gabriel stepped down first, boots quiet on the stone. "Best not to draw more attention to this motorcar than we already have."

That caught her attention—not the words, but the tone. She reached for the handle, but his hand was already there, offered to her yet again. He didn't rush her.

For the second time that day, she let her hand settle into his. His thumb brushed lightly across the back of her hand.

Oh, sir, I know that move.

She'd been unescorted with him all day—a scandal by any measure. Not that Alvie and Vivienne didn't care for propriety, but she'd slipped out before they could notice or object like she did the countless times with Rowen. Now here she was, alone with a man at a working-class pub as evening fell. The impropriety of it all should have horrified her, but instead it felt... liberating.

The pub door opened, and the world changed.

Inside, the air hit her like a wall: thick with sweat, beer, smoke, and sound. Not just noise, but life. The clatter of pint glasses, boots stomping in time with the music, the rise and fall of voices in a dozen regional brogues. Near the hearth, an Irish band tore through a jig that set the floorboards humming. Someone yelled. Someone laughed louder. Something shattered in the far corner. No one flinched.

This wasn't society. This was survival dressed in noise and whiskey.

No pleasantries. No pretense. And Dani loved it.

She moved through the crowd on Gabriel's heels, doing her best not to look at his shoulders. The way his coat flexed with every step. The way he took the lead. That part was harder to ignore.

O'Driscoll's was a museum of itself—faded posters peeling off wood-paneled walls, hand-painted signs advertising Guinness and Bass Ale, their slogans half-lost to time. Behind the bar, a tarnished mirror loomed, its gold lettering blurred with soot and fingerprints. A crooked sign near the door read: 'NO TRUST GIV-EN—SETTLE YOUR TAB OR SETTLE OUTSIDE'.

She snorted. *At least they're honest.*

Stealing a glance at Gabriel, she half-expected him to bristle at the lack of polish, maybe adjust his collar. But he didn't. He moved with quiet authority, nodding to men who greeted him with a familiarity that meant trust. A few clapped his shoulder. One just lifted his glass.

And then there were women. She noticed them, too. Their smiles. Their body language. Their focus. One, a blonde in a dress that screamed easy, slid a hand down Gabriel's arm as she leaned in, pressing her mouth close to his ear. Whatever she whispered earned a reaction.

The twist in Dani's stomach came fast and sharp. Her jaw clenched before she could stop it. *Not here for this.* Not to flinch when some woman touched him like he was hers. She had no claim, no reason to care.

But still. He was there with her. And it felt... *ick.*

Gabriel didn't let the blonde linger. He offered her a politely detached nod and kept moving, leading Dani past the din toward the back of the pub.

A booth waited for them in the corner, half-shadowed and quiet. A single candle burned low between them, its wax pooled thick around the base. Names and initials scarred the wood, carved deep into the grain. It felt old and honest.

Dani slid into the booth and leaned back. "Lovely place," she said, flat but not unkind.

He slid into the seat beside her, not across, removing his gloves slowly before laying them flat on the table. Neither had chosen the side that faced the wall. Whether it was caution or simple curiosity, neither seemed willing to turn their back on the room.

"A surprising admission," he said, amused. "I was under the impression you preferred more refined company."

"You mean the kind that doesn't smell like sweat and spilled stout?"

"Precisely."

"Well," she said, glancing around, "I really just wanted to get you alone to talk."

"But we are not alone," Gabriel hummed, his eyes drifting. "Merely an observation."

A barmaid appeared, wiping her hands on a faded apron. Dani didn't wait.

"House brew," she said.

Gabriel glanced at her, then nodded once. "The same."

"What, no fancy liquor?" she teased.

He leaned back, folding one arm across his chest. "I would not dare offend the establishment."

Their drinks arrived a moment later, thick mugs clunking against the table. The liquid inside gleamed dark and golden, sloshing near the rim.

Dani nudged one toward him with her knuckle. She knew what she was doing. The good old alcohol-first-on-an-empty-stomach trick.

"Drink."

He raised an eyebrow. "A rather forward request, Miss Wood."

She traced the rim of her mug with one fingertip, slow and soft.

"I don't drink alone. That's no fun."

Something flickered behind his eyes—interest? Maybe suspicion.

After a beat, he clicked his tongue, lifted his mug, and nodded.

"If I must."

She drank half in one go; The fire sliding down her throat, spreading through her chest, curling low in her belly. He drank his too, and she clinked her mug against his with a grin.

He smiled—sweet, but still too polite. Still too tightly wound. She needed the version of him that slipped up. So she ordered another round.

She leaned in slightly, arms resting on the table, posture easy and open—just enough to draw his eye. Not too much. Just enough.

When the next round came, she slid his mug toward him and winked.

His fingers tapped the table once, a tic she'd seen before when he was thinking. There it was again. A glance directed at her lips and the quick look away. His grip tightening on his mug like it might run from him.

She smiled.

Gotcha.

She took another sip, slower this time. Her voice got higher, flirtier and more feminine. "Mr. Dunwich... I'm not exactly the lady you think I am."

A bead of sweat slipped down her collarbone, catching the candlelight.

Gabriel swallowed. When he spoke, his voice had roughened, the edges gone hoarse. "That is... quite evident."

The alcohol was doing its job, but more than that, so was the moment. His posture, always so straight, shifting. Shoulders looser. Movements slower. That tight restraint he wore like a uniform peeled away.

Dani watched it happen like clockwork, coming undone. Her plan was working. It should have felt like victory.

It didn't.

The way he looked at her now unsettled her. Like he hadn't decided whether she was a risk or a reward.

And just beneath the heat, beneath the beer-soft haze, a name stirred in the back of her mind.

Rowen.

She shook her head.

Focus. Getting information.

She played her hand, leaning in just enough to blur the line between flirtation and intent. Her fingers traced the edge of his where it rested on the table—light, almost careless.

They sat and drank for what felt like a half an hour of conversation.

"Tell me, Mr. Dunwich, do you ever grow tired of being so... proper?"

Gabriel gave a quiet huff, shaking his head like she'd asked if the sky ever tired of being blue. "You assume I have a choice."

He pulled his hand back—not out of offense, but with a careful awareness of watching eyes. Polite to a fault. But she caught the pause, the flicker of hesitation.

Dani tilted her head, watching him over the edge of her nose, neck long and bare in the candlelight.

"Everyone has a choice."

He studied her, then smiled slower this time.

"And what would you have me do instead, Miss Wood?"

The question felt like a proposition.

Her stomach flipped. *Shit. This is actually working.*

She leaned in a little more, matching his tone. "Well... for starters, you could tell me what you know about the trinket boxes."

There was a shift. Subtle tension in his shoulders, the way his fingers stilled on the table. He knew something. But instead of answering, he smiled.

"You truly don't tire of this game, do you?"

"It's not a game."

"Oh, but it is." His gaze dropped briefly to her mouth. "And you, Miss Wood, are playing it quite well."

She swallowed hard. The alcohol was blurring the edges of her thoughts, making everything feel warmer, hazier. A flash of Rowen's face surfaced in her mind—guilt tried to claw its way up, but the beer pushed it back down. Gabriel's masculine presence, the way he filled the space beside her, the low rumble of his voice—her body was responding despite herself. The drink made it harder to fight, harder to care. She was trying to unravel him, not the other way around. Her plan was slipping sideways, but she pressed forward, resolve wobbling but intact.

Her hand reached for the edge of his coat, fingers grazing the fabric in a casual tug. He didn't stop her. Their faces were close now, the hormones beating between them in that dark corner, soft shadows catching along his jawline and casting firelight on lips that were dangerously inviting.

She hadn't thought this far ahead.

Plan A was seduction.

There was no Plan B.

But she could adapt. She always adapted.

Her voice fell to a sweet whisper. "Gabriel..."

He gasped quietly. She caught it and smiled to herself.

Gotcha again.

She leaned closer until her lips grazed the edge of his jaw. Just a breath, just a tease, but close enough to count. Then she went in for the kill.

"Mr. Dunwich," she purred against his skin, "I need to find a trinket box. The one I told you about—one that hums and glows. Do you have any idea where I can find another one?"

A long, electric silence crackled between them. His pulse beat hard at his throat. Her breath brushed his lips, closer, closer, almost on the edge of a kiss...

Then he let out a soft, utterly unexpected giggle.

She pulled back, blinking. "What the fuck?"

He tilted his head back, eyes shining, and laughed again—an unguarded laugh that didn't belong in a dark corner booth surrounded by secrets. It was boyish. Mischievous. So bizarrely out of character, she could only stare.

"Are you—" she started, but the words stuck. "Are you laughing at me?"

He tried to compose himself, but another chuckle slipped out. He pressed two fingers to his lips like that might hold it in. It didn't.

"Oh my god," she said flatly, dragging her hand back. "You're drunk."

She'd prepared for anything—evasion, misdirection, even careful lies. What she hadn't expected was laughter.

He blinked up at her, dazed and swaying, his grin too wide for comfort. "Miss Wood," he slurred, syrupy and languid, "you are quite enchanting."

She dragged a hand down her face with a groan. "Jesus."

Whether he didn't hear her or simply didn't care, he lurched forward, lips aimed in the general direction of hers in a tragically unsubtle attempt at a kiss.

She jerked back just in time. "Alright, Mr. Darcy. Relax."

Undeterred, Gabriel pouted—a genuine, drunken sulk, like a child denied dessert. "Miss Wood, I... I told you..." he trailed off, trying to focus. "I do not know what box you are speaking of, but I do know how to kiss."

"You're lying," she said sharply.

He just grinned, sloppy and maddening.

And then, without warning, he straightened—wobbly but determined. "Would you care to see the upstairs residence of my shop?"

Dani sat back, surprised by the shift. But she gathered herself with unrelenting resolve. *If I can get inside his shop when he's sleeping, I can poke around.*

"What would you like to do at your residence?" she asked, trying to keep her tone light.

But everything in Gabriel changed. His posture locked. His expression cleared—too fast. The fog didn't fade; it snapped. She had cracked something open far sooner than intended.

She recalibrated. Her posture softened, her eyes gentled, her voice slipped into something coaxing. She reached across the table, took his hand, and placed it over her heart—dangerously close to her breasts. His hand twitched in an almost squeezing motion, reflex.

"Gabriel," she whispered, "it's loud in here. We've both had too much. I don't want to go home yet. So let's go to your residence."

Gabriel froze, realizing the deadly combination being played. She had used his first name. His eyes darted to where her hand guided his, then to her face. A rush of color flooded his cheeks. He choked on his exhale—not with desire, but panic.

He never expected to get this far so easily. For a man of his class in this time, such a suggestion was scandalous. Dani watched the gears jam in his head as he tried to compute what she'd just done.

Then, abruptly, he stood too fast, knocking his knee against the table. "I must... ingest a meal," he blurted, stiff and mechanical, then turned and bolted toward the bar.

She exhaled, heart pounding—relief, for now. She'd made progress... and yet gotten nowhere.

And now I have to go to his place. At night.

And everyone knows what happens when two attractive, half-drunk people who've been flirting end up alone at night.

But so be it.

Whatever it takes to find a way to get home.

Then a shadow fell over the table. Dani looked up and froze.

Rowen.

Ice bloomed in her chest. She didn't need to guess. One look was enough. Rowen's sharp, composed edges had cracked wide open. She wasn't angry—she was furious. And worse, hurt. Dani felt it hit like a gut punch.

Around them, the pub roared on with music, laughter, and voices rising in drunken songs. But it all blurred. The only thing Dani could see was the storm in Rowen's eyes.

I'm in trouble.

"What," Rowen growled, voice low, "do you mean by this?"

Dani opened her mouth. "I—"

Rowen's gaze shifted to the empty seat next to Dani.

She didn't need to say it. She'd seen enough—maybe not everything, but enough to fill in the blanks. Dani leaning in, Gabriel's flushed face, the body language that screamed louder than words ever could. And the part that cut deepest? Dani hadn't stopped. Not when she had the chance.

But it wasn't just rage tightening Rowen's expression now. It was revulsion. It passed across her face so fast Dani almost missed it, but it was there. Cold, clear, and unmistakable.

I have disgusted her. Oh, my God. She thinks we are together.

Panic wrapped around Dani's chest like a vice. "Rowen, please. Not now. Can we talk tomorrow?"

Rowen remained silent, dismissing the conversation in her mind and turning to leave. But fate had other plans as she walked straight into Gabriel and his mincemeat pie. The splatter was immediate. Warm, sticky filling smeared across her suit, trailing down onto the floor in lumpy streaks. The scent of cloves and meat filled the air like grotesque perfume.

The world kept moving. Drinks poured, feet stomped, voices rose. Dani's sense of reality narrowed into a frozen snapshot.

Gabriel stared down at the mess. Then up. First to the ruined plate, then to Rowen's trembling form. Her fists clenched at her sides, her breath fast and shallow. Dani didn't breathe.

"Mr. Dunwich," Rowen said through gritted teeth.

"Mr. Quinn," Gabriel snapped back, the name sharp as glass.

The haze that had softened Gabriel was gone. In its place, the polished mask clicked back with terrifying ease. He adjusted his coat, brushing at his lapels, then exhaled once. If there was anything to snap you out of a buzz, this was it.

"Miss Wood," he said, his voice cutting. "What precisely is going on here?"

Fantastic. I've really fucked myself this time.

Her stomach dropped. She darted her eyes between Rowen, who was still burning, and Gabriel, whose patience was clearly gone.

Things were unraveling fast.

Gabriel turned to Rowen, that cool, cutting intelligence returning. "And why, sir, are our actions of such personal concern to you?"

Dani scrambled. "Rowen is—" She hesitated.

Half a second. But it was enough.

Gabriel's eyes darkened. "You're lying."

"I swear, Gabriel, it's not what you think—"

He didn't wait for her to finish. With the grace of someone long practiced in disappointment, he set his now empty plate down, the sound dull and final.

The ruined pie sat between them like a monument to her failure.

"I do not take kindly to being made sport of, Miss Wood." His voice stayed even, but something sat underneath... disappointment.

Dani didn't expect it to hit as hard as it did. She told herself it shouldn't matter. But the way he looked at her cut deeper than she liked.

The Gabriel she'd charmed, poked at, teased into letting his guard down—that version was gone. In his place stood a man guarding his pride with steel and silence. A man who no longer saw her as curious.

He turned and walked away without another word. And with him went her chance at the truth.

Dani clenched her fists, jaw tight. *Damn it. Damn it. Damn it.*

Then Rowen's hand was firmly on her arm. She didn't speak or wait—she just pulled.

Dani stumbled to her feet, barely catching her breath as Rowen dragged her through the noise, past the drinkers and dancers and shouting men, into the shadowed hall near the back.

The moment the door clicked shut behind them, Rowen spun.

"Would you care," Rowen said, her voice brittle, "to explain what that was?"

Dani yanked her arm free. "You wouldn't believe me. You didn't even believe me when I said I was from the future."

Rowen let out a laugh—sharp, joyless. "And what I just saw? That needs no explanation?" She stepped in, her voice dropping to a hiss, every word a blade.

"We spent the night wrapped around each other. You looked at me like I mattered. And now I find you here, lips nearly on his?" She spat the word.

Her chest rose and fell fast, but her eyes were clear. Not rage. Not jealousy. Hurt.

And for once, Dani had no words.

She'd meant to unravel Gabriel, not Rowen.

A lump pressed hard in her throat. "Rowen, I—"

But Rowen wasn't done. She stepped in so close Dani could feel the heat of her fury. "Tell me, Miss Wood," she gritted, "was this all some charming little game?"

Dani's stomach bottomed out. "Was what?"

Rowen's fists clenched, nails biting into her palms. "Me. Was I part of the con?"

The word hit like a slap.

Dani dragged a hand through her hair. "That's not what this is."

"No? Then what is it?"

Dani had no answer.

She couldn't tell Rowen the truth because she simply refused to believe it. Every move she made was to find a way back home. She didn't want to make Rowen's struggles seem insignificant. She was spiraling, clinging to the last remnants of her reality. So instead, she backed away.

"I need to go home," Dani muttered.

Rowen remained in her spot. Her shoulders rose and then settled, as if she were holding back something. A tear rolled down her right cheek. The tense silence crackled between them.

Finally, Rowen nodded—a short, resigned gesture. "Yes," she said, her voice clipped. "I'll take you."

She paused at the door, glancing back once. For a fleeting moment, the anger subsided, revealing an unfamiliar emotion beneath the fury.

"You will explain yourself," she said softly this time. "I detest secrets."

Dani let out a dry, bitter laugh. "That's ironic."

Rowen froze, shoulders going rigid.

For a moment, Dani thought she might speak. But whatever words formed, Rowen swallowed them down. Her jaw tightened. Her eyes shifted away. Then she turned, her steps controlled but taut as she led the way out.

Dani followed, silent now, through the fading noise of the pub, past the clink of glasses, the pulse of the band, the fire's warmth. She didn't look back. The mess she'd made would still be there, burning behind her nightmares.

The cold hit harder outside. It wasn't even that sharp, not really, but after the heat of the pub, it felt like punishment.

She followed Rowen in silence to the waiting buggy. Neither of them spoke as they climbed in. The door shut with a soft thud, and the silence inside the cabin swelled. No music. No voices. Just the creak of wheels and the distant clatter of hooves on stone.

They sat on the small bench. Not far apart, but not close either. Dani watched the streets roll by—the warm glow of tavern windows, couples walking arm in arm, the comfortable chaos of people living their lives. Rowen watched nothing at all.

In the dim carriage light, Dani caught glimpses of Rowen's profile. Her jaw was sharply set, and she folded her hands with precision in her lap. But it was her eyes that made Dani's stomach clench—distant, calculating, like she was working through some internal equation.

She's thinking about something. Something final.

Dani wanted to say something. Anything. An apology? Explaining it wasn't what it looked like? That she still didn't know what they were supposed to be? She almost said her name. Just Rowen. But the word jammed in her throat.

The silence stretched, heavy and suffocating. Each turn of the wheels felt like a countdown. Each street they passed another step away from whatever they'd had on that sleeping porch.

Rowen's fingers drummed once against her knee—a soft, rhythmic pattern that sounded almost like resignation. When she spoke, her voice was steady, eerily calm.

"My mother always said that some choices are imposed on us." She didn't look at Dani. "We simply convince ourselves we had a say in the matter."

The words sent ice through Dani's veins. There was something too peaceful about the way Rowen said it, like she'd come to terms with something terrible.

"Rowen—"

"Sometimes," Rowen continued, still staring out the window, "the path forward bec omes... clearer. When illusions fall away."

Illusions. The word hit like a physical blow.

Dani opened her mouth to protest, to explain, but Rowen's expression had shifted into something unreachable. She looked like someone who had just decided—not about forgiveness or anger, but about something much more permanent.

Oh God. She's giving up. On us. On whatever this was.

"What are you saying?" Dani whispered.

Rowen finally turned to meet her eyes. The pain was still there, but underneath it was something worse—acceptance. The kind that came after hope died.

"I'm saying, Miss Wood, that perhaps we've both been fooling ourselves about what was possible between us."

The buggy slowed as the Barrington mansion came into view. Rowen's hands smoothed her skirts with mechanical precision, like she was already preparing to step back into her carefully constructed life.

"There are... practical considerations," she hissed. "Responsibilities that perhaps I've been neglecting in favor of... fantasy."

Practical considerations. Responsibilities.

A chill that had nothing to do with the night air settled in Dani's bones. It was about more than just tonight. This was about Rowen choosing duty over desire, safety over risk. This was about her walking away from everything they'd discovered about each other.

When the buggy finally came to a halt outside the imposing mansion, Rowen remained motionless for a long moment. She controlled her breathing as if readying herself for an unpleasant task.

Dani hesitated, fingers resting on the handle. She turned halfway, desperate to say something that might bridge the chasm that had opened between them.

"Rowen, please—"

"Goodnight, Miss Wood." The formality hit like a door slamming shut. "I do hope you find what you're searching for."

There was a finality in those words that made Dani's chest tighten. Not just goodbye for tonight, but goodbye to whatever they'd been becoming.

Dani opened the door and stepped down into the cold. The buggy pulled away immediately, wheels grinding over gravel. Rowen didn't look back, her silhouette straight and resolute in the carriage window as it disappeared into the darkness.

Standing alone in the drive, Dani felt the shift like a physical thing.

Whatever we were becoming—it's gone now.

And Dani had no one to blame but herself.

19

THE TIME MERCHANT

EDWARDIAN ERA

"You're sulking," Vivienne said without looking up, the silver needle flashing through linen like a blade.

Dani flipped the magazine shut with a sigh and tossed it onto the velvet sofa beside her.

"I'm not sulking," she muttered.

"Brooding, then."

Dani didn't answer. The low-glowing lamps threw soft gold across the parlor, but the tea-scented warmth did nothing to settle the pit in her stomach.

A week of radio silence. A week since the O'Driscoll's disaster, and Gabriel wasn't returning her messages while Rowen might as well have vanished from the earth. She'd wondered if she'd die of old age in this house, trapped in corsets and calling cards forever.

She had screwed up completely. Gabriel was furious, Rowen was furious, and she had no allies, no plan, no scholars, and no clue how to fix any of it.

Dani pressed her eyelids together tightly, forcing the thought away.

The silver needle flashed in and out of the fabric like a tiny blade.

"You look as if you need to get some air in the garden." Vivienne said, not bothering to glance up.

Dani realized she'd been staring blankly at the ridiculous fashion magazine in her lap. She flipped it back open and scoffed. "Just trying to imagine myself stuffed into one of these contraptions."

Vivienne's needle paused for half a breath. "A lady's appearance reflects her character, Danielle. You would do well to remember that."

Dani rolled her eyes and bit back the urge to tell her that corsets weren't a personality trait. Instead, she leaned further into the sofa, letting the warm fabric swallow her whole.

Across the room, Laurel's pen scratched against the thick parchment, her hand moving with quick efficiency. Christmas meals, seating charts, and event planning. Dani had never seen someone so committed to controlling a holiday. That she could work here, in the family's space rather than the servants' quarters, was unusual.

Yet no one batted an eye.

Alvie, meanwhile, sat in an armchair by the fire, watching the flames dance with a look of quiet amusement.

"You know," he mused, swirling his brandy, "you're settling into this family quite well, Danielle. One might think you never intended to leave."

"Maybe I won't," Dani said, half-smiling since her leads and options to find a way home was dead.

"You're lucky, you know. This house. These people. You could do considerably worse." Alvie raised his glass in a half-toast. "Honestly, I hope you never find your way back."

Laurel's pen halted mid-line.

Her head lifted fast, eyes sharp. "That is a wildly inappropriate thing to say, Mr. Barrington."

He grinned, clearly pleased with himself. "Come now, Laurel. You must admit—it's been more interesting since she arrived."

Laurel placed the pen down with care. "She has a family. People who may look for her."

Vivienne gave a soft exhale, something close to a laugh. Her eyes never left her sewing. She didn't correct him. Didn't join the defense.

Because she didn't need to.

Everyone here already knew.

Dani caught it. That strange tension threading through the room—not new, just exposed.

Alvie swirled his drink, still watching Dani. "Quite strange," he said, "how much it bothers you, Laurel. Miss Wood has taken nothing from you... unless you think someone else has filled your position."

Laurel's spine straightened. "Don't be ridiculous."

Alvie leaned back in his chair. "I've always had a habit of taking in strays."

The words landed with a bang.

Vivienne's hand paused, needle suspended.

Laurel stared straight ahead.

Nothing else moved.

Vivienne's stitching resumed, smooth as ever. "Speaking of offspring."

The room snapped back into motion. A quiet shuffle of movement near the doorway drew Dani's attention. Shannon.

She hovered just inside the parlor, hands neatly clasped in front of her, her expression carefully controlled. But Dani saw it. The way her shoulders tensed. The way Alvie looked away.

Oh. Oh, shit.

Dani's mind raced.

The resemblance. Shannon was the person Alvie trusted more than anyone. That he had taken her in so easily, without question.

She had been right all along—Shannon is his daughter, and Vivienne had just confirmed it without saying a word. It didn't need an explanation. Is this the arrangement? Vivienne kept the name, Laurel got what remained, and they all lived with it. A love child, a mistake folded into the fabric of their lives.

Shannon didn't react or even glance at him. Instead, she kept her focus on Vivienne. "Mrs. Barrington, may I have a word with Miss Wood?"

Vivienne barely looked up from her sewing. "Of course."

Dani stood and followed Shannon out into the corridor, the warmth of the parlor fading as they climbed the narrow servants' stairs to the upper quarters. Shannon led her into the shared living space, where a small, wrapped parcel sat on the worn wooden table.

Turning, Shannon offered a small, wrapped parcel. "A delivery boy came." She tapped the label with a gloved finger. "It is addressed to you."

Dani took the package, the paper cool against her fingertips. Something about it felt weird. She undid the twine with careful fingers, peeling back the layers of brown paper to reveal something small and metallic. A mechanical case. She turned it over in her hands. The craftsmanship was intricate—etched metal, tiny gears, delicate details that felt too familiar.

Her heart stuttered. A trinket box.

Her mind raced as she turned it over, fingers grazing the delicate gears and engravings. The design looked identical to the trinket box that had started this whole mess, but with a different opening mechanism.

"What is it?" Shannon asked while peering over Dani's shoulder.

"I think I know who made it." Dani swiped her fingers over the engravings on the lid down to the side where she softly pressed the small button.

The reaction was instant—a faint click, a quiet whir, and then light burst to life, casting sepia-toned images onto the ceiling. The projection flared outward, distorting slightly before resolving into a moving scene that made Shannon gasp and step back.

Dani didn't move. Holograms and high-tech displays weren't shocking to her, but Shannon looked like she was about to pass out.

The projection shifted.

Downtown Portland. Bustling crowds. Cars and horse-drawn buggies. Women in layered skirts, men tipping their hats. The sun shone, bouncing off polished storefronts.

Then it jumped out of focus.

Pioneer Square park. A wooden bench.

Two figures.

A man and a woman.

The woman laughed as she scooted close beside him.

Shannon's voice came out barely above a whisper. "What is this magic?"

The man in the recording turned his head.

For the next few agonizing seconds, the distortion gradually eased and sharpened, allowing her to recognize him clearly. *Rowen.*

Beatrice leaned in and placed a soft, long kiss on his lips. His arms, the same arms that held Dani, wrapped around her waist.

Dani felt the world tilt.

A hard lump rose in Dani's throat. Her heart kicked like a trapped bird.

The projection cut out, leaving them in sudden silence. The mechanical case slipped from her fingers and hit the floor with a metallic crack while the image of Rowen and Beatrice echoed through her skull like a punch to the ribs. Her eyes burned, but she couldn't move, couldn't process what she'd just seen.

Shannon stepped close, her voice careful. "Miss?"

Dani backed away, slow and shaky.

"Miss Wood," Shannon said again, more insistent. "Perhaps you should—"

She didn't hear the rest.

She turned, snatched the case off the floor, and hurled it.

It shattered against the parquet. The lid skittered across the room.

The door flew open.

Edmund appeared like he'd materialized out of the air, panic written all over him with eyes locked on Shannon, like he'd feared the worst.

His eyes shot between Dani, the shattered device, and Shannon, who met his stare with a silent warning.

"Excuse us," Shannon said, her voice abrupt but calm. "Just... leave us."

Edmund wavered. Hero instincts alive and twitching. But Shannon's look allowed no argument, and after a beat, he stepped back through the door, leaving behind the fractured quiet.

The moment he was gone, Dani's eyes welled with pools of hot tears, breaching the lashes and painting her cheeks. She hunched forward; arms wrapped tight around her middle. Shannon rested a hand between her shoulder blades, drawing slow, quiet circles.

"Come now," she said gently. "You should wash up and get some rest."

Dani didn't argue. Her body moved on autopilot, numb to the hallways and hush of the house as Shannon guided her down to her room. She barely felt the stairs beneath her feet.

But the second she sat on the edge of her bed, the numbness cracked.

Rowen's kiss with Beatrice looped through her mind like a jagged refrain. And worse, the questions followed.

Rowen's final decision in the buggy that night, her words about duty. Was that her saying she was going to be with Beatrice? But why?

Dani had tempted Gabe for access—for answers. Not for desire, well, mostly. Not for love. But that didn't matter now. Rowen had seen strategy; she'd seen betrayal. And Beatrice? She'd seen an opportunity and stepped right into the space Dani burned wide open.

Dani let out a strangled noise, somewhere between a laugh and a sob, and pressed the heels of her palms into her eyes.

Okay, universe. Message received. Loud and clear. Getting her heart kicked in wasn't part of the plan. But maybe it should've been. She deserved it for getting her lips that close to Gabe.

But then her eyes fell to the shattered device Shannon brought to the room and placed on the dresser. The impossibly intricate gears and delicate craftsmanship. Only one man-made machines like that. Only one man could've made this box.

She wiped her face with her sleeves, smearing away both tears and the last remnants of her pride. All this time, he'd been stringing her along, pretending to be oblivious. But she was done. No more playing it safe, no more strategy, or waiting. Tomorrow, she will force him to give her answers; she'll extract the truth herself because sending that box was a messed up thing to do.

"Where's Gabriel?" Dani stormed through the door of the clockery, ignoring the chime overhead.

The old man behind the counter stiffened. His eyes flicked toward the door to the back room—confirmation enough.

Dani shoved past him.

Dust curled in a shaft of light from a bare bulb overhead. Shelves cluttered with gears and cracked blueprints lined the walls. But it was the bookcase—slightly ajar—that drew her in.

A heavy footstep behind her. The old man's hand shot out.

She spun on him. "Touch me and I'll scream loud enough to bring the street running. And when they get here? I'll ruin you."

His hand dropped.

She turned back and pulled the bookcase open. Cold air rushed out. A staircase led into the darkness below, steep and narrow. The scent of damp stone and burning metal filled her nose.

Gripping the railing, she descended.

The basement stretched wider than the shop above, its stone walls blackened with soot and age. Workbenches lined the space in chaotic arrangement—some cluttered with brass gears and delicate springs, others bearing half-assembled contraptions that seemed to defy the century they occupied. The air hung thick with the scent of oil, metal shavings, and something else... ozone, like the aftermath of lightning.

A fire burned low in an ornate hearth that looked transplanted from some grand manor, its flames casting dancing shadows across walls lined with blueprints, sketches, and what appeared to be newspaper clippings from decades she couldn't identify. The light flickered over a figure seated in a leather armchair that had seen better centuries, smoke curling lazily from a cigarette between his fingers.

He didn't turn when she reached the bottom of the stairs, though she could see his reflection in a cracked mirror propped against the far wall. The profile was unmistakable—Gabriel's strong jaw, the same aristocratic nose—but something was different about the way he held himself.

"Well, well," he said, voice carrying an accent she couldn't place—cultured but with edges that belonged to no single era. "The infamous Miss Wood finally decides to visit the bowels of my establishment."

She froze on the last step. That voice was familiar yet foreign, like hearing a song played in the wrong key.

"You know who I am."

"Oh, darling." He took a long drag from his cigarette, still not turning. "I know far more about you than you might be comfortable with. The question is—what brings you to my little sanctuary of impossibilities?"

The casual endearment made her skin crawl. No one in 1905 spoke like that, certainly not to a woman they'd never met.

"I'm looking for Gabriel Dunwich."

"Mm." He flicked ash into a crystal tumbler that definitely didn't belong in this century. "And what makes you think I'd know where to find such a person?"

"Because this is his shop."

A low chuckle rumbled from the chair. "Is it? How delightfully simple you are." Finally, he turned, and Dani's breath caught in her throat.

Gabriel's face stared back at her, but wrong in every conceivable way. The same intelligent eyes held none of Gabriel's careful restraint—instead, they glittered with predatory amusement. The mouth that had spoken so formally, so precisely, now curved in a smile that belonged in a jazz club or a speakeasy, not an Edwardian clockmaker's basement.

"You look like your brain just short-circuited," he said, rising from the chair with a fluid grace that made Gabriel's measured movements seem quaint by comparison. Black clothing covered him completely—a fitted jacket that looked futuristic, trousers that hugged his form with modern precision, and heavy black boots with thick soles and industrial buckles that were certainly not available in 1905. Everything about him screamed anachronism.

"What are you?" she whispered.

"Now that," he said, producing a silver flask from somewhere in his impossible coat, "is a much more interesting question than who." He unscrewed the cap with a theatrical flourish. "Jack Daniel's? Something familiar in this sea of primitive spirits."

The scent hit her—pure, undiluted whiskey that tasted of home and modernity. Her mouth watered despite herself.

"Who the fuck are you?" she managed, trying to inject steel into her voice.

He laughed, the sound rich and genuinely delighted. "Oh, I do love a woman with a mouth on her. So refreshing after all the simpering misses of this tedious era." He gestured to his face with lazy fingers. "Take a guess, sweet thing. Same canvas, different artist."

Her mind reeled. The resemblance was impossible—not just similar, but identical down to the smallest freckle. Yet everything else screamed difference. This man moved like he'd never known constraint, spoke like the twentieth century lived in his throat, and looked at her like she was prey he was deciding whether to devour.

"You're not Gabriel."

"Aren't I?" He tilted his head, studying her with unsettling intensity. "Depends entirely on your definition. I have his face, his memories... well, some of them. Though I've picked up quite a few extras along the way." He gestured vaguely upward. "The original recipe is upstairs brain rotting. We call him Sr.—or 'Dad' when I'm feeling particularly charitable. I'm Enver."

He circled her, slow and deliberate, like a shark testing the waters. "The real question, Miss Wood, is what you're willing to do to get the answers you so desperately seek."

"I just want to know where Gabriel is."

"Do you?" He stopped in front of her, close enough that she could smell tobacco and whiskey and something else—electricity, like standing too close to power lines. "Or do you want to know about the little trinket that brought you here? About the lights you've been seeing? About why reality keeps... shifting around you?"

Her heart hammered against her ribs. "How do you—"

"Know about that?" His smile turned sharp. "Oh, darling. I know about many things. The question is whether you're prepared to pay for that knowledge."

He moved to one workbench, fingers trailing over devices that seemed to hum with their own internal light. "Information, you see, is a currency far more valuable than gold. Especially information about time."

"What do you want?"

"Now we're getting somewhere." He turned back to her, flask raised in mock salute. "I want to know why a perfectly modern girl like you is so interested in my friend Gabriel. I want to know what you did to put such delicious misery in his eyes. And I want to know..." His gaze raked over her with uncomfortable intensity. "What you're willing to sacrifice to get home?"

The words hung in the air between them like a challenge. Dani felt the weight of the basement pressing down on her—all that stone and shadow and impossible machinery. This man, whatever he was, held answers she needed. But everything about him screamed danger.

"Fine," she said, lifting her chin. "But you answer my questions, too."

She stared, stunned. "You're..."

"A time traveler? Guilty. Been bouncing around decades like a pinball. The '80s were wild. You'd love the cocaine." He grinned. "Your little girlfriend up there? She's adorable, by the way. All that 'proper gentleman' bullshit. What a dumpster fire."

Dani's blood chilled. "You know about—"

"That she's a woman? Please." He rolled his eyes. "I've seen drag kings in the 1920s Berlin and cross-dressing spies in World War Two. Takes one to know one, sweetheart."

The casual way he said it, like Rowen's secret, was just another amusing tidbit, made her want to hit him.

"You sent that box," she said, the pieces clicking together. "The recording."

His smile turned sharp. "Guilty again. A little love letter, you could say."

"You thought destroying me was funny?"

"I thought you deserved it." His voice hardened. "You broke Gabriel's heart. Poor bastard was ready to tell you everything, and you played him like a fiddle. So yeah, I thought you should know what your precious Rowen was up to while you were busy seducing my friend."

She downed the drink he'd poured her, welcoming the burn. "You don't know why I did it."

"Don't I? You want to know how you landed here? Buckle up, buttercup."

She held out her glass. "Please. Enlighten me."

"Five years ago, I'm fixing a watch, and this guy shows up out of thin air. Hoodie, logo tee, goggle shades—not exactly 1900 attire. You remember the black-and-white photo that was all the rage? That's him."

She blinked. "The time travelling hipster guy?"

"2030. Aerospace program. He ripped himself through time, trying to prevent some climate disaster. Lucky for him, he landed on this very street in front of the Clockery."

"Let me guess, you helped him?"

"In exchange for the blueprints to his tech, I helped get him home. After that, I started selling time travel to the highest bidder." He didn't even blink, swirling his flask like he was discussing the weather. "Why do you think some people die young and others seem to live forever? Why do some always win—wars, elections, investments—and others lose? Time is just another currency, darling. You either have it, or someone else owns it. Capitalism at its finest."

Dani stood, pacing. "What about the lights and things I've been seeing for years? Things that appear and disappear?"

Enver's eyes sharpened with interest. "You've noticed. Time loops creating different versions of a person cause converging realities. Those who have traveled, like you—you see through the veil. It's thinner for us. What looks like ghosts are actually moments where two times briefly touch."

"I'm not going crazy?"

"No. The more loops, the more versions, the more convergence points." He gestured vaguely at the air. "Reality tears at the seams when we meddle too much, and Gabriel made one hell of a cosmic whoopsie. That's why there are three of us running around—me, Sr. upstairs, and one more poor bastard native to this timeline who you absolutely destroyed at that pub."

So the reason she'd seen the lights back in the present was because she'd already traveled into the past. She'd already lived in 1905. The loop was already in motion. Which meant, technically, all of this had already happened. *What a complete mind-fuck.*

Her eyes landed on the wall of identical wooden boxes. "And these?"

"Unfinished. I haven't produced any new boxes in three years. Well, since..." He trailed off, motioning toward another closed door behind him. "We don't let customers see what happens when you push time too far. There's a man in there who's lived the same day for forty years. Thought he could relive his wedding night. Now he doesn't remember if he's married or just pretending."

Dani swallowed.

"And a woman came in last winter—paid everything she had to rewind an hour. Wanted to unsay something cruel. The box malfunctioned. She rewound a week. Her son was never born."

A sickness crawled into her chest. This wasn't just a trinket or a portal—it was a system. A luxury for the rich. A punishment for the poor.

"I just need one that works properly," she said. "I want to go home."

Enver sighed, stepping beside her. He picked up a box and began adjusting its gears.

"Some are doorways," he said. "This one's a time accelerator."

He turned a key. On the workbench, an apple aged to rot in seconds. He pulled the key out, and the effect stopped.

"The one you need does more. It travels."

She looked at the box in her hands.

"This isn't random," he said. "Each dial is a time coordinate. Set it wrong, and you'll end up anywhere—or nowhere."

"And the key?"

He opened a hidden panel, revealing interlocking gears. "It winds the mechanism. Locks in the destination. Turn it without tuning it first, and you get what's left over. That's how you got here."

Dani's breath quickened. "If I turn it now—"

"We could end up in Rome, 1920s Paris, or two minutes from now in this same room. That's the trick, Dani," Enver said, his voice suddenly softer. "People think time is theirs. That it belongs to them. But it never did. It's always belonged to someone who could afford to bend it."

She yanked her hands back. "No, thanks."

"That's why I tune it. You can't just pick a date—you need a frequency strong enough to pull you through."

"Cut the cryptic bullshit. You obviously enjoy having something I need, so what's it going to cost me? And don't say my soul—I'm pretty sure I left that in the future."

He looked her over, and for a moment, something almost like respect flickered in his eyes. "You've got a spine, I'll give you that. Even when you're absolutely terrified and probably questioning your sanity."

"Try again."

"Fair enough. Points for honesty." He shrugged, but there was something almost fond in his expression now. "You can start by answering some questions. Think of it as a friendly interrogation."

She crossed her arms. "Fine. What do you want?"

"Do you know where Cleo Irvington is?"

Her body went rigid.

"Yes. Mary's great-grandmother. Why?" she answered.

"Mary," he repeated. "Where is Cleo?" His smirk had faded for the first time.

"Buried in the cemetery by St. Johns Bridge. Mary inherited everything."

It was grief or regret that crossed his face.

"That's not where I looked," he murmured. "So that's how the box got to you, I bet. But the key... that's still a mystery."

Before she could ask more, footsteps pounded down the stairs.

Gabriel appeared in the doorway and his eyes locked on hers. Cold. Angry.

Enver didn't move. "And here comes the rescue party."

"She's coming with me," Gabriel snapped.

Dani didn't have time to react as Gabriel grabbed her arm.

"No! Let me go!"

His grip was firm but careful—he didn't trust himself to let go.

They passed the old man at the counter, who waved dreamily. "Bye, little lark. Love you."

"Please, Gabriel," she rasped.

He didn't reply while he pulled her into the street.

20

WHAT WE SETTLE FOR

EDWARDIAN ERA

She looked back at the door to the clockery as it slammed shut.

Gabriel grabbed her wrist and pulled her down the side of the building, his pace urgent. No words passed his lips—he was brooding.

Right. He's obviously still furious about O'Driscoll's, she thought.

She yanked her arm, but he didn't let go.

"Don't worry, I get it. You think I played you."

Still no response.

She laughed bitterly. "Oh for God's sake, what? Is it because I went looking for answers?"

"Hold your tongue," he said under his breath.

She jerked away. "Of course. Heaven forbid I get some answers."

"I said, be quiet." His voice wasn't angry now—it was taut. And something about the way he said it made her freeze. "We shall not speak out here!"

It wasn't rage coursing through him. It looked more like fear. He wasn't dragging her away as punishment—he was dragging her away to get her out of sight. Pushing open a narrow green door tucked between crates at the rear of the building; He motioned her inside.

"Now," he muttered.

She stepped into the hidden entrance reluctantly, and the door slammed behind her.

Inside, the quiet was jarring. Polished floors gleamed beneath Persian rugs. Brass sconces cast a warm light over elegant wood trim, and vivid green damask wallpaper covered the walls, its bold floral patterns trailing up a private staircase.

It was elegant. Expensive. Too expensive for a simple clockmaker.

Of course. The sale of trinket boxes.

"You've been living in this?" she spat.

He turned on her, face pale and thunderous. "You went down there alone. With him."

She braced herself. "I didn't know he was down there—I was looking for you. But guess what? It worked out; he actually gave me answers."

"He provided lies."

"He gave me more than you have!"

"That man—Enver—is not to be trusted. He is what remains when everything decent is hollowed out. I would have us survive this!"

"I would have my life back!" She shouted, chest heaving.

"You do not comprehend the damage this man has wrought," his voice fraying now. "He has altered people. Time. Broken entire versions of us and everyone we hold dear in his pursuit."

"Pursuit of what?"

He looked away, biting his knuckles.

"Exactly," she muttered, hand to her temple, fingers trembling as words poured forth. "You keep claiming to protect me, but you won't even say what I'm supposed to fear. Quit keeping me trapped in this stone-age fever dream!" She shook her head with helpless anger. "I want to go home!"

"What of Rowen? Are you hoping to take her home?" he replied quietly.

Dani stiffened. He knows more than I expected.

"She hates me. And Beatrice has already swooped in. So, it's over. Now I'm stuck here to watch their happy ending. Thanks for that."

He stepped forward, closing the distance between them. Each movement shrank the space until she stumbled backward, her breath quickening with every inch until her back met the cold, unforgiving wall. His arm rose smoothly, resting beside her head, caging her in place.

"I protect you from a monster—a man who bends time as if it were clay, who would send you anywhere but home if given the chance. I cannot trust him. Nor can I trust that box to carry you safely."

He was too close. Just like in O'Driscoll's.

The hallway was silent. Empty. She could hear the ticking of his grandfather clock at the base of the stairs.

The neckline of her dress suddenly felt tighter. Her cheeks flushed. Her heart slammed against her ribs.

There it was again, that impossible, magnetic pull she'd tried so hard to ignore. It wrapped around her, sharp and familiar—his scent curling through her like smoke. His jaw was all hard lines and restrained fury. The sweep of his dark hair caught the light as he moved, and those pale eyes burned with something far more dangerous than anger: longing.

A conflict between her instincts and self-control paralyzed her. The desire to flee battled against her need for physical connection. She grasped for the reasons she'd kept her distance, but they dissolved like ash. All that remained was the question: Who would make the first move?

"I do not belong in this time. You only want me because I am a novelty. This isn't real, Gabriel." She forced herself to look away, turning her face toward the door.

He caught her chin and tilted her back to him. It was firm. Possessive. The gesture alone sent a jolt straight through her. His eyes dropped to her mouth, then returned to her eyes.

"I have known other women. With you, I do not want control—I want to tear your clothes off."

She avoided his eyes, reality preventing her from making contact. Sadly, from a physiological perspective, her body had already betrayed her—a pulsating sensation between her legs, intense and slippery. This wasn't affection; it was hormones, proximity, and the way tension like this lit up her nerves.

The fight inside her collapsed, messy and fast. *Fuck it.* She leaned in, just enough. Her lips curled into a dangerous smile, and a taunt tumbled out.

"Do it."

He froze for half a second. Now that he had permission, he had to summon the nerve.

Inhaling deeply, his eyes fluttered shut as he leaned in, his lips finding hers in an explosion of a kiss. It wasn't soft or careful—it was raw, frantic, full of panic and grief. She kissed him back hard, mouths open, teeth clashing. His ascot hit the floor. Her dress bunched in his fists.

She could feel his hardness against her as his body pressed close. His hands skimmed her arms, calloused fingers grazing skin. She gasped from surprise and grabbed his coat, pulling him closer, anchoring herself to him.

He kissed her like he meant it. Like he needed her to burn.

"I am hopelessly in love with you," he confessed, his voice velvet against her ear.

"Don't," she warned, though her fingers tightened in his hair. "You people call everything love. This is infatuation, Gabriel. I can't give you what you think you want."

He didn't respond with words. A shuddering gasp escaped her as her back bowed, a silent moan trapped in her throat. Fingers curling in his shirt. He pulled up her dress, pressing his hard length against her through her undergarments, the friction against her clit making her arch into him. Her tilting and thrusting hips made him rock hard, and the pressure between her legs against her warm center intensified.

"If you allow me to continue, I shall not stop once I am inside you. I will ruin your propriety," he whispered.

"Shut up," she replied. "Just—don't talk. Not right now."

Years ago, her propriety slipped out the window. Propriety had saved no one from heartbreak. Rules hadn't stopped Rowen from walking away. So, what was the point?

"Propriety can go to hell," she growled.

His palms pressed against her remaining thigh, lifting her slightly as he pushed her harder against the wall. The wainscoting dug into her back, the physical discomfort a welcome distraction. When a loud moan tore from her throat, he paused for a breathless beat.

"We must go upstairs." His voice was strained, maintaining that ridiculous formality that should have annoyed her, but somehow made this easier. It made him feel less real, more like a character in some costume drama.

"Then take me," she answered.

He didn't release her immediately, instead pressing his forehead against hers, his breathing heavy. The endearment was so sweet, but damn it! She wasn't looking for love. She was looking for oblivion.

His arm circled her waist, guiding her toward the grand staircase. Each step up felt like a decision—not a good one, but a decision. She knew what Rowen would say. She was running from pain instead of facing it, and this wouldn't help but only make everything messier. But Rowen had forfeited her right to an opinion the moment she'd refused to listen. The portraits of his ancestors watched with painted disapproval as she followed him down the lavishly decorated hallway to his bedroom.

"I have imagined bringing you here," he admitted softly, his hand on the doorknob. "Though never quite under these circumstances."

She swallowed hard. "What circumstances did you imagine?"

"Perhaps with fewer shouts and more... intention." His eyes met hers. "I may be a man of another time, but I recognize a wounded heart when I see one."

She felt exposed suddenly, more naked than any physical undressing could accomplish. "Are you changing your mind?"

"Not in the slightest," he replied, opening the door. "Merely acknowledging the terrain."

The bedroom door swung open to reveal a space frozen in time—heavy velvet curtains, a massive four-poster bed, and an elegant fainting couch positioned near the window. The antique dresser held a clutter of pocket watches, cufflinks, small brass clocks, and silver-handled brushes.

"I wasn't expecting company this evening," he said, suddenly self-conscious.

"I don't care," she replied honestly, and reached for him.

She kissed him roughly, backing him toward the dresser with unexpected force. His surprise quickly gave way to enthusiasm as he fumbled with the remaining buttons and hooks of her dress and corset. The garment fell open, and his eyes glowed appreciatively.

"Heaven help me... your muscles, someone carved you from marble," he breathed. Her toned body was unlike anything he had ever seen on a woman.

His hands were everywhere now, sliding over her exposed skin with growing confidence. She closed her eyes, imagining different hands: smaller, softer, more meaningful. Rowen's hands. Rowen's mouth. It should have made her stop, this intrusive comparison, but it only fueled her determination.

Lifting her suddenly, he sat her on the edge of the dresser. Several of his precious timepieces toppled to the floor with metallic clatters. He didn't seem to notice.

"I do hope you'll forgive my impetuousness," he murmured as his fingers worked the rest of her dress off. "I find myself rather overcome."

"Less talking," she instructed, helping him with his remaining clothes. "More action."

His eyebrows rose at her directness, but he complied eagerly, removing his own jacket and waistcoat with practiced efficiency. When he finally pressed against her, skin-to-skin, she felt a flicker of genuine desire cut through the emotional fog.

"Christ," slipped past her lips as his hungry mouth closed over her breast. He kneaded the soft swell, flicking her nipple with his tongue, then drifted lower, palms gliding over the hard lines of her abdomen. Hooking both hands beneath her thighs, he pried them wider to mold his hips to hers. The dresser's chilled wood bit into her back, only intensifying the molten throb building between her legs.

"I have wanted you from the moment I saw you," he whispered against her collarbone.

She didn't reply, didn't want to encourage the sentimentality. Instead, she reached between them and grabbed his cock, making her intentions clear. He groaned, the sound vibrating through the room.

"Shall we?" he suggested, glancing meaningfully toward the fainting couch.

Nodding, she allowed him to guide her. The velvet upholstery was cool against her back as he positioned himself above her, his eyes hungry.

"Are you quite certain this is what you desire?"

For a moment, she almost laughed at his formality, at the absurdity of their situation. Instead, she pulled him down against her again, answering with her body by tilting her hips in a rolling motion.

"Fucking shut up and take me," she insisted.

When he finally entered her, the initial discomfort was sharper than she'd expected. It had been a long time since she'd been with a man. Rowen would have probably gone more slowly, she thought.

He gasped, his hands gripping tightly on her hips as he established a rhythm. "You feel divine."

She closed her eyes, focusing on the physical sensations rather than his words.

But this wasn't about pleasure—not really. It was about feeling something other than emptiness, even if that something was just a physical sensation bordering on pain.

He withdrew and moved down her body, kissing down her abs as he positioned his lips between her legs.

The first touch of his tongue was messy and poorly rhythmic. She closed her eyes, trying to surrender to the sensation. But his technique was all wrong—too direct in places that needed subtlety, too gentle where she craved pressure. Nothing like Rowen's knowing touch, which had always found exactly the right rhythm, the perfect spot.

After several minutes of his well-intentioned but misguided efforts, frustration overtook her. This wasn't working. The comparison was too stark and present in her mind.

"Stop," she snapped.

He looked up, concern etched across his features. "Have I offended you?"

"No, just—" She pushed herself up on her elbows. "I need something else."

Understanding dawned in his eyes. "What would please you?"

She considered for a moment, then decided. "Take me from behind," she instructed.

"As you wish," he replied, helping her rise from the chaise lounge.

She positioned herself at the edge of his four-poster bed, bending forward until her forearms rested against the embroidered coverlet. That vulnerable position should have made her uncomfortable, but it felt like precisely what she needed—something raw and primal that couldn't be confused with making love.

He stood behind her, his hands tracing the curve of her spine with unexpected tenderness.

When he finally positioned himself and pushed inside her, the angle was different—deeper, more intense, pushing an unintended moan from her lips.

He gasped, his hands gripping tightly on her hips as he established a rhythm. "It would be heaven to release inside you."

"Don't" she replied with a muffled sound as her cheek pressed against the pillow.

Focusing on the physical sensations rather than his words, she closed her eyes. In this position, with her face hidden from him, she could pretend more easily. Could imagine different hands on her skin. Different words in her ear. His movements grew more urgent, less controlled. She knew he wouldn't last long—could feel it in the increasingly erratic thrusts of his hips, the tightening of his fingers on her skin.

In her mind, it was Rowen above her—Rowen inside her. The fantasy was imperfect but necessary.

As he pulled out and shuddered against her backside, his release was accompanied by a muffled, strangled moan against her shoulder. The entire encounter had lasted perhaps twenty minutes.

He collapsed beside her on the bed, panting. Reality seeped back in. The comparison was stark and unavoidable. This had been... something. A distraction. A release. But not everything. Not even close.

"That was..." he began, searching for words.

"Yeah," she agreed noncommittally.

Staring at the ceiling, she thought of Rowen again. Remembering their laughter until sunrise.

This had been exactly what she'd expected: quick, sufficient, ultimately empty. But it had served its purpose for a moment.

Pulling back slightly, Gabriel rested his forehead against hers, his lips parted. His chest rose and fell unsteadily. Lost in thought, he paused for a long moment—a genius with the constant whirring of ideas in his head, like wheels turning and spinning.

An icy dread washed over her as she wondered if Enver would burst through the door at any moment. Did Enver and the old man, amidst the quiet hum of the shop, hear them upstairs? How awkward would it be when she left? She'd used the vertical trolley downhill, so no buggy was waiting. Her mind trailed into endless thoughts, only to be broken by his head lifting with the softest expression.

"Marry me," he said.

She blinked. "What?"

His hand drifted down to hers, thumb brushing over her knuckles like a whisper.

"If you consent to marry me, I shall see you safely home myself. That I can guarantee. You will have time—perhaps a night, or two at most—to make your farewells and see to whatever matters require your attention."

"And in return?" she asked.

"Return with me and help me break the cycle—by staying. It is the only way. No more madness. We put an end to it. Together."

Dani stared at him. At the wreckage of her choice.

What cycle? What was he talking about? The time loops? The multiple versions of people? Enver's explanation raced through her mind, but an interruption prevented him from clarifying Gabriel's pursuit and goals.

"What cycle?" she asked.

"Enver did not tell you?"

"No, because you interrupted."

Gabriel's jaw tightened. For a moment, she thought he might explain. Instead, he simply asked again,

"Do you accept?"

She stared at him, weighing her options. Rowen was done with her. There was nothing left for her in this time—no allies, no answers, no hope of fixing what she'd broken. She wanted to go home more than she wanted her next breath. And what did she have to lose? Her dignity was already in tatters.

"Fine.""

"You accept?" His eyes smiled.

"Yes. But when we arrive—I see them alone. No explanations. No shadowing me. I do this on my terms."

He nodded once. "It is a bargain."

She stepped back, adjusting her clothes with shaking hands. Her voice felt like a stranger when she said, "I need to get home."

He held her gaze a beat too long, then bent to kiss her hand with a tender smile. It wasn't hungry or possessive, It was... grateful.

She returned his smile, careful and sweet—a practiced expression meant to reassure—but it couldn't warm the hollow in her eyes. And somehow, that made it worse.

Because he didn't know she planned to leave him the moment they reached the present. No matter what he said, no matter how gently he looked at her, she was ready to shove him back through the portal if it came to that.

He suspected nothing.

And she was already rehearsing the betrayal.

A week had passed since the proposal, and Dani had avoided him with the grace of a hunted fox. Not too distant—never enough to draw suspicion—but always just out of reach. Gabriel, to his credit, had not pressed.

Tuesday, they walked the length of Washington Park. He strolled with a cane he didn't need, all coat and tailored elegance, while she scuffed along in worn boots and climbed the nearest tree just to prove she could. He laughed, astonished, when she dropped from the lowest branch with a pinecone in one hand and dirt on her knees. "You are," he'd said, "without rival, the most unusual woman I have ever met."

And Thursday on a holiday when everyone was elsewhere—fishing.

She had expected silence. Instead, he talked nearly the entire time, albeit gently, in that lilting accent that made everything sound like it belonged in a leather-bound novel.

"You truly mean to handle the rod without gloves?" he asked, watching as she baited the hook with a wriggling worm and no hesitation.

"Do I look like the sort of girl who wears gloves?" she replied, cocking a brow at him.

He examined her muddy sleeves, the windblown braid, and the cut on her thumb. "No," he said at last. "No, Miss Wood, you look like the sort of girl who wrestles wolves for fun and wins."

She grinned. "Flattery won't catch you a trout."

"I would gladly settle for catching your heart instead," he said, eyes holding hers—then came the wink, sudden and striking, a flash of handsomeness so quick it left her blinking.

God. He said things like that—just casually. Like it wasn't enough that he was beautiful and brilliant, and patient in a way most men weren't. He had to be clever, too.

With a cast of her line, she attempted to ignore his lingering eyes. She wasn't trying to be alluring. She had wet boots, his old trousers, a crooked hat, and blood on her sleeve from unhooking a fish. But he watched her as if she were doing something exquisite. Not feminine. Not graceful. Just... rare.

He handed her his rod at one point. "Here," he said, as she wiped her hands on the borrowed trousers. "Would you mind reeling this in? I fear a fish has outsmarted me."

She took the rod from him, but her foot slipped on the muddy bank. She pitched forward.

He moved fast.

One arm caught her waist, the other steadied the rod, and he pulled her close startling her, breathless, her face inches from his.

He didn't let go right away.

"Careful, Miss Wood," he laughed. "I nearly lost you and the fish."

She raised a brow. "Which one would've hurt more?"

He pretended to consider it. "The fish, perhaps. You would surely resurface just to gloat."

She smirked. "I absolutely would."

His hand stayed at her back—grounding her. He didn't quite want the moment to end. His eyes swept her face, quieter now. "I do say," he said, "you accomplish things quite backwards."

"Backwards?"

"You wear my old trousers, out-fish me, scale a riverbank like it is nothing—and somehow continue to strengthen the steel cold chains on my heart."

She blinked, surprised.

Then: "You rehearsed that."

"I am afraid not. Perhaps I should have."

There was no pressure in it—just the warm, calm glow of someone who admired her exactly as she was.

She didn't know whether to shake her head or laugh.

"You're ridiculous," she teased. "Do you flirt like this with everyone who can bait their own hook?"

He leaned in just a little more. The riverbank narrowed.

"Only with those whose laughter and spirit haunt my thoughts."

Dani's grip on the fishing rod tightened, the only thing keeping her grounded in the present moment. Heat crept up her neck; she felt her cheeks flush, despite herself. That was... unexpectedly poetic. Hot, even.

She gently shook her head, brushing off the feeling and forcing a smile. "I need to change; it's cold," she interrupted.

"Very well. Let us get you back into proper clothes before taking you home," he responded.

He guided her to an abandoned fishing shed on the far riverbank.

The shed door creaked behind her, half-open to the golden haze of the late afternoon. He stood just outside, sleeves rolled up, fishing gear slung over one shoulder. He held her folded dress in his hands.

"You may require this," he said, voice soft but pointed.

She turned. The white shirt he'd lent her hung open at the collar, half-unbuttoned, showing her cleavage, sleeves rolled to her elbows. Mud streaked her calves. Her hair was damp at the edges from the mist off the river. She reached for the dress, but didn't take it yet.

Gabriel stepped inside.

He said nothing, simply watching her with a quiet intensity that filled the small space like charged air. The silence sent pulses down Dani's spine, and as reason battled with impulse, a whirlwind of thoughts raced through her mind. Slowly, almost reluctantly, one side won. To hell with it.

She lifted an eyebrow and looked toward the door. A signal to close it.

The door clicked shut behind him.

She didn't stop him. Not when he reached out, not when his fingers brushed her arm. Not when he kissed her, deep and sure, the press of his mouth stealing whatever stubborn part of her was still pretending this wouldn't happen. She let him.

Hands roamed like he was mapping her—down her ribs, over the flat plane of her tight abs, slipping around to her back. Her shirt slid off her shoulders. He pressed closer. The heat of his body and the faint scent of river water and cedar clung to him.

Rowen's name flickered through her like a pulse, but she shoved it down. He felt nice in his own way, and it wasn't completely unbearable. He was gorgeous, well-spoken, smelled nice, and his charm was rubbing off on her. This filled the void; this would do.

Her body responded with effortless heat, slickness blooming as his hands slid lower. One of her legs rose instinctively when his palm swept down her thigh—he caught it, cradling it against his hip like something precious. Then his fingers found her. Large and strong. He worked her open slowly, learning her with touch instead of sight, with devotion instead of skill. Every motion silently pleaded: Let me give this to you your way, since you prefer women. And maybe this was foolish. Despite that, he wanted to show her what it meant to be wanted in this way. Wanted by him.

She tilted her head back against the rough beam, staring at the ceiling so she wouldn't have to look at him and face what she was doing. Just release, relief from her thoughts and her pain.

He stroked deeper, teasing and coaxing, until she nearly reached the edge. Her hand slid down, brushing against her throbbing clit, rubbing the place that would bring her release while he thrust his large fingers inside her.

She didn't stop. Her breathing labored, chest rising and falling, as warmth pooled low, gathering like a storm as he kissed her breasts.

When she came against his touch, she let go, shuddering in the quiet space between them.

They kissed softly. He pulled her hand down to the hardness that had built beneath his trousers, but she couldn't. She felt a kiss was all she could give him back that felt somewhat real in this moment.

Gabriel's voice broke the silence. "I find you most lovely."

She didn't answer at first. Her throat felt raw. Her heart was worse than it had been moments before.

"I... I need to... change," she whispered, stumbling over her words.

He nodded, stepping back. Handed her the dress without touching her again. Turned away, as if to give her space.

She dressed in silence. Buttoned each piece like armor. Hair damp, fingers shaking just slightly.

She'd meant for this to be nothing. Just a moment—just something to feel other than hollow. But now, there was something else there. A shift she couldn't ignore.

Despite herself, Gabriel had grown on her.

Everything she thought she'd figured out about herself felt blurred. Confusing. Dani had always known what she liked and who she was. But now—now she wasn't so sure.

Could you care for two people at once, even if what you felt for each of them was nothing alike?

What she felt for Rowen was sharp and electric, and real. Unshakable. She was the one who tempted her.

But Gabriel—Gabriel was handsome, clever, and unexpectedly gentle. Though her heart belonged to someone else—and though she'd always preferred women—there was a strange fondness blooming. Not love. Not even desire, exactly. Just a warmth. A comfort. A space she hadn't realized she'd left empty until he stepped into it.

She glanced at his back, at the quiet way he stood there, waiting. Respectful. Present.

This wasn't who she was. But it had happened.

And maybe facing that truth was the hardest part—the truth that she had once believed not everything inside her was as fixed. Maybe the lines she'd drawn about herself weren't rules, just scaffolding. And now they were splintering under what she felt.

Still, that verse had haunted her for days. The one about kissing a million boys in bars and feeling nothing at all. She'd kissed the boy from the bar now—pressed her body to his, let him hold the loneliness for a while.

And the song was right.

None of it quieted what lived inside her. None of it changed what she'd lost. To silence that ache—the one that knew Rowen's name—she'd have to stop the world itself.

She'd have to go home.

21

THE GILDED CAGE

EDWARDIAN ERA

Before heading out for Vivienne's first Christmas charity party of the season, Dani slipped into the kitchen and stole a cookie off a cooling rack—something with ginger and molasses that stuck to her teeth. She didn't trust the catering at a turn-of-the-century opera house. Probably oysters. Definitely things wrapped in meat. The cookie would have to hold her.

The evening's affair would take place in the lavish surroundings of the Portland Opera House, instead of the grand ballroom at the Barrington Estate.

The opera house was one of Portland's finest, though it had fallen on hard times in recent years. Vivienne chose it for her grand affair partly as a charitable gesture and partly to strengthen her standing among the city's elite. The evening doubled as a fundraiser, with prominent guests donating generously to keep the theater's productions alive.

The scent of perfume and cigar smoke mingled with the warmth of too many bodies pressed into the echoing space. Laughter, champagne, and the swell of the orchestra filled the gilded hall, but Dani felt suffocated.

She didn't want to be here. Above all, she wished to avoid further reminders of her mortality. She still hadn't told Alvie and Vivienne about her and Gabriel's agreement, and that secret was getting harder to maintain.

The party was being held on the grand stage of the theater itself, where guests in shimmering silk and tailored suits moved in a restless tide. Those wishing for more intimate conversations occupied the plush, velvet-covered seats beyond the stage, while others wandered through the high box seats, whispering behind lace fans and cigars. Portland's elite focused their attention on Dani. She felt curious eyes weighing on her with suspicion.

Vivienne had tried to keep her close, weaving her through introductions like a prized doll.

Vivienne looked every bit the Edwardian ideal, wrapped in red silk velvet. Rosettes trimmed the off-the-shoulder neckline, their soft shimmer echoing the fabric's subtle sheen. The fitted bodice flattered her powerful frame, and the train trailed behind her in quiet, fluid grace. Without saying a word, she commanded the room.

"Smile, Miss Wood. Shoulders back. Remember, grace is a woman's greatest asset."

Dani nodded, the picture of a polite guest. They'd stuffed her into an ivory silk House of Worth gown, embroidered with gold thread and delicate floral flourishes. She felt like a dressed-up chicken—plucked, trussed, and ready for the carving knife.

Inside the opera house, the gilded cage felt even tighter. The glittering crowd sparkled with wealth and ambition, their smiles all hollow. A haunting soprano aria floated above them—rich, mournful, and aching. Dani knew the feeling well: beautiful, utterly trapped, and selling her soul to get home.

She needed air, so she left through a side door, the marble corridor muffling the sounds from the party. Near the powder room, she found a dim alcove. A flash of movement caught her attention just as her hand reached the door—not quite light, not quite shadow, but something in between.

She paused, focusing harder. There it was again, shimmering at the edge of her vision like heat waves off the summer pavement. Enver's words echoed in her mind: moments where two times briefly touch. Reality tearing at the seams.

She stepped closer, trying to make sense of what she was seeing. The shimmer intensified for a heartbeat, then faded completely, leaving her staring at nothing but empty air.

"Converging realities," she whispered to herself, her stomach dropping. She was seeing through the veil—proof that she'd already lived this, that the time loop was in motion.

Shaking her head, she forced herself to move forward. She had enough to worry about without chasing ghosts from other timelines.

But as she stepped deeper into the alcove, she realized she wasn't alone. Tucked into the shadowed corner, two figures stood entwined—Shannon and Edmund. His hand rested at the small of her back, his lips brushing against hers in a tender, stolen kiss. They looked happy, lost in their own world, unaware of anyone else. Dani's heart swelled, an unexpected warmth spreading through her.

"Oi, lovebirds—save it for after shift. Before someone important catches you," she grinned, but there was no bite in it. Just enough to startle them back into reality.

Then she turned away, cutting off the moment entirely. Whatever tenderness they'd found, she wasn't about to let them get caught.

She lingered in the marble corridor, letting the muffled sounds of the party wash over her like distant thunder. The cool air felt like a small mercy against her skin. She'd come out here to breathe, to escape the suffocating weight of smiles and small talk, and now she had to go back in there and pretend she cared about any of it.

She pressed her back against the wall, closing her eyes for a moment. How many more hours of this? How many more nights of playing dress-up in someone else's life while her real world slipped further away?

The thought of Gabriel's promise flickered through her mind—home, if she played her part. But first, she had to survive this glittering hell.

Footsteps echoed down the corridor, and Dani opened her eyes. A tall woman with golden hair emerged from the theater, moving with confident strides that were just a little too long, a little too purposeful for the delicate steps expected of ladies in 1905. Her shoulders sat square, her chin held at an angle that suggested she was used to meeting the world head-on rather than deferring to it.

The woman's eyes found Dani's and held them, and now in the brighter lighting Dani realized it was the woman from the club. The same hungry eyes that Rowen had kept her from getting to know. Clarissa. A slow, crooked smile spread across her face—not the practiced simper of polite society, but something genuine and predatory. Appreciative. The look that said she saw exactly what she was looking at and liked it very much.

Dani felt the heat rise in her cheeks. There was no mistaking that look. No pretending it was anything other than what it was.

Clarissa continued past her toward the powder room, and Dani couldn't help but watch the way she moved—that subtle swagger, the way her tailored gown couldn't quite disguise the masculine confidence in her stride. It was like watching someone who'd learned to wear femininity but never quite bought into it.

Just as Clarissa reached the powder room door, she placed her hand on the handle and turned back, catching Dani still staring.

Oh shit.

Dani spun around quickly, mortified at being caught, and immediately collided with a decorative plant stand. The brass pot wobbled precariously as she steadied it, her face burning with embarrassment.

Time to go back and pretend.

As she stepped back into the glittering chaos of the theater, the noise and light surged around her, masking the quiet twist in her gut.

Vivienne appeared at her elbow almost immediately, steering her back into the social whirlwind. "There you are, dear. Come, you simply must meet Mr. Hartwell—he owns half the lumber mills in Oregon."

The next hour passed in a blur of introductions. Mr. Hartwell and his simpering wife who spoke only of their latest European vacation. The Ashfords, who owned a shipping company and insisted on explaining every detail of their newest vessel. Mrs. Pemberton, whose husband controlled the city's largest bank and who sized up Dani like she was calculating her net worth.

Dani smiled, nodded, made appropriate comments about the weather and the opera season. It wasn't so bad, really—just tedious. She'd learned the rhythm of it: compliment the ladies on their gowns, defer to the men's business, talk, laugh at jokes that weren't funny.

But then, out of the corner of her eye, she felt someone watching her.

She turned slightly and spotted Clarissa. But now, a complete transformation had overtaken her. Gone was any hint of the predatory confidence Dani had seen earlier. Instead, she stood among a cluster of well-dressed men, fitting right in with their world. She threw her head back, guffawing at something one of them had said, a lit cigar held casually between her fingers like it belonged there. Her posture was relaxed, masculine, completely at ease in their company.

The transformation was startling. She could code-switch like a master, slipping between worlds as easily as changing clothes.

She watched Dani—not with idle curiosity, but with that same look from the club. Dani turned away, not sure what unsettled her more: the men sizing her up like a prize... or Clarissa who was.

She overheard a cluster of men near the balcony, swirling their brandy, their voices carrying just enough for her to catch snippets.

"That's why I've ensured my dear daughter is properly settled. A fine match with Rowen Quinn, head of the Workers' Union. Smart boy, that one. But now? We shall have control of that union in no time. The workers respect him; he's influential in the lowly circles I cannot easily reach."

Engaged. The word hit Dani like a sledgehammer to the chest. Her breath caught in her throat, and for a moment, the theater seemed to tilt on its axis. Not courting. Not exploring a potential match. Engaged.

When had this happened? How long had they been planning this while she was... what? Hanging out on sleeping porches, smudging mud on each other's faces, sharing stolen kisses that felt like the most real thing in this entire century? Her mind raced backward—Beatrice leaving the elevator at the department store that first day; Beatrice possessively holding Rowen's arm; and Rowen escorting her to that ball as if it were already decided. And those words in the buggy, about practical considerations and responsibilities she'd been neglecting in favor of fantasy.

Had Rowen been with Beatrice this entire time? Had she been that naïve, that blind? Or had Rowen been playing on both sides, keeping Dani as some secret dalliance while building a proper life with someone socially acceptable?

The casual cruelty of hearing it discussed like a business merger—because that's exactly what it was—made her stomach lurch. She'd known it was over between them, had told herself she'd accepted it, but this felt like being gutted with a rusty blade.

The men tipped their brandies and congratulated him.

"We are all forever in your debt. Here's to evading ruin, you sly old dog." A man with soft brown hair slicked to the side announced.

Dani's hands clenched into fists at her sides. She'd expected Rowen to move on, but not like this. Not as some business transaction. The disappointment crashed over her, followed immediately by a rage so sharp it took her breath away.

Dani rounded the corner and stopped short, Beatrice coming into full view within the group.

Beatrice's laugh was brittle. "Is that all you see, Father? A business arrangement?"

"What else should I see?" There was genuine confusion in his voice as he smiled and tried to keep the group's spirits up, avoiding a public fight.

"Perhaps the fact that I—" Beatrice stopped, composing herself. "Never mind. I have done as you asked, as I always do."

Ashdown's expression softened unexpectedly as he escorted her away from the group. "I'll be back, gentlemen. Keep your glasses full!"

The men cheered and laughed.

He reached out, surprisingly gently adjusting a cameo at Beatrice's throat. "Your mother wore this on our wedding day," he breathed. "Did I ever tell you that?"

"Every time I wear it," Beatrice replied, her voice gentler now.

"She would have been proud of you. The sacrifices you make for this family..." His voice trailed off, and in a blink, he looked older, wearier. "I know it is difficult being my daughter."

"It isn't entirely difficult, Papa," she said, though her eyes told a different story.

"When I was your age," he continued, "I wanted to be a botanist. Did you know that? I had notebooks full of pressed flowers and seeds." He gestured to the orchids surrounding them. "I preferred wild specimens—plants that survived against all odds."

"Surviving against all odds. I'm quite skilled at that myself as of late," she snarked.

He didn't acknowledge the little jab. "There was never time. After my father died, the business required my full attention." He straightened his cuffs. "As it now requires yours. Quinn's union connections are vital if we're to weather the coming changes."

"And if I had chosen someone else?" Beatrice asked, a rare challenge in her voice.

He considered her for a long time. "Family comes first, Beatrice. It always has." He touched her cheek briefly. "But if it brings you any comfort... your mother chose me, and in time, she found happiness in that choice."

As he walked away, Dani glimpsed Beatrice's face. Her careful mask had slipped, revealing something raw—love, complicated and deep, for a father she admired but feared disappointing.

But wait. Dani's mind began piecing things together. If Beatrice was just doing this out of duty, why had she looked so possessive at that ball? Why the jealousy when other women talked to Rowen? And that kiss in the projection—Beatrice had to know Rowen's secret by now, didn't she? You don't get that close to someone without figuring it out. So, if she knew, and she still kissed her... was she actually enjoying this? Having the town's most wanted bachelor on her arm, all the other ladies seething with envy. Not knowing the truth was far more complicated?

Maybe it wasn't just duty. Maybe Beatrice was getting exactly what she wanted—the prestige, the prize, and the satisfaction of winning.

As Ashdown rejoined the group, Beatrice's eyes swept the room and landed directly on Dani. A knowing smile played at her lips.

"I do hope," Beatrice said, her voice carrying just loud enough for Dani to hear, "that all of Rowen's... previous distractions... understand that such diversions are now quite impossible. A man of his standing requires absolute discretion in his associations."

The men chuckled, oblivious to the venom in her words.

"Quite right," one of them agreed. "He can keep his close-knit relations with the workers, but anything else would be imprudent."

Dani's hands clenched into fists. She needed something to do with them before she did something truly stupid. A passing waiter offered a silver tray of delicate refreshments, and she grabbed a sugar cookie without thinking—the same ginger and molasses kind she'd stolen from the kitchen earlier.

Something inside Dani snapped.

Before she could stop herself, her hand whipped forward, sending a sugar cookie flying toward the group of men and striking the loud-mouthed bastard directly on the side of his head.

The laughter cut short.

Brandy sloshed in his glass as he turned sharply, eyes scanning the room.

Dani ducked behind a decorative pillar, pressing a hand over her mouth.

I need to get out of here before I throw up.

Without another thought, she turned on her heel and slipped through the grand doors into the night.

The crisp night air struck her like a slap, sharp and sobering. Outside the opera house, the streets were quieter—the grandeur and revelry sealed behind velvet-draped walls. But farther down the avenue, the riffraff gathered in dim-lit corners, laughter spilling from alleyways. A distant violin threaded its mournful tune through the low hum of late-night conversations. A horse-drawn buggy clattered by its driver indifferent, barely casting her a glance.

Tears streamed down her face, flames of angry heat creeping up her neck as her hair whipped haphazardly out of its refined fastenings. She was running from them, from all of it.

Before she realized it, she'd reached Skidmore Fountain. In the present day, this was Saturday Market. But today it was entirely different.

The area was alive with movement—men in heavy coats whispered over cigars, well-dressed patrons slipped behind red-curtained doors, and women in elaborate gowns lounged in doorways, their sly smiles adding to the intrigue. The air was thick with the scent of damp stone, perfume, and the faint, salty smell of the Willamette River.

She barely noticed when she caught the attention of a well-dressed man, his slicked-back hair glinting under the streetlight. He took a step toward her, eyes trailing over her with interest.

"Are you quite lost, my dear?" His voice was smooth, but there was something about it that made her skin crawl.

Dani squared her shoulders, refusing to step back. "No," she said coolly. "I was just leaving. Unless you're offering directions, move along, buddy."

The man chuckled, blocking her path. "You ought not to be wandering these streets unescorted, madam. A lady such as yourself should be in more refined company."

"And you think that company should be you?" she shot back, deadpan. "I'd rather take my chances with a sewer rat, thanks."

The man smirked, clearly enjoying himself. "A sharp tongue on this one. You ought to be careful, darling. This part of town isn't kind to highfalutin girls like you."

His hand shot out, grabbing her elbow with intent to drag her toward the shadows between buildings. But Dani spun fast, breaking free of his grip and driving her fist hard into his chest. He staggered back, gasping.

"Touch me again and you'll lose more than your breath," she snarled.

A familiar presence stalked behind her, and a voice shot through the dark.

"She already has company, and I would wager she has little patience for the likes of you." Dani turned to see Rowen, standing just behind her. She looked different here, under the glow of streetlights in a well-cut tuxedo. More like herself.

The man raised an eyebrow but took a step back. "Ah, well, no offense meant, sir," he muttered, tipping his hat before slinking off into the crowd.

Dani watched him go, then glanced at Rowen with a wry half-smile. "You really couldn't let me have that one?"

Rowen's mouth tilted. "What can I say? I have a flair for dramatic rescues."

"I noticed. Very gallant. Next time, let me get a second swing off—then swoop in."

"I shall wait until he's halfway through a black eye," Rowen replied. "More fair."

They stood there for a beat, the city folding in around them—voices, footsteps, the buzz of lights—but neither moved.

"I saw you bolt from the opera house," Rowen said quietly. "Just as I was arriving. The anger in your shoulders was impossible to miss."

Dani scoffed. "You literally followed me?"

"Something told me to." Rowen's voice was soft. "Left the party behind without a second thought."

Dani glanced at her sidelong. "So, what's the etiquette when someone crashes your almost-street-fight?" Using humor as her shield.

"I believe the custom is to offer her a seat." Rowen nodded toward a bench by the fountain. Dani hesitated a second too long before following.

They sat. Not close, but not far, either. Just enough space for the ache to settle between them.

"Been a while," Dani said.

Rowen didn't look over. "I wasn't sure if you wanted to see me."

"I didn't," Dani said. Then added, softer, "Ugh, I still do."

Rowen's lips curved—barely.

They lapsed into silence.

A child darted past them in the shadows—too young to be out this late, but this was clearly the rough side of town where different rules applied.

Somewhere, a door creaked shut.

Dani shifted, straightening her legs. "So... engaged." She let the word hang in the air, testing its weight. "That's quite a development."

Rowen's shoulders tensed. "Dani..."

"No, it's lovely, really." Her voice was soft, almost wondering. "I always wondered what it was like to marry a self-serving spoiled child. I guess you'll find out."

She picked at a loose thread on her dress, not looking at Rowen. "Do you practice it? The way you can just... compartmentalize people? Or does it come naturally?"

"That isn't what happened."

Dani finally looked up, and her smile was heartbreaking. "Isn't it, though? Because from where I'm sitting, it feels like I was just the intermission between acts. You put my hand between your legs for shits sake."

Rowen arched an eyebrow, then reached into her coat and pulled out the familiar notebook. The sight of it made something twist in Dani's chest.

"Seriously?" she asked. "You're journaling mid-emotional standoff?"

"It helps me think," Rowen murmured, pen already moving.

"Great. Meanwhile, I'm over here white knuckling the space-time continuum."

Rowen paused in her scribbling, then looked over. "Would you rather I speak without understanding the shape of what I feel?"

Dani didn't answer. Not directly. She watched Rowen's fingers, watched the way her hand shook just slightly when she closed the book.

"Women like us don't get happy endings in 1905," Rowen said after a beat. Not bitter. Not angry. Just... tired.

Dani exhaled, leaning back against the bench. "We get secrecy. Smoke and mirrors. Marriage to men who'll keep our names out of the scandal sheets."

"And long nights in someone else's arms, pretending not to know who we really want." Rowen's head fell back, eyes finding the stars. "It's ridiculous."

"It's not like that where I come from. I was hoping to show you."

"Salem is still Salem."

Now wasn't the time to overcomplicate things—to try explaining what her world truly meant, or the unspeakable things she'd done to ease her own pain. That conversation would come later. The urge sat there anyway, low and restless. But this was good. Just being next to Rowen.

They fell quiet. The space between them crackled with electricity—every slight movement amplified in the stillness. Rowen shifting her weight. Dani's fingers drumming against stone. Their knees almost touching. Almost.

Rowen hadn't responded to her earlier words, but Dani could feel her tension, the way she held herself like she was fighting some internal battle.

Dani turned just enough to watch her. "You could have kissed me just now. Touched me."

"I still could." Rowen's voice was barely audible. "But I don't trust what it would do to me."

Dani's throat tightened. She let the silence ache.

Then she said, almost to the dark: "Well, you've done it. You salted my heart and carved your piece."

Rowen's head dropped, eyes closing. "Don't," she whispered.

"Why not?" Dani's voice cracked, quiet and raw. "It's true."

Rowen turned toward her, expression sharp and pained, mouth parted like she might say something—anything—but she didn't.

She didn't have to.

Their faces were so close.

If either of them moved just half an inch, it would all fall apart.

Despite that, neither of them looked away.

Rowen leaned in.

Dani tilted up.

Dani closed her eyes, anticipating the kiss. When she opened them, Rowen's lips were right there—her favorite feature, soft and perfectly shaped. But in her peripheral vision, a figure was coming into focus, steaming down the street toward them with unmistakable purpose.

"You have no business being here, Dani." The voice hit like a slap.

Dani jolted, breath tearing from her lungs as Laurel materialized before them, spine straight as steel, eyes like flint.

She crossed into their space with the precision of a blade through silk.

"And frankly, I have had quite enough of this. Shannon was never so willful, and you know well that Alvie would scarcely condone her gallivanting about at such an hour. If the footmen had not noticed you leaving the ball and brought me to find you, you may have disappeared completely without my intervention." Her tone softened.

Dani's lips parted as further confirmation settled in her eyes. There it is, Shannon's his daughter. Laurel hesitated, her mouth pressed into a taut line, wanting to take back her words. But Dani's smile said all that needed saying. And with that, the pot of family secrets simmered ever louder.

"Laurel," Dani said, shifting from her thoughts. "I just needed some air."

Laurel looked to Rowen, then back to Dani, her expression tinged with worry. "This is hardly the place for either of you," she said firmly. "Sir, surely you have more pressing matters to attend to this evening. And you," she turned to Dani, "have obligations as well."

Dani let out an exasperated sigh, her irritation bubbling beneath her composure. Laurel had once again dismantled a fragile moment of connection. Dani cast a furtive glance toward Rowen, searching for traces of reassurance. Rowen, composed as ever, inclined her head slightly, her voice low and resolute. "We shall speak again." Her eyes burned. "I will find you."

Laurel fell into step beside Dani, casting one last look over her shoulder as Rowen receded into shadow. "Honestly," she murmured, smoothing a wrinkle from her glove, "the company one finds near the docks these days... rivals only the Godfather."

Dani blinked. The name lodged like a thorn. *The Godfather?* She glanced at Laurel, but the woman's expression was unreadable—poised, elegant, entirely in control. Too in control.

Laurel changed the subject and continued, "Well, it seems news of your engagement is coursing through that theater with all the fervor of a scandal sheet. A dreadful shame, truly. It seems someone dashed my last hope for happiness."

Rowen pushed a small, forced smile. "A pity, truly. I had no notion my engagement would break so many hearts. Had I known Miss Laurel, I might have delayed the inevitable just to spare you the anguish."

Dani rolled her eyes at the exchange, but she couldn't ignore the way Rowen hung back, her presence now life-sucking.

They approached the opera house doors. The sounds of laughter and music swelled once more, a stark reminder of the night she was about to endure.

I have nothing else to stay here for.

She straightened her shoulders and walked inside the Opera house. The night was far from over. Forced smiles, hollow congratulations. She'd have to watch Rowen and Beatrice accept Portland's praise as if it meant something. A performance, like everything else in this world.

Rowen waited a pace before entering, then went straight to Beatrice's side. Dani watched with disgust as she slipped seamlessly back into the role of devoted fiancé. When her eyes found Dani's across the room, she saw the pain flicker there for just a moment—her eyelids shuttering like she was closing off whatever they'd shared by the fountain. Then she looked away and smiled at Ashdown's group, the mask clicking perfectly back into place.

Dani didn't get far into the space.

"Miss Wood."

The sharp eyes from earlier, Clarissa. From across the room, she caught Rowen watching the interaction, her expression horrified.

"I daresay someone has forgotten their manners," the woman said with a refined smile. "Clarissa."

"Danielle," she replied, cautious but steady.

"Yes, I'm aware. I asked around." Clarissa's smile deepened, more amused than warm. "You've made quite the impression already—though not nearly so dramatic as our dear Rowen and her intended."

"I'm not really in the mood for conversation," Dani said, trying to step past.

"I don't intend to make one. Just a quiet hallway and a few words."

Dani looked past her, toward the theater. Laughter. Champagne. Beatrice touching Rowen's arm like she owned her. Dani's stomach turned.

"A few minutes," she said.

Clarissa nodded. "This way."

Clarissa led her past the velvet curtains and into a quiet corridor off the theater. Behind them, the music and clinking glasses faded into a dull hum.

No need to look back. But Rowen did.

Still standing beside Beatrice, half-finished champagne in hand, she froze. Eyes locked on the two of them. Clearly worried.

They stopped beneath a wall sconce. "Will this do?" Clarissa asked.

"It's as good as anywhere else." Dani dropped onto the bench, arms crossed.

Clarissa smoothed her gown and sat beside her, posture sharp but relaxed, eyes forward. "I thought it best we speak, just the two of us. I've a habit of noticing things others miss."

No response.

"I gather it wasn't a long affair," she said.

"It wasn't an affair."

"It looked like one."

Dani gave her a sideways look. "You always this nosy?"

"I've been called worse." A small smile. "The way she claimed you, that was a first."

Nothing from Dani.

"I knew her when we were small. Scruffy little thing. Wretched with a brush, always sneaking out in trousers. She wore her hair tied back like a boy's. Her mother cried over it. But Rowen's never been one for rules." A beat. "Dressing as a man isn't a costume for her; it's second nature."

The backstory was touching, more than Dani expected.

"It appears she may have played a game with you," Clarissa added.

The silence dragged.

"If it's comfort you are after... I offer mine freely."

She rested her gloved hand on the bench between them. "You are—if you'll forgive the boldness—possibly the most arresting woman I've seen in years."

Her eyes drifted toward the theater. "And if it's vengeance you're after… tangling with me would land it right where it hurts. For the both of us."

A pause. "We were the closest of friends once."

Dani stared at her hand. Her pulse jumped.

"As much as the old me would have impulsively jumped on your offer. I can't."

Clarissa didn't move. "The offer is always open, you know where to find me."

Dani stood. "Thank you for the…offer."

Clarissa rose, too, observing her.

"It was very nice to meet you," Dani added, quieter now. "Truly. I'm just… not feeling well. I think I need to go."

Clarissa gave a slight nod. "You've made my acquaintance, Miss Wood. Do call on me—should your body need intimate attention, or you are seeking a special friend."

No goodbye. Just movement—back through the corridor, her shoes tapping on the tile.

Inside, the theater buzzed. Beatrice was still on Rowen's arm, laughing at something she didn't mean.

That was enough.

Out front, Jacques adjusted his gloves near the buggy line.

"I want to go home," she said. "Now."

22

SWEET DESTRUCTION

EDWARDIAN ERA

Dani had cried herself to sleep. After Edmund dropped her off, the tears came in waves—first the angry ones, hot and bitter, then the hollow kind that left her feeling wrung out and raw. In her rage, she wanted to tear the silk gown clean off her body, but the intricate fastenings fought back. She wrestled with buttons and hooks, her fingers clumsy with fury and exhaustion, until the dress finally gave way and puddled at her feet. Without thinking, she caught the expensive fabric with her toe and launched it soccer-style across the room, where it landed in a crumpled heap at the foot of her bed.

Pulling on one of the loose cotton nightgowns Shannon had left for her felt like shedding a costume she'd never wanted to wear. Too drained to care about her smeared makeup or tangled hair, she collapsed onto the bed, the soft linen a welcome comfort against her tear-stained skin. The last thing she remembered was staring at the ceiling, replaying every annoying moment from the opera house until exhaustion finally pulled her under.

Hours later, she woke to a sound. Subtle, barely there—yet it dragged her from sleep with a clutch of unease. She wasn't alone. Near-darkness cloaked the bed, with shadows glimmering along the walls from the low-burning fire. Earlier, when Shannon and the rest of the family had arrived home from the event, she'd padded through the room, her movements soft and habitual, tending the flames and tugging the curtains half-closed.

Dani had been half asleep, paying no attention. Maybe Shannon was back? In her grogginess, time eluded her.

But something felt wrong now. Tilted. Altered. Something unnatural permeated the still air.

The covers bunched halfway over her ears had muffled the quiet—but not enough. She still caught it. A faint out-of-place sound. The friction of fabric swishing against fabric. The soft exhale of someone trying too hard to be silent.

She didn't move or blink. Just listened, every nerve suddenly alert despite the fog of sleep.

Then—another creak. Not the restless groan of settling wood, but a shoe rolling down a step as the floorboards strained beneath someone's weight.

Her breath locked tightly behind her ribs. Muscles tensed. Fingers dug into the blanket until her knuckles blanched from her grip.

The sleeping porch. It had to be the sleeping porch. Someone had climbed up from the garden, through the trellis maybe, and was making their way across the small space toward her room.

Agonizingly slowly, she turned her head toward the dark, because moving too fast might give it a reason to strike. A shape resolved in the dimness.

Her stomach dropped straight through the mattress.

Oh, hell no.

A figure, tall and lean, inching toward the bed with the patience of a cat. A slight dip in the mattress marked the weight settling on its edge, followed by a shift as the figure inched closer.

She almost screamed, ready to throw hands, before the smell registered. Cedar smoke and something warm beneath it—bergamot, maybe, and the faint scent of night air clinging to fabric.

"Who are you!?" she snapped, voice cutting through the thick dark.

As the figure moved closer, the pale light from the dying fire illuminated a cheekbone and bright eyes studying her.

"I said I would find you alone, did I not?" Rowen's voice was velvet-wrapped steel.

"What in the serial killer nonsense was that?! Rowen, I nearly died! My soul left my body! You can't just materialize like some demon!"

"Apologies." Rowen scooted back a little.

"How did you..." Dani trailed off.

"Shannon." The single word carried a hint of apology.

Traitor, co-conspirator, and wingman with the timing of a Greek tragedy, Dani thought.

"At the opera house. While you were..." Rowen's voice faltered slightly. "While you were speaking with Clarissa I arranged to come."

So she must have panicked.

"But, why here—"

"Allow me to speak," Rowen said, cutting in softly, "before the courage leaves me entirely." She leaned her head closer to Dani, extending her neck.

Dani's eyes locked onto that maddening pulse in the long column of it—where skin met the curve of Rowen's shoulder. She wanted to rest her cheek there, feel that beat against her skin again. Proof that Rowen was here. That she's not dreaming.

"I am to marry Beatrice because her family shall provide for my mother's care," she said, not meeting Dani's eyes. "It is not born of love, but necessity. Survival, if you will." Her voice grew quieter, more strained. "That evening at the charity ball... when I bid three hundred dollars for your company... it was most imprudent of me, and it left me utterly ruined financially. Yet I could not bear the notion of another claiming even a moment of your attention. The very thought of you bestowing your affections upon someone else, of becoming... attached to another... it was unbearable."

Something took Dani's breath away. *Three hundred dollars*, she didn't realize at the time—is a fortune in 1905.

"The morning following, while I sat contemplating my financial ruin, Lord Ashdown presented himself at my door with his proposition. He had been waiting and observing, knowing precisely when I should be at my most vulnerable. His intent was quite clear: to stop any possibility between us before it might properly take root." Rowen's voice grew quieter. "But I didn't give him his answer straightaway. I rather thought... well, I wished to see you, to be near you, to know you better. I wanted desperately to feel what it might be like to be yours." Her hands clenched in the bedsheets. "For a brief moment, I thought I might devise some solution—some way to avoid his offer. I found myself quite torn between my sentiments for you and my duty to Mother. But then, that evening at O'Driscoll's..."

Dani shifted uneasily against the pillows.

"I witnessed you in his company that evening, and it confirmed my gravest apprehensions. I became utterly convinced... convinced that I was merely a momentary diversion for your amusement."

"I came here to bid you farewell. I required... one truthful moment between us. To speak with complete candor. To conclude this matter with dignity." Rowen's voice cracked at the edges. "I believed myself capable of such restraint. But now—"

Rowen shifted, the blankets crumpling beneath her. Dani lifted a hand and brushed back the strands of hair that had slipped loose across Rowen's temple. But Rowen caught her wrist. Not to stop her. To anchor her.

She pressed Dani's palm to her cheek; her lashes fluttered closed as if the touch hurt and healed her all at once. A single tear slid free, warm against Dani's hand.

Fuck.

The ache inside Dani snapped loose. She leaned in. No thought, no logic. Just gravity and her traitorous heart. Her lips found Rowen's, and the kiss landed like a plea and a goodbye.

Rowen kissed her back. Shaking. Another tear slipped between their mouths. She broke the kiss just to breathe Dani in, again and again, as if oxygen lived only where Dani was.

Dani returned the kiss slower, softer, pouring all the emotions she'd held back into the connection between them. Every tear she'd shed earlier, every ache that had torn through her chest—it all flowed into this moment, as if she could transfer the depth of her feelings through touch alone.

Her left hand slid down, catching Rowen's wrist in a gentle hold—and froze. Cool metal pressed against her skin. Hard and unforgiving. Her eyes dropped. A new gold ring catching the low firelight right where it shouldn't be. A slow, cold wave rolled down her spine.

Are you kidding me right now? Is that an engagement ring? Already?

Everything slammed back into place.

The room spun like it was suddenly too full. She sat there silently like a complete idiot, every logical thought punching the emergency exit.

Push her away, her mind screamed.

The fog of heat and want evaporated, stripped down to the truth she'd been avoiding for days.

She yanked back, shoving Rowen by the shoulders firmly enough to make a space between them. Her voice came low: "We shouldn't do this, Rowen."

Rowen's chest heaved, eyes still heavy-lidded and unfocused from the kiss. She blinked hard, trying to surface from the haze of want that had nearly consumed them both. "I... forgive me, I..." Her breath came unsteady, words scattered as she struggled to collect herself.

"Your fiancée, Beatrice." The name sliced through the air like a blade, cutting through whatever spell had held them.

She was so angry, knowing that if Rowen hadn't been so cold that night, hadn't shut her out so completely, she might never have let Gabriel soothe her pain. Pain that wouldn't have existed at all if Rowen had just listened to her explain herself.

"Am I just supposed to forget about this? It's magnetic, it's all I think about. How can I go home and forget about you?" She didn't bother softening the blow. Didn't want to.

The very suggestion of forgetting physically pained Rowen. "You speak again of leaving... as if such a thing were truly possible?" There was disbelief in her voice, a gentle skepticism that still couldn't quite accept Dani's claims about the future.

Then Dani—too honest for her own good—looked her straight in the eye. "I have done unspeakable things to get back to my time, and if you're here to close our chapter, I need to know, for finality's sake... what I am to you." The second the words left her mouth, she regretted them. It was too open and vulnerable.

"I am merely trying to survive!" Rowen's voice split the quiet like lightning.

They both winced and looked toward the door, waiting for someone to charge in.

But no one came.

And then, softer. "I have told you already. My whole life has been a performance. One misstep, and everything falls apart. You do not understand what is at stake. Not just for me—for my mother."

"You'll say everything except what I mean to you. So, this is it then? I guess we're done here." The words came out harsher than Dani intended, but she was past caring. She rolled away from Rowen, pulling the bedcovers up to her chin like armor against whatever came next. It wasn't mature—hell, it was childish—but it was the only barrier she could think of to stop herself from doing something stupid. Like tearing off her clothes and forgetting why this was wrong. The magnetic pull between them was still there, thrumming under her skin, and if she didn't put distance between them right now, she was going to do something they'd both regret. That landed like another slap.

But then she heard it. A soft, broken sound that made her stomach clench. Rowen was crying—not the controlled tears of earlier, but quiet, shuddering sobs that seemed to tear from somewhere deep inside her chest.

Dani's resolve crumbled. She pulled the blanket down and turned back around to face her.

Rowen had gone completely still, as if the slam of Dani's words had struck her like a physical blow. This kind of messy, raw confrontation, impossible to deflect politely, doesn't suit her. Nothing about Dani was proper, and it left Rowen defenseless.

Dani stared at Rowen's tear-streaked face, the way her jaw quivered as she tried to maintain some semblance of composure. Firelight spilled over her skin, painting the hollow of her throat in gold, and despite everything, Dani felt her breath shudder. All she could think about was pressing her lips to that vulnerable spot where Rowen's pulse fluttered like a trapped bird, hoping to erase her pain.

"You do not mean *nothing*," Rowen said, barely audibly. It probably cost her everything to say it.

Dani's heart ached at those words, revealing a possibility she had been too afraid to consider. *Hope*—dangerous, reckless hope that maybe this wasn't over after all. And like she always did when cornered, but offered even the smallest lifeline, she started talking. Fast. Desperate to explain, to fix what she'd broken before it was too late.

"The night at O'Driscoll's—" she started, then stopped, struggling to find the right words. "Look, I was trying to get information out of him. He has this... technology that could get me home. But then you just... vanished on me. And then someone sent me this projection of you and Beatrice in Pioneer Park, kissing, and I thought..." she trailed off, running her hands through her hair.

"God, I was such a wreck. I was desperate to get home, and I felt like you'd been playing games with my heart this whole time. So, when someone offered comfort, when I was feeling destroyed..." She looked down at her hands. "I let it happen. I let someone touch the parts of me that were still bleeding from you. And I hate I did."

Rowen stared at her, processing every word, and Dani's heart hammered as she waited for judgment, for anger, for anything. The seconds felt like hours as Rowen's expression shifted, something unreadable rolling across her features.

In the unbearable silence, Dani shifted anxiously, her hand moving to fidget with the loose front bow of her nightgown. The fabric slipped lower on her shoulder, exposing the curve of her collarbone in the firelight. She didn't realize what she was doing—just needed something to do with her nervous energy—but when she looked up, Rowen's pupils had dilated, fixed on that exposed skin.

"I can no longer resist you," Rowen said, her voice barely above a breath.

She leaned in—one hand braced against the mattress, the other rising to press Dani gently into the headboard, anchoring her there with an urgency that bordered on desperation.

A picture frame toppled from the nightstand and hit the floor with a sharp, splintering crack.

Neither of them moved.

The silence that followed was knife tight.

They listened—

For footsteps in the hall.

For the creak of disapproval.

For the world to catch them breaking it.

But nothing came.

A chilling stillness, each tick of the clock echoing like a hammer blow.

Dani turned her face away from Rowen, and a curtain of hair slipped loose around her eyes. When she looked back, her lashes were wet with unshed tears clinging to her lower lids. Her whole body felt like a live wire, strung tight with tension. And Rowen—Rowen looked no steadier, her own composure hanging by a thread.

They were both going in circles, wasting time and unraveling in the process.

"I…" She released a shaky breath, and the confession poured out. "Heaven help me—your eyes undo me." She inhaled sharply and straightened her shoulders, restoring her composure. "If you have been seeking solace in Miss Clarissa's embrace to ease your suffering, I shall forgive you. But I cannot bear to know particulars, for if I do, I fear I may reduce her to ash."

Dani exhaled slowly, caught between arousal and guilt. Rowen's jealousy is intoxicating—the raw, possessive edge in her voice sent heat pulsing through her veins. But beneath the rush, something twisted sharp in her chest.

It isn't Clarissa. It's Gabriel.

The truth pressed at her throat—thick, aching, dangerous. Her engagement, the mistakes, the shame of what she'd done. She could say it now. Should say it.

But this moment—this fragile, borrowed moment—might be the last she ever has with Rowen. And she knows, without a doubt, that the truth would ruin it.

So she will bite it back. Let the silence hold her sin.

Just a little longer.

Her best option is to tell Rowen exactly how she feels before it's too late.

"You have completely consumed me," Dani whispered. "Every single day since I met you, I've tried to convince myself that what I felt wasn't real. That I could just... push it away and move on. But God, Rowen, you're everything. You've gotten under my skin so deep that I don't know where you end and I begin." Her voice grew softer. "You've ruined me for anyone else, and the terrifying part is... I don't want to be fixed. I burn for you."

Rowen didn't speak. Her eyes shimmered in the low light, locked on Dani's mouth.

Dani looked up again, raw and wide open.

"Because..." Her throat closed around the rest. It felt like a glass edge, the next words dangerous and irreversible. "I think... I think I'm in lov..."

Rowen leaned in swiftly, kissing Dani before the words could escape her lips. "Do not," she shuddered. "If you say it, this becomes real, and then I can no longer pretend you are not everything I fear losing."

This was the edge, and Dani had been here before.

Cornered and confined by an oppressive silence, the words now wedged in her mind instead of escaping her lips. And this was always when she made her worst decisions. When reason abandoned her, and instinct seized control. When the primal urge to consume consumed her.

Let Beatrice have her vows, her name, her ring, her lie. But this? This first act of virginal undoing? It will belong to me.

She felt the shift settle over her—that terrifying calm before the strike of the match against the stone. Her pulse slowed, steadied. She could almost taste the ruin she was about to unleash. Her lips curved into something feral. A Cheshire cat's grin morphed into a slow smile. Not forgiveness or compassion, pure claim.

Fingers found the first button at Rowen's collar. A quiet click as it slipped free. Then another. And another. Each one undone, like breaking open a lock.

The shirt fell away beneath Dani's hands—loose, helpless. Underneath, the white cotton binding wrapped tight around Rowen's chest, the fabric that helped create the masculine silhouette that fooled the world.

Dani's fingers found the edge, unwinding the long strip of cloth with careful reverence. Layer by layer, until Rowen's true form revealed.

Rowen's chest rose, bare and trembling, nipples hardened to the touch.

Dani leaned in, palms warm as they cupped each breast. Her thumbs grazed over sensitive peaks—light, teasing strokes that dragged a low sound from Rowen's throat.

She kissed her deeply through it all, unhurried and possessive, before trailing her mouth along Rowen's jaw and down the column of her throat. When she pressed a soft kiss right over the pulse she'd been watching earlier, Rowen's head tipped back in surrender, a quiet gasp escaping her lips. She continued her path lower, lips brushing the tender space between her breasts, and felt Rowen shudder beneath her touch.

Dani placed another kiss lower still, just under the swell of one breast where the skin was soft and hidden and wholly untouched, and Rowen's breath fractured completely. Her hands hovered uselessly at her sides at first, fingers twitching as if they couldn't decide where to land, until finally they found Dani's waist—tentative and uncertain before curling tighter with growing confidence. When Rowen pulled her on top, thumbs digging possessively into her hips, Dani knew she had all the invitation she needed. The bed dipped beneath them as she straddled Rowen.

The nightgown rode up higher, bunching at the crease of her hips and leaving the long length of her gorgeous thighs bare against Rowen's torso, warm skin grazing skin with every subtle movement.

Rowen's hands descended lower, grasping the softness of Dani's thighs. Her fingers sank in; she couldn't believe she was allowed this much.

"God, I need you so much it hurts," Dani moaned, the words torn from somewhere deep in her chest.

Rowen went completely still, a slow, visible flush creeping across her cheeks as her eyes dropped to where Dani straddled her. When she spoke, her voice was rough with want.

"Your thighs... they are tempting me to further damnation."

Her dark sexual confidence from the speak easy no longer existed. It was absolutely clear this was Rowen's first time with a woman—the nervous tremor in her hands, the way she looked at Dani like she was both a miracle and a terrifying mystery. There were no guidebooks for this moment, no quiet chapter tucked away in any finishing school manual that explained what to do when the woman you adored sat upon you like this.

Hesitantly, she reached up; Her shaking hands hovering above the delicate lace bow at Dani's chest. Then, as if gathering her courage, she tugged the bow loose in one sharp pull. The gown gave way instantly, and Dani's breasts spilled free, nipples pink and hard, stood erect in the wavering darkness.

"Wait," Dani whispered, dismounting from Rowen and moving to the side of the bed. Bare feet padded across the cold floor as she moved through the hushed stillness of the room.

First, she reached for the bedroom door and turned the lock with a soft click.

Rowen sat up slowly, her eyes dragged down Dani's naked muscular body in hungry, disbelieving passes as she walked.

Then Dani crossed to the sleeping porch, fingers brushing the frame as she eased it shut, bolting it from the inside.

Only then did she return, her gaze never leaving Rowen's. She climbed back onto the bed and sank onto the pillows on her back.

Flushed and beautiful, her pink nipples peaked tight in the cool air, legs parted to reveal the soft pink bloom of her center.

Rowen's throat worked as she swallowed hard.

Dani lay there, every inch bare and unbothered, commanding, with nothing but a look.

And Rowen, with all her inexperience, came apart.

Her fingers hovered near Dani's breast, close enough to perceive the heat radiating from her skin, but not yet brave enough to touch.

"If you would permit me..." Rowen added, quieter still, "I should very much like to feel you."

Dani's teeth caught the corner of her lip, holding there for a breath.

Following this, she gave the slightest nod.

Rowen's hand lowered, cupping Dani's breast softly in her palm.

And for one suspended second, she remained there.

Wide-eyed and barely breathing.

Her fingers tightened, pressing into the soft, full, perfectly round breast, leaving her utterly destroyed.

The space between Rowen's legs throbbed until the smallest part of it strained tight, swollen, and unbearably sensitive.

Her hand roamed, slow and careful—ribs, waist, hip—squeezing as she went. Mapping Dani's body and learning it by heart.

She paused at her stomach, fingers curling against the soft skin.

"How am I supposed to marry anyone else when I've already given every part of me to you?" Rowen breathed.

Dani pushed Rowen's fingers lower, finding the slick heat of her center—wet and waiting. Everything else dropped away as Rowen gasped sharply and Dani felt her soul practically leave her body. She shifted her hips, guiding Rowen's fingers into unhurried, precise circles, showing her the rhythm her body already ached for.

But Rowen caught a spot harder than intended—too dry, too much—and Dani yelped sharply. Rowen's whole body snapped still, frozen as panic flared across her face, believing she had broken something precious. A tremor passed through her hands as she had already begun retreating, but Dani's thumb traced the edge of her lips, offering nothing but trust. Rowen's breath shook, but this time she let Dani lead, her eyes closed in quiet satisfaction.

Rowen looks absolutely adorable like this, she thought. Eager yet awkward, nervous as hell but trying so hard to please. The combination was devastating, and Dani ached with the need to feel her deeper, to guide those trembling fingers exactly where she needed them most.

She led Rowen carefully, dragging her hand along her inner thighs before settling those tentative fingers lower than before, right at her entrance. When Dani pressed Rowen's fingertips against herself—a slow, sticky tap into the dampness—Rowen's hands shook barely perceptibly, but enough to crack the composed mask she'd been holding onto. She was still terrified, but Dani didn't let go, holding her steady as Rowen's eyes widened when her fingers grazed that intimate opening for the first time.

Rowen, still terrified, pressed in, and the smallest breach had Dani gasping, her hips tilting up involuntarily. She could feel Dani's ribbed walls grip around her fingers, tightly pulling her in as if she belonged there.

"Rowen," Dani managed, her head tipping back into the pillows as Rowen pushed a little deeper, noting the way Dani's body gave way for her—the flutter and squeeze around her fingers like nothing she'd ever imagined.

She moved again slowly, learning, intuitively watching Dani unravel beneath her, and it emboldened her. When she pressed deeper and accidentally curved her fingers slightly, Dani's moan was instant, her hips rolling softly to chase the movement, greedy for every inch. She found a rhythm then, pumping her fingers in and out with care, dragging them slowly to feel every texture while Dani's thighs trembled and her jaw went slack.

"You're gonna—" Dani's voice broke off, sharp and breathless. She rocked up against Rowen's hand, pushing her in deeper.

Rowen knew she'd never recover from this—seeing the way she affected Dani was addicting, too good, with Dani's body shaking and wound tight around her fingers, hips bucking in a rhythmic roll. But Dani didn't want to reach that point yet, couldn't come, not like this. She grabbed Rowen by the wrist, dragging her hand out slowly, slick fingers trailing wetness down her thigh.

Then she surged up—all muscle, all control—catching Rowen by the waist and flipping her clean onto her back with effortless ease. Rowen hit the mattress with a soft, startled sound, breath stolen straight from her chest as Dani followed, crawling over her like a storm rolling in.

She hovered there, every dark wave of her hair slipping forward around gorgeous round bare breasts that still heaved from breathlessness. One hand pressed flat to Rowen's stomach, pinning her, and Rowen's body quivered beneath her fingertips. She should have felt scared, but Dani's strength, that devastating silhouette—it only made her want more.

Dani leaned in, her upper body lowering until her bare chest pressed flush against Rowen's, the soft drag of their nipples brushing as she shifted, making Rowen gasp. She steadied herself with one hand braced beside Rowen's ribs, maintaining her position to keep the pressure perfect, while her other hand didn't hesitate—sliding straight down to pop the trouser button open without ceremony before slipping inside, palm flat, moving in slow circles over Rowen's center. The slick glide of her folds, the hard throb beneath, all of it pulled into motion with every slow rotation.

But Dani didn't go straight for her clit—absolutely not, not yet. Rowen was brand new, raw, overwired, and Dani wanted her to burn with every swipe, slowly, without overwhelming her too soon. It was working: Rowen's hips twitched under her hand, her breath breaking apart in staggered, little gasps that told Dani everything she needed to know.

"Proper girl... letting me ruin you like this," Dani breathed into Rowen's throat, whatever control she had burning alive in the wreckage of Rowen Quinn and her scared but utterly ruinous, pleasured looks. Her hands moved to Rowen's remaining clothes, working the fastenings with urgent fingers until she could push the trousers down and away. "Spread your legs," Dani rasped. "I need to feel you."

Startled, Rowen spread her legs without hesitation as Dani moved slowly at first, positioning herself above Rowen on her knees, wrapping a leg underneath her and one on top so their wet centers could align intimately. Rowen gasped—she hadn't realized that women could do that.

Dani rocked against her with the slow, steady pressure of slick against slick until Rowen's head tipped back on instinct, a raw sound tearing from her throat. Rowen looked like she'd forgotten how to breathe, watching Dani's breasts bounce with the motion as their bodies locked together, the hard, throbbing swells of them catching again and again while kissing each other, until Dani's legs shook. She came hard then, clenching and grinding down against Rowen with a soundless gasp, eyes squeezed shut, heart flying as the aftershocks hit slow—thighs twitching, breath panting, sweat cooling against her skin.

When she blinked down through the haze, she nearly lost it all over again. Rowen was shaking beneath her, mouth parted, eyes wide with that stunned, awed look—like Dani had just rewritten her entire goddamn world.

Sweet thing.

But Dani wasn't done—not until Rowen came too. "Stand up for me," she ordered, and Rowen's brow knit curiously, reluctantly, as she rose on unsteady legs. Dani dropped to the floor and sat back against the edge of the bed like she'd planned this from the start, waiting and watching. "Put your right leg up," she told her, tapping her shoulder. "Right here." Out of shyness, Rowen bent down to kiss Dani before awkwardly lifting her leg to her shoulder, balancing over her—as if this wasn't the first filthy thing she'd done tonight. "Now," Dani said, eyes heavy, tracing her tongue along her bottom lip, "take my face."

A beat. Two. "Oh... heavens above," was all Rowen could muster, and Dani smiled at the breathless awe in her voice. Rowen shifted forward then, hips unsteady, moving against Dani's mouth with cautious pressure—she didn't know what she was doing, only that it felt devastatingly good as Dani flattened her tongue, dragging it in slow, pressured passes over the soft heat of her folds, giving Rowen time to adjust.

When Dani's lips closed over Rowen's clit, Rowen lost it completely—her whole body jolting as if lightning had struck her, "Goodness!" punching out of her as her hands scrambled down into Dani's hair, uncertain whether to pull her closer or shove her away.

Nobody had told her it would feel like this, like drowning and flying at once, as Dani sucked her into her mouth, gently but firm, pulsing her slowly with just the right pressure. For ten endless, exquisite minutes, Dani worked her with patient devotion, learning every response, every shudder, building the tension until Rowen was barely coherent.

"Dani—I," she gasped, her hips stuttering before her shoulders trembled as she arched forward, and then she came spilling into Dani's mouth, completely undone. Dani stayed right there through it all, licking her through the waves like she owned this part of Rowen now, claiming every tremor and gasp as her own.

When Rowen finally crumbled and half-collapsed, dropping to her knees, she caught Dani's face in both hands and kissed her with desperation. "I daresay... I shall never recover," she whispered against Dani's lips, the quiet collapse of someone who had never been allowed to feel this much.

They sank down together, hearts still beating out of rhythm as breathing slowly returned to normal. Dani laid with her head on Rowen's chest, listening to the steady thrum of her heartbeat. The fire had burned down to red embers.

It was then that Rowen spoke, her voice soft and almost confessional: "It sounds quite absurd, I know... but I think I have written versions of you in my dreams for years."

The words hit Dani harder than anything Rowen had done with her hands. She was still furious about the ring, still angry about Beatrice, still enraged by all of it—but none of it mattered when Rowen touched her like this. And Dani knew, with terrifying certainty, that she was in love with her.

Hope bloomed in her chest, fierce and sudden. If this indicated Rowen changing her mind—if tonight meant what Dani desperately wanted it to mean—then maybe she could find another way. Regardless of the agreement she'd made with Gabe, she could figure out how to get that box from him, find her way home. Maybe even bring Rowen through the portal with her. They could be together, really together, away from all this Edwardian propriety and hopeless marriages. There had to be a way.

But exhaustion continued to pull at Dani even as she refused to surrender to sleep. "Stay with me," she whispered, and Rowen's fingertips drifted along her skin in gentle patterns, a sigh brushing through Dani's hair—warm and full of longing and regret in equal measure. Then, as the last embers died and true darkness settled over them, sleep finally claimed them both, still wrapped around each other as if letting go might break the spell that had given them this one perfect, stolen night.

Her body was heavy with sleep's warmth. Eyes closed, she savored the weight of blankets and the soft mattress beneath her.

The memory crashed over her—Rowen's touch, scent, hushed confessions in darkness.

Dani's eyes flew open, her hand reaching instinctively beside her.

Empty.

The sheets were cool, as if no one had lain there at all. Only the faintest impression on the pillow suggested she hadn't dreamed it. That, and the scent of cedar and bergamot—a trace so faint she might have imagined it.

She sat up slowly, pushing tangled hair from her face. The bedroom looked exactly as before—fireplace reduced to glowing embers; nightgown draped over the chair. Nothing suggested the world had shifted, yet she felt it everywhere. In her body's tender ache, in phantom touches that lingered.

So why come to her at all if she was still marrying Beatrice?

A soft knock startled her. "Yes?"

"It's only me, miss. I've brought your morning tea." Shannon's voice, muffled through wood.

"Come in."

Shannon entered with quiet efficiency, steam rising from the china teapot. Her eyes flickered to the rumpled bed, the discarded nightgown, but her expression remained neutral.

"Did you sleep well, miss?"

Heat rose in Dani's cheeks. "Yeah. Thanks." She paused, studying Shannon's carefully composed face. "And thank you for... last night. For helping her find her way here."

The faintest smile tugged at Shannon's lips. "I'm sure I don't know what you mean, miss."

"You little shit," Dani said, but there was warmth in it.

Shannon's smile widened just a fraction as she moved to stoke the fire. "Is there anything else you require, miss?"

Dani shook her head. Once Shannon left, she threw back the covers and rose on unsteady legs. Her reflection showed a stranger—flushed cheeks, tangled hair, eyes too bright. She looked haunted.

She needed answers. Needed to know why Rowen had unraveled in her arms only to vanish again.

As she reached for the tea, something small and white caught her eye—nestled against the teapot's base. A folded note, so tiny she might have missed it. With trembling fingers, she unfolded it.

The handwriting was scribbled, quickly written without proper punctuation, but still elegant—unmistakably Rowen's:

> D
>
> *Forgive my absence there are matters I must attend to that cannot wait. What I feel for you is real. Touching you and being touched by you was the most perfect thing I have ever known. But for my mother's sake I must honor my engagement to Beatrice. I know you will understand.*
>
> R

Dani read it again, slower, the words blurring as her hands shook. The paper crinkled in her grip. *I know you will understand.*

Like hell she understood. Her chest felt like it was caving in, breath coming short. Rowen had the audacity to tell her their night together was perfect, then walk away because of duty? And assume Dani would just... what? Smile and wave her off to marry someone else?

The note fluttered to the floor as Dani pressed her palms against her eyes, trying to stop the burning behind them.

She folded the note and tucked it into her nightstand drawer. Outside, Portland was waking—chimney smoke rising against the morning sky, distant sounds of horses and staff moving about. The world continued its march, oblivious to her pain.

She reached for her tea, the cup's warmth steadying her hands. If this was Rowen's idea of goodbye, it was the hardest one she could imagine. To give her a taste of what they could be, only to walk toward a life with Beatrice? A special kind of cruelty.

"You cruel, infuriating little shit," she muttered, the endearment carrying both affection and genuine anger.

Dani wasn't about to be held hostage by someone who wouldn't choose her. If Rowen was determined to go through with this engagement, then Dani would find a way forward, too. And that meant home, alone.

She hardened herself against Rowen, despite the pull she felt. Even if it meant burying last night's memory.

23

GODSPEED

EDWARDIAN ERA

Alvie snapped the newspaper shut, slapping it onto the breakfast table. "Quite enough nonsense in this town. We shall retire to the mountains for a month."

Vivienne arched a delicate brow, her fork pausing mid-air. "A month? Alvie, we have commitments to uphold."

"The mountains will do us good—fresh air, respite from this ceaseless tedium." He straightened in his chair. "Besides, the motor car has finally arrived, and I intend to put it properly through its paces. I am considering inviting several couples to join us. The hunting lodge boasts ten fine bedrooms, after all."

He plucked a sugar cube and dropped it into his tea. "The blasted game lift at the lodge has been giving us trouble again. Edmund, please come to my study after breakfast. We should also ask Gabriel Dunwich of Dunwich and Sons to join us—he's the only one who really understands the lodge's game lift pulley system; it's jammed. Without it, we shall struggle to process the venison we hunt."

Dani stirred her tea without looking. A week of feigned illness, a week of ignoring Gabe's calls. Cedar. Bergamot. Empty sheets. And now—his name, sharp as a blade.

"What?" Her spoon clattered against the saucer. "Gabriel?"

"Indeed. He fashioned the mechanism and levers with his own hands—most ingenious work. Prudent, he comes to assist. He can stay for a bit as well—I've got some other things for him to fix."

Well, shit. Here we go.

"Actually, I've been meaning to tell you both something."

Vivienne set down her fork. "Go on, dear."

Dani swallowed hard, her throat suddenly dry. The words seemed to stick somewhere between her chest and her mouth. She glanced at their expectant faces, then down at her hands.

"I'm engaged," her tone filled with shame, "To Gabriel."

Silence flooded the table. Alvie's eyes studied her face—the forced brightness, the way her hands fidgeted with her napkin. Concern shifted across his features before he composed himself.

"Well," he said finally, a hearty laugh breaking through his hesitation. "Splendid! Though I must say, Gabriel is rather bold neglecting to ask for my blessing first."

Heat crept up Dani's neck. She hadn't expected this—the warmth in his voice, the way he looked at her like... like a father might. "Oh, I... I didn't think... I'm just a guest here, so I didn't expect—"

"Nonsense, my dear." Alvie's voice softened. "You are family to us now. We love you as our own daughter." He reached across to pat her hand gently. "Gabriel ought to have known better, but no matter. I dare say this shall be a most exhilarating holiday indeed."

The words hit her unexpectedly hard. *Family.* After months of feeling displaced, unmoored, here was this man claiming her as his own. Guilt twisted in her stomach—if only he knew why she was really marrying Gabriel.

Vivienne studied Dani with sharp eyes. "Well, that is rather unexpected. Tell me, when did this courtship begin? I confess I had noticed no particular... attachment."

"It's been... recent."

"How recent?" Vivienne's smile was polite, predatory. "Surely such momentous decisions require considerable thought."

Dani shifted in her seat. "We've known each other for—"

"And where exactly did you meet Mr. Dunwich? Portland society is quite small, yet I don't recall seeing you together at any functions."

"Vivienne," Alvie warned gently.

But Vivienne continued. "I merely find it curious that a young woman would accept a proposal from a gentleman she's scarcely seen with in public. One wonders what sort of... understanding you might have reached."

The implication floated through the dining room. Dani's face burned.

"Come now, Vivienne, let the girl be," Alvie chuckled. "She has demonstrated commendable independence."

Vivienne's lips pressed into a thin line, but she relented. "Very well. Nevertheless, congratulations, dear."

Dani tried to smile, but her thoughts had already drifted. *Would Rowen care if she found out?* She pushed her plate aside.

"I need to go into town before we leave."

Vivienne tilted her head. "Oh? And what pressing engagement calls you to town, dear?"

"I need a proper coat. Won't last long in the mountains without one."

"A sensible decision. I shall have Shannon accompany you."

"That's unnecessary. Just a quick trip."

"Very well. But whilst you are there, have Edmund collect my dress order."

Dani nodded, rising. If she was going with Gabriel for a month to the mountains, surely Rowen would or herself would be married by the time they returned. She had to see Rowen—*one last time.*

The department store's warmth struck her like a slap. Heavy perfume, steaming wool, whispered silk. Images from their first meeting flashed—Rowen's intent eyes, her nervousness, the laughs they'd shared trying on clothes. She had barely registered anything since she had stepped from the coach, her boots striking hard against the wet pavement.

Images from that night flashed through her mind as she rode the elevator up—Rowen's silhouette in her bed, unexpected and breathless; the press of lips against her neck; whispered confessions neither had any right to make. That devastating morning had come with the slap of reality—Rowen had a fiancée waiting, a life already promised to another. Despite her efforts, Dani found herself chasing after something she couldn't possess. She had to make one final attempt, one last chance to convince Rowen.

She moved without thought off the elevator, unaware of her limbs, because some force had taken control and propelled her forward. She scanned the sea of corseted figures. Sharp profile, piercing eyes. *Her.*

But Rowen wasn't there.

A woman in a high-collared dress stood behind the counter, her expression indicating that she had just sensed something particularly unpleasant. Despite her efficiency in folding the linens, her eyes remained fixed on Dani, displaying undisguised curiosity.

"Excuse me," Dani said, adjusting her voice. "I was hoping to find Rowen Quinn. Is he in today?"

The clerk's eyes softened slightly at Dani's evident distress, but curiosity soon overpowered sympathy. "Mr. Quinn?"

Dani gave her a look.

"Oh." A knowing smile crept in. "You're a bit late."

Dani's chest went tight. "Late for what?"

The woman leaned on the counter, inspecting her. "He's not in, I'm afraid."

"But he still works here?"

A pause.

"Well..." The clerk glanced left, then right, as if someone might overhear. "That depends on how one defines 'still.'"

Dani said nothing. Just waited.

The woman's expression brightened as if she'd been waiting for that exact silence. "It's all been rather irregular. Here one day, quite vanished the next. No warning, no farewell, not even a goodbye luncheon, which, I assure you, is most unusual. We do try to keep things proper."

Something inside her tilted. Dani gripped the counter.

The clerk's voice dropped, confidential now. "You're not the first to come looking. Girls have been pouring in since he left. Teary, dramatic types. Clutching gloves and begging for answers."

So many ladies? Christ, was Rowen running some kind of Victorian heartbreak factory? Buy one flutter of hope, get your dignity crushed free.

"Left," Dani echoed.

"Oh yes. Packed up and cleared out midweek. Quite the scandal, honestly." She lowered her voice conspiratorially. "Especially given the rumors of a fiancée. One would think he'd be more discreet—he's certainly upset half the female population of Portland."

"Did he leave a forwarding address?"

"No, I'm afraid Mr. Quinn left quite suddenly. But between ourselves, such hasty departures often follow... indiscretions. Though I heard he has friends at that establishment on Morrison Street—you know, the sort of place."

The pub. Of course.

Dani nodded stiffly, then turned away. She drifted toward a rack of gloves, staring through them, breathing hard. The store buzzed around her—polite laughter, the rustle of fabric, the click of heels. All too loud. A pair of well-dressed women near the hat display had stopped their conversation to watch her, their eyes sharp with curiosity. Another woman by the ribbons whispered something to her companion, both glancing her way. She could feel their stares like pinpricks on her skin.

This isn't some modern-day meltdown in a Target parking lot where you could ugly cry beside your car and vanish into blessed anonymity. This was 1905. People noticed. People talked. And in a week, some society column would probably print a polite, flowery version of *Miss Wood Suffers Very Public Hysteria Over Handsome Tailor, Sources Say*—and somehow, Vivienne would have it framed.

Dani pressed her palms to her eyes then squared her shoulders and walked back to the counter, voice steadier this time. "I need to collect a dress order for Vivienne Barrington. And one winter coat, please. I don't care what it looks like."

The clerk straightened at once, professionalism snapping into place. "Of course, madam. Right away."

Minutes later, Dani carried the wrapped dress to the waiting buggy, handing it up to Edmund before tossing the coat angrily inside. His face creased with concern.

"Everything alright, miss?"

She managed a weak smile. "Yeah, just... shopping's more exhausting than I thought."

Edmund didn't press. "Right then. Home it is."

The Barrington Estate's foyer felt stifling when Dani stepped inside, Edmund following behind with her coat and Vivienne's dress. The warmth couldn't touch the hollow ache where hope had been just an hour before.

"Ah, there you are, dear!" Vivienne appeared from the parlor, eyes immediately going to the wrapped package in Edmund's arms. "Did you manage to find everything you needed?"

"Your dress is ready," Dani said flatly, gesturing to Edmund. "And I got a coat."

Vivienne's eyes narrowed. "How lovely. Edmund, see that my dress is properly hung in the wardrobe. And Miss Wood's coat as well."

"Of course, ma'am." Edmund nodded, though his concerned glance lingered on Dani before he headed toward the stairs.

"You look rather pale, dear," Vivienne observed, stepping closer. "Perhaps some tea would—"

"Miss Wood."

Alvie's voice cut through the exchange. He stood in the study doorway; the usual mischief vanished from his eyes. "Might I have a word? A matter of some importance has arisen."

Vivienne glanced between them, curiosity stretching across her features, but she stepped back gracefully. "Of course. I shall see to the arrangements for dinner."

Dani followed him down the dim corridor, something in his posture—the set of his shoulders, the way he moved with unusual purpose—warning her this wasn't about social pleasantries.

The study door closed behind them with a soft click. Rich redwood paneling gleamed in the fading light of early evening. Leather-bound books lined the walls from floor to ceiling, and a crystal decanter caught the firelight on the side table. The fire crackled softly in the hearth, casting dancing shadows across the Persian rug.

Above the mantel hung a portrait of downtown Portland, and on Alvie's desk—Rowen's gift lay open, pages catching the firelight.

Alvie moved to the decanter, pouring amber liquid into a crystal glass. He didn't offer her one—a small reminder of the time she was in.

"How was your shopping expedition?" he asked, though something in his tone suggested the question was merely polite prelude to weightier matters. "I received a rather interesting telephone call from Miss Morewood. Her acquaintance at the department store seemed quite concerned about your... state."

She hadn't been wrong—word really did travel fast in 1905. And since Miss Morewood was as wealthy as Alvie, she didn't have to wait for a letter to spread her gossip. She could just pick up her shiny new telephone and tattle immediately..

"I'm fine," she said, brushing it off with a smile, then under her breath muttered, "Alexander Graham Bell's greatest invention: the snitch machine."

Alvie's eyes remained steadfast, unwavering in their gaze as he held hers. His steady and unblinking stare seemed to challenge her to speak further, as he raised his glass for a sip.

Finally, she gave in, the truth tumbling out. "I... I went to find Rowen, actually. I needed to speak with him."

Alvie paused, glass halfway to his lips. "Ah. I rather suspected as much." He set the drink down untouched. "I couldn't help but notice his rather generous bid of three hundred dollars at the charity ball. And the way you two looked at one another... well, it was quite apparent there were feelings involved. A delicate situation indeed, given his engagement to Miss Ashdown."

A flush rose to her throat. "Was it that obvious?"

"My dear, you two practically set the ballroom ablaze with those looks."

"Well, it doesn't matter now anyway. When I got to the department store, the clerk said he'd vanished. Just up and quit mid-week without notice." Dani's voice grew strained. "I'm worried he may have run off somewhere."

His eyes lost their warmth. "Running off may be the least of our concerns." He moved toward a massive hunting painting, placing his palm against the gilded frame. The panel swung open, revealing a hidden safe. "Given your engagement to Gabriel, I find myself compelled to discuss certain matters of considerable importance," he said. "There are circumstances of both you and Mr. Dunwich that you may not fully comprehend. I confess, my dear, that I have not been entirely forthcoming." He paused, meeting her eyes directly. "I have an idea of how you got here—indeed, I have suspected since nearly the moment you graced our threshold."

Inside the safe, on velvet, lay a metal box identical to Mary's.

"How...?"

Her legs went unsteady. She gripped the back of the nearest chair, knuckles white against the leather. All this time—every conversation, every shared meal, every moment I thought I was fooling them—he'd known.

Alvie lifted the box carefully from its resting place and crossed to where she stood. "Perhaps you'd care to examine it?"

With trembling fingers, Dani took the box. It felt lighter than Mary's—hollow, almost. She traced the familiar engravings, then lifted the lid. Unlike Mary's box, filled with intricate gears and crystalline components that seemed to pulse with their own light, this one contained only empty velvet compartments and a few crude metal pieces.

"It's different," she breathed, setting it gently on the side table beside her chair.

"How long?" she whispered.

He turned to face her, firelight deepening the lines around his eyes. "The resemblance was unmistakable when you arrived. To Vivienne. To myself. And then you slipped the Barrington name."

She shook her head, trying to process it. "And that box?"

"I unfortunately funded their creation. Gabriel approached me with plans for projection boxes—devices that would show moving pictures. But then his partner arrived. A man named Enver who transformed the concept entirely."

This explains the projection box Enver sent me, showing Rowen and Beatrice kissing in the park.

"And instead of a projection box, you ended up inadvertently investing in time travel."

"I wasn't the only one. Gabriel courted several wealthy acquaintances. This was merely a prototype." He placed it on his desk. "This one does not work—and I'm glad. Once they functioned as time portals, I heard stories. The sorrow they wrought."

"Why didn't you just tell me?"

"How does an Edwardian gentleman inquire if a young woman has traveled through time?" A bitter laugh escaped him. "Propriety demanded I gather evidence first—your fascination with the Clockery, your peculiar mannerisms, and now this sudden engagement to Gabriel. It all confirmed my suspicions." His expression grew grave. "But even entertaining such thoughts publicly would brand me a lunatic. And you—in 1905, my dear, claims of time travel could see you committed to an asylum. The fewer souls who know of such things, the safer we all remain."

"So you just watched me?"

"I protected you the only way I knew how—with silence." He joined her at the hearth. "Society would hardly welcome you if they knew. Even Vivienne believed you might be my offspring and with my quick acceptance, it made things easier for you to integrate until I could figure things out. Even if it meant allowing society to think I had not one bastard child, but two."

The weight of his sacrifice hit her—like a falling piano, only less musical and more existential. While she'd been flailing through the dumpster fire of time travel and figuring herself out, Alvie had been quietly shielding her from disasters she hadn't even thought to worry about. The asylum. His social ruin. Basically, a one-way ticket to Edwardian cancellation.

"You risked everything," she mumbled. "For a stranger. That can't be the only reason."

He poured himself another measure of whiskey. "I admit, I partly feared your confirmation would lead to your eventual departure. I realized I hadn't prepared for that possibility."

The tenderness in his voice made her chest ache.

"I didn't mean to keep it from you," she said quietly. "I dropped into a strange century, had to decode the culture, and spent a solid week terrified I'd get Salem-witched if I said the wrong thing."

A breath of a smile. "I got my box from Mary—Cleo's great-great granddaughter. I've been looking for another one ever since. Trying to get home."

The glass froze halfway to his lips. "Cleo..." He stumbled into a chair. "She has a granddaughter?"

"And I'm your great-great-granddaughter."

Neither of them spoke. The only sounds were the ticking clock and the soft pop of embers in the fireplace. Outside, birds chirped in the gathering dusk, oblivious.

He shifted toward the doorway, half-expecting Vivienne to appear and confirm the impossible. The color had drained from his face, leaving him pale beneath his sun-worn complexion.

"I knew something was familiar," he finally said, his voice quiet and rough. "When I laid eyes upon you. But this..." He set down his untouched drink with a trembling hand. "To think all this time, I was playing host to my own blood."

He moved to the window, pulling back the heavy velvet curtain to stare into the darkness beyond. His reflection stared back—a ghost superimposed on the evening sky.

"Vivienne believed you to be my child at first—a mistake, a love child. It was only later I realized you had arrived using a box. That's why I encouraged her to embrace you so quickly, so completely. Why she insisted on securing you a marriage—to marry you off and out of my care. Keep her occupied until I could figure out something."

Dani sank deeper into her chair, overwhelmed by the magnitude of it all. But there was more in his expression—something he hadn't yet revealed.

"Perhaps we should continue this conversation somewhere more comfortable," Alvie suggested gently, noting how she trembled. "The parlor fire is warmer, and I believe we both need a moment to collect ourselves."

She nodded, watching as he grabbed the crystal decanter from the side table. At her questioning look, he gave a wry smile. "I suspect I'll need to finish this entire bottle after the revelations of this evening."

They walked through the quiet halls to the parlor, Alvie cradling the decanter like precious cargo.

In the parlor, Dani settled into the wing chair, tucking her feet beneath her. A few pins had come loose during their conversation, and she absently pushed a strand of hair behind her ear. The firelight cast shifting patterns across the room, making everything feel slightly unreal—fitting, given what they'd just discussed.

Alvie set the decanter on the side table between their chairs, pouring himself another generous measure. "Have you considered what happens when one meddles with time?" He stood at the mantel, his silhouette tall against the dancing flames.

"You mean paradoxes? Changing the future?"

"Not just the future. The lives of those around you." Setting down his glass with a soft clink, he leaned forward, his signet ring catching the light as he gestured. "Every small action creates ripples. The woman who serves your tea might not meet her husband because you requested Earl Grey instead of Darjeeling, changing her schedule by mere minutes. The child from that union might become a doctor who saves countless lives... or a criminal who takes them."

"And no one's ever mapped what happens if two timelines bleed into each other. I pray you never have to find out."

"Shit. Do you think I've done irreversible damage?" She leaned forward, hands clasped tightly in her lap.

"I believe we must acknowledge our power to reshape destinies beyond our own." His eyes found hers. "When Gabriel first approached me with his projection box idea, curiosity blinded me. I never considered the moral weight of what Enver was creating, and absolutely didn't expect the devices would evolve beyond simple projections. You must be careful."

She swallowed hard, the fire suddenly too warm on her skin. "If I stay here...if I continue changing things...people I know might never exist."

"Or exist differently. Including, perhaps, yourself." He turned to prod the fire with a brass poker, sending sparks upward in a flaky constellation.

"Had I known your true identity, I might have reconsidered giving you such a loose leash. Knowing we're related means you could affect my own family line—and perhaps the nature of the activities in which we involved you." He reclaimed his seat opposite her. "But what's done is done."

She'd told him everything—or enough. Regarding her arrival in the box. About wanting to get home. About Gabe and their deal. The words had spilled from her like water, unstoppable once the dam had broken.

"There's something else, isn't there?" she asked quietly, reading the tension in his posture. "Something about Rowen."

Alvie's jaw tightened. His fingers drummed against the arm of his chair as he chose his words carefully. "The labor meetings. Rowen's involvement with the workers. My interest in such matters."

"I didn't know you were involved."

"I've been working to protect him, you see." The words came out strained. "Lord Ashdown has been using Rowen's ailing mother as leverage—forcing this engagement to control both Rowen and his influence with the workers."

Dani's breath caught. Through the open door, she could glimpse Alvie's study across the hall, where Rowen's book lay open on the desk. Even from here, she remembered seeing the margins filled with Alvie's careful handwriting—corrections and suggestions in red ink across pages titled "Strike Plans for Common Workers: A Guide." The evidence of his quiet support made her chest tighten.

"You've been fighting Ashdown?"

"Quietly. Carefully." He rose and moved to the fireplace, staring into the flames. "Rowen's voice with the laborers is powerful, pure. Ashdown seeks to corrupt that, make him his puppet. The man mistreats his workers terribly—unsafe conditions, poverty wages—and instead of making it right, he wants to use Rowen's gift for words and public speaking to pacify them. To convince them their suffering is noble."

"That's vile." Dani's hands tightened in her lap.

"Indeed. The engagement suits his aims—a respectable union that keeps Rowen within reach and grants him the appearance of virtue while tightening his grip on the workers he claims to champion. When truly, he'd do better to treat them with fairness from the outset, as any man of principle ought to. He's surrounded himself with a small circle of wealthy allies, all equally guilty, all hoping Ashdown will silence the unrest before it touches their own businesses."

"So, your support of the labor movement..."

"Has been partly strategic, yes. To keep Rowen free to advocate for workers rather than becoming Ashdown's political instrument." He turned back to her, expression grave.

"I've been playing the long game, longer than anyone realized—trying to break his hold over the young man without destroying his mother."

The revelation hit Dani like a physical blow. All this time, while she'd been consumed with her own feelings for Rowen, Alvie quietly orchestrated a campaign to save him from a different kind of imprisonment.

"But now, with Rowen's sudden departure," Alvie continued, his voice lowering, "the balance has shifted considerably. It places him in grave peril. Ashdown is no man to suffer defiance lightly. Should he learn that Rowen has slipped from his grasp—and might even speak against him..."

"He'll come after him," Dani finished, her voice hollow.

Alvie studied her face, noting something she wasn't saying. "There's something more, isn't there? About Mr. Quinn."

She hesitated, throat tight. She'd been carrying this secret, protecting Rowen's identity even as her heart broke. But Alvie had trusted her with so much—his knowledge of time travel, his family secrets, his quiet campaign to protect Rowen.

"Rowen isn't a man. She's a woman. Disguised. And..." She took a breath. "I love her. I wanted to take her back with me. Somewhere we wouldn't have to hide."

Alvie went still. The fire crackled in the silence as he processed this revelation. When he finally spoke, his voice was careful, unhurried.

"I see." He set down his glass with precision. "That is... that explains much." A long pause. "In my years supporting those who society deems lesser—the workers, the poor—I've learned that the world's rigid rules often cause quite more suffering than they prevent."

He met her eyes then, and she saw not disgust but a weary understanding. "You must know how dangerous this knowledge is. Not just for you, but for her."

"I know." Her voice came out small.

"And yet you trust me with it." His expression softened. "My dear girl, you've shown more courage in this moment than most show in a lifetime." His voice grew thick. "I cannot pretend to fully understand, but I know what it is to long for person, and a different world than the one we're given."

Relief washed over her. "Which makes this whole Gabriel thing messier."

"I'd imagine so." He responded, "And if Rowen asks you to stay?"

"I have a family—my father, your great grandson," she replied. "They still live in this house. They're restoring it—slowly and carefully. With all the inheritance tied up in your downtown properties, it's hard and taking time... but it's worth it. There's so much I can tell you. But I remember what you said about altering history."

She paused, then gestured toward the decanter—an unspoken request. After everything they'd just laid bare, he understood: the rules of 1905 didn't quite apply to her. With a quiet nod, he poured the amber liquid into a crystal glass and handed it over. Dani knocked it back in one swift motion, a crooked smile tugging at her lips.

"Delicious," she said, voice warm with defiance. Finally. Only took revealing I was a time traveler, his great-great-granddaughter, and in love with a cross-dressing woman to earn a drink.

"You know, when the boxes first began working—when they weren't myth anymore but real, functional—I did not seek love. Or destiny. I simply wanted to be rather more clever with my fortune," he added.

Dani's brows furrowed. "You used one?"

"I did, indeed. Like the rest of my circle, I was curious. Most of them wanted to peek at the market, cheat time, and come back richer. But I was different. I wanted to see if my investments paid off—if the Barrington name endured. And it did. Just... not in the way I expected." He paused, his expression darkening. "Ashdown also has a box."

Dani went still. "Wait—what?" The casual way he'd mentioned it made her stomach drop. "Ashdown has one? How is that even possible?"

"This problem is too big for just the two of us to solve. We'd need an entire battle plan." He held up a hand before she could respond. "What's important now is you and getting home. I shall handle it." He wiped his brow and composed himself. "But back to my story—when I used the box, I wasn't like the others in my circle. I ended up in 1972. A summer garden party at our family's estate—though by then, it was hardly ours in the way it once had been. She was playing the violin. Laurel. Hair wild, posture perfect, wearing colours I'd never imagined on a woman. And she played like she didn't belong to anyone but the music."

"... Laurel?" Dani's voice was distant, still processing the bombshell about Ashdown.

He nodded. "I was supposed to return that night. I didn't. I kept coming back. Again, and again. We fell in love, and then she was pregnant. I couldn't leave her behind. I told her about the box, about my life—and I brought her here. Back with me."

"Wait—Laurel's from the seventies?" She asked, astonished. The wheels in her mind whirled and turned at this new revelation. "The godfather joke. At Skidmore Fountain.

"I thought—God, I thought she was just eccentric." She shook her head, dazed. "She's like me. A transplant. A fake."

"No. Not a fake." He replied sorrowfully. "Just... misplaced. Like you. She didn't know I was married. I kept that from her for too long. Vivienne's devastation became apparent when we arrived in 1905. But propriety bound us all. Time made things complicated, but in the end, we made peace with the arrangement."

"Awkward?" Dani asked.

"She became head housekeeper. Silent partner in the household. Never tried to unseat Vivienne. Said it wasn't her place. We raised our daughter, Shannon, in the home. As a servant, yes, but never unloved. Vivienne couldn't bring herself to fully accept her, but she saw the girl was educated. Cared for."

"That's why she always looked... apart. And Vivienne was always so cold to her."

Alvie nodded slowly. "It was a quiet tragedy, but also, in its own way, a sort of family. I am no stranger to not fitting society's norms—I fear you and I are much alike in that regard."

His fingers drummed against the arm of his chair. "You remind me of her, you know. Someone who belonged to one world but longed for another."

"What happened to them?" She leaned forward, the chair creaking beneath her.

A faint, wry smile touched his lips as he drifted toward the portrait above the mantel. "She made a choice. And lived with it."

He turned, resolve settling into his expression. "This is quite the predicament. We must find Rowen." His voice lowered, carrying a quiet urgency. "For his... pardon me, her very safety."

Dani straightened, resolve settling behind her eyes. "I know where to start. The pub, O'Driscoll's, on Morrison Street. The clerk said Rowen had friends there—someone might know where she's gone."

"Quite sensible. The taverns are where working men speak freely." Alvie reached for his coat. "I shall escort you, naturally. Such places are hardly—"

"Actually, no." Dani held up a hand. "I appreciate it, but on Burnside, during my night shifts bartending last summer, I've seen far worse than just a few belligerent drunks. I'll be fine."

Alvie's shoulders eased, and he gave a slow nod. His gaze lingered on her a moment longer—part caution, part quiet admiration.

"You're not gonna try to stop me?" She straightened, smoothing her skirts, preparing to rise.

He chuckled, "Would it work if I did?"

"Nah, probably not." She replied.

"Be careful, my dear," he said as she rose, grabbing her coat from where it lay draped over the settee. "You love her that deeply?"

"More than I thought I could." She shrugged into the garment, fingers working the buttons easily, even with their unfamiliar style.

He blinked at her, disbelief softening into a muttered aside. "A public house? At night? Unaccompanied... My granddaughter." He shook his head slowly. "Miss Wood, ladies of this era simply do not do such things."

She turned slowly, dramatic, her skirts kicking up like a dust storm. "Well, partner..." she drawled, tipping an imaginary hat, "I reckon I ain't from around these parts, now, am I?"

He smiled, a flicker of pride behind his eyes, and raised his glass in a quiet salute. "Godspeed."

24

AN UNEXPECTED FRIEND

EDWARDIAN ERA

She pushed forward, scanning the faces through the dim haze. The clerk had said Rowen had friends here—someone had to know where she'd gone.

O'Driscoll's pressed in around her, bodies swarming with heat, sweat, and the sharp tang of whiskey. Laughter rolled through the air, a smothering chorus beneath the low lamplight. The wooden beams overhead disappeared into a smoke-drenched ceiling, darkened by decades of pipe tobacco and coal fires. The scent of ale and damp wool clogged her lungs as she stepped further into the murky interior.

She hadn't even realized how hard she was breathing until someone shouldered into her, jostling her forward.

"Watch it," a man grumbled, glancing at her before returning to his drink.

Barely noticing because she was scanning the faces. Searching. Hoping.

A shift of movement near the bar caught her eye—a familiar sharp profile, golden hair long enough to brush a stiff collar. Her stomach flipped.

Unaware of the men in her way, she surged forward, twisting past broad shoulders and half-lifted glasses. Someone scoffed as she pushed through. A hand brushed against her waist—not by accident—but she wrenched away before she could even register the anger bubbling up.

She reached for the figure's shoulder; Breath locked in her throat. Rowen.

"Rowen!" she gasped, yanking them around.

Her stomach plummeted.

It wasn't her.

The stranger blinked at her, startled. He was too old, broad, or ugly—a man in his mid-thirties, brows knitted in confusion. His drink sloshed over the rim of his glass.

"The hell do you think you're doing?" a voice barked behind him.

She stumbled back, mortified. "I—sorry, I thought you were—"

"Leave off, Tom," another voice cut in. "Can't you see the lady made a mistake?"

Dani turned toward the speaker and froze. Near the back corner, hunched over a pint with shoulders broad beneath worn wool—the docker from the tunnels. The one with the scarred hands who'd been deep in conversation with Rowen that night.

Maybe her luck hadn't completely run out.

Dani wove through the crowd, ignoring the curious looks and occasional comments. A woman alone in a pub was unusual enough. A well-dressed woman? That was asking for trouble.

"Excuse me," she said, sliding onto the stool beside him.

The man glanced up, taking in her fine dress and careful posture. His eyes narrowed. "Well, well. What's a lady of your standing doing in a place like this? We don't take kindly to society types coming down here to gawk at the working class."

"I'm not here to gawk. I'm looking for someone."

"Course you are." He turned back to his drink. "Let me guess—lost your way from some tea party?"

"I need to find Rowen Quinn. It's important."

He snorted, returning to his drink. "Important for who, then?"

"Please. The department store said he'd vanished, just up and quit—"

"Vanished?" The man's laugh was rough as sandpaper. "Quinn ain't vanished. He's home, far as I know."

Dani's heart stuttered. "Home? But the clerk made it sound like—"

"Like he'd run off?" He shook his head. "Nah. Just keeping his head down, isn't he? Smart, considering his new engagement to that Ashdown girl. Won't need to work again, will he? Finally got someone on the inside who understands us workers."

Dani's stomach turned. "You think that engagement is good for the workers?"

The man's eyes lit up. "Course it is! Rowen's one of us. Now he'll have Ashdown's ear, won't he? Maybe things'll finally change 'round here."

Oh God, Dani thought, they do not know what Ashdown is really capable of.

"Where does he live?"

The man's expression hardened. "You're not the first to come asking, and you won't be the last. But we don't give out that information, miss."

"I'm not trying to cause trouble. I just need to—"

"Listen here." He turned to face her fully, voice dropping low. "Quinn's done more for us workers than any fancy gentleman ever has. We protect our own, we do. You want to find him? He'll find you if he wants to be found."

The finality in his tone left no room for argument. Dani slumped on the stool, defeat washing over her. Another dead end.

"Can I at least buy you a drink?" she asked weakly. "For your trouble?"

He studied her for a long moment, then nodded. "Whiskey. And one for yourself—you look like you need it."

Two hours later, Dani had graduated from needing a drink to needing someone to point her toward the door. The pub had transformed into a warm, blurry cocoon where nothing hurt as much.

"An' then—" she gestured wildly with her glass, sloshing whiskey dangerously close to the edge, "—then she says, 'Mr. Quinn's not in' like I'm some... some desperate lovesick... which I'm NOT, by the way."

The docker—Jimmy, she'd learned—nodded sagely, well into his sixth pint. "Course not."

"I'm getting MARRIED. To a very nice... scientist... person. Tomorrow we're going to the mountains, and then I'm going HOME." She emphasized the last word by slamming her glass down. "Home where women can vote and wear pants and kiss whoever they damn well please without ending up in an asylum."

Jimmy blinked slowly. "Asylum?"

"Did I say Asylum? I meant... Oregon. Different Oregon. Far away Oregon." She waved vaguely eastward. Or was that westward? Direction had become negotiable.

Someone started up a drinking song near the bar, and Dani joined in, even though she only knew half the words. The melody was close enough to something she'd heard in movies. She swayed on her stool, raising her glass high with the rest of them.

Through the haze of voices and smoke, something caught her eye. A familiar figure in a corner booth, watching her with undisguised amusement.

She stopped mid-verse. "Oh, fuck me sideways."

Jimmy followed her gaze. "Know him, do you?"

"Unfortunately." She squinted at Enver. "How long has he been lurking there like some Edwardian Snape?"

"Been there since before you started your second bottle, miss."

She watched him across the room, laughing at something a barmaid whispered in his ear. That familiar lazy chuckle made her skin crawl. The barmaid—the same one who'd been all over Gabe at the last pub visit—clearly thought she had her regular client. No wonder Gabe dismissed her advances. Where Gabe would sit rigid with proper posture, this one sprawled against the booth seat like he owned the place. He had undone his waistcoat buttons and loosened his cravat. Just enough to be indecent.

"No, it's alright." She waved him off. "He's like a bad penny—always turning up where he's not wanted. Besides, I'm too drunk to care if he's dangerous."

Enver arrived just as she finished, eyebrows raised. "Comparing me to currency? How flattering. Though I prefer to think of myself as a rare coin—valuable and hard to get rid of."

He settled against the bar beside her. "Verse three of 'Whiskey in the Jar' was a little flat, by the way."

"My harmony is PERFECT." She slid off the stool—or rather, the stool ejected her, and she landed upright through sheer drunken physics. She turned to Jimmy, sliding money under his glass. "Thanks for the company."

"Anytime, miss. You watch yourself now."

She swayed slightly, then focused on Enver. "What are you doing here?"

"Watching you systematically destroy your liver. It's like performance art." He gestured back toward his booth. "Join me before you fall over."

She navigated the treacherous journey back to his corner booth, collapsing into the wooden seat with zero grace. The booth still held the warmth from where he'd been sprawled, and she could smell his cologne—something expensive and vaguely sinister. "Shouldn't you be off... sciencing? Making more of those fucking boxes? Ruining lives?"

"It's past midnight, darling. Even mad scientists need their beauty sleep." He signaled the bartender for another round. "Though this is far more entertaining."

"Nothing about tonight is entertaining." She leaned forward until her forehead met the sticky table with a dull thunk. Then, with poor rhythm, she began gently banging her head against it. Thunk. Thunk. Thunk. "I'm stuck here." Thunk. "In the wrong century." Thunk. "Engaged to your dimensional twin or whatever he is." Thunk. "And the one person I—" She stopped mid-thunk, leaving her forehead pressed to the wood. "Doesn't matter. She made her choice."

Enver leaned back, studying her with those too-clever eyes. "Ah. So that's what this is about. Our mysterious Mr. Quinn."

She raised her head from the table. "How did you—"

"Please. You've been moping about him for weeks. Also, you just spent twenty minutes telling Jimmy over there about your 'definitely not desperate' search for him."

"I hate you." She let her forehead drop back to the table with another thunk.

"No, you don't." He pushed the fresh whiskey toward her. "You hate that I'm right."

She lifted her head and grabbed the glass, glaring at him over the rim. "You know what? Fine. Yes. I fell for someone I can't have—" She gestured wildly with the glass, whiskey sloshing dangerously close to the edge. "—and tomorrow I'm running away to the mountains with your copy—" Another dramatic gesture sent liquid tilting precariously. Enver's eyes tracked the glass like a man watching a lit fuse. "—I'll get married so I can go home, say goodbye to my parents, and then come back—" The whiskey nearly crested the rim. "—and miserably watch the woman I can't have enjoy her newfound life with horse-face McGee. Happy?"

"Ecstatic." He gently reached over and steadied her glass before she could baptize the table. "This marriage, built on mutual desperation and timeline shenanigans, must thrill Gabriel."

She knocked back the entire glass in one go, then slammed it down. "He's getting what he wants. I'm getting what I want. Everyone wins."

"Except you look like someone just shot your dog."

"I don't have a dog."

"Metaphorically shot your metaphorical dog."

Despite herself, Dani snorted. She pointed at him accusingly, then brought her wrist back to wipe her mouth. "You're the worst."

"I've been told." He raised his glass. "To terrible decisions and the people who make them."

She clinked her empty glass against his, perhaps a bit too forcefully. "To going home and forgetting this total nightmare."

"Home." He tested the word. "Tell me about this magical life of yours."

"Why? So you can come visit and bother me there?"

"So I can understand why you're so eager to leave." His tone was light, but something twinkled beneath it. "Must be quite special to walk away from all this."

"All this?" She gestured at the grimy pub. "Yeah, I'll really miss the lack of women's rights and pickled mystery meat."

"You know what I mean."

She did. And that was the problem. The shot was hitting her hard now, making everything feel too sharp and too blurry at once. "In my time," she said slowly, fighting to keep the words from slurring, "I can be myself. Wear what I want. Love who I want." Her voice cracked.

Enver was quiet for a moment. "And Gabriel knows about all of this? About Quinn?"

"God, no. Not all of it." She tilted her head back to stare at the ceiling, trying to steady herself against the slow spin of the room. "He knows I want to go home. That's all he needs to know."

"Mm." Enver swirled his glass thoughtfully. "And he's promised to take you back? Just like that?"

"We have an arrangement." She kept her voice carefully neutral. "He gets what he wants, I get what I want."

"How transactional."

"I want to go home." The words came out fiercer than intended. "That's all that matters now."

"If you say so." But his expression suggested he didn't quite believe her.

She tilted her head back again; the room doing a lazy waltz. "Water. I need water."

Enver motioned to the barmaid, who brought over a glass. Dani grabbed it and started gulping like she'd been wandering the desert for days, water dribbling down her chin, making ungodly slurping noises.

"Christ," Enver muttered, watching her drain the glass. "I hope you're more talented with your mouth than the way you drink."

She choked, spraying water. "Excuse me?"

"Just an observation." He smirked. "You know, in another life, we might have been friends."

"In another life, you wouldn't have helped trap me here."

"Fair point." He tilted his head. "Though technically, I helped create the way home. Glass half full?"

She slammed the empty water glass down and motioned frantically at the barmaid for another. "Glass fully empty. And also broken. And possibly poisoned."

He laughed—a genuine sound that transformed his face. For a moment, she could see why some version of her in some timeline had fallen for some version of him.

The barmaid delivered another water, which Dani attacked with the same desperate enthusiasm.

"God, we're a mess," she muttered between gulps.

"The absolute worst." He agreed cheerfully. "Another round?"

"No." She waved him off, still clutching her water glass. "I'm way past my limit. I need food. Something with potatoes. Nothing with tails or eyes."

Enver flagged down the barmaid. "The lady requires sustenance. Heavy on the potatoes, light on the questionable meat."

"Shepherd's pie, then?" the barmaid suggested.

"Perfect. As long as the shepherd's not actually in it." Dani squinted suspiciously, looking over to Enver. "You never know in this century."

Twenty minutes of her picking at her food and him nursing his drink, then the pub door opened.

"Rounds for everyone!" The voice boomed across the room like thunder.

Dani's blood went cold, then hot, then cold again.

Lord Ashdown swept in all expensive wool and political smile. Behind him—

Oh, hell no. Her fingers tightened on her glass.

Rowen stood in her perfectly tailored men's clothes, that careful masculine stride. Beatrice draped on her arm like an expensive accessory, glowing with the satisfaction of a woman who'd won.

"Is that—?" Enver started following her gaze.

"Her Fiancé," Dani said in a mocking, singsong voice, making exaggerated air quotes. "The future Mrs. Ashdown. Or wait, no—Rowen's the one pretending to be the mister. God, this timeline's exhausting."

"My daughter is engaged," Ashdown continued, beaming at the cheering crowd, "and we shall see a wedding soon!"

The pub erupted. Free drinks had that effect.

Dani couldn't breathe. Couldn't think. Could only watch as Rowen smiled and nodded, playing the part perfectly.

The devoted fiancé.

The reformed radical.

Ashdown's perfect puppet.

"Breathe," Enver murmured beside her.

Rowen was laughing at something Beatrice whispered, head tilted in that way Dani knew so well, her jawline catching the light. Then Beatrice leaned in to kiss her cheek, and Rowen—

Rowen turned into it, catching Beatrice's lips with her own in a brief but tender kiss. When they pulled apart, Rowen's smile was warm, her hand coming up to brush a strand of hair from Beatrice's face with practiced intimacy.

The gesture was so natural, so easy. Like they'd done it a thousand times before.

Dani watched Rowen whisper something that made Beatrice blush and swat her arm playfully. Rowen caught Beatrice's hand, bringing it to her lips in a gentlemanly kiss that had Beatrice giggling.

They looked... happy. Genuinely, perfectly happy.

She would never choose me, Dani realized with crushing clarity.

Something inside her snapped.

A bitter taste coated her tongue as she swallowed. She had been so, so stupid.

The thought sharpened—anger curling hot around the grief.

The pub spun around her. She should leave. She should.

But she didn't.

Through the haze of whiskey and hurt, she felt it—eyes on her.

Her gaze locked with Rowen's from across the crowded pub. For one suspended moment, everything else fell away. Just them. Just this. All the things they couldn't say suspended in a long agonizing moment.

That look activated Dani's self-destructive, retaliatory reflex—one she was well known for back home. She wasn't proud of it.

Her hands moved before her brain caught up. She turned—Enver was right there. Too close. Too convenient.

She grabbed his lapels and yanked him forward, crashing her mouth against his with all the grace of a freight train.

For a second, he froze. Then—because he was still Enver, chaos incarnate and a shameless opportunist, his grip firmed on her waist, steadying her, grounding her. He kissed her back like he'd been expecting this all along.

But it was all wrong. Too rough, too desperate, too much teeth and whiskey and fury. Nothing like—

No. She wouldn't think about that.

She kissed him harder, pouring all her rage and hurt into it. Let everyone see. Allow them to gossip. Let them judge.

Let *her* see.

Enver's hand brushed her jaw, tilting her face toward him. His fingers were rougher than Rowen's, his mouth firmer, and his shape entirely wrong—not slender, not careful, not her.

The pub noise faded to white static. Someone whistled. Someone else laughed. She didn't care.

When she finally pulled back, gasping, Enver's eyes were wide.

"Well," he managed. "That was—"

She turned and found Rowen's eyes again.

Then Beatrice followed Rowen's gaze. Her pretty face twisted with disgust. "Isn't that the Barrington girl? How common. Making such a display."

Rowen said nothing.

Did nothing.

Just... stared.

You salted my heart and carved your piece. The words from Skidmore Fountain slammed into her brain all over again.

"We're leaving," she announced, grabbing Enver's hand.

"Are we?" He sounded dazed. "Alright then."

She dragged him toward the door, not caring who saw, not caring what they thought. Let Portland's gossip mill run itself ragged.

The cold air hit like a slap. She stumbled forward, releasing his hand, gulping in the sharp cold night. Her legs kept moving, putting distance between her and that pub, between her and the image of Rowen's face.

"Dani—" Enver called behind her.

She didn't stop. Couldn't stop. The cobblestones blurred beneath her feet as she half-ran, half-stumbled down the empty street. Her breath came in ragged gasps that had nothing to do with exertion.

When she finally stopped, she was in some alley she didn't recognize, walls pressing in on both sides. The silence was deafening after the pub's chaos.

Then it hit her. All of it.

A sound tore from her throat—raw, primal, furious. She screamed into the darkness until her voice cracked, until her lungs burned.

"FUCK!" She slammed her palm against the brick wall. "Fuck, fuck, FUCK!"

"Feel better?" Enver's voice came from the alley entrance. He'd followed her, of course he had.

She whirled on him; tears she hadn't realized were falling streaking her face. "Don't. Just don't."

"Wasn't planning to." He leaned against the wall, keeping his distance. "Scream away. God knows this city could use more honesty."

Another sob wrenched from her chest. She pressed her palms against her eyes, trying to stop the flood. "What the hell is wrong with me? I just—I kissed you to hurt her. I used you like some kind of... of weapon."

"Yes, you did." His voice was surprisingly gentle. "Rather effectively, too. Enver rocked back on his heels facing her, rolling his shoulders.

"Well," he drawled, running a hand through his hair, "You kiss like a warning label. I respect that."

She shot him a look.

"Is this what rock bottom looks like? Kissing all the Gabes like I have a quota to meet?!" She shoved at his chest, but he caught her wrists carefully. "I'm a disaster. I'm a fucking disaster who ruins everything I touch."

"You're coming off an alcohol binge and heartbroken." He released her hands. "Hardly a criminal combination."

"I'm pathetic." The words came out broken. "Standing there watching her with—with horse-face McGee, pretending to be happy. And she just... she didn't even fight. Said nothing. Just watched me make a fool of myself."

"Come here." He opened his arms.

"No." She stumbled back. "No, I don't need—I don't want—"

But her body betrayed her, collapsing forward. He caught her, holding her steady while she sobbed into his unfortunately expensive waistcoat. He smelled like whiskey and tobacco and all the wrong things, but he was solid and warm and there.

"This is so fucked up," she mumbled against his chest. "You look just like him but you're not him and I kissed you—"

"Breathe."

She did, gulping air between sobs. "I hate this. I hate all of this."

"I know."

They stood there in the alley, her crying herself empty while he held her up. When the sobs finally quieted to hiccups, she pulled back, grabbed his sleeve, and wiped her face on it.

"Did you just—" He looked down at his now-damp sleeve in horror.

"My crying already ruined your shirt." She sniffled, going for the other sleeve. "Might as well complete the set."

"This is a thirty-dollar waistcoat!"

"Should've thought of that before you offered comfort." She gave one final wipe. "There. Much better."

"God." She laughed, but it sounded hollow. "That little voice that tells me to blow shit up impulsively. I ruin everything when backed into a corner!"

"You're gloriously self-destructive."

Despite everything, she snorted. "Gloriously?"

"You kissed me in front of half of Portland's working class to spite your secret lover. If that's not glorious destruction, I don't know what is."

"The upside," he added with a wry smile, "is that I'm a replica of the man you promised to marry. Everyone will just think you are lovebirds who couldn't keep their hands off each other."

"Oh god." She groaned. "That's going to make tomorrow's gossip even worse. I wouldn't doubt Ashdown calls Alvie before I even make it home." She rolled her eyes. "That seems to be the trend around here—gossip travels faster than horses."

"It was. Terrible judgment, excellent execution." His voice shifted, something darker threading through. "Though if it helps, we all have someone who was never ours. Someone we'd burn the world down for, even knowing they'd never choose us."

She studied his face in the dim light. "Speaking from experience?"

"Perhaps." He straightened his ruined waistcoat. "But that's a tragedy for another evening."

"Thanks. For... whatever this was."

"Chaos management?" He wiped his dirty coat. "I'm surprisingly good at it."

They started walking, her steps steadier now. The crying had burned through some of the alcohol, leaving her feeling empty but clearer.

"I've been so stupid. Thinking if I just... if I waited, or fought harder, or found the right words..." She shook her head. "But she made her choice. She's been making it every day since I met her."

"People rarely change. They just reveal what they always were."

"Yeah." She wrapped her arms around herself. "Yeah, I'm starting to get that."

They walked in silence for a while; the city sleeping around them. When they reached a corner she recognized, Dani stopped.

"I'm done," she said, and the words felt like a vow. "I'm going to marry your brother, go home, and forget any of this happened."

"Simple as that?"

"Simple as that." She met his eyes.

She turned to go, then looked back. "Enver? We're never talking about tonight again."

"What tonight?" He gave her a mock bow. "I spent the evening drinking alone, as always."

"Good."

She left him there, walking back to catch the trolley up the hill to the Barrington house with new resolve. Rowen had made her choice. Now Dani had made hers.

25

LET THE PAST KEEP HER

EDWARDIAN ERA

The rain tapped against the kitchen windows, a soft percussion that underscored the clatter of plates and the low hum of morning conversation. The scent of fresh bread and strong tea filled the space.

Dani perched on a worn stool at the long kitchen table, its surface scarred by years of bread dough, butcher's cuts, and hurried breakfasts. Crumbs clung to the grooves as she absently tore at a piece of toast. The smell of yeast and wood smoke made her hungover stomach turn. Nearby, Shannon moved in a simple rhythm, crooning as she stirred something at the stove, her travel case already packed by the door. Edmund had set his beside it—they'd all be making the journey to the lodge together.

"You've barely touched your breakfast, Dani," Shannon said gently, passing her a fresh cup of tea. "It'll be a long day. You'll need your strength."

Dani offered a small smile in return. "I'm working on it."

She had a terrible hangover. A hangover that didn't welcome food.

Across the table, Laurel dipped a spoon into her porridge with surprising grace.

"You know," Laurel said, studying Dani with those too-knowing eyes, "the mountains will do you good. Fresh air. Peace and quiet. Sometimes you just need to get back to where you once belonged."

Dani nearly choked on her tea. "Did you just quote the Beatles at me?"

Laurel's spoon paused halfway to her mouth. For a moment, they just stared at each other.

"I do not know what you mean," Laurel said carefully. "It is just something my... mother used to say."

"Right." Dani set down her cup. "Your mother. Who loved... traditional folk songs."

"Exactly." Laurel's eyes glinted. "Very traditional. Nothing revolutionary about them at all."

Shannon glanced between them, confused. "What are you two talking about?"

"Nothing, dear," Laurel said smoothly. "Just an old woman's nonsense."

The kitchen door swung open, and Edmund stepped in, brushing rain from his coat sleeves. "Have I stumbled into a henhouse, or may a gentleman trouble himself for a piece of toast?"

"You may sit," Laurel replied, already sliding a plate across the table. "But only if you don't talk politics before tea."

Edmund settled in beside Dani with a grateful sigh. "A reasonable condition. Though we should load the automobile soon. The weather won't improve, and it's a long drive to Government Camp."

The four of them sat in companionable rhythm—pouring tea, trading barbs, letting the warm kitchen push back the dreariness outside. It wasn't home. But it felt like something close to it.

In the foyer, Alvie stood near the grand entrance, gesturing animatedly to the footmen about the logistics of their trip. Trunks and cases were being loaded onto the automobile—Shannon's modest bag, Edmund's careful packing, and enough provisions for a month in the mountains.

When Dani entered the foyer, Alvie turned, his sharp blue eyes sweeping over her. For a beat, he said nothing, just took in her stiff posture and the exhaustion that weighed on her shoulders.

Vivienne appeared at the top of the staircase, wrapped in an elegant robe. Her movements were graceful, but Dani caught the subtle way her hand drifted to her stomach—a protective gesture, almost unconscious.

"Alvie," Vivienne's voice carried down like silk. "I'm afraid I won't be accompanying you to the lodge after all."

He frowned, moving to the bottom of the stairs. "But darling, we discussed—"

"I know." She descended slowly, each step carefully. "But I visited Dr. Morrison yesterday, and he's confirmed what I suspected." Her hand settled more firmly on her midsection. "We're going to have a child."

The foyer went silent. Even the footmen paused at their work.

Alvie's face transformed—surprise melting into joy. He bounded up the stairs to meet her, taking her hands gently. "Vivienne, my dear—"

"The doctor insists I avoid travel, especially over rough roads." She smiled, but Dani saw the calculation behind it. "You understand, of course. The child must come first."

"Of course, of course." Alvie kissed her hands. "We'll postpone—"

"Nonsense. You have guests coming. Gabriel needs to repair that infernal game lift. Business doesn't stop for biology." Her eyes found Dani over Alvie's shoulder. "Besides, Miss Wood needs this holiday. Look at her—she's positively wan."

Dani's throat tightened. The realization hit like a stone dropped into still water. This baby would be her grandfather. This moment, right here, was her family taking shape across time.

She swallowed hard, stepping closer. "Vivienne... congratulations. And take care of yourself, alright?" Her voice wavered, but she forced a smile. "And—thank you. For everything."

Vivienne tilted her head, amusement flickering in her eyes. "Oh, Dani, you sound as though you're saying goodbye forever. It's only a month in the mountains."

"I know. I just..." Dani took a slow breath. "With the wedding coming and everything changing... I wanted to make sure you knew how grateful I am. For taking me in. For treating me like family when I was just a stranger who showed up at your door."

Something shifted in Vivienne's expression—a flicker of understanding, perhaps. She descended the remaining stairs and reached out, brushing a loose strand of hair from Dani's face. The touch was soft. Maternal.

"You were never just a stranger, dear." Her voice dropped low enough that only Dani could hear. "Somehow, I think we both know that."

The words hung between them, heavy with unspoken truth.

"Now," Vivienne said more loudly, stepping back. "Do try to keep Alvie from any truly dangerous schemes. And ensure that Shannon doesn't work too hard—she has a tendency to forget she's human and not a machine."

"I'll do my best."

Vivienne's lips quirked. "No, you won't. You'll likely encourage whatever mischief presents itself. But I suppose that's why Alvie's so fond of you." She placed a hand on Dani's cheek. "Be well, my dear. Whatever comes next."

Alvie brightened suddenly, still holding Vivienne's hand. "Danielle, what do you think? You have such modern sensibilities—what would you name our child?"

The question caught Dani off guard, her throat tightening. She looked between them—her great-great-grandparents, though Vivienne didn't know it.

"Well," she said slowly, "if it's a boy... Henry. It's a strong name. Classic." Her voice wavered slightly. "And if it's a girl... Louise. Both timeless."

"Henry," Vivienne tested the name thoughtfully. "I rather like that."

"Though I have a feeling," Dani added softly, then awkwardly gestured toward Vivienne's midsection, "it'll be a boy. Because of the, uh, way you're carrying... it? Him? The... baby."

She winced at her own fumbling. "That's a thing, right? How you can tell? The carrying thing?"

Vivienne looked amused. "Old wives' tales, dear."

"Right. Those." Dani cleared her throat. "Still. My money's on Henry."

Alvie turned slightly away from Vivienne and gave Dani the briefest wink—a silent acknowledgment of everything unspoken between them. He knew she was giving them her grandfather's name.

"Henry Barrington," Alvie said warmly. "It has a fine ring to it."

Dani wanted to say something—something real. Something final. She wanted to call Vivienne "grandmother." But the words stuck in her throat. Instead, she just nodded, memorizing this moment when her family's future was taking shape in the past.

Having loaded the automobile, Alvie helped Dani up while Edmund assisted Shannon. The engine rumbled to life, startling a flock of pigeons from the eaves.

As they pulled away from the curb, Alvie studied Dani's face. "You were out quite late last night, I gather."

"Gossip travels fast."

"Indeed. Miss Morewood telephoned this morning. It seems there was quite the to-do at O'Driscoll's—her gardener was in attendance. Something regarding a finely dressed miss who bore an uncanny resemblance to yourself and a dark-haired gentleman causing quite the stir?" His tone was light, but concern lurked beneath.

Dani kept her eyes on the passing houses. "Did you know Ashdown was there? Making announcements about Rowen's engagement?"

Alvie's jaw tightened. "So you found her."

"She was never missing." Dani's voice came out hollow. "She's exactly where she wants to be. Where he wants her to be. Playing the perfect fiancé while he parades her around to win over the workers."

"Daniell—"

"It's fine." She cut him off. "I mean, it's not fine, but it's... done. She made her choice."

The motor car rumbled east out of Portland, following the Columbia River Highway's precursor—still just a rough wagon road that would make any modern driver weep. They passed through small settlements that clung to the riverbank: Troutdale, where the Sandy River merged with the Columbia, its sawmill sending up plumes of smoke; Corbett, barely more than a general store and a cluster of weathered houses.

Edmund drove while Shannon dozed against the window. The road climbed away from the river into dense stands of Douglas fir and cedar, their trunks so massive that the automobile looked like a toy beneath them. Every few miles brought another logging camp, the air sharp with the scent of fresh-cut timber and wood smoke.

"The workers think Rowen's engagement is good for them," Dani said suddenly. "They think she'll have Ashdown's ear. They do not know he's using her."

Alvie sighed. "Ashdown is cleverer than I gave him credit for. And now, with Rowen under his control..."

"We can't save someone who doesn't want to be saved." The words tasted bitter. "I learned that last night."

At Brightwood—if you could call three buildings and a post office a town—they stopped to add water to the radiator, the engine steaming like a kettle. The landscape grew wilder as they climbed, the forest pressing in on both sides. Mount Hood loomed ahead when the trees broke, its glaciers glowing pink in the afternoon light.

By the time they reached Government Camp—little more than a few rough cabins—the temperature had dropped twenty degrees, and patches of snow appeared beneath the trees.

"Almost there," Alvie said, trying to lighten the mood. "Gabriel arrived yesterday to begin repairs. Several other couples will join us throughout the week."

Dani nodded absently. Tomorrow she'd have to face Gabriel. *Play the excited fiancée. Pretend everything was going according to plan.*

But today, watching the forest swallow the last glimpses of Portland behind them, she let herself breathe.

The motor coughed and wheezed up the final incline toward the lodge, and Dani closed her eyes.

26

WEDDING BELLS AND REGRETS

EDWARDIAN ERA - ROWEN

The church bells tolled, sending waves of sound rippling through the city streets. Inside, the air was dense with candle smoke and the heavy scent of roses, their petals arranged in perfect spirals along the pews. Guests whispered behind gloved hands, their voices an undercurrent to the organ's somber hum.

Rowen stood at the altar, spine rigid, hands locked behind her back to keep from shaking. The volume of the wedding suit pressed against her bound chest, each breath constricted, shallow.

She could still run.

The thought flashed like a lit flame. She could push through the side door, sprint into the alleyway. The fabric of her carefully constructed life would unravel in seconds, but she'd be free.

Then she saw her mother in the front row, gloved hands folded neatly in her lap. Those familiar, weary eyes held a quiet plea.

The church doors creaked open.

Beatrice floated forward in white silk and lace; her veil casting shadows across delicate features. Beautiful. Perfect. Everything a man like "Rowen Quinn" should want.

Each step echoed through the church like a countdown. Ten steps. Nine. Eight.

A memory intruded—three weeks ago, Pioneer Square, on an unseasonably sunny December afternoon. They'd been walking through downtown after lunch, Beatrice's hand tucked properly in the crook of Rowen's arm. Just another performance in her endless series of performances.

"Shall we sit?" Beatrice had suggested, gesturing to a bench near the fountain.

They'd settled onto the worn wood, watching the city flow around them—merchants hawking wares, couples strolling, children chasing pigeons. Rowen had relaxed, letting the afternoon sun warm her face.

"It's pleasant, isn't it?" Beatrice said. "Being able to walk together like this. In public."

"Yes." Rowen had kept her voice carefully neutral, masculine.

"Though I imagine it must be fatiguing." Beatrice smoothed her skirts, eyes still on the passing crowd. "Always playing a part. Never being able to truly ease."

Something in her tone made Rowen's shoulders tense. "I do not know what you mean."

"Do you not?" Beatrice turned then, studying Rowen with those perceptive eyes. "I've known for a while. The way you sit—knees always properly together even in men's clothing. How you flinch when other men clap you on the shoulder. The careful way you never fully relax, even when you think no one's watching."

Rowen's world swayed. This was it—exposure, ruin, her mother thrown into the streets—

"I know you are of the gentler sex," Beatrice said simply. "And I do not have a mind to care."

"I—" Rowen's voice came out strangled. "Beatrice—"

She reached over, placing her gloved hand over Rowen's. "Did you think I could not tell? I've spent my whole life studying people, learning what they want, what they hide. You're very good at your charade, but not perfect."

"Why didn't you—" Rowen replied. "Why didn't you expose me? Why didn't you run?"

"Because I want you regardless." Beatrice's fingers tightened. "Do you understand? I want you as you are. And I'll admit..." Her smile turned sharp. "There's something delicious about having what every other woman in Portland wants. They all throw themselves at the mysterious Rowen Quinn, and I'm the one who gets to take you home."

Rowen's stomach dropped. This wasn't relief—it was another cage, just with different bars. She was a trophy, a prize to be won. Her mind raced, searching for escape routes that didn't exist.

"Does your father—"

"No. And he won't. This is between us." Beatrice shifted closer on the bench. "I'll be a good wife to you. Keep your secret. Share your bed. Give Father the alliance he wants. All I ask in return…"

Rowen's stomach dropped. This wasn't relief—it was another cage, just with different bars. Her mind raced, searching for escape routes that didn't exist.

She leaned in, and Rowen's whole body went rigid, suddenly aware of how public they were, how many eyes might watch, how completely trapped she was.

"…is that you're mine. Completely."

Then Beatrice kissed her. There, in Pioneer Square, in full view of anyone who cared to look. It was soft but possessive, gentle but inescapable.

Rowen forced herself not to pull away. Her mother needed this. The workers needed her on the inside. She had to play along. But her mind screamed with thoughts of Dani—sharp wit and modern boldness, the way she laughed, the way she'd felt in Rowen's arms that night at the fountain.

This is wrong. This is all wrong.

Her body moved mechanically, responding just enough to make it convincing. Her hand came up to Beatrice's jaw because that's what a besotted fiancé would do. But inside, everything recoiled.

When they pulled apart, Beatrice was smiling—a cat with cream. "See? Not so diffi-cult."

"Right." Rowen's voice came out steadily somehow. "Not difficult at all."

Beatrice's fingers traced along Rowen's collar. "I'm not entirely certain how women… engage with each other intimately. But I have a feeling you'll show me." Her voice dropped lower. "I've been curious for quite some time, though I'd never dare admit such a thing in polite company."

Rowen's blood ran cold. This wasn't just about possession or status—Beatrice saw her as an experiment, a way to explore desires she couldn't otherwise acknowledge.

"Beatrice—"

"Shh." She pressed a finger to Rowen's lips. "We have our whole lives to figure it out. Starting with our wedding night, I'm quite looking forward to it."

What Rowen didn't know, couldn't know, was that Enver stood across the square with his projection device, capturing every moment. The kiss that would later shatter Dani's heart had felt, in that moment, like the last door slamming shut on Rowen's future.

Three steps now. Two. One.

Beatrice reached the altar. The priest began his droning sermon about duty and bonds. Rowen barely heard him over the thundering in her ears.

"Do you, Rowen Quinn, take this woman..."

The words blurred together. She nodded when prompted, spoke when required. The ring slid onto her finger like a shackle.

"You may kiss the bride."

Rowen leaned in, pressing her lips briefly to Beatrice's—mechanical, hollow. But Beatrice caught her jaw, holding her there a moment longer, making sure everyone saw. Making sure Rowen understood she was hers.

The reception hall glowed under crystal chandeliers, laughter bubbling from every corner. Rowen moved through the congratulations like a ghost, champagne turning to ash on her tongue.

"You look so handsome," Mrs. Whitmore gushed. "So happy!"

"Thank you." The words came automatically. Rowen turned away, unable to maintain the smile.

"Such a lovely couple," another voice cooed. "You must be over the moon!"

"Absolutely." Each lie scraped her throat raw.

She needed air. Space. Anything to keep from screaming.

Then she heard it—gossip slipping through the crowd like poison.

"Did you hear about the Barrington, girl? Seen at Morrison's public house, kissing some gentleman quite inappropriately..."

"Shocking behavior! Though I heard it was her fiancé—that Dunwich fellow. They've gone to the Barrington Hunting Lodge on Mt. Hood for a whole month. I do wonder if they shall be wed there. The Lovingtons went with them I heard."

"Still, in public like that? Oh yes, the Lovingtons will give a full report indeed. I wonder how *quaint* it shall be. No proper lady would..."

The champagne flute trembled in Rowen's hand.

Dani.

Another memory crashed over her—two weeks ago, the engagement party at Ashdown's estate. Portland's elite circulating through rooms heavy with cigar smoke while she'd stood beside Beatrice, playing the devoted fiancé.

"Quinn here understands the working class," Ashdown had said to his investors, hand heavy on Rowen's shoulder. "Been quite helpful in... managing expectations at the docks."

She'd forced a smile then, still believing she could influence him from the inside. Still naïve enough to think patience and strategy could turn his policies toward justice.

"The beauty is, they trust him," Ashdown had continued, eyes glinting. "When we need to... adjust certain policies, who better to explain why it's necessary?"

"Indeed," one man had chuckled. "Nothing like having one of their own to keep them in line."

"Exactly." Ashdown's grip had tightened. "The workers deserve stability. Order. Someone to explain why strikes only hurt their families. Wouldn't you agree, Quinn?"

The threat was subtle, but clear. Rowen had thought of her mother, frail in her sickbed. "Of course."

"Good man." Ashdown had patted her shoulder. "Gentlemen, if you'll excuse us, I believe we should make an appearance at the public house. Show the workers we're men of the people."

That's when she'd known. She wasn't going to change anything. She was just another tool in his collection.

The pub had been packed with people and laughter when they'd arrived. Ashdown playing man-of-the-people while Beatrice clutched Rowen's arm possessively. She'd been maintaining her facade, smiling at the workers who thought she was their champion, when movement near the bar had caught her eye.

Dani. Wild-haired and flushed with drink, looking like everything Rowen wanted and couldn't have.

For one breathless moment, their eyes had met across the crowd. Rowen had seen recognition dawn on Dani's face, saw her freeze mid-conversation.

She'd turned to the man beside her—Gabriel—and yanked him down into a kiss that was all teeth and desperation and fury.

Rowen's world had stopped.

She'd watched Dani pour everything into that kiss, watched her make a spectacle of choosing someone else. Anyone else. The message was clear: You chose her. So, I choose him.

"Isn't that the Barrington girl?" Beatrice had murmured, fingers tightening on Rowen's arm. "How common. Making such a display."

Rowen hadn't answered. Couldn't.

"Good thing we're getting married," Beatrice had continued, voice honeyed with victory. "No more distractions."

Now, standing in her wedding reception, Rowen forced down another sip of champagne. Two weeks. Dani had been gone two weeks, presumably with that man. Probably married by now. Happy.

The thought shouldn't hurt. Rowen had made her choice.

But it did.

That night, the bridal suite felt like a tomb. Velvet drapes pooled in corners where candlelight couldn't reach. The massive bed loomed like an altar of its own.

And beyond the door, servants waited. Listening. Tradition demanded proof of movement, sounds, and evidence of a properly consummated marriage.

Beatrice stood at the mirror, carefully removing pins from her elaborate hairstyle. Each movement was deliberate, unhurried.

"They're listening," she said conversationally. "We should give them what they expect."

Rowen remained by the fireplace; wine glass clutched like a shield. Her third. Maybe fourth. Not enough.

"Beatrice—"

"Come here." It wasn't a request.

Rowen's feet moved of their own accord. Everything felt distant, unreal. This couldn't be her life. This couldn't be happening.

Beatrice turned, reaching up to loosen Rowen's cravat. "I've been very patient," she murmured. "But I'm your wife now. And I intend to have what's mine."

Outside, footsteps shifted in the hallway.

Waiting.

Listening.

And Rowen closed her eyes, letting the last piece of herself die quietly in the dark.

Beatrice crossed the room slowly, stopping before her. Her hand reached for Rowen's collar but hesitated midair.

"I shall not ask you to feel something you do not," whispered. "But I would have you know... I desire this. I desire you."

Rowen lowered her eyes.

"I can't feel what I should. But I'll still give you what I have left."

"You don't have to be genuine. You just have to stay."

Beatrice had expected clumsiness. Awkward silence. Perhaps even indifference. What she had not expected was the touch of hands that knew precisely where to go. The quiet reverence of a mouth that found the tender places beneath her ear, her throat, then lower still.

"You... you have done this before," she managed, voice barely above a whisper.

Rowen paused for the briefest second, then answered with quiet certainty.

"Yes."

Beatrice exhaled shakily, a half-laugh catching in her throat. "Merciful heavens..." She had a fair idea of *who* had taught her such things. And it left a taste in her mouth that was not quite jealousy, but far from comfort.

She had expected a polite disrobing. Awkward silence beneath dim lighting. Perhaps even a turned back while she extinguished the lamps and endured the deed, however necessary.

What she hadn't expected was the press of Rowen's fingers against the laces at her back—or the way Rowen slipped her hands aside when she fumbled with her own corset.

The gown loosened. Then the chemise. Silk slid to the floor with a thud. Beatrice stood bared to the firelight, her breath shallow in the warm hush of the room. Her arms fluttered, not sure whether to cover herself or stand her ground.

No words escaped Rowen's lips. She simply looked—just looked—for way too long.

Her body was not like Dani's. Lovely, yes—but it stirred no fire in Rowen. No ache. She felt nothing but dryness... and shame for it.

Unfastening her waistcoat, Rowen shed her shirt. Her body, though compact and toned, was unmistakably feminine now.

Beatrice did not flinch. She knew. That was never the issue. What mattered to Beatrice was the claim. None of the town's ladies could have her. She would be the one on Rowen's arm. The one whispered about behind fans and over tea. Admired. Envied. Untouchable.

Beatrice's voice cracked.

"You're so very... certain of how to do this."

"Not of much," Rowen murmured, swiping her bangs that had fallen to her eyes. "Only what is required of me."

Then she kissed her, her tongue sweeping Beatrice's mouth, tongues meeting.

It was not chaste.

Beatrice gasped into the contact, her fingers tightening on Rowen's bare shoulders. No one had ever kissed her like this. Like Rowen knew exactly how to unravel her... and had done so before.

There was heat, yes—but no hunger.

Only a kind of duty, executed beautifully.

Rowen's lips traced her jaw, then her throat, then lower—until Beatrice's breath became a broken rhythm.

She was guided—not gently, but without room for protest—down onto the bed.

Rowen followed, pausing only to pull back the quilt.

Beatrice's bare skin met the cool linen, and she shivered—not from the cold, but from the way she was being handled.

"Tell me if you wish me to stop," Rowen murmured, hovering above her. Her hand cupped Beatrice's breast, thumb brushing over the nipple until it drew tight under her touch. "Say the word, and I shall leave you untouched."

Beatrice let out a helpless noise.

"That would be unkind," she whispered. "You mustn't stop now."

The kisses trailed lower. Down her ribs. Her belly. Her inner thighs. The pace was maddening.

Rowen did not speak again. Her mouth was already between Beatrice's thighs and properly well-bred Beatrice was dissolving under the touch of someone she had married for show, who now knew her body better than she did. She didn't know whether to be scandalized or grateful.

Rowen finally put her mouth on her. Beatrice cried out and grabbed fistfuls of the sheets. Her hips bucked once, then again, until Rowen's hands slid beneath her thighs to hold her tightly in place.

"Tell me you want me too," Beatrice moaned.

Rowen didn't answer. She didn't want to.

"Say it! I need it." Beatrice urged, her voice breaking.

A pause. Then, rough and breathless between licks— "I want you."

She pressed on—tongue circling, pressing, stroking with an unshakable rhythm.

One arm kept Beatrice pinned to the bed while the other slipped between her legs, finding her slick, open, and utterly overwhelmed.

Rowen stilled—just for a heartbeat.

She'd expected resistance. Blood, maybe. The fragile catch of something that would mark this as a first.

But there was none.

She was already open.

Not from her. Not from this.

Of course she had.

Beatrice had already given herself to a man.

The realization bloomed and vanished all at once, swept away in the tide of Beatrice's gasping breaths.

Beatrice moaned beneath her, slick and shivering, her pleasure mounting in waves.

She was falling. Drowning. Coming apart.

When her climax hit, it was not the dainty flutter she'd once imagined it might be. It was sharp, keening, almost embarrassing. She came with a sob, her body trembling so hard she curled in on herself, Rowen's name slipping from her lips like a revelation.

Still holding on, Rowen breathed hard against a thigh, her mouth damp with proof of everything she reluctantly did.

The realization bloomed and vanished all at once, swept away in the tide of Beatrice's gasping breaths.

Beatrice moaned beneath her, slick and shivering, her pleasure mounting in waves.

She was falling. Drowning. Coming apart.

When her climax hit, it was not the dainty flutter she'd once imagined it might be. It was sharp, keening, almost embarrassing. She came with a sob, her body trembling so hard she curled in on herself, Rowen's name slipping from her lips like a revelation.

Still holding on, Rowen breathed hard against a thigh, her mouth damp with proof of everything she reluctantly did.

Beatrice sighed beside her, sated and serene.

"I've never—well. No one's ever brought me to such an end before." Her voice was soft, almost dreamlike.

Rowen felt used.

"One does hear of such things... in whispers," Beatrice murmured, gaze drifting toward the ceiling. A small smile tugged at her lips. "But I confess, I didn't quite believe." She exhaled, quiet and full of wonder. "I daresay I didn't know it could feel like that."

Rowen still couldn't bring herself to look at her.

The night had been long drawn out in gasps and sighs, Beatrice clinging to her like a woman starved. Rowen gave what she could. Again, and again. Hands, mouth, breath. Until her body was sore and her soul scraped raw.

She had not slept. Not truly.

Beatrice had drifted off near dawn, one arm flung lazily across the pillow, her smile still soft with dreams. The fire had gone cold. The lamps dimmed. Even so, Rowen lay wide-eyed, aching with the wrongness of it all.

I have given her what she desired, but it was not mine to give. She deserves someone who might love her without regret. And I... I have none left to give.

By the time the staff stirred in the halls—teacarts rolling, footfalls muffled on carpet—it was past midmorning.

Rowen dressed in silence.

Her skin still burned with the memory of Beatrice's body, but her mind was elsewhere. Somewhere far away. Somewhere green-eyed and impossible to forget. She had wrestled with it long enough.

Duty. Pride. Fear. None of it mattered anymore.

Clarity broke through, sharp and final.

She would do it.

Damn the risk.

Damn the cost.

Forgive me, Mother, I'll find another way. Forgive me, Beatrice.

She spun sharply, her vision threatening to blur.

She had to get out.

Now.

The next thing she knew, she was moving.

Out the door.

Down the steps.

The streets of Portland splayed out before her—muted shapes and distant voices lost in the storm that had gathered in her heart.

She was not walking.

She was running.

27

FALLING THROUGH FOREVER

EDWARDIAN ERA

The hunting lodge was nestled deep within the leaf-laden forest, framed by towering evergreens. Days had passed since their arrival, and the isolation settled over Dani like a blanket. It gave her time—too much time—to think.

Each morning, she walked alongside Alvie, trekking through the landscape, their boots crunching against the leaves as they hunted, fished, and gathered firewood. Alvie, in his element, loved exploring and being in nature.

Gabe was never far behind. He had an irritating knack for showing up when she thought she'd finally gotten a moment to herself. At first, she ignored him, but as the days carried on, she begrudgingly tolerated his presence. He wasn't awful company—not entirely. In some ways, he reminded her of Alvie, quick-witted and confident but with an edge that kept her guessing.

She'd let him into her bed—a mistake born of loneliness and the ache Rowen left behind. His touch was skilled, his body familiar now, but it was like trying to fill an ocean with a teaspoon. Still, when he looked at her like that...

Later that afternoon, he took her to the back of the lodge to show her Alvie's game winch, a rusting contraption he had spent the past day repairing. "See, the mechanism here was stuck," he explained, crouching beside it. "Needed some oil and a bit of finesse."

Dani knelt beside him, watching as he adjusted the gears. "You are always this handy?"

He shot her a sideways glance. "Clockmakers must be. But yes, I was always repairing things as a child. My father used to—" He stopped abruptly, clearing his throat. "Nevertheless, it should work now."

"Great." She stood, brushing dirt off her knees. "Alvie will be thrilled."

He stood as well, moving closer than necessary. "You've dirt on your cheek."

Before she could respond, his thumb brushed across her cheekbone. The touch lingered.

"Thanks," she said, stepping back. "We should head in."

"Dani." His voice had that quality again—soft, hopeful. "Might I..."

She knew what was coming. Saw it in the way he leaned toward her, the way his eyes dropped to her mouth.

Play the part, she reminded herself. *Just enough to keep him believing.*

She tilted her face up, letting him kiss her. It was gentle, worshipful almost—the kiss of a man who thought he was holding something precious. When he pulled back, his eyes were bright with an emotion she didn't want to see.

"You're extraordinary," he murmured.

"Gabe—"

"I know, I know." He smiled ruefully. "We must head in." He took her hand, pressing it briefly to his lips. "I've waited this long to find you."

The sincerity in his voice made her stomach twist with guilt.

"We should really get back," she said, gently extracting her hand. "Before Alvie sends a search party."

"Of course." He offered his arm, ever the gentleman. "May I escort you?"

She took it, because refusing would raise questions. As they walked, he chatted about improvements he planned for the lodge, his voice warm with enthusiasm. She made appropriate noises, smiled when expected, even laughed at one of his jokes.

Just a few more weeks, she told herself. *Then married. Then done.*

But his adoration pressed against her like a physical thing, making each small deception feel heavier than the last.

That evening, the grand dinner begun inside the lodge. The scent of roasted venison, rich gravies, fresh-baked bread, and spiced puddings filled the dining hall, all set against the flickering candlelight of the chandeliers. Twelve couples filled the lodge—Alvie's attempt at making this feel less like exile and more like a house party. Their chatter provided perfect cover for her racing thoughts.

Alvie's guests filled the long table, men he had known since his university days. They were much like him—old-money, business investors with stakes in various enterprises across town. Their wives, dressed in extravagant silks and pearls, perched at their sides with carefully composed expressions, making it clear they had no intention of staying at the hunting lodge longer than necessary.

While the men hunted, drank, and shared stories of their successes, the women remained indoors, whispering among themselves, their delicate fingers never brushing against the rough edges of the world outside. In contrast, Dani spent her days in the thick of it—chopping wood, riding out in the snow, tracking game with Alvie and Gabe.

As the meal progressed, the conversation drifted from town gossip to recent events—news of the Russo-Japanese War dominating discussion, debates over the construction of new rail lines, and hushed mentions of political unrest in Russia. The men spoke in deep, assured tones, their words laced with certainty like the world would always remain under their control.

Dani looked over at Gabe, fingers idly twirling the stem of her wineglass.

"Boring," she mouthed, lips barely moving.

He offered a crooked smile. Beneath the table, his hand slid over hers, fingers curling around in a firm touch.

She startled—but didn't pull away.

Instead, warmth crept through her body. A quiet comfort in the middle of all this aristocratic pretense.

Maybe it was the wine.

Maybe it was just that he was... there.

The evening carried on, and eventually, the inevitable came—the toasts. Alvie stood first, his glass raised high. "To my Danielle and young Gabriel. A fine match, indeed! May your union bring prosperity and—"

"A merry household!" one of Alvie's friends cut in, raising his glass with a boisterous laugh. "Come now, have you two shared the joys of courting?"

Dani choked slightly on her drink, eyes widening as the table erupted into laughter.

Gabe, ever the charmer, gave an easy grin. "Ah, sir, a gentleman never speaks of such things in present company," he lifted his glass, smoothly diverting attention as the laughter swelled, his words leaving just enough suggestion to satisfy the room's curiosity. Then, beneath the table, he gave Dani's hand a light squeeze, a silent "Look what I did—I saved you."

Dani let out a breath she hadn't realized she was holding, casting him a glance of reluctant appreciation. The night wore on, filled with singing, clinking glasses, and an air of joviality that dulled the edges of her doubts.

But the act was wearing thin.

The dinner finally over, the song and laughter faded as guests retired to their rooms. The hall was quieter now, and the warmth of the fire bathed the corridors in a gentle, amber glow.

Gabe walked beside Dani, his steps unhurried, his presence steady. When they reached her door, he hesitated before facing her. His hand lifted, brushing a stray lock of hair from her cheek before tilting her chin gently upward.

He kissed her again, slow and confident. And this time, she didn't question it. She was almost home.

Dani stiffened. "Gabe—" She pulled back, stepping away, arms crossing over herself to ward off the sudden cold pressing in at the edges of her mind. "I need to change out of this dress to lounge by the fire for the rest of the evening."

Gabe studied her, his sharp blue eyes searching for something beneath the surface. Then, with a polite dip of his head, he stepped back. "As you wish. I, too, feel the need to make myself useful—perhaps I shall see to the game lift once more. After all, a man's hands were not made for idleness.

His words were effortless, but there was something in his tone—something restrained. She knew he was giving her an easy exit, letting her go without making her say what she couldn't. The disappointment in his eyes was brief.

She slipped inside, closing the door softly and resting her forehead against the wood. A relentless thrum coursed through her—not from excitement, but the sharp reminder of what she wanted and couldn't have.

She changed into a deep burgundy silk tea gown with an embroidered dark green overlay, high neckline. She released her long brown wavy hair, letting it fall freely over her shoulders; it was no longer confined by the careful pins she had worn during dinner.

Stepping back out into the hunting lodge's grand day room, she let the warmth of the fire wash over her, though it did little to settle the turmoil in her thoughts. She picked up the book she had been reading earlier, its leather cover cool against her fingertips. She sank into one of the overstuffed chairs, pretending to read while letting the soft murmurs of conversation fill the surrounding space.

Alvie sat across from her, nursing his brandy, his attention lost in the firelight. Two of his old university friends hung back, their voices low and unhurried as they reminisced about days past. The atmosphere was relaxed, steeped in the familiar ease of old friends sharing quiet company.

For an hour, Dani remained there, flipping pages until she barely registered, listening to the comforting sounds of Alvie's occasional chuckle and the rhythmic clink of glasses against the side table. It was calm. It was easy. And then the door swung open, the cold rushing in with an unforgiving bite.

Gabe stepped inside, shaking dampness from his coat. His boots left wet imprints across the wooden floor. He approached the gathering with an easy stride, offering Alvie a nod.

"How's the game lift coming along?" Alvie asked, taking a sip of his brandy.

"Almost done," Gabe replied smoothly, tugging off his gloves. "Should be operational by tomorrow."

"Good, good," Alvie nodded approvingly, then gestured toward one of the side rooms. "I've a clock in the guest quarters that could also use some attention. When you've the time."

"Yeah, no worries. I can check it out later—should be an easy fix," Gabe replied.

Dani, who had been absently poking at the fire, froze.

Yeah? Since when does Gabe say 'no worries'?

Slowly, she turned, studying him. Gabe caught her expression and gave her a quick, almost imperceptible nod before tilting his head toward the far side of the lodge. Without a word, he started walking.

Dani followed.

The noise of the lodge faded as they stepped into the shadowed corner, away from curious ears. She crossed her arms. "What the hell is going on?"

Enver rolled his shoulders, shaking off the weight of the situation. "Look, before you freak out—"

"What the hell are you doing here? Where's Gabe?"

"Oh, he's fine. He's just taking a little nap. Chloroform's surprisingly effective. He'll be up in a few hours," he replied.

Her mouth dropped. "You knocked Gabe out?"

"I helped him take a break. Call it a... creative solution." He shrugged, voice turning more serious. "I had to step in, Dani. He would never take no as an answer—not really. He was always going to bring you back here after your goodbye. That was the real trap. He's going to keep you here—marry you, impregnate you and tie you down. Because letting you go? That was never an option for him."

Dani's breath caught. "That's not true."

He leveled her with a look. "You know it is. I traveled last night and saw your future together." His voice dropped. "I saw you die, Dani. Some disease—consumption, typhoid, I don't know—something they can't cure here. Gabe knew. In that timeline, he knew and kept you, anyway. He'd rather have you for two years than lose you at all."

The room felt smaller. Dani opened her mouth to argue, but the certainty in his eyes stopped her.

"You must go back," Enver continued, his voice lowering. "If you stay, things will change. The timeline—Cleo, Mary—everything shifts. You can't stay."

Her eyes turned skeptical. "Why do you care so much?"

"Because I spent my entire life chasing something I couldn't fix." His voice cracked. "Cleo. I thought she loved me. I thought we were meant to be. And then, one day, she was gone."

As Enver described the romance, Dani's mind was no longer in the wet clearing but inside a gilded ballroom. Golden chandeliers cast light over glittering gowns and crisp tuxedos. Laughter and music filled the air.

At the edge of the dance floor, Cleo stood frozen, champagne flute untouched in her gloved hand. She was watching Alvie Barrington move effortlessly across the floor, twirling Vivienne in a graceful waltz—the woman he had chosen, the woman who now wore the future Cleo had once imagined for herself.

Cleo's throat burned. She turned away, rejection slicing deeper than expected. Then she saw him.

Enver stood near the brandy cart, posing as Gabriel to sell his time travel services to the wealthy. His dark hair swept back in waves, charming and brilliant with just enough mystery to intrigue. He spoke of time as something tangible, something to be crafted and bent.

Cleo lifted her chin and walked straight toward him.

She made herself indispensable. In his workshop, surrounded by the smell of burning metal and ticking gears, she watched him craft box after box for the elite. When Enver's fingers hovered over the dials of one particular device, he whispered, "This one is for us."

Cleo's smile stretched from ear to ear.

The world cracked open. They fell.

When Cleo's feet hit solid ground, everything was different. Automobiles roared past, neon lights blazed, jazz spilled from hidden speakeasies. A newspaper fluttered at her feet: 1930.

But the thrill faded. Months passed, each heavier than the last. The dazzling lights of the 1930s couldn't mask the suffocating reality of their relationship. After another strained dinner, Cleo slipped away to Enver's workshop. The watch he'd given her pulsed with a familiar glow—a signal connected to their time machine.

That night, she stole their box. As the portal flared to life, she didn't hesitate. She vanished into a future where he could never follow.

The ballroom dissolved back into the damp clearing.

"Cleo took the watch," Enver said, his voice hollow. "It was supposed to notify me whenever the trinket box moved through time. Without it, I couldn't know if she was jumping or had just... stopped. Settled somewhere. Died. So I kept looking. I built a few watches, but they don't work as well." He gestured vaguely at his wrist.

"I stopped making the boxes after she disappeared three years ago. Those who purchased them still have theirs, I have two, and then there's yours in the present."

For the first time, Dani saw the exhaustion behind his arrogance, the weight of years spent chasing something forever out of reach.

"After you told me where she was buried I jumped to Portland and Cleo's grave," he whispered. "Saw that Cleo had lived a full life. A family. She was happy. She didn't truly love me." His expression softened. "And I finally understood—I no longer needed her. My search was over."

Dani sucked in a sharp breath. "The lights I saw every year with Mary, shimmering over the river on September 21st—that was you."

"Yeah." He studied her. "Time isn't a line when you mess with it—it's layers. The ripple effect kicked in the instant I first visited her grave. Every future version of me carrying that grief would come back to this exact spot. You were seeing the echoes before you knew what they meant."

"I spent so many years wondering about those lights," she whispered. "And it was you."

"In infinite loops," he confirmed. "But here's what's strange—in this timeline, Cleo hasn't happened yet. The events are out of order, and I think it's because of your arrival. In the timeline I know, she falls for me. But here, she's meant to fall for Gabriel instead. I traveled moths ago when you arrived , confused about the timeline and saw it. She shows up in six months."

Understanding dawned in Dani's eyes.

"Gabriel knows this, I shouldn't have warned him. He's hoping that marrying you, making you stay, would disrupt the timeline permanently. Keep the loop broken." Enver's voice dropped. "He's seen what grief did to me. He doesn't want to become what I became—mad with loss, chasing ghosts through time."

The lodge door banged open in the distance. Footsteps.

"Someone's coming," Dani whispered.

They turned to see Alvie approaching, his expression unreadable in the moonlight. Behind him, another figure emerged from the shadows.

She forgot how to breathe.

Rowen stood there, breathless, water droplets dusting her shoulders. Her blue eyes found Dani's, wild and desperate.

"How did you..." Dani started.

"Gossips at my wedding, giving quite detailed accounts of Alvie's hunting party," Rowen said, her voice strained. "Finding you was simple enough—there's only one road to Government Camp."

A fierce pounding filled Dani's chest. She'd thought it was over. That Rowen had made her choice. But here she was, looking desperate and beautiful and everything Dani had been trying to forget.

Alvie sighed. "I believe I'll return to the lodge. Whatever happens here is between you young people." He caught Dani's eye meaningfully before disappearing back inside.

"Danielle, I must speak with you." Rowen stepped closer, her breath visible in the cold air. "I married Beatrice. My mother is secure, well cared for. That was the purpose of it all. But the only thing that shall sever a marriage such as mine is death. If I were to disappear, they would presume me dead. We could leave for Salem. Vanish entirely. No one would seek us."

She moved closer still, desperation bright in her eyes. "Please don't marry this man. Your heart belongs to me."

Enver glanced at Dani with barely concealed amusement at Rowen calling him Gabe.

Dani's eyes widened, tears blurring her vision. "Don't say that. You don't get to say that now."

"Why do you resist me?"

"Because we both know I don't belong here."

Rowen closed the space between them, her fingers trembling as she grasped Dani's hand. "Tell me honestly—can you resist me? Can you look me in the eyes and truly say this isn't exactly where you belong?"

A sharp ache twisted in Dani's chest. "Rowen, it's not that simple—"

"But it is exactly that simple," Rowen interrupted fiercely, her voice breaking. "You were never meant for him, nor was I meant for Beatrice. I did what I had to for my mother's sake, but it means nothing now. I can endure anything—any loss, any pain—but I cannot endure losing you." She drew in a ragged breath. "I love you, Dani. My heart is yours, entirely and irreversibly. You nearly confessed your love once—do not silence it now."

"I beg you, darling, deny me no longer," Rowen whispered, tears threatening to spill.

Darling. The word hit Dani like a tidal wave. Rowen never spoke that way, but now she revealed such tender vulnerability.

Enver cleared his throat. "As sincerely touching as this is, we really don't have time." He twisted the key in the box. The gears clicked into place. The air rippled. A swirling vortex of light and shadow burst forth, warping the surrounding space. "Time's up, friend. Portal's open."

Rowen's eyes widened in shock. "What—what is that?"

"Proof," Dani said softly. "Everything I told you was true."

"You..." Rowen stared at Enver, taking in his modern mannerisms with new understanding. "You're not from here either."

"Nope. I am from everywhere and nowhere." Enver grabbed Dani's wrist. "She needs to leave. Now."

"No!" Rowen lunged forward, grabbing Dani's other arm. "Please, let us run away to Salem or the East Coast, I do not care!"

The portal's pull, growing stronger, trapped Dani between them. "Rowen, I need to leave."

"This makes little sense!"

"It doesn't matter if it makes sense," Enver said urgently. "If she stays, she dies. That's what I saw. That's what happens."

The portal's pull intensified. Dani's feet began sliding toward it.

Rowen's grip tightened desperately. "Then I'm going with you!"

"Rowen, no—"

But it was too late. The portal's force yanked Dani backward. With Rowen still holding on, the portal's force pulled her along. In that split second, Rowen made her choice—not letting go, following Dani into the unknown.

Just before the world collapsed around her, Dani caught sight of Alvie standing in the lodge doorway, his expression knowing and sad.

"Grandpa!" she screamed, the word bursting from her before she could stop it.

His eyes widened in understanding just as the portal snapped shut.

The world exploded into color, time unraveling around them, folding and twisting as they plummeted through the void.

Falling.

Falling.

Together.

28

THE LIGHT GAZER

PRESENT DAY

The Barrington house stood quiet in the December darkness, early evening settling over the estate like a heavy blanket. Inside, Mary lay in Dani's bed, having escaped there after dinner. It was only 8 PM, but she'd been going to bed earlier and earlier lately—what was the point of staying awake?

She'd been sleeping here since October, telling herself it was to help with the research, to be close to Dani's things. Her own apartment was still occupied with a renter across town. The truth was simpler and more pathetic—she couldn't let go.

The bedside clock read 8:47 PM when the burning started.

Mary jolted awake from her half-doze, gasping. The watch on her wrist wasn't just warm—it was searing hot, like metal left in the summer sun. She'd never felt it do this before, not even the night Dani vanished.

"What the hell—"

She stumbled out of bed, fumbling for the lamp. The watch face glowed beneath the glass, gears spinning so fast they blurred. The burning intensified, shooting up her arm like electricity.

Still disoriented, she staggered to the bedroom door and out onto the landing. The huge staircase windows that overlooked the grounds blazed with pulsing blue light—like lightning, but rhythmic, measured. Proximity, she's close to it.

The clearing. It was coming from the clearing.

"No way. No fucking way."

Mary flew down the stairs, not bothering with shoes, just a coat. From the library, she could hear George call out, "Mary? What's wrong?" But she didn't stop to answer.

She yanked open the front door just as another pulse of blue light washed across the grounds, throwing twisted shadows from the trees.

The watch burned hotter. The gears screamed.

She ran.

Frozen grass crunched beneath her socks. Her breath came in sharp gasps, lungs burning from the cold. But she didn't slow. Couldn't slow. Because she knew—with absolute certainty—what that light meant.

The portal was open.

Two figures crashed into the clearing, landing hard among the fallen leaves. Their sudden arrival was as startling as thunder in a clear sky.

Mary stumbled backward, disbelief washing over her. The watch burned hot in her palm for an instant, then dimmed abruptly, its glow fading to nothing.

Silence.

Then, a rough inhale broke the quiet.

"Dani?"

The name barely escaped Mary's lips before Dani groaned, shifting slowly onto her elbows.

The earth beneath her felt impossibly solid. The air smelled foreign yet familiar. Slowly, Dani's eyes fluttered open, adjusting to the dim starlight.

She knew that voice.

"Mary?"

Mary stood a few feet away, her coat half-unzipped, eyes wide with shock. She took in Dani's appearance—the corset, the dirt-streaked petticoat, the Edwardian boots—and then her gaze shifted.

Rowen lay beside her, jacket torn, breathing heavily and shivering against the cold ground.

Mary's mouth fell open. "What the actual—"

A broad, relieved grin broke across Dani's face.

Rowen turned toward her, wild-eyed and disbelieving. Then she too smiled broadly.

They smiled like idiots. Like survivors.

Their hands found each other, gripping tightly, confirming that this was real.

A laugh burst from Dani's lips—real and joyful.

Mary watched their hands link, and something sharp twisted low in her chest. It wasn't just shock. Or joy. Or even relief that Dani was alive.

It was the feeling of something breaking loose inside her—something she'd spent years packing into quiet boxes labeled just friendship and don't ruin this.

Dani had always been hers—in sleepovers, in grief, in lazy Saturday mornings that bled into afternoon. She'd held Dani in every way but the one that mattered most.

And now someone else was holding her.

A girl with a torn jacket and fire in her eyes.

The kind of girl Mary would've fallen for in a different life—had she let herself look.

But she hadn't.

Not until this second.

Not until it was already too late.

Her head snapped between the two women, her voice rising sharply. "Excuse me? Would someone like to explain why you two just fell from the freaking sky looking like some historical takeover?"

Dani wheezed, breathless with adrenaline and joy.

She grabbed Rowen's hand firmly, pulling her upright. "Come on," she gasped urgently. "We have to get to the house."

Mary scrambled after them, shouting questions into the night. "Wait—what's the hurry? Who is that? Why do you smell like a history museum—"

But Dani didn't slow.

Rowen didn't let go.

And together, they ran.

The front door creaked open just as Dani reached the porch—not flung open dramatically, but cautiously, someone had heard a noise, they couldn't quite place.

Teresa and George had been in the library, a fire crackling low in the hearth, when they heard the muffled sound of footsteps—rushed, frantic—on the entrance stairs. Teresa set her teacup down mid-sip, exchanging a look with George as she rose.

They stepped into the foyer just in time to see the heavy doors swing wider.

And there she was.

Dani, breathless, muddy boots dripping onto the marble floors, cheeks flushed red from cold and adrenaline. Beside her stood Mary, coat askew, and someone else—a stranger—clutching Dani's hand.

Rowen looked a mess. Torn jacket. Windblown hair. Dirt smudged across her face.

"Oh my god—Dani," Teresa squealed.

She surged forward before Dani could speak, arms thrown wide and eyes shimmering with disbelief. The hug crushed what little breath Dani had left. "Hi, Mom," she mumbled into her shoulder.

A blur of orange fur shot across the marble floor—Fat Fluffy Toaster, all fifteen pounds of him, launching himself at Dani's legs like a furry missile. He climbed halfway up her muddy petticoat, claws digging through fabric as he purred loud enough to wake the dead.

"Toaster!" Dani laughed, scooping up the massive tabby who immediately began headbutting her chin with aggressive affection. "I missed you too, buddy."

And then George was there, slower but no less stunned. He stared for a beat, like he needed to confirm his daughter was real.

"You look like hell," he said, his voice catching.

Dani laughed, "I missed you too."

And then her dad was there pulling her into a second hug, solid and too much all at once. "We didn't know where you'd gone," he said quietly, worried that speaking it too loudly might break her. We thought—God, we didn't know what to think."

Behind her, Mary stood at the threshold, wide-eyed and still catching her breath. Rowen stood just a step behind, unsure, like she wasn't sure she belonged there. Dani reached back instinctively, lacing their fingers together pulling her forward.

As Rowen stepped further into the foyer, her eyes went wide. The stain on the wall, the dingy edges of the flooring. She turned slowly, taking in the subtle changes: a heating vent where a radiator had been, light switches on the walls, Teresa's modern coat hanging on the same Edwardian coat rack.

"My God," Rowen breathed, her free hand reaching out to touch the wall. "It's the same, but..." Her gaze traveled to George's jeans, Teresa's cable-knit sweater, the TV visible through the parlor doorway. "Everything's different."

"This is Rowen," she said, voice soft. "She's, well, she came back with me."

Teresa's eyes scanned from their joined hands to Rowen's face. That motherly kind of recognition settled across her features. "You must be exhausted," she said gently, "and you smell like... a museum."

Dani managed a breathless laugh, still gripping Rowen's hand.

George blinked at the mud pooling on the marble beneath their boots. "Let's get you both inside before the floor takes the worst of it."

Teresa nodded, brushing beads of rain off her daughter's shoulders. "Come. The living room is still warm from the fire. We'll get you dry clothes and something hot to drink. We have so much to ask."

As Dani stepped fully into the stair landing near Alvie's portrait, her eyes drifted upward toward Vivienne's above it. She swore—just for a second—their expressions had softened. Not eerie or haunted, just... warm.

"You wouldn't believe the last few days," her dad said, running a hand through his hair as he closed the foyer pocket doors. "Thanks to Mary, it's all starting to make sense."

Teresa gave Dani a quick squeeze on the arm and excused herself, disappearing down the back hall toward the laundry room. She returned several minutes later, arms full of oversized hoodies and sweatpants. "Here—these should work for both of you. You can change in the downstairs entry bath."

Dani and Rowen slipped into the small tiled bathroom, the steam from the radiator fogging against the mirror. They kicked off their muddy boots and shed their heavy coats, damp with snow and time.

They just stood there naked, facing each other silently.

Rowen tilted her head, eyes curving with a crooked smile over Dani's bare breasts. A sharp bite caught her lower lip as she took in the view—Dani's golden hair damp and tousled, red cheeks flushed from heat and nerves.

A beat passed. Neither moved, just looks.

With an attempt at levity Rowen joked "So... this is what passes for modern clothing?" her voice low. "The quality is appalling. The stitching—utterly careless."

Dani snorted softly. "You'll pull them off better than I do. You always do."

Rowen tugged the hoodie over her head. The oversized fabric swallowed her narrow shoulders, the sleeves falling too far past her wrists. She pushed her long bangs behind her ears, strands sticking to her cheek, and looked up through her lashes.

And just like that—it wasn't funny anymore. It wasn't awkward.

It was devastating.

A hunger in them shifted.

Neither of them hesitated this time.

Dani reached first, pulling Rowen in. Their mouths met in a breathless, urgent kiss. Her back collided with the porcelain sink as Rowen pressed her hips against her, wrapping her hands around Dani's waist reaching her plump cheeks she'd been aching to squeeze.

The kiss was feverish, clumsy, greedy. The one Rowen had imagined while Beatrice's mouth had stolen hers, the only thing that had kept her from breaking.

Her hand slipped down Dani's behind, tracing the soft curve of her leg crease before sliding in front between her legs.

Dani gasped into the kiss, her leg instinctively rising to give more access. Rowen's fingers found her wetness and slowly slid inside. Dani kissed harder, her body trembling. The sensation of Rowen finally, finally touching her again was electric.

Her mouth parted with a soft cry—but Rowen's hand slid gently over her lips, silencing her. She leaned in close, her golden lashes lowering as she gave the smallest shake of her head—*no.*

Then came the quietest sound from Rowen's mouth:

"Shhh…"

It slipped out with devastating calm, her lips pursing so prettily Dani nearly lost her mind.

That look was wickedly confident, and it was everything.

Dani nearly came undone just watching her. *I've brought back the death of me.*

Dani's eyes fluttered shut, her breath muffled beneath Rowen's palm. The quiet hum of their bodies pressing together filled the space, intoxicating and reckless.

And then—

Knock-knock-knock.

"Everything fit in there?" Mary's voice rang through the door, falsely casual. "Just checking. Totally not trying to interrupt anything."

Dani groaned against Rowen's shoulder.

Rowen bit back a grin. "I am certain she *was* trying to interrupt."

Dani pulled back just enough to whisper, "She's never going to let us live this down."

"I hope not," Rowen said, tugging the hoodie's drawstrings with a mischievous glint. "I dare say, I like it here."

"What do you mean?"

Before Rowen could answer, another knock tapped lightly on the door, Teresa's voice following behind it. "If you're dressed, we've got tea waiting."

Dani shot Rowen a final, defiantly breathless look as Rowen slowly withdrew her fingers. Without a word, Rowen leaned in and pressed a tender kiss to her forehead. A silent reward. "I love you."

Before Dani could even form a reply, Rowen turned and opened the door. Warm light spilled from the hall as they stepped out, feet padded now in thick socks. Mary leaned against the wall nearby, arms crossed, she knew exactly what had just happened.

No one said anything, but the raised brow she shot Dani said plenty.

They followed Mary back to the living room, the sound of their footsteps muffled by old rugs.

George looked up from the fireplace as they entered, giving a nod of approval at their changed clothes. "There we go. A little less Gilded Age, a little more Oregon in December."

Nodding, Teresa gestured toward the side pocket doors, which stood partially open to reveal the library beyond. Inside, books, notes, and old papers lay scattered across the long table. "Mary's been here. She told us everything—about the watch, the glowing box, the timelines. It all sounded like madness at first, but..."

George cut in; eyes sharp now with frantic fascination. "But then I remembered some things. Records passed down from grandfather Alvie. He wrote about a girl named Danielle. Said she would come from nowhere and change everything. That her arrival would mark a shift in time itself."

Dani's mouth went dry.

"He said she'd arrive at night with a key on her necklace," her dad continued. "Then Mary showed us what she'd found, and it all clicked. Everything Alvie left behind wasn't poetic nonsense—it was a roadmap. She connected Alvie, Cleo, and Gabriel through the journals and records."

Stepping away from the table, Teresa picked up an envelope from a stack near the journals. "There's more," she said softly. "This was left with the journals. It's addressed to you—Alvie said it was to be opened the day you returned after disappearing."

With unsteady hands, Dani grabbed the envelope. Her name curved across the front in Alvie's unmistakable handwriting. She waited for half a second, then slipped her thumb beneath the seal.

The letter unfolded with a soft rustle.

Her eyes tracked the words.

Stopped.

Widened.

"He... he left money," she breathed. "A lot of it."

My Dearest Danielle,

If this letter has found its way to your hands, then I must assume I am no longer among the living. Do not be distressed, my dear girl there is no need for sorrow, nor tears. Take comfort in knowing I have resolved your predicament.

The matter of the estate (the funds entangled in property) has been thoroughly seen to. You are no longer burdened. Send my love to your father and mother.

With all my enduring love and deepest affection, your devoted grandfather,

Alvie

George leaned in, eyes watering, "enough to save the house. More than enough for paying off college, the repairs, everything."

"He planned for all of it," Dani replied, barely above a whisper. A warm hand landed on her shoulder—her mother's.

The doorbell rang, cutting through the moment. George frowned, checking his watch. "Who could that be at this hour?"

He returned moments later with a well-dressed woman carrying a leather portfolio. She looked to be in her forties, professional but warm, with kind eyes behind designer glasses.

"Ms. Wood? I'm Sarah Chen from the Wood-Barrington Trust. We've been monitoring the property for your return." She glanced at the key around Dani's neck. "That's one of the verification items mentioned in our charter."

Dani's hand went to the key automatically. "I'm sorry, what trust?"

"Forever Forward Foundation serves individuals whose love and identity exist beyond society's traditional boundaries established in your name in 1906. You're listed as the founding beneficiary." Sarah smiled. "Mr. Barrington left very specific instructions. We were to wait for your return, no matter how long it took."

The room went silent. Even Mary, who'd been hovering in the doorway, stepped fully inside.

"A foundation?" Dani's voice came out strangled.

Sarah opened her portfolio, spreading documents across the already cluttered table. "The Forever Forward Foundation. Currently managing assets of approximately forty-seven million dollars." I didn't want to believe any of it, but for my salary, I'll believe anything.

Dani's teacup crashed to the floor.

"The original endowment was modest," Sarah continued, seemingly unbothered by the shattered china, "but Mr. Barrington had remarkable foresight. He invested in Ford, General Electric, and somehow—though our historians can't explain it—bought Coca-Cola stock before it went public."

George laughed, slightly hysterical. "He knew things, didn't he?"

"We've funded safe houses, legal advocacy, and historical preservation for over a century."

Sarah pulled out another document. "The foundation specifically names George Barrington as co-beneficiary."

"We own several properties throughout Portland, including the building that was once Meier & Frank department store. It's now a community center." Sarah confirmed.

"He... he... um... did all this?" Dani sank into a chair, overwhelmed her hands shaking.

"There's one more thing." Sarah pulled out a sealed envelope, older than the others. "This was to be given to you personally upon your return."

With shaking hands, Dani opened it.

> *P.S. You will find I have taken certain liberties with my investments. You taught me that progress without love is merely machinery. Let those who come after you know they are not alone. You never were. Also, Rowen's mother is well taken care of, I've seen to it.*
>
> *Love, A.B.*

Tears streamed down Dani's face. Rowen's hand found hers, squeezing tightly.

"The foundation has a board meeting next week," Sarah whispered. "As the founding beneficiary, you have a permanent seat. Both of you do." She looked at George. "Mr. Barrington was quite insistent that George be given equal authority."

"You said you've been monitoring the property?" Dani managed.

Sarah nodded. "The foundation owns this house. We've been maintaining it, waiting for your return. The 'financial troubles' were... a cover story. We couldn't exactly explain we were waiting for a time traveler."

George sat down heavily. "You mean the house was never actually in danger?"

"Never. Though we let certain parties believe it was, to maintain the timeline Mr. Barrington described." Sarah gathered her papers. "I'll leave you to process this. My card is on the table. Call when you're ready to tour the foundation's facilities."

A stunned laugh slipped out of Dani. "Of course he did." She turned toward his smaller cameo portrait on the living room wall—Alvie and his hunting dogs smiling like he knew exactly what he'd done. One thing that changed in the timeline. Like this was his in on the joke.

"Wait," Dani said, blinking. "How long have you been working this out? What happened to me."

Teresa let out a slow breath. "When we realized something had to do with the trinket box from your nightstand."

"You were trying to open it?"

"We tried everything. Eventually, I figured out how to work the dials, but we didn't have a key. We thought maybe—if we could just get it open..." George replied.

"You were trying to open a portal."

He nodded. "Exactly."

For a second, everything around her dropped into silence.

They hadn't just waited for her. They'd been fighting for answers. The story hadn't paused while she was gone—it had been unfolding here the entire time.

And now she was standing in the middle of it, Mary had been at the center of it all. Quietly, behind the scenes, she'd been handing them every missing piece.

Rowen shifted beside her, eyes scanning the cluttered table, the notes, the boxes, the books. "It appears your family is quite... tenacious."

"You have no idea." Dani huffed.

Teresa gave Rowen a once-over. "Did you jump through after her?"

Caught off guard, Rowen's brows lifted. "It was the only sensible thing to do."

George shook his head in disbelief. "Jumping through a damn portal after our daughter—that's one hell of a first impression." the tone sincere now.

"What year did you say you came from?" Teresa finally eased back, brushing a stray curl from her daughter's face before her eyes found Rowen again.

"Ah... 1905." Rowen blinked, clearly still adjusting to modern light switches and throw pillows.

"Shoot. I was betting on 1900, exactly. Should've written it down." George laughed.

Teresa tilted her head, her smile turning sly. "And who exactly are you to our daughter, then?"

Dani opened her mouth, but Rowen beat her to it—voice formal. "Merely someone most fortunate to have made her acquaintance—one who is indebted to her in ways I may never sufficiently express."

"That sounds suspiciously romantic." Teresa teased.

Dani's cheeks burned. "Mom—"

But Teresa was already grinning.

Her dad stepped in every time the practical one. "What did you do? Back then, I mean."

Rowen folded her hands neatly in front of her. "I was, by trade, a tailor and seller of fine dresses—entrusted with the oversight of an entire floor in a rather distinguished department store. I also held the position of chairman of the workers' union, a duty I took most seriously. And yet, in the quiet hours of the evening, I would often turn my thoughts to the written word. Mostly fiction... modest little tales, scarcely read by anyone at all, but dear to me nonetheless."

"You never told me that." Dani squealed.

Rowen shrugged modestly. "You had troubles enough of your own."

"A tailor and a writer? Oh, I like you," Teresa said, lighting up.

"I knew it," George added, nodding with genuine admiration. "That explains how you looked at that jacket I left on the coat rack. I saw you sizing up the stitching."

Rowen smiled. "Old habits."

"Is that why you're dressed as a man?" Teresa asked, tilting her head.

"Well..." Rowen started, but Dani quickly jumped in, not about to let a complicated backstory derail the welcome-home moment.

"She has impeccable style, Mother. We can chat about the details later."

"Impeccable?" Teresa raised an eyebrow. "Now that's a word. I think time has changed you, Dani—you seem more grown up and confident." She gave her daughter a proud smile.

From the side, Mary stood quietly, arms crossed. She didn't say a word, but her eyes were on Rowen, taking her in. The way her blonde short hair lay above her hear perfectly tousled, how she somehow looked regal in the borrowed hoodie and sweatpants like custom-tailored couture, how Dani kept unconsciously leaning toward her, touching her wrist, brushing their hands together like magnets that didn't know how to stay apart.

Of course, Rowen was charming, elegant, accomplished, and perfectly undone in that effortless way that made people lean in without realizing why.

Mary's jaw twitched—not anger, not exactly, but something else nestled in her chest, a feeling she is now acutely aware she should examine. Then she caught Dani smiling at Rowen—soft, full, in a way she'd never seen before—and for the first time, the truth hit with a clarity she wasn't prepared to face. *Why does this bother me so much?*

The living room eventually faded into gentle laughter and dimmed lights—Dani nestled between her parents on the couch, Rowen drifting the bookcases, electronics, and knick knacks nearby, quietly taking in this strange new world. Mary reappeared from down the hall, arms crossed, head tilted.

"So," came her casual voice, edged with something sharper, "anyone hungry?"

Dani perked up. "I don't even remember the last thing I ate. Was it soup? It was definitely soup."

"I'll make pasta." Mary's smile widened, just slightly smug.

"Oh my God, yes."

"I'll make it vegetarian," Mary added, glancing at Rowen with too much casualness.

Rowen raised a brow. "Vegetarian? These are things you haven't told me as."

"She's been one since high school," Mary said, already moving toward the kitchen. "Kind of her thing."

Rowen followed behind, her steps slow and reverent. Her hand grazed the wall, landing on the light switch, a relic from another era. Her eyes flicked toward the recessed lights, the thermostat, and the family photos lining the hallway. When the microwave beeped, she flinched—just slightly.

"What... was that?"

"That," Dani laughed, "was the microwave. It's a tiny metal box that uses science to ruin leftovers."

Rowen gave a low, thoughtful hum. "Your century is absurd."

Mary opened the fridge and pulled out a few ingredients. "It's called progress."

Rowen edged toward the refrigerator, then paused. Dani opened the door for her.

"Oh," Rowen murmured, peering in. "It's colder than I expected."

"That's the fridge," Mary chimed, tossing pasta onto the counter. "Keeps food from rotting. Revolutionary stuff, I know."

Rowen turned back to Dani. "And you... eat this way often?"

"She does," Mary answered before Dani could. "I used to make this pasta all the time after finals. It's kind of a comfort food thing."

Rowen nodded slowly. "It smells... comforting."

"She used to say it was the only thing that made her feel normal during the chaos," Mary added lightly, but something was pointed behind the words.

"Well," Rowen said, voice smooth, "I imagine chaos follows her often."

Dani leaned against the counter, chuckling. "You're both acting like I'm some tragic soup heroine."

"You're just easy to take care of," Mary said, stirring the pan.

"And difficult to forget," Rowen added smoothly, not looking away from Dani.

Mary didn't respond—just stirred harder.

Eventually, Mary slid a plate in front of Dani. "Here. This one is yours."

"And the biggest portion, thank you." Dani's smile softened.

Rowen clocked it—every beat of familiarity, the comfortable shorthand between them.

Mary set another plate down, this one for Rowen. "I didn't know how much you'd prefer."

"Much appreciated," Rowen replied coolly, taking her seat. "I'm more accustomed to soup and bread from a hearth."

"No hearth here," Mary said, forcing a polite smile. "But we do have Wi-Fi."

Rowen blinked. "A... what?"

"Don't even try to explain," Dani cut in. "It'll melt her brain."

Rowen tilted her head, amused. "Then I shall remain blissfully ignorant."

Another beat of silence.

"So..." Mary said, voice carefully neutral, "are you staying long?"

Dani hesitated. "Honestly? We just got here."

Rowen didn't say a word—just brushed her hand beneath the table, fingers sliding against Dani's. A quiet, grounding touch.

Mary noticed.

And just like that, dinner turned into a silent battlefield—polite conversation masking a steady undercurrent of something heavier.

After the dishes were cleared—primarily by Mary, who moved quickly, waving off any help—Dani yawned. "Alright. I'm officially dead inside. I need sleep."

"The guest rooms made up; your father finished it while you were gone; I have been staying in your room," Mary said smoothly. Rowen, you're welcome to the guest room."

A pause. Subtle but *very* loaded.

It wasn't meant to sting—but it did.

The truth lingered behind her teeth like a ghost: I slept in your room every night because I couldn't bear being anywhere else. Not just because Dani was missing. But because she wasn't ready to imagine Dani with anyone else.

Rowen looked at Dani, who caught her hint and tried not to combust. "Actually... I should stay with Rowen; this isn't her century."

Mary didn't say much—just nodded a little too tightly. "Right. Sure."

"All this technology is quite dizzying, I think I shall faint," Rowen said, trying to break the tension. Dani laughing at the inside joke.

Visibly irritated by not being included in this inside joke, Mary replied, "Well, then you should head up to bed," grabbing the last of the dishes. "Dani, do you want to stay up and chat?"

Dani didn't miss the signs in her expression—the quiet, bruised ache she didn't want to express. "I should probably go to bed, too. We've had an insane 24 hours."

Rowen hesitated. "If it's inappropriate—"

"It's not," Dani said, maybe a little too fast. "You're fine. Come on."

They left Mary in the hallway, arms crossed, watching them disappear together.

Her arms stayed crossed—but only to keep herself from unraveling.

She stood in the quiet long after the door shut, frozen in place, gut hollowed by the soft sound of laughter trailing. Dani's laughter.

It used to belong to her.

And now it didn't.

Dani's room felt surreal.

Not because Rowen was there sitting gingerly on the edge of her bed but because it was hers. Her posters were on the walls, her messy stack of books was still leaning dangerously on her nightstand, and a hoodie was slung over the desk chair. All of it screaming *home* while Rowen sat in the middle like a time-warped daydream made real.

Rowen ran her fingers along the bookshelf, brushing lightly over a faded copy of Pride and Prejudice, a cracked mug holding pens, and a candle labeled "Bergamot + Smoke." She paused, lifting it to her nose.

"Well," she muttered, "you have my scent, let me have yours."

Her gaze wandered to the vanity. A few cologne bottles stood in a tidy row, one clearly more used than the rest. She picked it up, gave the label a squint.

"Issey Miyake," she read aloud, then smiled. "Of course mens cologne."

She sprayed a little into the air and stepped through it like muscle memory. "Now let me smell you," she said softly, more to herself than anything.

She sniffed her sleeve and laughed again, shaking her head. "Incredible." Rowen set the bottle back, not quite ready to let go of the experience.

"This is your sanctuary," she said softly, a smile playing at her lips. "And you chose my scent without ever knowing me. How utterly remarkable."

Dani flopped back onto the bed. "More like my disaster nest, but sure." She grinned wickedly. "Maybe that's the only reason I was attracted to you—just following my nose like some lovesick bloodhound."

Rowen chuckled. "It is a curious thing... I spent so long imagining your world, crafting it in my mind. And now that I stand within it, I wonder how I ever believed I understood you at all."

Dani rolled onto her side, propping her head on her arm. "How are you really doing with all this modern stuff?"

"Your world is extraordinary," Rowen said softly. "Lights that never flicker, ice that never melts, warmth without fire. Yet what strikes me most is not your technology."

"What then?"

"Mary. She has been sleeping in your bed, dwelling in your sanctuary. In my time, we would call such devotion something other than friendship."

Dani went very still. "Mary doesn't... she likes guys. She's always dating guys." But even as she said it, pieces started clicking together—the way Mary had always kept her at arm's length, the careful distance, the sleeping in her bed for months.

"Does she?" Rowen asked quietly.

"I...don't think...so" Dani replied, still questioning it.

As if summoned by their voices, Toaster appeared in the doorway, orange and black fur catching the lamplight. He surveyed the scene with typical feline judgment before padding over to leap onto the bed with surprising grace for his size. Without ceremony, he settled himself directly between them, purring like a small engine.

"And who might this distinguished gentleman be?" Rowen asked, tentatively reaching out to scratch behind his ears.

"That's Toaster. He's basically the real owner of this house." Dani grinned as the cat immediately rolled over to expose his belly, clearly smitten with their new guest. "He's got excellent taste in people."

The room felt cozy and calm with them in it. Dani's eyes trailed over to the desk, the pens, the books, the notepads.

Then, gently, Dani asked, "What did you do with your little notepads?"

Rowen blinked. "I wrote Union propaganda. Editorials. Novels, chiefly. Yet I never dared confess that part. It always seemed a secret best kept, a thing quite beyond what was expected of me."

Dani sat up a little straighter. "You write entire books?"

Rowen nodded. "In another life, I imagined myself an authoress. I did attempt a novel and sent it for publishing."

Dani's brow lifted. "Wait—*what*? Why am I just hearing about this now?"

"I sent it off, nothing more." Rowen responded.

"What was it called?" Dani asked, already sitting up.

Rowen hesitated. "The Light Gazer."

Dani paused.

Without a word, she scrambled to her desk, yanked her laptop open, and typed fast, fingers flying across the keyboard.

"No way," she breathed. "Rowen—this is real. It's right here. *The Light Gazer.* It's on Amazon."

Rowen's brows furrowed. "The forest?"

Half laughing, Dani snorted. "No—it's a giant digital marketplace. You can buy almost anything with a few clicks. It's like... a modern miracle and a capitalist nightmare wrapped in one."

She turned the screen toward Rowen. "You're telling me *you* wrote this? Because this book... this is a New York Times Classics Bestseller."

Rowen stared at the screen agape. "I used a pen name, but yes. That was mine."

They sat there in stunned silence, the glow of the laptop screen reflecting in their eyes. A strange, full-circle warmth bloomed between them—soft, bittersweet, and magical.

"This synopsis—it's us. Rowen... this is our story."

Reaching for Dani's hand, Rowen threaded their fingers together gently. "I wrote it while we were courting," she said. "I submitted the manuscript to several publishers the day I left for the hunting lodge. I left before I would hear back... well, before everything."

Dani swallowed hard, blinking back tears. She hovered the mouse over the title again and then slowly moved to the 'Buy Now.' button at the bottom. *Click.*

For a second, Dani didn't function. That sentence struck a chord deep within her brain.

She'd been kissed. She'd been wanted. She'd been pursued. But this?

This was another level.

Her pulse thundered between her legs. Her throat burned. That was the most achingly beautiful, *damningly romantic* thing anyone had ever done.

A book. *Rowen had written a whole fucking book.* With no hope. No promise of a happy ending. Just longing.

It clicked something loose inside Dani. Snapped some final thread of restraint.

She turned to face Rowen, eyes hungry.

"Close the door."

The latch clicked. Rowen came to her without hesitation.

Dani kissed her like she needed to remember the taste. No warning, no patience—just intensity and hunger. They moved together, fluid and frantic, peeling off layers in breathless bursts. Skin met skin. Hands shook. There was no room for shame here. Only demands.

Dani leaned in, lips brushing Rowen's ear. "You trust me?"

Rowen nodded, her voice bobbing in her throat. "Goodness, Miss Wood. Yes."

"It's just Dani, remember?" Dani whispered, pressing a kiss to Rowen's temple. "Lay back for me, Miss Quinn," an impish grin spread across her face.

Rowen obeyed, heart hammering. She wasn't sure she could breathe, let alone speak.

Dani kissed her again, tenderly, as she gently guided her down into the pillows. Rowen felt the warmth of Dani's fingers as they briefly rested on her thigh before retreating.

A quiet creak. The open of a drawer. Then a sound she didn't recognize: the thick slide of leather, the sharp click of metal buckles.

Rowen lifted her head and froze.

Dani stood at the foot of the bed, hips low, ripped abdominals tight, wearing something Rowen had no name for. A harness. Black, worn-in, and *strapped with length*. Her length.

It sat proudly between Dani's thighs like it belonged there.

Rowensucked in a sharp breath. "What... what is that?"

Dani just smirked. "Inspiration for your next book."

She stepped closer, slow and sultry. Her hands smoothed over Rowen's legs as she climbed back onto the bed.

Rowen stared stunned, disoriented, and *burning*. Her mouth opened, but nothing came out.

People whispered about pleasure behind closed doors in her world, barely mentioning it even in marriage. And now here was Dani, all modern, muscular, and hungry, wearing her desire on her hips.

"Can that—?" Rowen breathed. "Can *you*... with *that*—?"

"Oh, I can," Dani said, settling between her legs.

Rowen swallowed hard, chest heaving. "I didn't know women could—"

Bending down, Dani kissed her passionately, murmuring, "You're on the verge of discovering our modern capabilities."

Dani climbed back over her, letting the tip drag along Rowen's slick entrance, teasing with her fingers until Rowen's hips lifted of their own accord.

Shifting back, Dani angled just enough to reach up and gather her long, wavy brown hair into a loose twist. She secured it into a messy knot at the back of her head. A few strands slipped free, curling against her cheek, softening her jaw and casting shadows over her face, but nothing could dim those eyes. Hungry. Green. Glinting like embers in the dark.

And then she smiled. A ferocious account of unrestrained chaos.

"You're sure?" Dani breathed through a crooked grin.

Rowen nodded, breathless. "Show me your world."

The first push made Rowen gasp—high and full of disbelief. She clutched at Dani's arms, fingers digging in as she adjusted to the sudden, impossible fullness.

"Hell," she whimpered, eyes wide, lips parted.

Dani held still, cradling her face. "Inhale, sweetheart. You're doing so fucking good."

Rowen trembled beneath her.

Then Dani moved.

A slow pull, a deeper push—rhythmic and wet. Every thrust coaxed a new sound from Rowen's throat until her moans turned to begging. Her legs wrapped tight around Dani's waist, trying to pull her deeper.

Dani kissed her, rocked into her, speaking against her mouth, "Every version of me—every timeline, every place—I'd still end up here. Inside you. Loving you like this."

Rowen shattered with a cry, spine arched, body clenching around her.

Dani didn't stop. She fucked her through it—harder now, gasping against her neck. Their bodies met in a slick, wet rhythm, skin glistening under the dim light. Gasping breaths mingled with the scent of sweat and exertion, hands tangled, fingers gripping tightly. Warmth radiated between them, a damp heat clinging to their skin.

When Rowen came again, she sobbed Dani's name like it was the only thing tethering her to this timeline.

And Dani held her—thrusting, kissing, until neither of them knew where one ended and the other began.

A pitiful meowing broke through their breathing.

Toaster sat pressed against the door, orange fur on end, staring at them with wide, horrified eyes. He pawed frantically at the wood, claws making tiny scratching sounds as he tried to escape whatever traumatic symphony he'd just endured.

"Oh shit," Dani wheezed, still catching her breath. "Sorry, nugget."

Rowen buried her face in Dani's shoulder, shaking with silent laughter. "I believe we've scarred the poor creature for life."

Toaster let out another yowl, as if to confirm, and scrabbled harder at the door.

"Alright," Dani laughed, slipping out of bed to open it. "Freedom, you drama queen."

The cat shot from the room like his tail was on fire, leaving them dissolving into giggles.

Taking off the strap, Dani tossed it to the desk chair and crawled back into the bed. Bodies limp. Sheets a tangled mess.

Rowen curled onto her side, fingers brushing Dani's cut obliques. "My very own Helen of Troy," she whispered, eyes still heavy-lidded, "I would burn a thousand cities for you."

Dani smiled. "This is exactly how I envisioned us."

Rowen grinned and kissed her again, nice and slow.

Dani tucked the curtain bangs behind Rowen's ear. "Rowen."

She looked up, quiet and open.

"I love you," Rowen said first.

Dani kissed her temple. "I love you too."

Outside, the world waited. But here, there was only this and sleep.

Dani stirred between tangled sheets, still drunk on afterglow. Her breath carried the ghost of Rowen's skin, her body humming with the sweet ache of thorough attention. The evidence of their night lingered in the air—heat and moisture, the phantom rhythm of Rowen's mouth mapping every inch of her.

She reached across the bed, seeking warmth.

Her hand met cold linen. Empty space where Rowen should have been.

Before panic could take root, sound shattered the morning quiet.

Bang. Bang bang.

"DANI!" Mary's voice hit like a sledgehammer to the chest. "DANI, WAKE UP!" Another slam against the door—frenzied and desperate. "SHE'S HERE! DANI! SHE'S TAKING HER!"

Dani bolted upright, electricity shooting through her spine. "What—?"

The room was off. Rowen's hoodie still puddled on the floor where it had fallen last night. Her borrowed clothes lay untouched on the chair. The pillow beside Dani showed no impression, as if no one had ever been there at all. Toaster stood to stretch woken from his sleep, hair on end.

"Rowen?" The name scraped raw from her throat as she stumbled toward the door, wearing nothing but an oversized t-shirt and mismatched socks.

She yanked it open. Mary stood in the hallway, chest heaving, drenched in panic ridden sweat. The antique watch at her wrist blazed so hot it sent wisps of steam curling against her skin. When their eyes met, Dani saw her own terror reflected back.

"She's downstairs," Mary gasped. "A portal—it opened in the foyer. The box, they've taken—Rowen's..."

Dani didn't wait for the rest. She grabbed Mary's wrist and they tore down the stairs together, her socked feet skidding treacherously across polished hardwood. Her shoulder slammed into the banister as they rounded the corner.

The house itself seemed to scream. A low harmonic filled the air—like an orchestra tuning before tragedy struck. Light bent around corners where physics said it shouldn't, and the vintage wallpaper rippled like water. Time itself felt elastic, stretching and contracting with each heartbeat.

Above them, Dani's parents burst from their bedroom. Teresa stood frozen at the landing, her face a mask of disbelief.

"Oh my God!" she shrieked at George. "Do something! Get the gun!"

George rushed back toward their closet where the gun safe waited, but Dani already knew the truth with crystalline clarity: they were too late. No earthly weapon could touch what was happening below. This was a game with different rules, and they'd been outmaneuvered from the start. The figures were at the goal with a clear shot.

At the foot of the staircase, reality had torn itself apart. Searing blue light yawned across the marble foyer like a wound in the world. An ornate trinket box hovered in midair, its mechanical heart pulsing with blue otherworldly energy. A wide portal gaped, revealing a doorway to another place through its glow; it wasn't modern.

Memory struck like lightning.

Alvie's words in the parlor, sharp with warning: *"Ashdown also has a box."*

Lord Ashdown. Beatrice's father. The pieces clicked into place with sickening certainty that this wasn't some cosmic accident. This was a calculated retrieval, planned and executed with military precision.

And there, framed by the tear in space itself, stood Beatrice.

She cut an imposing figure draped in midnight silk, every inch the aristocrat's daughter. Beside her, a hulking man servant held a limp form slung over his shoulder like a sack of grain.

"ROWEN!" Dani's voice cracked as she stumbled forward, disbelief warring with rage.

Rowen hung unconscious in the servant's grip, her head lolling at an unnatural angle, blonde hair falling like a curtain across her face. Her bare toes dragged against the marble with each of the man's steps.

Beatrice's voice cut through the chaos with devastating calm. "She doesn't belong to you. You are... nothing."

"No." The word escaped Dani as barely a whisper. "No, no, no."

Behind her, George fumbled with the gun's loading mechanism while Teresa watched in mounting horror. The mundane terror of suburban parents faced with the impossible.

Dani lunged forward, but the air itself burned blue-white around the portal's edge. The barrier shimmered like the surface of some hellish lake, beautiful and utterly impassable.

Beatrice took a careful step backward, her smile sharp enough to cut glass.

Something primal snapped inside Dani's chest.

"OH, HELL NO."

She whirled toward Mary, fingers digging into her shoulders hard enough to bruise. "GRAB MY BOX! NOW!"

But Beatrice was already moving. With that same wicked smile curving her lips, she stepped through the rift as casually as walking through a doorway taking Rowen with her into the blue.

The portal began to collapse. Light cracked across the walls like breaking glass, and the crystal chandelier overhead groaned under some invisible weight. The tear in reality shrank with each passing second.

Dani screamed a sound torn from her very soul and ran straight for the dying light.

Everything went white.

About the Author

Amanda Luper

Amanda is a LGBTQ+ fiction author originally from Portland, Oregon, now living in Alaska. A lifelong lover of history—particularly the Egypt, Tudor, and Victorian eras—she blends romance, time travel, and queer identity into lush, emotionally resonant stories.

Her debut novel, *The Light Gazer*, began with a dream in 2014—two girls, a forgotten century, and the feeling of falling in love for the first time. She wrote it down the next morning and spent the next decade bringing Dani and Rowen's story to life between her full-time job and work as a wedding photographer.

When she's not writing or capturing real-life love stories through her lens, she's wandering the world with the woman who inspired every heartbeat she ever wrote, exploring new countries, and chasing golden hour light with a camera in hand.

CONTINUE THE STORY

Follow Amanda on Instagram @amandaluperbooks and stay tuned for book two in the
Arnautica Series! "The Key Between Hours."
Press inquiries please email amandaluperbooks@outlook.com